Jago Ransleigh.

She wondered to what kind of a man such a name belonged, for thus far she knew but little of her employer's character—and that he had loved a woman called Tamsyn, who had fallen to her death at this wild, haunting place where she, Verity, now stood.

Tamsyn...Tamsyn... The name appeared to echo softly, eerily, once more.

Unwittingly, as she gazed down at the strand below, at the frothy, soughing sea rushing in to break upon the rocky, shingled beach, Verity suddenly shivered violently.

It was only the cold and wet that caused her distress, she told herself uncompromisingly after a moment— that, and her wild, fanciful imagination, no doubt. Envisioning Lady St. Aubyn's body sprawled pitifully on the jutting crags, she was hearing things.

Still, for some unknown reason, as she turned away, stricken and uneasy, it was all Verity could do to prevent herself from running toward the manor—and all the while, she felt as though someone watched her steadily until she was out of sight.

REBECCA BRANDEWYNE

THE LOVE KNOT

MIRA®

THE LOVE KNOT

MIRA and the Star Colophon are trademarks used under license and registered
in Australia, New Zealand, Philippines, United States Patent and Trademark
Office and in other countries.

ISBN 0-7394-3483-7

Printed in U.S.A.

For my husband, John,
the best man I've ever known,
and who shared Cornwall with me.
With all my heart and love.

THE PLAYERS

IN CORNWALL:

At St. Aubyn Manor:

Lord Jago Ransleigh,
  Earl of St. Aubyn
His deceased wife:
  Lady Tamsyn Kenhebres Ransleigh,
  Countess of St. Aubyn
Their twin children:
  Lady Meliora
  Lord Bastian
His cousin:
  Colonel Hugh Sherbourne,
   a dragoon guard
The Earl's Household Staff:
The upper servants:
  Mr. Drummond,
   the steward
  Mrs. Wickersham,
   the housekeeper
  Mr. Ashfield,
   the earl's valet
  Mr. Peacock, the butler
  Mr. Lathrop, the groom
   of the chambers
The lower servants:
  Loveday, a chambermaid
  Bessie, a housemaid
  Ned, a footman
  Trueth, a nurse
  Cook, a cook
  Howel, a coachman
  Other servants

At Jamaica Inn:

Miss Verity Collier,
  a governess
A mysterious stranger

On the Moors:

Black Jack Raven,
  a highwayman

At St. Aubyn Lodge:

Lady Kenhebres,
  the earl's mother-in-law
Her servants:
  Eval and Doryty Ythnow

Other Personages:

Miss Gwendolyn Marchmont,
  a lady
Miss Katherine Nightingale,
  a lady
Fouquet, a French spy

CONTENTS

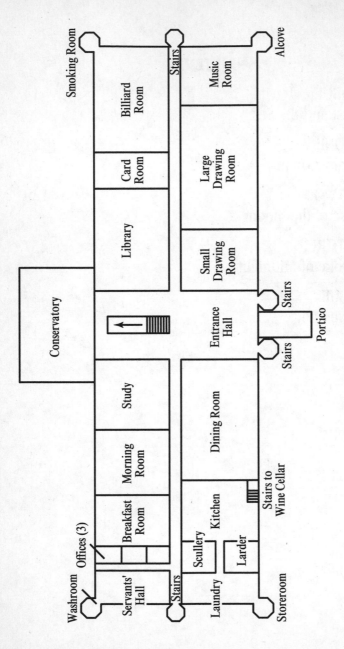

St Aubyn. (Ground Floor.) Scale 1" = 40'

Floor plan by John Cox.

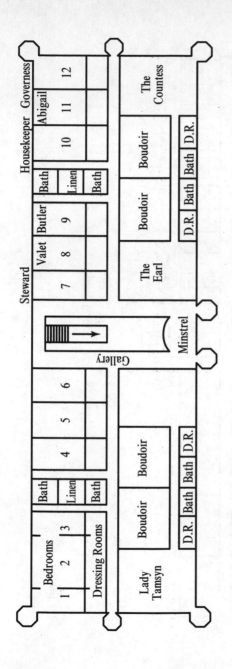

St Aubyn. (First Floor.) Scale 1" = 40'

Floor plan by John Cox.

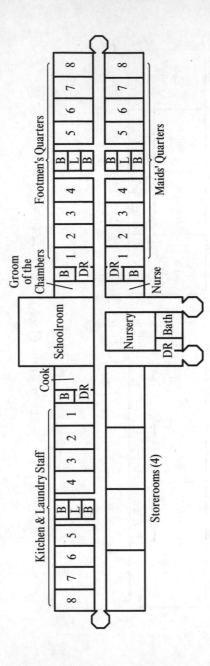

St Aubyn. (Second Floor.) Scale 1" = 40'

Floor plan by John Cox.

The Love Knot

The Highwayman rides no more the hightoby,
The hightoby no more he rides,
With silver rapier a'gleam in the pale moonlight
And two pistols at his sides.

He lost his heart to a fey silkie lass,
Who danced 'neath the rise o' the moon,
Sealskin hair a'tangling in the wind,
As she played her haunting tune.

From the mist and the sea, she crept to the shore,
At the stroke of the midnight hour.
With oil paints and brush, she cast her spell
In her dark, enchanted bower.

She burned a bright candle for her love,
Sought his image in the mirror, where
She braided a crimson silk love knot
Into her long brown hair.

So the Highwayman rides no more the hightoby,
For his heart was stolen away.
Now, he dwells forever in the Otherworld
With his dark silkie lass so fey.

Prologue

The Mist and the Sea

Of what is't fools make such vain keeping?
Sin their conception, their birth, weeping:
Their life, a general mist of error,
Their death, a hideous storm of terror.

> *The Duchess of Malfi (1623), act IV*
> —John Webster

From want of regular rests, I have been rather
narvus,
And the passage in *Lear*—"Do you not hear
the sea?"—
has haunted me intensely.

> *Letter to John Hamilton Reynolds*
> —John Keats

Frightful Cliffs of Fall

O the mind, mind has mountains; cliffs of fall
Frightful, sheer, no-man-fathomed.

> *Poems (1918). No. 64, Carrion Comfort*
> —Gerard Manley Hopkins

Whoever fights monsters should see to it that
in the process he does not become a monster.
And when you look long into an abyss,
the abyss also looks into you.

> *Thus Spake Zarathustra*
> —Friedrich Wilhelm Nietzsche

What the hammer? What the chain?
In what furnace was thy brain?
What the anvil? What dread grasp
Dare its deadly terrors clasp?

> *Songs of Experience (1794). The Tiger*
> —William Blake

The Cliffs at the Edge of the Sea
Cornwall, England, 1802

Sometimes, on a wintry eve years later, when the wind was high and blew like a torrent among the rustling trees of the park, and the moon was hazily ringed and tossed among ghostily drifting clouds; when the ocean along the treacherous rocky coast maddened and roiled, and swept, white-foamed, over the deceptive reefs and shingled beaches, the grey rain came hard, and the gossamer mist cloaked the hills, the moors and the marshlands of Cornwall, there were those who would remember this perilous night when Verity Collier stood poised at the edge of the precipitous black cliffs that crumbled down to the sea far below, staring, petrified, into the hideous dark abyss that had always haunted her—and that bore the face of her own terror.

Always—ever since she had been a child—she had been absolutely terrified of heights.

She did not know why—for who can explain the fears, often irrational, that lurk in the mind of a child, some of them, to be sure, to be sheepishly laughed at in later years and easily cast off, but others never to be outgrown and left behind. Rather, these last—the worst of all—seem only to slither like serpents through the dark, labyrinthine chasms of the adult brain, there to conceal and entrench themselves even more profoundly and securely in their hiding places, whence to strike viciously and poisonously when least expected.

Those evil fangs that now pierced Verity sank deeply, their venom surging like a fever through her blood, leaving her dizzy, disoriented and faint. Her head swam sickeningly; her heart pounded as though it would at any moment burst from her breast; and her nerves stretched as taut as harp strings, vibrating rackingly with fright. Her mouth and throat were so dry that she could not swallow, while, conversely, the rest of her body sweated so profusely that, more than once, she unwittingly wiped her palms upon her skirts buffeted by the rising wind that whipped and tore mercilessly at her hair and garments.

Her knees shook violently, weakened until, at last, they completely gave way beneath her, and she slid down heavily upon them, bowing her head and closing her eyes, the blood roaring in her ears and the earth tilting wildly, nauseatingly, all around her, as though it had somehow spun out of control upon its very axis.

Dimly, in some dark corner of her mind, she was aware that the grassy ground was damp beneath her knees, and that from the manor far behind her echoed the high, thin, pitiful screams of a child. But the other, far below her, was silent.

Oh, God, was he dead?

At that thought, she felt her heart lurch as sickeningly as her head reeled, then turn over painfully in her breast, constricting as though encircled by the crushing coils of some monstrous snake. No, she could not—*would* not—believe that. He was alive.

Please God, he was still alive.

But his muteness terrified her even more than the shrieks of the other, stinging her like a cruel goad, bringing her to her senses.

Taking a long, deep breath to steady herself, Verity raised her head, although she did not yet open her eyes, and stretched out her arms blindly before her, deliberately, determinedly, pushing herself upward, until she stood once more at the edge of the cliffs that hove up over the sea. Then, finally, her heart in her throat, she forced herself to open her eyes again, prepared now for the crazy rotation of the earth, which made the pale stars seem to rush from the black sky into the churning ocean below, white with froth and from which spume rose to kiss her lips with its brine as cold as death.

Fearfully, once more cognizant of the shrill, haunting screams from behind her, she dared to glance back over one shoulder. By the wan silvery light of the diffuse full moon that shone in the darkly clouded firmament, she spied a man in white running toward her purposefully from the distant manor, his arm upraised, wildly brandishing a meat cleaver whose sharp blade gleamed menacingly when struck by the moonbeams showering from the heavens, in concert with the light rain.

Cook, gone mad with rage—and no help for her here, or for the silent child, either.

Turning back to the cliffs, Verity gazed down, stricken, at the steep, narrow track, slick with mizzle, that wound its way, like the undulating serpent at the root of her terror, through a jumble of boulders, smaller rocks, and wet, moldering earth to the shingled beach below. No, she could not do it...could not descend that dark, insidious footpath—with its uncertain fate at the end.

But she must.

There was no other way.

Resolutely, breathing hard, she set one wholly unsteady foot upon the precarious trail, and then the other, her great terror of heights such that, eventually, she wound up clambering and clawing her way down the hazardous track, finally, to her everlasting horror, losing her grip on the damp rocks to which she tried so desperately to cling.

Down—

Down—

Down—

Verity fell, a long, wailing scream of agony and fear tearing from her unnaturally parched throat as she tumbled headlong down the dark, jagged, crumbling cliffs—into the gaping maw of the black abyss of her own terror....

Book One

The Highwayman

The wind was a torrent of darkness among the
gusty trees,
The moon was a ghostly galleon tossed upon
cloudy seas,
The road was a ribbon of moonlight over the
purple moor,
And the highwayman came riding—
    Riding—riding—
The highwayman came riding, up to the old inn
door.

He'd a French cocked hat on his forehead, a
bunch of lace at his chin,
A coat of the claret velvet, and breeches of
brown doeskin;
They fitted with never a wrinkle: his boots were
up to the thigh!
And he rode with a jeweled twinkle,
    His pistol butts a-twinkle,
His rapier hilt a-twinkle, under the jeweled sky.

The Highwayman
—Alfred Noyes

One

Jamaica Inn

There is nothing which has yet been
contrived by man by which so much
happiness is produced as by a good
tavern or inn.

> *Letter, March 21, 1776*
> —Samuel Johnson

Whoe'er has traveled life's dull round,
Whate'er his various tour has been,
May sigh to think how oft he found
His warmest welcome at an inn.

> *Written on a Window of an Inn at Henley*
> —William Shenstone

Jamaica Inn, Bodmin Moor
Cornwall, England, 1802

Near the small hamlet of Bolventor and shadowed by Tolborough Tor, the centuries-old inn—originally erected in 1547 and named the New Inn but later rebuilt in the mid-1700s and now called Jamaica Inn—stood like a great, grim, forbidding ogre upon the top of the harsh, barren hill that loomed just ahead of the sturdy but inelegant post chaise lumbering along the turnpike road that ran between the towns of Launceston and Bodmin, across the very heart of the desolate, windswept Bodmin Moor. Through the descending dusk and the gloomy windows, wet with drizzle and mist, of the public coach as it rounded a slight bend in the narrow, curving road, then began its clambering ascent toward the crest and the inn, Verity Collier got her first glimpse of the latter, and it was anything but welcoming. At the realization, she shivered.

Was ever there a bleaker and more cheerless sight? she wondered wearily, her spirits, already low and daunted, sinking still further as she spied the wayside resting place where the Earl of St. Aubyn's driver was to meet her. Almost, she wished she had not come.

Huddled forlornly and alone inside the drafty, damp vehicle, she thought it seemed forever since she had last been thoroughly warm and dry, although, in reality, it was only since she had left Derbyshire a few days ago, when she had embarked upon her trip to St. Aubyn, the solitary manor that was to be her new home. It lay not far from the towns of St. Ives and Penzance, near Land's End, in southwestern Cornwall. There, she was to be governess to the widower Earl of St. Aubyn's two young twin children, Meliora and Bastian.

Given how distant and secluded the manor was, Verity's new position was not the most sought after, for there were not many females of her age and erudition who wished to be sequestered away in the remote wilds of Cornwall. Even so, she was ultimately glad of the post. Although not lacking in testimonials from Trowbridge School, the semicharitable institution for girls in which she had been reared and educated, progressing there from pupil to teacher, still, her relative youth and inexperience had been held against her by many prospective employers. For quite some time, Verity had worried that she would never find other work and thus might not ever be able to leave Trowbridge, a stern, austere environment in which she had known very little joy over the years.

But then, fortuitously, she had spied the Earl of

St. Aubyn's advertisement in the Derby *Mercury,*
and she had written to apply for the position he had
offered: the tuition of his twin children, aged seven,
at a salary of fifty pounds per annum, along with
room and board. The yearly wage alone had seemed
a princely sum to Verity, who had earned far less
than half that amount at Trowbridge. So although she
had hoped for something nearer to London and society, and the thought of Cornwall's wildness and
isolation had given her pause, still, she had known
beggars could not be choosers, and in the end, she
had dispatched a letter detailing her qualifications for
the job, together with her references from Trowbridge.

Shortly after that, she had received a reply from
the Earl's housekeeper, Mrs. Wickersham, stating
that the post was hers and outlining arrangements for
her to travel to St. Aubyn within the fortnight. That
was how Verity had come to be sitting in the ponderous coach, hastening across the Cornish moors on
this biting and uncongenial afternoon now fading
into twilight.

It was only the thought of her having at last escaped from Trowbridge, and of the fifty pounds per
annum, along with room and board, promised her in
her new position that sustained her. She must dwell
on those advantages to her situation, Verity chided
herself sternly, and not on its more disheartening aspects. But still, as the vehicle in which she journeyed
drew nearer to Jamaica Inn, she could not quell her
burgeoning distress, and her fiercely sought-after resolution faltered so, that she nearly wept.

She was acclimated to the fine, soft rains and pastoral green hills of Derbyshire. Cornwall was as inhospitable, godforsaken and alien to her as the moon would have proved, had she been able to set foot upon it.

In every direction, high, rugged tors with names like Rough Tor, Brown Willy and Kilmar Tor, brindled with outcrops and slabs of glowering granite set at all odd angles, crouched like hulking, predatory beasts over the stark, savage terrain—the wild, isolated moors and stagnant, peaty marshlands that stretched away endlessly to the tumultuous grey-green ocean beyond. Amid the stony hills, sweeping heaths and boggy hollows, strange, atavistic rock formations christened with equally strange names like the Cheesewring and the Hurlers rose, and still waters like the Dozmary Pool, into which it was claimed King Arthur's sword Excalibur had been thrown, nestled. Trees were sparse, and those few that did cling tenaciously to life here were gnarled and distorted—bent and twisted by the ceaseless wind into tortured, fantastic shapes that made them appear like dark demons standing sentinel beneath the miasmal sky. Sodden, stunted heather and broom bowed beneath the inclement elements, and from the earthen tops of the low, dirt-filled stone fences peculiar to Cornwall and creating a chessboard of the land, bushy evergreen gorse sprouted to spread its long, creeping tendrils like grasping fingers among the crevices of the rocks. The chill gusts that blew in from the soughing sea carried ghostly, diaphanous billows of mist with them, and smelled of brine and peat.

The day hastened toward darkness and a hard rain yet to come, but ahead, upon the summit of the hill up which the post chaise now inexorably rumbled, Jamaica Inn towered in dour defiance of the gloaming and of the brumous, lowering clouds that bruised the sky. To the west of and well back from the slender ribbon of road, the sepulchral old inn stood— foursquare to the four winds, exposed to all the unforgiving elements. Composed of two solid stories of grey slate set with a center portico and small windows, capped by a roof from which tall, smoking chimneys jutted skyward at either end, it was flanked north and south by two large outbuildings, so that the three edifices together formed a courtyard, cobbled and reached by a long, brown-grass-banked, pebbled drive over which the high wheels of the public coach chuntered and bounced as it finally turned off the road to roll to a swaying halt before the sheltered inn door.

The place was nothing at all like the quaint, charming, homey country inns to which Verity was accustomed. Instead, like an imposing, austere Norman castle, Jamaica Inn had been built to endure, to withstand the erosive elements and any other determined onslaughts upon it—and so it had succeeded in doing.

After collecting Verity's single, stout, black leather-bound trunk from atop the vehicle, then climbing down from his box, the driver swung wide the creaking-hinged door of the post chaise and unfolded its wooden steps so that she could descend. This, she did hesitantly, however, mistrusting the look of both the dismal, disconsolate inn and its cobblestone courtyard, hazardously slick with raindrops that glistened in the wavering torchlight cast by the iron sconces mounted on either side of the porch.

Even under the best of circumstances, Verity would have had no desire to enter the inn alone. Now, in light of her flagging spirits and lack of pertinacity at this instant, the thought was sheer anathema to her. However, as no one approached to greet her, as expected, it seemed she had little other choice but to inquire within. So at last, reluctantly, modestly lifting her skirts in a futile attempt to avoid their dragging in the puddles that pooled in the courtyard, she carefully traversed the short distance to the portico. Then, with difficulty, she cracked open the heavy wooden door and slowly stepped inside.

At once, her nostrils were assailed with the strong, mingled odors of soured ale and mulled wine, of stale tobacco smoke and greasy cooking fires, of dank wood and leather, and of musty fabric. As her eyes gradually adjusted to the dim candlelight within the place, Verity observed that she stood in the main taproom. Although of fairly good size, it was made to appear smaller and, incongruously, somehow cozier by its low ceiling—once whitewashed but now turned a dingy yellow-grey from age and smoke— by the dark-stained wood of its furnishings, and by the leaden flagstone floor. A substantial, highly polished bar behind which hung a huge, murky mirror and shelves stacked high with a wide assortment of bottles ran along the entire wall to her left. Elsewhere around the taproom was set an array of crude tables with a motley collection of equally crude benches, stools and chairs, most of which were occupied by other customers—the vast majority of them male... miners from the nearby quarry and farmers from the ancient outlying cottages, Verity deduced, from the plain, rough, unkempt look of the men.

For an interminable minute, as they spied her standing tentatively on the threshold, they fell silent, viewing her with a bizarre mixture of curiosity, speculation, lewdness, slyness and the hard distrust of those who have lived all their lives in a tight-knit society firmly closed to outsiders. In the face of their stares and stillness, the last remnants of Verity's courage nearly deserted her. But, then, as they observed that she was but a lone female traveler, harmless enough, and of no great beauty or riches, besides, the men returned to their previous pursuits, and their unfamiliar Cornish accents, along with their boisterous talk and raucous laughter, once more dinned in the taproom and her ears.

Greatly relieved at no longer being an object of attention, Verity turned to the bar, where questions put to the barkeep elicited the most welcome information that arrangements had been made for her arrival, and paid for in advance, so that she was not only to have the use of the inn's parlor, but also there to be served supper while she waited for the Earl's coachman to collect her. Upon her receipt of all this news, a porter was duly summoned; her trunk was fetched from the courtyard; and she was shown through the inn's rabbit warren of dark passages and rooms to the parlor, where, much to her gratitude, a fire blazed cheerfully in the stone hearth.

Quickly advancing toward it appreciatively, Verity laid aside her black beaver muff and her reticule, then numbly stripped off her thin woolen gloves, clammy from the mizzle, and fastidiously hung them on the brass fender to dry. Stretching her slender hands out to the crepitant flames, she involuntarily sighed deeply with pleasure as the heat began bit by bit to permeate her entire being. After a time, when the worst of the chill had left her icy fingers, she removed her black, beaver-trimmed bonnet and black merino mantle, as well, spreading the latter on one of the two wing chairs by the fire, in the hope that much of its dampness would be eradicated by the blaze before she must once more venture outside to brave the elements. Then, tiredly seating herself in the opposite chair, she took stock of her surroundings.

By the dim light of the flames in the hearth and of the few burning candles casting long, eerily dancing shadows on the walls and in the four corners, she saw that like the taproom, the parlor was practicable but unimaginative and unrefined. Its mélange of couches, chairs, footstools, tables and carpets, while comfortable enough to one who had known precious little of that commodity in her twenty-odd years, had obviously seen far better days. The upholstery and rugs were aged and stained by time and use, and the carved-wood furnishings were dulled and marred from the same causes. A thin coat of pale-grey dust lay like a pall over all, and here and there, silvery cobwebs hung like shimmering ropes of crystal from chandeliers.

All in all, it was not a particularly inspiring sight. Still, Verity mused, the chamber was currently private, not likely to be wanted by anyone else this early in the evening, and it would serve her own small needs well enough for the short while that she would require its use—besides which, it would be churlish and ill-advised of her to lodge any complaint about the Earl's transactions. Most employers, she knew full well, would not have so far troubled themselves on her behalf, nor paid the reckoning for it, either. So for these things alone, she was inordinately thankful and easily able to overlook the parlor's vagrancies. It was enough that, at least for the time being, she was warm, starting to dry out and sheltered from the oppressive elements—and presently to be fed, too, she realized thankfully, as, without warning, a young maid appeared on the parlor threshold, bearing a crockery-laden wooden tray that she sat gingerly upon a low table before Verity. Then, after inquiring as to whether anything else was wanted and learning that it was not, the lass departed, leaving Verity to her solitary supper.

As the enticing aromas of hot tea and food reached her nostrils, she became acutely aware of her hunger, of the fact that she had not eaten since breaking her fast that morning. Surveying the repast, she discovered that in addition to the inevitable and welcome teapot covered with its cozy, there was a large plate replete with hunks of gravy-drenched mutton, boiled potatoes and cooked carrots; a smaller plate upon which reposed a thick slice of fresh, crusty bread spread with butter; and a little dish of stewed apples smothered with the rich, clotted cream for which Cornwall and its neighbor Devon were famous. Verity's mouth watered in anticipation. She was not to starve, at any rate.

But before she could even pour herself a cup of tea, flint and steel suddenly scraped and sparked in one darkly obscured corner of the room, causing her to jump and cry out softly. Her heart thudded in her breast, and one hand flew to her throat.

"My profoundest apologies, madam." A low, seemingly disembodied male voice resonated from the deep shadows. "It was not my intention to startle you."

"Perhaps not. However, you—you ought to have made your presence known immediately upon my being conducted to the parlor, sir, instead of permitting me to believe I was alone," Verity remonstrated tartly, peering suspiciously toward the corner, annoyed that she was unable to discern her accoster clearly, and frightened and indignant at the unpleasant notion that she had been stealthily spied on for quite some time.

"I fear that in defense of my unseemly silence, I must plead the fact that until the arrival of the maid with your supper, I was fast asleep in my chair, blissfully unaware that anyone besides me now occupied the chamber." By this time, the spark that had so unnerved Verity had been applied to the end of a thin, foreignly fragrant, dark-brown cheroot, which, although it glowed bright orange as the speaker smoked, did nothing to illuminate his visage. "However, you are quite right in thinking I should have bestirred myself much sooner, so I beg your pardon, madam—and now beg it yet again in light of my further remissness. I should also have inquired as to whether or not you objected to my indulging my predilection for a good cigar. It may be that you would wish me to refrain or else to withdraw to other quarters."

"No, indeed. I would not ask you to forgo your pleasure on my own account, sir, and as I cannot in all good conscience and truth state that I have engaged the parlor privately, I can scarcely insist that you vacate it, either, especially when you were plainly here before I was."

"You are most kind." Once more, the man fell still. But then, after a moment, he continued. "Please, do not allow me to keep you from your meal, madam. Tea and food are best partaken hot, and you must be famished, besides, to be dining at this early hour."

"Yes, sir, I am. I've eaten nothing since this morning, when I boarded the post chaise to Cornwall. Nor am I accustomed to conversing with strangers. So, if you will please excuse me, I would be most grateful."

With hands that trembled slightly from a combination of dismay, fatigue and hunger, Verity reached for the teapot, removed its cozy and filled its accompanying cup to the brim. Only minutes past, she had delighted in her solitude. To have since discovered that she was not, in reality, the parlor's sole occupant had disquieted her. She had not thought to have an audience—much less an unfamiliar one—at her supper. The entire affair was made even more disturbing, somehow, by the fact that she could not see the interloper's face, although as her eyes adjusted from the fire in the grate to the somber half light within the room, she was finally able to make out something of his form and attire.

Whether he was young or old, she could not honestly judge, but she reckoned the former, given his apparent fitness and strength, for he had the tall, handsome, muscular physique of one who was neither aged nor infirm, neither slack nor idle. Broad shoulders and chest tapered to a firm, flat belly, lean hips and long legs. A well-tailored coat of rich claret velvet fitted him smoothly and smartly, beneath which he wore an elegant silk paisley waistcoat and a fine white cambric shirt with a jabot of lace that spilled like foam down its fore; more frothy lace adorned its cuffs. Soft brown doeskin breeches hugged his corded thighs, and high black leather jackboots encased his legs.

Yet, despite all this, Verity had the distinct impression that he was not quite the gentleman he might at first glance appear. For tucked into the black leather belt at his waist were a pair of dueling pistols whose highly polished butts gleamed in the semidarkness, and a silvery rapier hung at his side. But perhaps she misjudged him, she told herself, half-ashamed of her finding fault. For, from what she had thus far seen of Cornwall, she could well believe that accoutrements such as these were necessary on its savage moors and marshes. Nor was there aught in either the man's voice or demeanor to rouse her to cast aspersions upon his character. Still, she remained vaguely ill at ease as she sipped from her cup of tea, gratified by its steaming warmth but finding its flavor strange to her tongue, for it had a peculiar, almost smoky taste.

"It's the peat."

"I'm—I'm sorry...?" Verity said inquiringly, glancing once more toward the dusky corner, whence the stranger had again spoken.

"When you drank from the teacup, your expression was such that I deduced you found its flavor unfamiliar."

"Yes...yes, I did," she acknowledged slowly, surprised by his perception and more than a little unsettled at the idea that he must have been watching her very closely.

"In light of your evident curiosity, madam, I was emboldened to explain that the taste is due to the peat that permeates the waters hereabout."

"I see. Thank you for troubling to enlighten me, sir. I was indeed wondering at its cause, as you guessed."

"It was no bother, I assure you, madam. Although you have made clear that you are unused to conversing with those to whom you have not been properly introduced, I, for my own part, believe there can be no harm or offense, surely, in two solitary wayfarers, thrust together by circumstance, exchanging a few pleasantries to pass away the time, and further, meals are much more enjoyable, I have always thought, when accompanied by some congenial conversation.''

"You are quite right, of course,'' Verity conceded politely, after a moment, feeling chastened and abashed. "I apologize, sir, if my earlier behavior seemed...standoffish. I have had a rather long journey, and I am hungry and weary from it. I fear I am hardly good company, as a result.''

"Yet, still, more agreeable by far than that rough, bedraggled lot in the taproom. So do you apply yourself to your supper, madam, and with your consent, I will make what poor attempt I may at entertaining you with some enjoyable discourse.''

At that, feeling that to again demur could only prove churlish, Verity proceeded as requested, deciding that perhaps the interloper was simply lonely and in need of some amicable amusement. As he himself had indicated, given the situation, there could surely be no injury or impropriety in the two of them engaging in a light, impersonal colloquy, she thought, severely suppressing the strictures of her Trowbridge teachers as regarded the conduct of well-brought-up young women and that now echoed clamorously at the back of her mind. Fortuitously, after many unhappy years at the school, she had at long last managed to leave it far behind, and there were at Jamaica Inn, besides, any number of persons within earshot whom she could summon for assistance, should the stranger give her some cause to do so, she reasoned.

So, thankful for such a generous evening meal, Verity dined eagerly and well on the savory fare, while her nameless companion, as good as his word, set about to divert her. Seemingly content to remain anonymous in his Cimmerian corner, he made no attempt to introduce himself, nor to draw nearer to the crackling fire where she sat. Still, his low, mellifluous voice mesmerized her as he smoked the slim, exotic cheroots he favored, and told her tales tall and perhaps sometimes true to while away the time as she ate.

He was an excellent, witty raconteur and highly knowledgeable, it was soon evident, about Cornwall and its history. He filled her ears with wild, vividly recounted stories of the county's ancient Celtic peoples and their quaint traditions, many still determinedly clung to even now; of yesteryear land battles and violent shipwrecks on the deceptive Cornish reefs that hove up from the turbulent sea; and of chilling ghosts and stealthy smugglers. There had even been murder done at Jamaica Inn itself, he imparted, and eerie specters were rumored to haunt its dark, labyrinthine passages and rooms, while on many a night, "moon cursers" made their furtive ways across Bodmin Moor, Twelve Men Moor, East Moor and all the rest, contraband in hand.

Verity thought these all peculiar and disturbing topics, particularly as dinner dialogue. Yet in spite of that, she was utterly fascinated to learn about this savage and unfamiliar Cornwall that was to be her new home. She could have gone on listening to the stranger for hours. But finally, the last sips of her flavorful peaty tea were drunk; the last morsels on her earlier abundant tray were eaten; and the Earl of

St. Aubyn's coachman—"Howel, miss," he introduced himself taciturnly, touching his cap politely
but brusquely—entered the inn's parlor to collect her.

After donning her plain cloak, bonnet and gloves,
and gathering up her muff and reticule, Verity turned
to thank the man who had regaled her all through
her supper with his entertaining, however uncanny,
narrative—only to discover that he had silently and
mysteriously vanished.

"Well, that's odd. Where did he go, I wonder,
without even so much as a by-your-leave?" she murmured to herself, somewhat puzzled and piqued.

"Who, miss?" Howel asked, overhearing, as he
hefted her sturdy trunk to carry it outside to the waiting carriage.

"Why—the man who was sitting right over
there." She motioned toward the gloomy corner that
her unknown dinner companion had previously occupied.

"I saw no one, miss," the driver insisted, as he
started toward the parlor doorway, glancing neither
in the direction that Verity had indicated nor back at
her. "Thou art tired from thy long journey, an' 'appen Jamaica Inn be known fer its hauntin's, too. Art
thou comin'? 'Tis best if'n we dunnat bide here
o'erlong, fer there be a storm on t' way, an' we mun
hurry like t' divvil if'n 'tis not ta o'ertake us afore
we reach St. Aubyn. Thou've not yet seen one o' our
Cornish storms, miss, but they be summat wild an'
fierce, not fer t' likes o' thee ta be caught out in,
methinks."

Despite this caveat, Verity was reluctant to depart

from the inn, to abandon its warmth and dryness, and to venture back outside into the late-spring eve's chill and damp. In addition, she was more than a little curious about how and why her dinner companion had abruptly disappeared—how he had done so and why Howel had not only not seen him, but also alleged him perhaps to have been a ghost! Granted, the parlor was poorly illuminated, its corners long shadowed as a result. Still, the coachman ought to have observed the interloper's egress, she thought, for despite Howel's remarks, she could not imagine that she was so exhausted from her travels that she was envisioning specters nor had actually conversed with one at quite some length.

Still, despite the intrigue, there was neither time to investigate it nor even to dwell any further on the matter, for, her trunk in hand, the Earl's driver now strode rapidly through the dark rabbit warren of long passages and boxlike rooms that composed Jamaica Inn. If she did not make haste to follow, he would perhaps leave her behind! That notion seized hold of Verity most unpleasantly, and after quickly glancing about to be certain she had retrieved all her meager belongings, she hurried after him, passing once more through the noisy main taproom.

As the heavy old inn door groaned to a close behind her, muting the revelry within, she saw that the dusk had slipped away as quickly as it had come. Night had now fallen, and the moon had risen, glowing like a lustrous pearl in the black-velvet sky. Before her, swathed in drifting mist in the cobblestone courtyard, stood four fine black horses harnessed to a magnificent carriage fashioned of burnished ebony wood and boasting high, metal-rimmed wheels whose brightly painted yellow spokes shone in beautiful contrast in the pale silvery moonlight. An imposing, elaborately carved family coat of arms was mounted upon the door that Howel held open for her, lowering the steps so that she could ascend into the vehicle's interior.

After Verity had comfortably settled herself upon the plush purple-velvet bench within, the reticent coachman shut up the door and climbed up onto the box above. Then, with a brisk snap of his long whip and a brief shout to the team, they were off, hooves and wheels clattering upon the puddled cobblestones and then the long, pebbled drive to the ribbon of road beyond.

Behind them, Jamaica Inn continued to stand its grim, forbidding watch, the incongruously soft lamplight spilling from its windows growing increasingly dimmer with distance, until, at last, the inn seemed to wink suddenly into dark oblivion entirely.

Shuddering a little at that unnerving thought, Verity did not again look back.

Two

St. Aubyn Manor

In the black moon
of the highwaymen,
the spurs sing.

Song of the Rider, 1860 (Cancion de Jinete, 1860)
—Federico García Lorca

No coward soul is mine,
No trembler in the world's storm-troubled sphere.
I see Heaven's glories shine,
And faith shines equal, arming me from fear.

Last Lines
—Emily Brontë

Once Howel had assisted Verity into the carriage, he did not speak to her again, but instead sat silently upon the box above, his only words to the horses, whose long leather reins he handled with firmness and assurance, setting a steady but brisk pace, so that the coach made good time without exhausting the team. He was a strange, remote man, she thought, garbed in black livery topped by a stovepipe hat, tall and thin, with an austere face and a demeanor that did not invite communication, even had such been easily possible, which it wasn't, unless she wished to sit outside on the box with him, which she did not. Although solitary, the inside of the vehicle was much warmer, drier and more comfortable, with its closed windows and lushly cushioned purple-velvet seats. So she sat alone with her musings.

Verity did not know how long or how far they traveled from Jamaica Inn, whether or where they stopped to change horses along the way—only that she herself was so weary from her lengthy trip that she eventually dozed on and off for much of the trip, lulled by the rhythmic pounding of the steeds' hooves and churning of the equipage's wheels into a light but restful slumber. It was only as the coach picked up speed, finally attaining such an alarming rate that she was jolted wide-awake and nearly flung from the bench by an especially vicious bump, that despite her tiredness, she could no longer find any respite in sleep.

Sitting up and smoothing her appearance—for she had unconsciously curled up on the bench while she had napped—Verity tried to peer out the windows to see what was occurring. But these were obscured by drizzle and mist, so that only inky blackness and trickles of rain and brume met her frightened gaze. From outside, she could hear that the wind had risen, and the four-in-hand swayed nerve-rackingly on its supports as it barreled along the narrow, winding road. The storm that the coachman had warned her about earlier at Jamaica Inn must be drawing swiftly nearer, she realized. He was trying to outrun it— madly, it seemed, in the face of the keening gusts, unrelenting mizzle and dark, serpentine pebbled road.

For, as the glowering sky had earlier foreshad- owed, it was a primeval late-spring night, not fit for either man or beast—much less for Verity perched precariously in the expensive, gleaming ebony car- riage that now hurtled like a snarling hellhound along the serpentine ribbon of road uncoiling beneath neb- ulous moonlight across the wild, desolate Cornish moors.

The narrow dirt road, strewn with pebbles over which the high, yellow, metal-rimmed coach wheels clattered and crunched, was moist and slick from the light rain that drizzled and glistened like teardrops on the tiny stones. Floating ghostily among the drifting, foreboding pewter clouds massed and swollen in the firmament, the moon that, with long silvery talons, raked the bleak terrain, was full, ringed and eerily shimmering. The few stars that shone were softly dim and blurred. Beneath the pale, hazy glow emanating from the heavens, the moors, thick with evergreen gorse, stretched away to jagged, rocky cliffs that hove up at the land's end to crumble into the roiling, white-frothed ocean beyond. From the sea, spindrift-tinged wind and fog swept inland, wafting across the road, the bitter gusts causing the gossamer mist to flit and billow like a blown, cobwebbed shroud.

All in all, it was not a sight to inspire confidence in the onward-rushing vehicle's pale, lone occupant, and as she gazed out the murky, beveled-glass windows, trickling with rain and brume, of the well-appointed, well-sprung equipage in which she now traveled, Verity shivered. Unbidden, the ghost tales and stories of smugglers recounted to her earlier this evening by the dark, mysterious stranger at Jamaica Inn, where she had supped and then been collected by the opulent four-in-hand, returned to haunt her. Surely, there was naught to be afraid of, she tried desperately to reassure herself as she tightly clutched the leather safety strap within the carriage to keep from being thrown violently about the lavish interior. But still, the night and the velocity of coach were such that her fears would not be allayed.

Not for the first time, Verity wondered if the driver, Howel, were a madman, to be urging the four, beautifully matched black horses harnessed to the vehicle to such a reckless pace, on such an inhospitable eve—although she knew otherwise, since if he were not sane, she could not think he would be in the Earl of St. Aubyn's employ. Time and again, the coachman's long, snaking whip lashed out above the proud, finely shaped heads of the powerful, galloping steeds. In response, their hooves thundered upon the winding road, churning up clumps of sodden earth that splattered with dull thuds against the underbelly of the pelting equipage. From the beasts' besprent, lathered coats, flecks of white foam flew, glimmering like salty spume in the bleary, erratically flickering light cast by the brass lanterns bolted to either side of the four-in-hand's exterior. Almost, Verity yearned for the more sedate post chaise in which she had traveled the better part of her lengthy journey from Derbyshire to Cornwall—except that the public coach had been even draftier and not nearly as comfortable as the private carriage.

Yet even this last, despite all its sumptuousness, was not foolproof against the elements, and as the chill and briny damp crept in to penetrate her worn, modest pelisse and permeate her very bones, she shivered again.

At Jamaica Inn, Howel had told her that he feared that a storm was coming and said they must hurry if they were to reach St. Aubyn before it struck. Still, despite the warning, Verity had never dreamed that the last stretch of her long journey would be conducted at such a brash speed—frightening under normal circumstances and made even more so this eve by the drifting mist and dreary drizzle obscuring the slender road that twisted ahead. She did not know how the driver could seem so sure of the way. She herself felt certain that at any instant, the vehicle would veer uncontrollably off the road and suffer a horrible accident, crashing and overturning.

Even as the thought occurred to her, a sharp, alarming explosion suddenly split the night air, followed almost immediately by yet another loud report. Howel swore and then shouted, and his slithering whip cracked. The hooves of the horses pounded, and the equipage lurched terrifyingly on its spinning axles. Verity clung to the leather safety strap even more tightly, her heart now in her throat. She did not know what was happening, but she believed her worst fears had come to pass, that the four-in-hand indeed raced inexorably toward its doom.

But then, much to her surprise and relief, instead of brutally wrecking, the carriage abruptly jolted to such a vehement halt that despite her fierce grip on the strap, she was flung from the cushioned bench onto the hard, highly polished wooden floor of the coach. Stunned and battered by the rough fall, Verity simply sat there momentarily, trying to catch her breath and glad to be alive. Her gratitude at being relatively unhurt save for a few, minor bumps and bruises was unmercifully cut short, however, turning without warning to horror when, after slowly gathering her composure and hauling herself back up on to the velvet seat, she heard from outside the vehicle a low, authoritative voice imperiously demand, ''Stand an' deliver....''

Oh, my God, we are being held up! she recognized, horrified, as the highwayman's centuries-old command reached her ears. But before she could really even assimilate this idea, think what action to take to try to protect herself and her belongings, the equipage door was abruptly ripped open wide, and the four-in-hand's dangerous, brazen accoster stood without, one glimmering pistol, which he must have reloaded after firing both it and its twin just moments past, leveled at her threateningly.

Was there ever a more fearsome sight than the lone robber who confronted her? Verity could not imagine one. Tall, dark, muscular and thoroughly menacing, he wore a black silk hood that, except for its eye, nose and mouth holes, covered his face entirely beneath his black French cocked hat, and a black silk domino was buttoned up to his throat to conceal most of his clothing. A pair of soft brown doeskin breeches and high black leather jackboots adorned with glittering silver spurs completed his ensemble. He had his second pistol trained warningly on Howel, whom he had compelled down from the box, and a silvery rapier hung at his side. Nearby, a lone black stallion waited obediently for its master.

For the first time in her life, Verity almost fainted. Despite her uncompromising upbringing at Trowbridge, she had led a relatively sheltered existence among mostly females, never exposed to anything like this. In the face of this unfamiliar, masculine terror, she knew neither what to say nor to do. Sheer instinct alone caused her quickly and covertly to cram her reticule inside her muff, for it contained all of what little funds she had in this world, and she could not afford to have it stolen. Then, pale and trembling, she sat silently where she was—for what use to cringe in a corner, in the futile hope of going unseen?—resolutely attempting to compose herself and thrusting to the back of her mind all the disturbing stories the stranger at Jamaica Inn had recounted to her earlier tonight. Surely, murder was not the brigand's aim!

"What? Travelin' all alone, madam? With noan but a single, poor-spirited driver ta defend thee?" he drawled mockingly as he spied her. "What means this? Surely, one who possesses such a splendid carriage as this ought ta be attended by more'n one mere servant!"

"I—I fear you very much mistake the matter, sir." Verity explained simply, as she found her tongue at last, her chin lifting slightly with defiance as she gazed at the highwayman steadily, for although she was apprehensive, no coward's heart and soul were hers. Faith would sustain her, as it always had. "This fine coach is not mine. Rather, it belongs to the Earl of St. Aubyn, who dispatched it to Jamaica Inn to fetch me to his manor. I am but the new governess to his two children, so I've nothing of any value to be relieved of, and I therefore beg you to allow us to continue our journey unmolested. The driver has told me there is a storm coming, and indeed, the wind blows ever stronger, and the rain falls ever harder, so I've no good reason to doubt him. Nor have I any desire to be caught abroad in such foul weather."

"Nay, I'll wager not. 'Tis a pretty enough tale

thou spin, madam, an' I'm tempted ta believe it, fer 'tis true thou've not t' look o' some hoity-toity lady about thee. Still, 'tis a glint o' summat gold methinks I spy beneath yer pelisse, noan t' less, an' no mistake!''

A small, stricken gasp escaped from Verity's lips, and unwittingly, one gloved hand flew to her breast, to the filigree gold locket that lay there, suspended from a delicate gold chain hanging around her neck. Her fingers closed about the object tightly.

"You are a thief and rogue, sir, so I do not delude myself into thinking you are a gentleman," she stated coldly, with far more aplomb than she actually felt. "Nevertheless, I am persuaded you might play the role of one if you so chose. This locket can be of comparatively little worth to you, whilst I prize it highly for its sentiment. It belonged to my mother, who died when I was but a girl, and it is all I have left of her. If you wish it, then I am very much afraid that you must shoot me, because I could not bring myself to part with it otherwise.''

Much to Verity's surprise, although she quailed inwardly as she spoke, the robber, instead of discharging his pistol at her, as she had fully and hideously expected, threw back his head and laughed— a low, devilish sound that revealed even teeth that flashed whitely against his black mask.

"Divvil take me, but those art brave words fer so slender an' frail a lass, an' I do admire courage, madam! Still, I'll not be gone with nowt. I mun have summat fer all me trouble!''

So saying, he suddenly shoved both his pistols into

his black leather belt and, swaggering toward her, drew forth his rapier. Then, before Verity realized what he intended, with a swift, deft flick of his wrist, he skillfully cut off a lock of her soft dark-brown hair that had earlier been loosened from its neat chignon by the Cornish wind and so now peeped from beneath the brim of her bonnet. Catching the falling tress in his free hand, the arrogant, audacious highwayman tucked it into the pocket of his domino.

"Nivver let it be bandied about that Black Jack Raven took advantage o' so brave a young miss!" he insisted, with a bold grin and evident satisfaction at his own dubious gallantry. Then, to her further mortification, he abruptly, with his supple rapier, administered a couple of rapid, resounding and insulting whacks to Howel's backside. "Thou ought ta be ashamed o' yerself fer not takin' better care o' t' lass entrusted ta thy charge," he declared to the hapless but outraged coachman. "Now, get thee back on yer box, mate, an' drive on as if'n t' hounds o' hell harried hard yer heels, or else I shall not be responsible fer me actions!"

Howel needed no further urging. Stiff and mute with ill-concealed anger and indignation, he hauled himself back up onto the vehicle's box, gathering up the trailing leather reins.

"Till we meet again, madam." With a grand flourish, the brigand touched his rapier to his French cocked hat, saluting Verity, then swept her a low bow.

"Indeed, I most profoundly hope we shall *not*,

sir,'' she answered gravely, ''for it has been an experience I should not care to repeat.''

At that, the thief only laughed low and impudently again, then slammed shut the equipage door and tersely ordered the coachman onward. With a snarled oath and a sharp lashing of his whip above the finely molded heads of the horses, Howel set the team to a furious gallop, and the four-in-hand shot forward with a lurch that jounced Verity so rudely against the squabs of the seat within that the wind was nearly knocked from her. With some difficulty, in light of the carriage's speed, she righted herself, her heart thudding far too hard and fast in her breast. Was there ever a more dreadful day than this one had proved? she wondered, thoroughly distressed. A more fateful journey? And still, it was not yet ended!

Outside, the wind now suddenly moaned and shrieked like a banshee, and moments later, the drizzle metamorphosed into a hard rain that pelted the coach unmercifully, so that Verity thought poor Howel must be not only chilled to the bone, but also perilously blinded by the elements. How he kept the vehicle on the road, she did not know—except that the great, jagged tridents of lightning that now fitfully split the night sky must have helped to illuminate his path.

Once or twice, Verity attempted to look out the windows, in a vain attempt to calm her fears, which were threefold. The first was that the threatening highwayman, changing his mind and deciding he had not got enough for his trouble, after all, would now follow them, bent on some even worse mischief. The

second was that, unbeknown to her, the driver, exposed to the full fury of the breaking storm, would
be blown from the box, and that the equipage would
race on heedlessly without him. The last was that the
four-in-hand would crash and overturn, killing her
and Howel both! But despite the ominous flashes of
shattering, scintillating lightning, it was impossible
to discern anything clearly beyond the obscured
panes, so her anxiety continued unabated—and, indeed, was worsened by the violent claps of thunder
that smote the firmament fiercely.

She had been robbed! The awful realization suddenly swept over Verity like an inward-rushing
ocean breaker, ruthlessly battering her senses. While
it was true that, thankfully, the daring, insolent brig-
and had stolen neither her reticule nor her precious
locket, he *had* taken something even more intimate
from her—the silky dark-brown tress that he had so
artfully cut from her bonneted head. Involuntarily,
one hand crept up to her hair, to the right side where
the lock was missing. It was a miracle that he had
not put out her eye or scarred her face while seizing
his ill-gained trophy! she thought, shuddering at the
very idea. That he had not even so much as grazed
her with his rapier was obvious proof that his swordsmanship was superior.

Now, as Verity dwelled upon the thief, in the hope
of allaying her fears about Howel perched upon the
box—or perhaps not—and the carriage wrecking, it
slowly dawned on her that there had been several
similarities between the stranger at Jamaica Inn and
the formidable robber. Both had been garbed in soft

brown doeskin breeches and high black leather jack-boots—although her interlocutor had not worn spurs—and carried a pair of dueling pistols and a rapier. Was it possible the two men had been one and the same? No, surely not. Surely, the notion was the height of absurdity, a wild imagining born of her exhaustion and all she had been subjected to this night, Verity told herself firmly. The stranger's speech had been that of, if not a gentleman, at least an educated man, while the highwayman had spoken the rough dialect of the lower Cornish classes. And to what purpose would her interlocutor—having engaged her in conversation at some length over supper and thus learning something of her own self in the process—have set upon her, knowing full well that she possessed nothing worth stealing? That did not make any sense at all. Yet, still, she could not wholly thrust from her mind the odd notion that the stranger and the brigand were identical.

Without warning, there came a peculiar lull in the tumultuous storm, abruptly rousing Verity from her speculative and highly agitated reverie. The moors had given way at long last to stands of old trees that grew so thickly here that their gnarled branches heavy with greening leaves had interwoven to fashion a canopy over the road, thus largely protecting it from the gusting wind and driving rain; and as a result, much to her vast relief, the coach gradually slackened speed, then eventually—finally—turned off the main path entirely.

By the dim, glowing light cast by the lanterns bolted to either side of the vehicle, Verity had a fleeting impression of tall, imposing, dark-grey stone pillars flanking an open wrought-iron gate, and of a dark-grey stone lodge to the right just beyond, with soft candlelight shining—incongruously, it seemed—from its curtained windows. Then the equipage swept onward, clattering and weaving its way along a long, winding drive paved with crushed seashells and, like the road now left behind, covered with a canopy formed by the interleaved boughs of the ancient, looming, twisted Cornish elms that lined the grassy verge.

As yet another huge, serrated fork of lightning splintered the heavens and thunder boomed, Verity caught a glimpse of the manor itself through the sheeting rain. Three solid, grim, forbidding stories of the same dark-grey stone as its gate pillars and lodge, set just like Jamaica Inn, foursquare to the four winds, towered and battlemented, with a gabled roof, and lined with rows of dormers, oriels, and tall, mullioned casement windows with lozenged lead-glass panes, it resembled some ages-old fairy-tale castle aeons spellbound—although entangled with a profusion of clinging ivy rather than with fateful brier. Then the brilliant, erratic lightning dissipated, and the manor darkened all at once, as though it had of a sudden somehow been vehemently blotted from existence, snatched up by some unseen, titanic fist and hurtled into deepest nothingness.

Unwittingly, Verity shuddered. In some shadowy corner of her mind, she realized she had expected St. Aubyn to be graceful and stately—not this awful, fearsome place.

The four-in-hand rolled at last to a halt beneath its cavernous portico, irradiated by flickering brass lanterns hanging from the stout rafters above and affixed to either side of the massive oak portal. After collecting Verity's trunk, Howel clambered down from the box, opened the imposingly crested door of the carriage, then lowered the steps so that she could alight. Assisting her out into the blowing wind and rain that were little daunted by the porch roof, so that her cloak whipped wildly about her and droplets dampened her cheeks, he strangely, determinedly, held fast her hand for a moment, shouting at her to be heard above the storm.

"I mun apologize ta thee, miss, fer allowin' us ta be o'ertaken by t' 'ighwayman. 'Appen he were right, an' I ought ta have defended thee better. I be glad that he did nowt more'n steal a lock o' yer hair, although I know that mun have been quite grievous ta thee, e'en so. I do hope thou can find it within yerself not ta judge me too harshly an' ta forgive me fer me shortcomin's."

"Of course I can, Howel," Verity responded quickly, never having been one to hold a grudge and wishing to take shelter from the elements as soon as possible. "In all truth, there was really very little you could have done. The thief was heavily armed and clearly both highly skilled and experienced at employing his weapons. So things might have gone far worse than they actually did. But thankfully, in the end, there was no real harm done, other than to my pride and my hair, and the first will soon mend and the last grow back in time."

"Thank 'ee, miss. I be much obliged ta thee."
Releasing her then, the coachman touched his hand
to his cap respectfully before turning away to hammer the brass door knocker, fashioned in the shape
of a roaring lion's head, upon the heavy front door
of the manor.

Minutes later, the portal was flung open wide to
reveal two footmen in livery and a young, uniformed
housemaid, with a brass candlestick held high to light
the entrance hall beyond.

"Do come in, miss," the lass greeted Verity
brightly. "We have long been expectin' thee this eve,
an' grew quite worried when t' storm broke, fer fear
that thou would be caught in it. But, there, Howel
knows what he's about, so p'rhaps we ought not ta
have fretted so, after all. Fer here thou be, safe an'
sound—although it be a bad night, an' thou mun be
well nigh frozen from t' cold an' wet. Come in to t'
fire, miss, where thou may warm thyself."

The housemaid, whose name, Verity shortly
learned, was Bessie, then led the way through the
entrance hall and then a long passage to a small, snug
sitting room, where a cozy blaze burned in the stone
hearth. It was not at all an elaborate, elegant chamber, but, rather, a pleasant, cheerful one, with a mélange of old furniture—couches, chairs, footstools
and tables—that appeared to have been chosen principally for comfort and certainly not to impress.

Verity was much surprised, for this was not in the
least what she had expected to find in the Earl of St.
Aubyn's household, which she had initially imagined
would be expensively and, to one so unaccustomed

to finery, grandly furnished in baronial splendor, but which, after actually glimpsing the manor, she had half feared and fancied would instead be swathed in dust and cobwebs wrought by time and a pall cast by the evil spell of some unknown sorcerer. So it was that she had prepared herself to be awed and even frightened by St. Aubyn's interior. Instead, she found herself once more warmly welcomed.

For, from where she sat placidly in a wing chair before the crackling fire, a calico cat curled up beside her, a thin, elderly, bespectacled woman, neatly dressed in a plain black silk gown and a crisp white linen widow's cap that matched her freshly starched white linen apron, glanced up at Verity's entrance, then smiling and laying aside her embroidery on a nearby table, rose, sprightly stepping forward with her hands friendly outstretched.

"You must be Miss Collier, arrived at St. Aubyn at last. How do you do, my dear? I am Mrs. Wickersham, his lordship's housekeeper."

"I'm very pleased to meet you, ma'am," Verity replied, shaking hands and returning the smile.

"Come in, and sit down. Take my seat. It's closest to the fire, and you must be chilled to the bone on a night such as this. Away with you, puss!" Mrs. Wickersham shooed the cat from the wing chair. The creature stirred lazily, then lightly leaped down, yawning and stretching, before arranging itself on the braided rug in front of the grate.

"I would not wish to deprive you of your own comfort, ma'am."

"Oh, you must not bother yourself about that, my

dear,'' the housekeeper insisted. ''I'm quite warm enough, and I shall do very nicely in the rocker, I assure you. I did not wish to sit in it before, for fear that I should fall asleep. But now that you are come, I need not fret about that.'' Turning to the housemaid, she directed, ''Bessie, go into the kitchen and fetch Miss Collier something to eat and drink. I'm sure she must be hungry and thirsty after her long journey. Here are the keys to the larder.'' Taking a large brass chatelaine from the chain at her waist, the elderly woman handed it to the young housemaid.

''I'm most appreciative of your consideration, ma'am.'' Verity laid her muff and reticule on the table, then divested herself of her bonnet, pelisse and gloves. ''I confess it seems ages since I dined at Jamaica Inn.''

''I guessed as much. So I myself have found it to be on those rare occasions when I have made the trip from here to Launceston and back—although, fortunately, I have never done so on such an inhospitable night as this has proved to be. What an ordeal it must have been for you, my dear, traveling such a way in the midst of one of our storms.'' Mrs. Wickersham shook her head slowly with understanding and sympathy. ''I cannot imagine that it has endeared our Cornwall to you.''

''Whilst it is true that I am unused to such inclement weather, I hope I am made of sterner stuff than to be driven away by a strong wind and a hard rain, ma'am. In all truth, I believe I was more afraid of the furious pace of the coach than of the storm itself. I thought Howel must be blinded by the downpour, exposed to the elements as he was, and I still do not know how he kept us on the main road and from suffering an accident.''

"Ah, well, he is long accustomed to our storms, knows the road like the back of his hand and has an uncanny way with both horses and vehicles, besides.'' Taking up her embroidery, the housekeeper settled herself into the rocker opposite the wing chair and began once more to ply her needle. "Still, you could not have known all that, and even we who do know fretted for you, out and about on such a night, for there is always the possibility of something unforeseen occurring. But, there, all's well that ends well. You're safely arrived now, and that is all that matters.''

"Yes, ma'am.''

Bessie returned from the kitchen, bearing a tray laden with a teapot and accoutrements, a bowl of thick, appetizing stew and a plate with a generous slice of crusty bread liberally spread with butter. She set the whole upon the table, pouring tea from the pot into a mug and, after inquiring as to how it should be prepared, adding a little sugar and lemon.

"Thank you, Bessie. It all looks lovely,'' Verity observed, then, without any further ado, gratefully applied herself to the light repast.

"Will there be anythin' else, Mrs. Wickersham?'' the housemaid asked.

"Have the footmen taken Miss Collier's baggage upstairs to her room?''

"Aye, mum—straightaway, they did.''

"Then, no, that will be all. You may go, Bessie.''

"Thank 'ee, mum." After a slight curtsy to both women, the housemaid exited the hall.

Once Bessie had gone, the housekeeper chatted companionably to Verity, explaining that "his lordship," as she referred to the Earl, was currently away from home and that his two children, Meliora and Bastian, who were to be Verity's charges, were already abed.

"But you shall meet them both in the morning, and see the schoolroom then, also," the elderly woman said. "It is well stocked with all we believed needful. However, should you discover aught wanting, then you must let me know at once, and whatever else is required will be ordered immediately, for so his lordship instructed before he went away."

"That was very thoughtful and kind of him. However, I feel sure I shan't find anything lacking. What sort of children are Meliora and Bastian, ma'am? It would perhaps be helpful to me if I knew a little bit more about them and their interests before meeting them and undertaking their education. They are twins and seven years of age, as I recall. So they can neither of them have been long in the schoolroom."

"No, my dear. In fact, until now, they have both been in the nursery. Their mother died two years ago, and as his lordship and the youngsters were all greatly affected by her passing, it was thought best not to make any alterations for a time, which would further upset the children. So you will be their first and only experience with a governess—and, if all goes well, their last. For his lordship is not one, like some I have known, to be forever turning off his servants on a whim, without any just cause. Although there are those people who call him a proud, vain and arrogant man—and that, he may well be, in truth, for he is much changed and has turned ever more sober and inward since her ladyship's death—still, he is a fair and honorable master, and not without kindness when it suits him.''

"Are Meliora and Bastian much like him?'' Verity queried, pondering what she had thus far learned of her new employer, the Earl.

"Physically, yes, for they are all a black-haired, black-eyed lot, the St. Aubyns are, with wild dark Cornish and Breton blood mingled within them. Even so, you will find both youngsters quiet and well behaved, perhaps even too much so, I have thought for quite some while—for children ought to be children, I always say, and there's been precious little enough merriment in their lives since her ladyship died.'' Mrs. Wickersham paused, pressing her gentle lips together almost grimly for an instant, as though to prevent herself from saying anything further on this subject, and indeed, when she continued, it was to direct the conversation into another channel.

"But, there, I mustn't rattle on so, thoughtlessly keeping you from your bed when you must be utterly exhausted from your long journey and, now that you've finished your meal, wanting to retire, my dear. The hour has grown very late, for the clock has just now struck midnight. There will be plenty of time in the morning for you to meet Meliora and Bastian, and, since tomorrow is Saturday, for you to spend the weekend getting acquainted with them and forming your own initial impressions before beginning lessons on Monday. And, too, you will learn, by and by, how we get on here at the manor and, so, need not be overwhelmed with it all at once.''

With that, once more laying aside her embroidery, the housekeeper stood, snuffing the candles in the silver lamps one by one, then taking up a lone brass candlestick to light their way upstairs, as Verity gathered her belongings. She wondered whether, before seeking her bed, she ought to inform the elderly woman about the highwayman who had held up the Earl's equipage, but then, after consideration, she slowly decided against it. She did not want to start off her new position on the wrong foot, and she was uncertain whether the incident would make trouble for Howel, perhaps even causing him to be dismissed and thus inevitably setting all the servants against her. He had already apologized, and he would know better than she, besides, what ought to be done, whether a complaint should be lodged with the Earl or some other authority.

The matter thus settled in her mind, Verity followed Mrs. Wickersham through the long dark corridors of the manor to the entrance hall, thence up the grand, central oak staircase, with its highly polished and ornately carved balustrade, to the gallery above, whence the bedrooms emanated. The gallery, which overlooked the entrance hall below, ran around three sides; the fourth—to the front of the house—was slightly larger and gracefully curved to fashion a minstrel gallery, behind which a circular stained-glass window was set into the manor's exterior wall. Beyond, outside, the savage storm still raged, and as Verity and the housekeeper climbed the long flight of steps, coruscating lightning flared in the night sky, intermittently illuminating the entrance hall, staircase and galleries, flooding them with eerie splashes of color, so that they resembled something not of this world. As a result, Verity once more experienced the strange, disturbing impression that she had come to a fairy-tale castle that was not quite real.

Mrs. Wickersham, however, seemed unperturbed.

"I've put you in the east wing with the rest of the upper staff, in the bedroom but one from my own, my dear," she announced, as they reached the gallery and started down its length. "It is a rear chamber and not as spacious as the front bedrooms are. However, as it is much cozier and rather more private, and overlooks the gardens out back, which are quite beautiful when in bloom, I thought that perhaps you would much prefer it. I know I do."

"It sounds exactly so, ma'am," Verity agreed, pleased and touched by the housekeeper's consideration. "For in truth, my chamber at Trowbridge was such a dreary cubicle that I would feel lost and uncomfortable in some huge, luxurious apartment."

Plainly delighted that her choice had been so well received and approved, the elderly woman led Verity down a passage that branched to the east from the long gallery, finally coming to a halt before the closed door of the rear, corner bedroom. After turning the brass key in the lock, Mrs. Wickersham stepped inside, passing through a small antechamber, which was the dressing room, with tall, capacious wardrobes lining the walls on either side of the door, and at the center of whose floor sat Verity's trunk, waiting to be unpacked. Glancing swiftly but keenly around the bedroom itself to be quite certain all was properly in readiness for the new occupant, and upon observing that it was, the housekeeper nodded to herself with satisfaction. Then she bade Verity a gentle good-night and left her alone in the chamber.

Once on her own, Verity inventoried her surroundings, thrilled and marveling as she slowly moved from one thing to the next, touching and stroking fabric and wood, as though quite unsure if any of it were real, if perhaps this were actually a dream from which she would shortly awaken, only to find herself, in reality, back in her dull, miserable cell at Trowbridge.

If this was a small bedroom at St. Aubyn, then she would indeed, as she had earlier surmised, have rattled around like an ill-aimed marble in one of the manor's larger chambers, and so she was even gladder to have been given this one.

It was itself of a size to which she was thoroughly unaccustomed and boasted furnishings of which she had never before had the like. Against one wall stood a canopy bed high enough that it required a short flight of wooden steps to climb into it, and with bedclothes consisting of a heavy burgundy coverlet and bed curtains for warmth. It was bordered by twin night tables set with crystal lamps and, at its foot, by a bench with a comfortable cushion upholstered in a burgundy-and-gold-striped material. Opposite the bed was a fireplace with mantel, flanked by two small bookcases, which held a few books and some bric-a-brac. On one side of the wide doorway to the dressing room sat a graceful dressing table with a gilt-framed, beveled oval mirror above and a round, tufted and fringed stool of gold brocade beneath. On the other side was a commode with a square mirror above and a white porcelain washbasin, pitcher and chamber pot. The far end of the bedroom boasted two cozy wing chairs covered in a Scottish-plaid fabric, with a gateleg table between them, upon which stood yet a third crystal lamp. Gaily patterned chintz draperies hung at the windows; wallpaper with a delicate floral design set above dark oak-paneled wainscoting covered the walls; and a Persian carpet lay on the gleaming wooden floor. Candles burned in all the lamps; a small fire blazed cheerily in the grate; the coal bucket was full; and a warming pan heated on the hearth, so that her bedsheets should prove neither cold nor damp.

Best of all—and most appealing to Verity's vivid imagination—was the fact that, being the corner bedroom, the chamber opened into one of the eight octagonal towers that rose from the manor's corners and its east and west sides, and that also flanked its portico. Not large, the tower nook had been cleverly fitted all the way around with a built-in, ornately carved wooden coffer that served as not only additional storage, but also seating, being plushly cushioned in the same burgundy-and-gold-striped material as the bench at the foot of the bed. The niche was separated from the main chamber by a doorway at which, just as at that to the dressing room, hung burgundy velvet curtains, drawn back and tied with tasseled cords. Verity could not envision a more wonderful or more secluded hideaway for reading or sketching, two of her favorite pastimes.

For all this was she inordinately grateful, and all at once, her misgivings about having come to such a strange, wild, desolate place—where brutal storms battered the land, brigands rode the hightoby and inns and manors were grey, grim, and forbidding in nature—vanished.

She could bear a very great deal, indeed, Verity thought, sighing deeply with contentment, for such a bedroom as this.

Three

Journey's End, Life's Beginning

Youth, what man's age is like to be doth show;
We may our ends by our beginnings know.

Of Prudence
—Sir John Denham

In my end is my beginning.

Motto
—Mary, Queen of Scots

By fairy hands their knell is rung,
By forms unseen their dirge is sung;
There Honor comes, a pilgrim gray,
To bless the turf that wraps their clay,
And Freedom shall awhile repair,
To dwell a weeping hermit there!

Ode Written in the Year 1746
—William Collins

With great care, Verity placed her bonnet, muff, reticule and gloves on the single top shelf inside one of the wardrobes, then hung her mantle on one of its many pegs within. Her outer accoutrements looked very forlorn, she thought, inside the spacious compartment, which even the remainder of her clothing would not be able to fill. The idea that anyone should own enough garments so that there would be no room left within all the wardrobes put together astonished her, although she knew there were those who did. The Earl, no doubt, was such a one.

As she slowly knelt to unlock and open her trunk, she pondered all that she had learned about him tonight. Proud and arrogant, but fair and honorable, Mrs. Wickersham had said of him, and that he did not turn his servants off on a whim. That boded well for her, Verity realized, for as long as she performed her job competently and was not a troublemaker, she could be assured of a permanent position here at St. Aubyn for quite a long time, thus enjoying a secure future. Many governesses, she knew, were not nearly so fortunate as that.

Nor had it sounded as though either Meliora or

Bastian would prove a problem child. To the contrary, they were too subdued and could afford to be livelier, the housekeeper had averred. Thinking of this, Verity felt her heart go out to the two youngsters. Their mother's untimely death must have affected them very hard indeed. Since she had been but a five-year-old child herself when a shipwreck had claimed not only her own mother, but also her father, Verity could sympathize with the Earl's children. She would have a bond with them, she thought, that might prove a first step in winning their trust and liking, which she knew she must earn if she were to be able to effectively teach them.

Tiredness prevented Verity from completely unpacking her trunk, which she would do in the morning. For now, she removed only her essential toiletries, nightgown and wrapper. Her silver-backed mirror, brush and comb, inherited from her mother, she arranged on the dressing table, along with a small bottle of attar of roses. Her toothbrush found a home on the commode, while her nightgown and wrapper she laid on the bed, in preparation for retiring.

Then she undressed and, pouring water from the pitcher on the commode into its matching washbasin, laved her face and hands, and cleaned her teeth, glad to rinse away the residue of her travels. The cake of soft, sweetly scented soap and the sponge that had been provided for her use astounded and delighted her, for she was accustomed to harsh, lye soap, which burned the skin, and a coarse washcloth. Donning her nightgown, she unpinned her long dark-brown hair, which hung to her willowy waist, brushed it, then neatly plaited it into a single braid.

After that, Verity stoked the fire, even daring to add a little more coal to keep her warm through the night, for this was a luxury she had never before known, either—and surely, since the coal bucket was full, she was meant to employ its contents! Then she extinguished all the candles in the lamps and climbed the short little wooden flight of steps to the high canopy bed with its plump downy mattress, drawing the bed curtains closed about her.

In the darkness illuminated only by the flames on the hearth, she lay still, listening to the storm that continued to roil outside. If she were honest with herself, she must admit that despite its frightening ferocity, there was something about its wildness and savagery that, now, when she was no longer exposed to its full fury, spoke to some unknown thing deep inside her, which she had not heretofore recognized that she possessed.

As though taking some precious object from a treasure box, Verity gingerly examined this new, strange and somehow distressing aspect of her character. Perhaps it was only the events of this entire eve that had unsettled her, she decided at last, making her feel no longer quite herself, as though by coming here to Cornwall and St. Aubyn, so different from Derbyshire and Trowbridge, she had even now begun a process of transformation that would lead she knew not where. No, she would be better tomorrow, Verity insisted to herself, when her serenity and composure would once more return to her, and her life would go on as quietly and unremarkably as it had before.

She was too young and had lived too sheltered a life at Trowbridge to guess the real truth of the matter: that any significant change in circumstance usually results in a significant change, as well, in the one who experiences it.

And so, blissfully unaware, she finally slept.

Dawn brought a pale, sickly sun that struggled hard to pierce the mizzle—but without success. Although last night's storm had now blown over, thick, nebulous clouds continued to swirl in the lowering sky, spattering drizzle, and mist tinged with spindrift swept in from the sea, floating across the moors and marshes, and lying in the hollows of the land.

Rising from her bed and drawing the curtains at her windows, Verity gazed out through the lozenged lead-glass panes over a lawn, gardens and wooded park swathed in brume, which lent them a strange, otherworldly air, as though they might be the haunts of elves and fairies. Even as the idea occurred to her, she spied two diminutive figures, accompanied by a larger one, making their way along one of the serpentine flagstone garden paths. This, she realized, must surely be the twins, Meliora and Bastian, with their nurse, out for a morning walk.

Stepping to one side of the window so that they would not see her, Verity watched them for several long minutes. The youngsters did not run and play, as, despite Mrs. Wickersham's words to her last night about them, she had expected. Instead, they strolled sedately, almost gravely, in a manner that, while well behaved, was not at all childlike. Verity tried to think back to when her own parents had died, wondering how long she had grieved for them. She could not remember, but still, she thought that the two years the Earl's wife had now been deceased seemed an uncommonly long time for a household to remain even unofficially in mourning.

Even so, it appeared the Earl had at last decided that it was now time to leave the past behind and to move forward, time for Meliora and Bastian to graduate from the nursery to the schoolroom, and Verity was to help them make that change. In some respects, her job would be easier because the youngsters had never before had a governess, so they would not know if, lacking experience, she made mistakes. In other respects, it would be harder, because their minds were as yet untrained, and it was up to her to mold and educate them in accordance with the Earl's expectations and to his own wishes and satisfaction.

For a moment, that notion made Verity feel as though she had butterflies in her stomach. But then she determinedly reminded herself that, as first a pupil and then a teacher at Trowbridge, she had managed to win the approval of even the stern, exacting administrators of that grim and miserable institution. How much worse, then, could the Earl be, especially when his housekeeper had termed him a just man? Indeed, a man who did not stint on either candles or coal for those who served him was already more esteemed in Verity's own eyes than the Trowbridge administrators, who had grudged the institution's or-

phaned pupils so much as a candle stub and a few
lumps of coal or peat on even the darkest, coldest
nights. The Earl had sent his own carriage for her to
Jamaica Inn, too, and made and paid for all the arrangements there, as well, none of which he needed
to have done—and most employers would not have.
That was another mark in his favor.

Turning from the window, Verity undertook her
morning ablutions, then finished unpacking her trunk
and neatly putting away her belongings. She dressed
herself carefully in one of the three gowns she possessed—two of which were of plain black bombazine, the third and best of which was of pearl-grey
silk and thus much too fine to wear on any but special occasions. To the clean black gown she had
donned—the one she had not traveled in—Verity
added a fresh white linen tucker and a matching
apron, the latter of which she found useful to guard
against chalk, ink, paints and other such ilk associated with a schoolroom.

Undoing her long hair from its braid, she brushed it,
then wound it into its customary neat chignon at her
nape. Then, studying her reflection in the dressing-
table mirror, she observed with dismay how odd her
hair looked, with its tress cut short on the right side
by the highwayman, escaping from her hairpins. In
the end, there was no help for it but to cut the other
side, also, to make the two even, and then to curl the
shorter tendrils, so that they framed her oval face
softly. Verity could only hope she did not appear too
frivolous.

After that, she tidied her bedroom, then made her way along the long gallery to the front staircase leading down to the entrance hall. All the usual morning noises associated with a kitchen preparing—or washing up after—breakfast guided her in that general direction, and she came at last to the sitting room to which she had been conducted last night upon her arrival at the manor. Now, as then, Mrs. Wickersham sat within.

"Good morning, ma'am," Verity greeted her.

"Gracious, you're up early, my dear, even though I bade Loveday let you sleep, as I felt certain you would be worn out from your long journey."

"Thank you very much, ma'am. But as to my being up early, I beg to disagree, for indeed, I fear I must be the last one downstairs this morning. From my windows, I saw what I presume to have been Meliora and Bastian with their nurse outside in the gardens, and now, here you are before me, also. Am I too late for breakfast?"

"No, not at all. We have none of us yet eaten this morning, but now that you've come down, we shall. Trueth—who is the twins' nurse—will bring them inside just shortly, I'm sure. The upper staff always dines in the breakfast room, even in the evenings." The housekeeper indicated the room next door, where, through the open, adjoining pairs of French doors that flanked the Parian fireplace shared by the two chambers, Verity could see a round table and a sideboard in the process of being prepared for breakfast by some of the housemaids and footmen. "For the servants' hall is only for the lower staff. Trueth and the youngsters usually have trays sent up to the nursery, of course—although, sometimes, now that the children are older, they eat at the table with us, as they shall this morning, so you can meet them and grow a little acquainted. They are always a little company for me, too. But whilst there are the twins, and also Mr. Drummond, the steward; Mr. Ashfield, his lordship's valet; Mr. Peacock, the butler; and Mr. Lathrop, the groom of the chambers, it is simply not the same as having another woman of my own status and intelligence to converse with.'' The elderly woman sighed, then went on.

''It is sometimes difficult, I have always thought, being betwixt and between, neither grand enough for the dining room nor belonging in the servants' hall. For one must maintain a certain formality with one's betters and an equally certain distance with those over whom one has authority. So I am very glad you are come to St. Aubyn, my dear.''

''I am, too,'' Verity replied, smiling shyly with pleasure, realizing Mrs. Wickersham was lonely and thus eagerly looking forward to having someone of her own rank to talk to.

''However, I do have a bone to pick with you, Miss Collier!''

''Ma'am?''

''Indeed, I do.'' The housekeeper nodded gently, her eyes twinkling softly. ''For you never breathed a single word to me last night about his lordship's carriage having been set upon by a highwayman— and that Black Jack Raven himself, no less!''

''Oh! You must forgive me for the omission,

ma'am. I confess I had no wish to be the cause of any trouble for Howel, and since there was no real harm done and I was as yet a stranger to the household, I thought it best to allow him to take whatever action he deemed appropriate.''

"And so he has," the elderly woman explained. "He has told all, and word has been sent to the dragoon guards at Truro. Colonel Sherbourne is to call this afternoon for a full report. Black Jack Raven is the most notorious brigand in these parts, wanted high and low for his dastardly deeds, and the dragoons have sought his capture now for many long weeks!"

"My goodness! I had no idea, of course, that he was so very infamous!" Verity said.

"No, but he is—for since he commenced his lawless acts here in Cornwall some months ago, he has robbed many a poor, unwary coach and traveler, relieving them of their purses and other valuables. No one has proved safe from his thievery. I had not, however, thought Black Jack so bold as to attack his lordship's vehicle, but since he has now done so, it would seem he has grown even more dangerous and daring! Yet Howel claims the brazen robber behaved quite peculiarly to you, my dear.''

"Indeed, he did, ma'am," Verity confirmed. "For, fortunately, although I was frightened, I still somehow had the presence of mind to shove my reticule into my muff, so he would not know I had it, and when he would have insisted on stealing my locket, which belonged to my departed mother—God rest her soul—I told him I would not part with it, that he would have to shoot me to get it.''

"No! How very brave!''

"Foolhardy, more like, I have no doubt. In truth, I thought to have my life ended right then and there, ma'am. But instead, the wicked fellow only laughed, making me his compliments. Then, before I realized what he was about, he drew forth his rapier and—and cut off a lock of my hair! That is why you see it as it is now this morning, ma'am. As it looked very odd otherwise, I was forced to trim the opposite side to even the two, and there was naught for it but to curl the bits afterward, to try to give them some semblance of decency—although I fretted that the resulting effect was too frivolous for one in my position.''

"Not at all, my dear,'' Mrs. Wickersham hastened to reassure her. "So be at ease. It is a style quite becoming to you and, under the circumstances, cannot be thought of as other than a badge of courage!''

"Thank you, ma'am. I am most grateful to hear it.''

No more was said, for just then, Trueth, the nurse, entered the morning room, along with her two young charges, followed shortly by Messrs Drummond, Peacock and Lathrop—the steward, butler, and groom of the chambers, respectively. Mr. Ashfield, the valet, it seemed, was away with the Earl. Verity was introduced to all, and then their morning meal was served in the breakfast room, the plates and

bowls being set out for them on the sideboard by the
housemaids and footmen.

As Trueth intended to have a tray sent up for her
to the nursery, Verity was not able to speak long with
her, but made arrangements to do so later that day.
The three male authority figures of the household
were polite, but relatively uncommunicative, not being inclined to idle chitchat upon first meeting Verity, without having yet taken her measure. Having
greeted her, inquired as to her health and journey,
and remarked on the weather, they said little further.
She was then at leisure to direct her attention to Meliora and Bastian.

As she did so, Verity thought that perhaps her earlier, fanciful impression this morning was not so very
far off the mark, after all, for the appearance of the
twins was such that they might indeed have been
mistaken for fairy children, even without the benefit
of the mist that cloaked the gardens outside. Both
youngsters were small for their age, and delicate,
with dark skin and black eyes, these last seemingly
too large for their grave little faces.

Despite Verity's cheerful attempts to draw them
out, the twins spoke hardly at all, both being of a
nature shy and withdrawn, it seemed—although perhaps not naturally so, she suspected, given their
motherless circumstances. Still, they were avidly curious about her. Of that, she felt sure, for when they
thought she was not watching, they observed her
with a great deal of interest and speculation from
beneath the thick fringe of their long sooty lashes.
Had she sensed any hostility from the youngsters, she

would have been highly unnerved. As it was, she believed them uncertain and, oddly, even fearful where she was concerned, and as it had last night, her heart went out to them. They were poor, lost little souls, she thought—much as she herself had been at the deaths of her own parents.

Instinctively, Verity did not press the children and felt her reticence to have been the proper course of action when they regarded her less dauntedly. She had made a beginning that was well enough. In time, she would with caring and kindness win their hearts and favor, she reckoned.

After breakfast, Mrs. Wickersham proposed to show Verity the rest of the manor. "For I know what it is like to be in an unfamiliar place and not know one's way about," the housekeeper declared. "However, although large, St. Aubyn is most well laid out and thus difficult to lose one's way in. The two main passages on the ground floor are echoed on the first and second stories, and so from any of them, one can find the path to the central staircase in the entrance hall, where one may then orient oneself."

Continuing to chatter amiably, the elderly woman conducted Verity on a tour of the house. The original castle was nearly four centuries old and had been built facing south. Later, the wings had been renovated and expanded, and the gabled roof added, until the edifice, once square, had become not only rectangular in footprint, but also a strange—although not displeasing—mixture of architectural styles. On the ground floor, it was halved from front to back by the entrance hall, which, in medieval times, had used to be the great hall and was the central core of the entire manor, at the rear of which was a large conservatory filled with exotic plants of all kinds. From the entrance hall, two main corridors ran east and west, dividing both wings into north and south sides. At the far end of each of these passages, which each culminated in one of the manor's eight octagonal towers, were, as in those on flanking the portico, spiral staircases leading up to the first and second stories.

In the east wing, on the south side, were the small and the large drawing rooms, with two scts of French doors between them, which could be either opened or closed, depending upon the need for privacy or else for space to accommodate huge parties. Beyond the same kind of French doors that flanked the shared Parian fireplace at the opposite end of the large drawing room lay the music room, which boasted a grand piano and a gilded harp, and whose tower nook formed a small alcove for private tête-à-têtes. On the north side of the east wing were the library—in whose floor-to-ceiling bookcases, behind locked glass doors, sat rows of leather-bound books of every kind—the card room, and then the billiard room, whose own tower bay sported a smoking room.

In the west wing, on the south side, were the dining room, the kitchen—in which a set of stairs led down to the basement's wine cellar—and then, side by side, the larder and scullery, separated from each other by a short, narrow hall that led to the laundry, which had a small storeroom in its tower niche. On the north side of the west wing were the Earl's study and then the morning and breakfast rooms. Next to this last, but reached by means of a short passage that branched off from the main west corridor, were Messrs Drummond's and Peacock's and Mrs. Wickersham's offices all three in a row. Across from these lay the servants' hall, where the help dined, and tucked into its tower recess was a washroom for them.

It was, as Mrs. Wickersham had earlier observed, a most excellent arrangement, for among other things, the dining and breakfast rooms and servants' hall could all be easily served hot meals and other refreshments from the kitchen, with no inconvenience.

Eagerly Verity's gaze drank in the splendor of all the chambers, as the French doors to one after another were opened to reveal the grandeur within. The walls were all tinted in pale, elegant hues, with elaborate cornices, crown moldings, pillars, mantels and wainscoting—all intricately carved with grapes, vines, flowers and other motifs, the woods either painted pure white or else stained dark, depending upon each room's character and function. Chandeliers laden with crystal ropes and teardrop pendants were suspended from the ceilings; rich, heavy draperies hung at the windows; brilliantly colored tapestries and gilt-framed mirrors, pictures and portraits adorned the walls; and Persian carpets lay upon the floors. Fine wood furnishings of cherry, oak, mahogany, rosewood and satinwood, and couches, chairs, benches and ottomans upholstered in gorgeously grained leathers and chatoyant silks, satins, damasks and brocades filled the rooms. Alabaster Grecian and Roman statuettes and Bohemian-glass ornaments, Sèvres china and Dresden figurines, ormolu clocks and silver lamps and serving pieces, and Oriental screens and plants in brass, copper and Chinese-porcelain pots decorated the mantels, tables and floors.

"Oh! How very magnificent it all is!" Verity breathed, awed, for she had never before in her life seen the like. "And how carefully and well you maintain it, Mrs. Wickersham! I had thought that it would all be swathed in canvas sheets, to guard against dust, mildew and must in his lordship's absence. Yet it is all immaculately in readiness, as though he will come back at any moment. Is he expected soon, then?"

"I do not know. His lordship is often away, traveling—to London and the Continent. Even to such far-flung places as the West Indies, Egypt, India and the Orient, he has been. We never know when he will return. But he does not like to come home and find the manor all shut up like a tomb. So we keep it always as though he were in residence."

"His lordship is here but little, then, I take it?"

"In the past two years, since her ladyship died, yes, he has spent but very little time here," the housekeeper elucidated. "He loved her very much, so the place holds painful memories for him, I have no doubt. In addition, his lordship is attached to the War Office in some capacity—I know not what—and so, until the Treaty of Amiens was signed between Great Britain and France earlier this year, he was much away in connection with the war efforts. Perhaps now that that Corsican upstart Napoléon seems to have given up all his wicked designs upon us, we may get on with our lives in peace and quiet, without fearing to be murdered in our beds by French legions!''

"Let us hope so, indeed, ma'am!" Verity agreed earnestly.

Going upstairs from the ground floor to the first floor, the two women continued their tour of the manor. Here were to be found sixteen bedrooms— eight in the east wing and eight in the west, all with their own dressing rooms, and the four largest, which all faced south, having their own boudoirs, as well. In between each pair of the large chambers were two private baths. The twelve smaller bedrooms lined the north rear of the house and, in each wing, were set in threes off two short passages flanking two central, shared baths, between which was a large closet for linens and other storage. All the smaller chambers were furnished much like Verity's own, although done in different colors, while the larger bedrooms were even more opulent.

The last of these, in the west wing, was especially so, draped in shades of gold and icy blue, and bedecked with stunning furnishings and ornaments. In its boudoir, above the white-marble mantel, hung a huge portrait of the loveliest woman Verity had ever before seen. Golden-haired and pale-blue eyed, the lady was, with a distant, regal air, and clothed all in gossamer white and set amid a wintry bower, so that

she looked like some snowy, fairy-tale princess, forever frozen in time.

"That was his lordship's wife, the Lady Tamsyn—
God rest her soul," Mrs. Wickersham said, as she
noticed Verity's keen interest in the portrait. "This
was her apartment when she was alive, and his lordship's own was next door. But after her death, he
could not bear the sight of either of them and so
moved into the east wing. They are used only for his
guests now."

"Her ladyship was very beautiful! So fair and
stately—just like a queen! No wonder his lordship
loved her! How tragic that she was so young when
death claimed her. How did she die, ma'am?"

For an interminable moment, it seemed as though
the housekeeper would not answer, and Verity feared
that, unbeknown to her, she had inadvertently trodden upon some forbidden territory, and she hastened
to apologize.

"Please forgive me. I did not mean to pry."

"No, I know you didn't." The housekeeper shook
her head sadly, sighing. "It's not your fault, my dear.
It is only natural that you would be curious. It's just
that, here at St. Aubyn...we never talk of that dreadful night.... Still, perhaps it is best that you should
hear the whole, awful story now, and from my own
lips, so you will understand why matters are the way
they are here at the manor, and you will not seek to
question further—and of those to whom such would
prove inordinately painful." The elderly woman
paused, as though gathering her thoughts. Then, at
long last, in a low, hushed voice, so that her words

would not be discerned by any other save Verity, she related her sad tale.

"A strange, terrible accident, it was, that took her ladyship's life. The twins' nurse—not young Trueth, whom we have now, but another, older nurse, whose name was Doryty—fell asleep at her post. Unbeknown to us then, she was overly fond of a pint of porter, and that dire night, she evidently imbibed far more than her fair share." Mrs. Wickersham's lips thinned with severe disapproval at the memory. "Observing their nurse thus, the twins, who were only five years old at the time and a wild, mischievous pair then—not quiet and well behaved, as you see them now—took it in their fanciful heads to slip from their beds, creeping past Doryty, who slumbered and snored in a deep, drunken stupor in her chair. Somehow—it was never learned how—they then managed to sneak away from the house, bent on spying the fairies they had heard tell danced on the dewy grass whenever there was a ring around the misty moon."

"Oh, no!" Verity cried, upon hearing this.

"Yes, my dear. Truly, it was a miracle that no harm befell them, too. But, there, I get ahead of myself. To continue, her ladyship awoke—undoubtedly, it was a mother's instinct that bestirred her—and going upstairs to the nursery, she discovered her children's nurse far too heavily asleep to be wakened and that both the youngsters themselves were missing. Why her ladyship did not then rouse the entire manor, no one knows. Perhaps she intended to but then, upon retracing her steps to the gallery, noticed the front door standing open wide. In her diaphanous white nightgown and bare feet, she ran outside, looking like a ghost in the mist as she set off in search of the twins.

"When, rounding the house, she reached the back gardens, his lordship glimpsed what seemed an apparition from his study window—for he toiled late at his desk that night—and, curious, he hurried outside after it, realizing after a moment that it was his distraught wife. Her ladyship's mind was of a sensitive nature, and now, she was half out of it with worry for her children and what had become of them. In her great upset and grief, she raced on blindly through the gardens, toward the shore beyond, paying no heed to his lordship's calling her name and chasing after her. At the edge of the dangerous, crumbling cliffs along the sea, her ladyship slipped and stumbled on the wet grass, and, thus losing her footing, fell to the deadly rocks below. His lordship arrived too late to save her. Ever since, he has blamed himself for her death, and he and the poor twins, being found in the gardens afterward, were irrevocably changed from that fateful night to such as they all are now."

Here, the housekeeper ended her tragic revelations.

"Thank you, ma'am, for sharing the St. Aubyns' story with me," Verity stated softly, much moved. "You may trust to my discretion. I shall speak of it to no one."

"I know you will not, my dear. I would not have recounted the tale to you otherwise." Once more, the elderly woman paused. Then, abruptly shaking off her memories of the unhappy past, she asked, "Shall we continue our tour of St. Aubyn?"

The manor's second floor—which was not as spacious as the first two stories and, except for the central core, which housed the schoolroom and nursery, had sloped walls and ceilings—was a veritable rabbit warren of servants' quarters and attic storerooms. In the schoolroom, which Mrs. Wickersham had saved until the very last, Verity discovered the nurse, Trueth, along with Meliora and Bastian, waiting for her.

"Well, my dear, I shall leave you now to become better acquainted with Trueth and your young charges," the housekeeper announced to Verity, "and be about my own business, for I've plenty of work yet to do!"

"I hope I didn't take up too much of your time, ma'am," Verity said quickly, worried that perhaps she had.

"No, not at all. So please don't fret yourself on that account. I've enjoyed showing you the manor. Remember, you're to let me know if you require anything else for the schoolroom."

"Yes, I won't forget. Thank you so much, ma'am."

"It was my pleasure, my dear."

Once Mrs. Wickersham had left them, Verity spent some time chatting with Trueth, who was a sturdy, sensible young woman of good Cornish peasant stock. Between them, they arranged a schedule whereby Verity would give the twins their lessons during the morning hours, with her afternoons free, at which time the children would continue in the nursery with Trueth, for they were too young yet for a full day of classes and other activities.

"And of course, I will be happy to take them on afternoon walks or other outings, Trueth, so you may have some time to yourself, also."

"Thank 'ee, miss. 'Twill be much appreciated."

Matters thus settled, Trueth, too, departed, and Verity was left alone at last with the youngsters.

"Well, I suppose the first thing we ought to do together is to take stock of the schoolroom." She spoke quietly and smiled at them gently, for she could tell that now that their nurse was gone, they were apprehensive. "Would you like to help me do that?"

They glanced at each other silently, then nodded politely. But still, neither spoke.

"All right, then. Let's see what we have here. I expect it will be rather like a treasure hunt, don't you?"

Despite the fact that they only nodded again, Verity continued to talk to them, keeping her voice low but natural, as the three of them investigated the schoolroom. The glass doors of the bookcases were locked. However, Mrs. Wickersham had given Verity the key, and now, she turned it in the lock to reveal a plethora of elementary works suitable for children—books for reading, writing, arithmetic, history and geography. Other nearby, open shelves yielded such finds as tablets, sketch pads, and slates, as well as pens and ink, charcoal pencils, crayons and chalk. On one wall hung a large blackboard, and there were two sturdy easels supplied with brushes, watercolors and paper for painting. At the center of a table with chairs was a globe, and in one corner stood a cabinet piano of rosewood.

Spying this, Verity sat down upon its plumply cushioned bench, running her slender fingers experimentally over the black-and-white keys. Then, slowly, with feeling, she began from memory to play a beautiful, haunting melody, the first movement of a piece properly titled *Sonata quasi una Fantasia*—"Sonata almost a Fantasy"—but that, in later years, would be known simply as "Moonlight Sonata."

"Oh, madam, that was lovely!" Meliora whispered, when the new governess had finished playing and the last note had dulcetly died away.

Much to Verity's surprise, for she had dreamily lost herself in the melody, as she half turned on the piano bench at the unexpected sound of Meliora's voice in her ear, she saw that both of the twins had crept forward to stand very near to her, inexorably drawn by the music.

"It perhaps spoke to you, Meliora, as it does to me, no?" Verity queried gently.

"Yes, madam, it did."

"It is a piece of music called a sonata, written by a German composer named Ludwig von Beethoven and dedicated only last year by him to the Countess Giulietta Guicciardi, with whom he had fallen in love. Would you like to learn how to play it?"

"Is it—Is it possible that I could? You—You do not tease me, madam?"

"No, Meliora. It is one of the things I have come

to St. Aubyn to teach you…how to play this instrument, which is called a cabinet piano. Would you like to learn, also, Bastian?''

The boy nodded but did not speak, and although he was the older twin by one hour, as Verity had learned from Mrs. Wickersham earlier this morning during their tour of the manor, she knew that at this moment, Meliora was the braver.

''Excellent. I am very glad to hear it—and delighted to have two such promising young pupils! So, on Monday morning, we will begin our lessons together, during which time you will learn not only how to play the piano, but also many other skills and talents, such as reading, arithmetic, history and geography, how to speak French, Italian and German, and to sketch charcoal drawings and to paint watercolors. To you, Meliora, I will also teach fine needlework, and eventually, Bastian will be taught Latin and Greek, although for such things as those and other, more advanced studies, he will require a male tutor, will perhaps even go away to school someday—to Eton or Harrow or some other—when he is many years older than he is now. But for now, I will teach the two of you, and I hope we will become friends.''

''Thank you, madam,'' the girl said soberly. ''We shall both try very hard to please you.''

''Oh, I do not think you shall either of you have to try very hard, for you both please me already,'' Verity responded, her words rewarded with two shy, but genuine smiles. ''I am happy to be your new governess.''

"We have never had a governess before."

"I know. Shall I tell you a secret? Yes? I have never been a governess before, either. Before I came here to St. Aubyn, I was a teacher at a school called Trowbridge, in Derbyshire, which is a long way from Cornwall."

"Have you journeyed to many places, madam?" Meliora inquired.

"No, until a few days ago, I had never left Derbyshire. Indeed, I had never even traveled more than fifteen miles from Belper, which is a market town known for its nail making, cotton manufacturing and white-stone quarrying. But now, St. Aubyn is to be my home, and here, I hope to stay a while." Verity paused briefly. Then she continued, "And now, I believe we have seen all there is to see here in the schoolroom, and we have become a little better acquainted, have we not? So, since it is now nearly lunchtime and you must both be hungry, let us go downstairs and find out what Cook has for us."

Feeling as though she had done very well her first day, Verity then accompanied the children down to the breakfast room, where it was discovered that Cook had cold meats, cheeses and salads to offer. Messrs Drummond, Peacock and Lathrop apparently did not partake of the midday meal, so Verity, Mrs. Wickersham and the twins dined alone. As a result, the atmosphere was much more relaxed and congenial, and Verity was delighted when both she and the housekeeper managed to draw the youngsters into conversation, although, still, it was only Meliora who actually spoke, with Bastian only nodding in response to the dialogue.

Afterward, the children returned to Trueth and the nursery, while Verity was summoned to the small drawing room, to be interrogated by the dragoon guards' Colonel Sherbourne about the notorious highwayman Black Jack Raven.

Four

At the Edge of the Sea

Listen! You hear the grating roar
Of pebbles which the waves draw back, and fling,
At their return, up the high strand,
Begin, and cease, and then again begin,
With tremulous cadence slow, and bring
The eternal note of sadness in.

> *Dover Beach, st. 1*
> —Matthew Arnold

The sea of faith
Was once, too, at the full, and round earth's shore
Lay like the folds of a bright girdle furled;
But now I only hear
Its melancholy, long, withdrawing roar,
Retreating, to the breath
Of the night wind down the vast edges drear
And naked shingles of the world.

> *Dover Beach, st. 3*
> —Matthew Arnold

As the groom of the chambers, it was a part of Mr. Lathrop's responsibilities to greet visitors and announce them to the appropriate members of the household. So it was he who informed Verity that Colonel Sherbourne, of the dragoon guards, had arrived at St. Aubyn and was now waiting in the small drawing room for her to receive him.

"Please inform Colonel Sherbourne that I will be there directly," Verity told Mr. Lathrop.

"Very well, Miss Collier." He nodded to her briefly.

After checking her appearance in a mirror in the morning room, smoothing her chignon and gown and removing her apron and laying it to one side, she traversed the passage to the small drawing room.

While beautifully and elegantly appointed, the small drawing room was not as formal as its larger counterpart next door, and for this reason, Verity felt more comfortable in it than she did in the other. As she entered the chamber, she observed a tall, uniformed man standing, with his back to her, at the windows, gazing out over the sweeping front lawn and wooded park beyond.

"Colonel Sherbourne?"

"Yes, and no other! And you must be the new governess, Miss Collier, I presume." Turning from his perusal of the dismal weather outside and smiling, he made her a courteous bow, to which she responded with an equally polite curtsy.

"Won't you please sit down, Colonel?" She indicated a nearby chair, taking a seat herself. "May I offer you some refreshment? Some tea, perhaps, or something stronger?"

"Tea would be lovely, madam, thank you. I've ridden over from Truro, and so in all truth, I could do with something hot to warm me on a day such as this."

Ringing for a footman, Verity instructed him to fetch some tea, then once more directed her attention to the Colonel.

"I am so sorry, sir, that you were put to the trouble of coming here in such weather."

"You are perhaps not familiar with Cornwall, Miss Collier?"

"No, sir. Until only a few days ago, Derbyshire was my home—and, indeed, all I knew of the world."

"Forgive me, but I thought as much. Once you come to know Cornwall, you will realize that today's weather is not so very inclement as you might suppose. Those of us who live here are accustomed to the mizzle. However, have no fear, madam. We do have our share of sunny days, for we've a fair number of gardens to testify to that fact, even though it does not always seem as though sunshine favors us!

But perhaps, having suffered such a rude introduction to our county, you are now of a mind to pack up and return to Derbyshire posthaste!''

Verity smiled, for she liked Colonel Sherbourne immediately. A handsome man, with sandy-blond hair and twinkling cornflower-blue eyes, his manner was affable and charming, designed to put her at her ease.

''I am made of sterner stuff than perhaps I appear, Colonel,'' she rejoined firmly.

''Indeed, it must be so!'' he declared. ''For Lord St. Aubyn's coachman, Howel, has already given me an account of what transpired with the highwayman Black Jack Raven. However, I should like to have your own version of the unhappy event, also, Miss Collier, for your own perspective will have been different from Howel's, and it may be that you will have spied something that escaped his notice. Black Jack's a clever scoundrel, and I've chased him for quite some time now—without success, unfortunately, I confess. I should like very much to apprehend him.''

''I shall be glad to tell you my version of the incident and hope I may be of assistance to you, sir. However, I feel it only to fair to warn you that I will doubtless have very little to add to what Howel has already imparted to you. It all happened so fast...why, I daresay that scarcely more than a quarter of an hour passed from the time I heard the rogue's first shot until he abruptly demanded that we drive on! Besides which, he wore a black hood over his face and a black domino over his clothes, so I cannot even say what he looked like or much about how he was dressed.''

The tea that Verity had ordered earlier was now brought in by the footman Ned, along with an assortment of small sandwiches, biscuits and other sweets. As she did the honors, pouring the hot beverage into the china teacups and inquiring as to whether the Colonel preferred milk, sugar or lemon, Verity related how the brigand had set upon the carriage.

''There is not much more than that that I can tell you, sir,'' she insisted, once she had finished her tale. ''Except...''

''Except, what, Miss Collier?'' Colonel Sherbourne leaned forward eagerly in his chair, his blue eyes observing her keenly.

''Well, sir, I...I hardly know whether I should even mention it, for my impression is so vague that I am no doubt mistaken in it. But whilst I was at Jamaica Inn, waiting for Howel to arrive, I was shown to the parlor and there served an early supper.'' She paused.

''Yes? Please do go on, madam,'' he urged.

''Unbeknown to me at first, I was not alone in the parlor as I had at first thought. There was a man sitting in a shadowy corner...a stranger to me. After a time, he spoke to me. Initially, I attempted to discourage any conversation between us, because of course, we had not been properly introduced. Aware of my hesitation, however, the stranger maintained that there could surely be no harm or offense in two wayfarers such as ourselves engaging in a pleasant dialogue to pass away the time, and in truth, sir, it did seem to me that there could not be. So whilst I ate my supper, the stranger entertained me with many interesting, although…highly peculiar tales about Cornwall.''

''What kind of tales, Miss Collier?''

''Stories about ghosts and smugglers—and even about murder done at Jamaica Inn. Despite how it all disturbed me, I'll admit I found it all quite fascinating, even so. The stranger was a most excellent raconteur, and he appeared to be quite well versed in the history of the county. Now, Colonel, you must be wondering why I mention all this, so I shall try your patience no further, but satisfy your curiosity forthwith, without any further delay.

''The reason is because, later, it struck me that perhaps the stranger I encountered at Jamaica Inn and Black Jack Raven were one and the same man. I admit I do not know why I thought this, for apart from some similarity in build and dress, there was nothing about the two men that gave me any cause to connect them. Their speech was vastly different, for one thing. The stranger was well spoken, whilst the highwayman was not. Further, the stranger, having discoursed with me at some length at supper and learning I was en route to St. Aubyn, to serve as governess here, could not have reasonably supposed I possessed any money or valuables. Thus, the idea that he would have held up Lord St. Aubyn's coach seemed to me entirely insensible—and of this, at least, I am sure, the stranger at Jamaica Inn did not lack for intelligence. To the contrary, I should have said.''

''I see.'' His fair brow knitted in a frown, Colonel Sherbourne contemplated her words. ''Nevertheless, it is wholly possible to alter one's manner of speech,'' he pointed out, after a long moment. ''Still, although I intend no offense by the observation, madam, as you say, what would have been the stranger's purpose in robbing you? By your own admission, you had no money or valuables. And although I can hardly credit it, even Black Jack, I understand, permitted you to keep your mother's locket, whilst proving so shameless as to cut off a lock of your hair in recompense!''

''That is quite true, sir—however much it pains me to confess it!''

''Whilst this stranger at Jamaica Inn did nothing untoward at all?''

''No, sir. He was most polite and circumspect—except that he never told me his name, and I never saw his face, for he remained obscured in the dark corner throughout our colloquy.''

''Well, it is certainly all a very odd puzzle, Miss Collier, is it not?'' Colonel Sherbourne rose, preparing to take his leave of her. ''I thank you for agreeing to meet with me and to tell me about last night's unfortunate occurrence. I promise you I shall make every effort to apprehend the ruffian just as soon as possible.''

''I have every confidence that you will, Colonel. I only hope I have proved of assistance to you, in however small a fashion.''

"Indeed you have, madam. Every scrap of information that comes my way about Black Jack is of help to me. But, now, I must not trespass any further on the time that you have so generously spent with me this afternoon. It has been my pleasure. I shall hope to see you again under happier circumstances."

"Yes. Thank you, sir." Verity stood.

"No, please, Miss Collier. You need not trouble yourself to show me out. I know my way quite well, I assure you, for I have been often at St. Aubyn over the years. In fact, Jago and I grew up together. We are not only old friends, but also cousins."

"Jago?"

"Ah, my apologies for the informality. I was speaking of your new employer, Jago Ransleigh...Lord St. Aubyn."

After Colonel Sherbourne had ridden away, Verity was free for the remainder of the day. Having already seen the inside of the manor, she now determined that despite the light drizzle and mist that continued outside, and the chilly spring air, she would be brave and explore the grounds.

If what the Colonel had said was true—and she had no good reason at all for supposing it would not prove so—then it might be days before the inclement Cornish weather would relent, permitting the sun to shine brightly through. Besides which, a stroll would no doubt do her good, she reckoned. She was accustomed to walking on a regular basis, and these past few days, she had been cooped up in one vehicle or another, with very little exercise to speak of.

Thus decided, going upstairs to her bedroom, Verity donned her cloak, bonnet and gloves, and took her muff from the wardrobe, also, so that her hands would not freeze right through. Then she returned to the entrance hall and let herself out the front door. Once outside, she discovered that despite the mizzle and the nip in the spring air, she was warm enough in her outer accoutrements, and she strode briskly across the front lawn, pausing a short distance away to gaze back at the manor.

Verity had thought to find it less grim and forbidding in the daylight, less medieval and ensorcelled in appearance, but it was not so, and as she studied the house, she now realized this was because although attempts—such as expanding and renovating the wings and adding the gabled roof—had been made over the centuries to try to soften its facade, the fact that it had begun life as a fortress could not wholly be disguised. Nor did the solid grey Cornish slate of which it was fashioned lend itself to other than a dark, austere demeanor that made it seem somehow spellbound. Still, she could not deny that the manor somehow suited its wild setting.

Before it, the long, serpentine drive culminated in a circle, at the center of which stood a tall, grand stone fountain, surmounted with gargoyles from which water streamed into the large, fluted basin below. Cornish elms, yews, rhododendrons and flower beds abounded on the greening lawn. At the end of this began the park, which was heavily wooded with all manner of trees, some of which formed a rookery for blackbirds that fluttered uneasily and cawed noisily as they spied her, then at last rose up from the branches to wing their way skyward, a black, mobile cloud.

The manor sat upon a knoll, so that from the front lawn, Verity could see not only the park, but also valleys, meadows and fields beyond, and, in the distance, the spires and rooftops of two nearby, isolated villages tucked amid the rough hills, dense groves and sweeping moors and marshes that were Cornwall. Herds of placid, black-and-white cattle, woolly sheep, and, now and then, a goat or two grazed on the commons, and wild horses and ponies roamed the land.

As she strolled onward, entering the park, Verity's nostrils were assaulted by the fragrances of rich, damp loam, decaying wood and leaves, and other aromas not unpleasant and peculiar to copses wet with mizzle. Droplets dripped from the greening canopy of boughs, and drifting brume played will-o'-the-wisp among the trees and undergrowth. Well-trodden tracks and riding trails meandered their ways through the park, and the earth was soft and moist beneath her feet. Selecting a footpath at random, she wandered through the woods, occasionally chancing upon secluded gardens with wrought-iron gates set into hedgerows and bowers with benches for resting upon, until, finally, she came around to the rear of the manor.

Here, on the back lawn, the gardens were much more formally laid out, each with a different theme, and boasting fountains and reflecting pools, waterfalls and streams; stone obelisks, statues, birdbaths and benches; graceful gazebos, pergolas and even a small temple; and green arbors, topiaries and an intricate maze formed by close-clipped yews. Flagstone paths led from Elizabethan gardens to sunken gardens, from flower gardens to herb gardens, all of which eventually swept down to the rugged hills and crumbling cliffs along the shore of the ocean.

To one side lay the St. Aubyn family chapel and cemetery, with its ornate stone sepulchers with wrought-iron gates and wooden doors, and its granite tombstones with chiseled names and dates worn faint by the elements and time, beneath whose greening grass those long dead and buried lay. In one of the mausoleums, embellished with carved cherubim and grapevines, Lady St. Aubyn's poor, broken body reposed eternally at rest within a stone crypt. But here, Verity did not choose to intrude, feeling somehow, strangely, as though she trespassed.

Instead, she walked on until, at last, she came to the jagged cliffs at the edge of the sea. Yet, although both the savage vista and the murmuring billows spoke to her, just as the wild storm of the night before and Beethoven's sonata of this morning had, she still did not venture too near to the place where the terrain had eroded away to tumble down to the rough shingle and beach below. Not only did she not wish to slip and fall to her death—the way the Earl's late wife had done—but, also, Verity was absolutely terrified of heights. When exposed to them, she suffered vertigo so bad that she knew she could easily lose her balance and topple to the rocks below.

Perhaps Lady St. Aubyn had been afflicted with

the same sort of fear and dizziness when it came to heights, Verity mused. Mayhap that had contributed to her fall. Her tale was tragic, and for some mysterious reason, it had made a deep impression upon Verity. She could not seem to stop dwelling upon it.

*Tamsyn...Tamsyn...*the restless ocean seemed to whisper to her as its foaming waves rolled inland. It was a strange, beautiful name, she thought, one with which she was unfamiliar and so that she surmised was either of Cornish origin or else that was peculiar nowadays to Cornwall. And the name *Jago,* too, was unknown to her.

Jago Ransleigh.

She wondered to what kind of a man such a name belonged, for thus far, she knew but little of her employer's character—and that he had loved a woman called Tamsyn, who had fallen to her death at this wild, haunting place where she, Verity, now stood.

*Tamsyn...Tamsyn...*the name appeared to echo softly, eerily, once more.

Unwittingly, as she gazed down at the strand below, at the frothy, soughing sea rushing in to break upon the rocky, shingled beach, Verity suddenly shivered violently.

It was only the cold and wet that caused her distress, she told herself uncompromisingly, after a moment—that, and her wild, fanciful imagination, no doubt. Envisioning Lady St. Aubyn's body sprawled pitifully on the jutting crags, she was hearing things.

Still, for some unknown reason, as she turned

away, stricken and uneasy, it was all Verity could do
to prevent herself from running toward the manor—
and all the while, she felt as though someone
watched her steadily until she was out of sight.

Five

The Apparitions

There must be ghosts all over the world. They must be as countless as grains of the sands, it seems to me. And we are so miserably afraid of the light, all of us.

Ghosts
—Henrik Ibsen

It was down by the dank tarn of Auber,
In the ghoul-haunted woodland of Weir.

Ulalume
—Edgar Allan Poe

"Ghastly grim and ancient Raven wandering
    From the Nightly shore—
Tell me what thy lordly name is on the
    Night's Plutonian shore!"
Quoth the Raven, "Nevermore."

The Raven
—Edgar Allan Poe

As time passed at St. Aubyn manor, the months slipping by and spring giving way to summer, Verity's expectation that she and her life would presently return to their former serenity and composure was not proved wrong. Her days soon settled into a pattern that, while new to her, was eventually revealed to be no less dull and routine than that at Trowbridge had been—although infinitely more pleasant and agreeable. But still, despite this last, she felt almost cheated somehow, and if she were painfully honest with herself, she must admit that in leaving Trowbridge and Derbyshire behind, she had in some dim, hitherto unexamined corner of her mind secretly hoped to embark upon a life filled with at least some kind of adventure and excitement—something perhaps even wild and reckless to interrupt the unrelenting tedium of her days.

But there was nothing—except that, strangely, every now and then when she walked in the gardens, the park or along the cliffs at the edge of the ocean, Verity sometimes thought she heard again the eerie lament of *Tamsyn, Tamsyn* being cried on the wind or the sea, and she felt once more as though unseen eyes spied upon her, causing the fine hairs on her nape to prickle. But there was never anyone there, and at last, she decided that in her inexplicable longing for some escapade and stimulation, she was simply imagining things.

Although, at the time, she had been terrified of the speed at which the Earl's carriage had traveled when it had fetched her from Jamaica Inn, of the savage storm that had raged that night and of Black Jack Raven, the infamous highwayman who had held up the coach, now, in retrospect, it all seemed quite the most exhilarating thing that had ever before happened in her young life. From the safe distance created by time, Verity often reflected upon the memory—and felt she knew not what, only that she was vaguely restless and unsatisfied, as though there ought to be more to life than what she had thus far experienced.

Still, whenever it seemed as though these feelings would become too overpowering and difficult for her to bear, she would firmly tamp them down, determinedly refusing to dwell upon them, telling herself that this was life, and that those of her ilk could expect nothing more. It must be some anomalous flaw in her own poor character, she judged, that caused her to yearn for what was more than her fair lot, for none of the others in the household appeared to be troubled by such incomprehensible yearnings as plagued her.

Mrs. Wickersham continued as good-naturedly and placidly as she had been upon Verity's arrival, seldom cross or ruffled, and with never an unkind word for anybody, regardless of the provocation. The Messrs Drummond, Peacock and Lathrop, while unfailingly courteous and friendly enough, still maintained a certain dignity and reserve in their manner toward Verity, which did not encourage any particular closeness or confidences—except that, occasionally, the steward, Mr. Drummond, related to them all that he had received a business letter from their employer, Lord St. Aubyn, who had yet to return to the manor. Of the remainder of the staff, Verity soon grew most familiar with her chambermaid, Loveday, with the housemaid Bessie and the footman Ned, and with the nurse, Trueth.

Gradually, also, the more time the twins spent with Verity, the less apprehensive they became of her and the more talkative, although Meliora still spoke more often than Bastian, who persisted in being more subdued than his sister. During their lessons, Verity discovered that both children could read and write a little, and do a few sums, as well, so that she was not beginning entirely from scratch where they were concerned, but need only continue and encourage their progress. Once the youngsters warmed to her, she found them both to be intelligent, talented and obedient, with an innate curiosity that made them imminently teachable. They honestly wished to learn and, further, to win her approval.

In fact, although delighted by this last, Verity was sometimes equally puzzled and even disturbed by it, too, for she could not help but feel that it was wholly unnatural for two children to be so very obliging and eager to please. It was almost as though they were starved for attention and affection, although she knew both Mrs. Wickersham and Trueth spent considerable time with them and loved them dearly. Verity could only attribute the youngsters' behavior to their dead mother's tragedy. Perhaps they felt that by being disobedient and sneaking outside that tragic night, they had brought about her death, so that, now, they wished to do nothing wrong, to make no false step that would unwittingly lead to some fresh disaster.

Yes, that must be it, Verity inevitably thought, for there was no other plausible explanation. As a result, her heart continued to go out to the twins, and she increasingly developed a genuine affection and fondness for them. Yet, still, in this large, equable household filled with friendship, companionship and warmheartedness, she felt some strange loneliness and lack that would not be entirely banished, no matter how hard she tried, and that dismayed and shamed her whenever it beset her. For she knew she had no cause for ingratitude or complaint at St. Aubyn, where she was well treated and respected as a member of the upper household staff.

On her free afternoons, after her morning lessons with Meliora and Bastian, Verity undertook any number of tasks and pastimes, depending on what was needed. Sometimes, she assisted Mrs. Wickersham in the house or with cutting flowers in the gardens; at others, she kept the twins occupied so that Trueth could have some time to herself. When she was not busy with these endeavors, Verity took long walks in St. Aubyn's gardens and park, and even trekked across the rough hills and sweeping country-side, exploring. She grew accustomed to the Cornish mizzle and did not let it deter her. But with the on-slaught of summer, there were many finer days, when, by late morning, the sun shone brightly, and it was warm enough that she required only a light spencer instead of her pelisse.

Frequently then, carrying her easel, paint box and a small, folding canvas stool, Verity sought out some appealing landscape or seascape, and painted it in watercolors to amuse herself. Or else she packed an alfresco luncheon for herself and escaped to some isolated spot to read or daydream. Sometimes, she ran errands that took her into St. Ives, the nearest town of any size.

Set upon the northern shore of Cornwall, St. Ives was a bustling fishing town that sprawled amid the hills and cascaded down their sides to Smeatons Pier, the harbor, the beaches and the bays below, around which all manner of shops and pubs clustered, and narrow cobblestone streets and alleys twisted—the Downalong, the area was called. Here, hemp nets and ropes were hung out to dry; old men smoked pipes and otherwise idled on the harbor wall; and Cornish luggers with their distinctive dark-brown sails plied the waves, in search of pilchard, herring and mack-erel. The catch was salted, then packed into wooden barrels for export, while, in exchange, visiting ships brought timber and coal for the tin-mining industry that was also a part of Cornish commerce. Seagulls soared and called their strange, forlorn cries above

the harbor, and strutted along the beaches and labyrinthine streets, in search of food.

Verity adored going into St. Ives. Somehow, she
felt more alive there. She liked wandering around the
clamorous Downalong, with its raucous, milling
crowds, quaint, charming shops and unabashed street
vendors hawking their wares: "Cockles an' mussels,
alive, alive-o!" The crisp air always smelled of salt
from the sea, of fresh fish and crabs and other shell-
fish, and of new-baked breads and hot Cornish pasties—small pies filled with meat. From the Sloop, a
pub that had stood for five hundred years on the harbor, wafted the aromas of ale and tobacco smoke, to
mingle with the rest.

But there was one place to which Verity did not
go: St. Aubyn Lodge, the grey slate edifice that
guarded the manor's gates. Having inquired of Mrs.
Wickersham who lived there, she had been informed
that it was inhabited by the late Lady St. Aubyn's
widowed mother, Lady Kenhebres, and her servants,
Mr. and Mrs. Ythnow.

"They keep to themselves, mostly," the housekeeper had elucidated. "Lady Kenhebres is unwell
and requires quiet and rest. When Lady St. Aubyn
was alive, Lady Kenhebres lived in the manor, but
after her ladyship's death, his lordship felt that his
mother-in-law would be much more comfortable in
the lodge, away from unhappy memories and noise,
and there, she has stayed."

On more than one occasion, when Verity strolled
past the lodge, she thought she heard again the name
Tamsyn, Tamsyn soughing in her ears. The strange,

echoing plaint sounded so real that she glanced sharply around, unable to credit it to either the wind, the sea or her wild, fanciful imagination. But as usual, there was no one about, and the lodge was shut up tight, its curtains drawn over the windows, so that she could not even see inside. In the end, she went on, once more deciding that perhaps it was the ceaseless Cornish wind or the restless ocean, although even that explanation did not wholly satisfy her.

Once or twice, she spied Lady Kenhebres's servants, Mr. and Mrs. Ythnow, busy outside at some chore, but she could not believe that either one of them was responsible for the peculiar keening, either. They were both stout, hard-faced, dour, taciturn Cornish peasant stock, and rarely spoke beyond a short, sullen greeting that did not encourage her to linger, making attempts at polite conversation—not that Verity wished to. Whenever she passed them by, she could feel their eyes staring holes in her back, and she shivered, and thought them a very queer, unpleasant sort of couple. She frequently wondered why the Earl employed them. But, then, it was not just anyone who would have wanted to tend to a sick, elderly woman in Cornwall's desolate wilds.

Much more affable was Colonel Sherbourne, who made it his business to stop by St. Aubyn manor a few times a month, to relate any problems in the area and advise the household to exercise caution in this or that regard, and to see, among other things, how Verity was getting on and to make certain she had suffered no lasting ill effects from the Earl's carriage having been held up by Black Jack Raven. Unfortunately, however, it seemed that despite all the Colonel's best efforts, the notorious highwayman had still not been captured and brought to justice.

"Truly, he is as sly and clever a scoundrel as they come, is Black Jack Raven," Colonel Sherbourne insisted one day to Verity. "However, eventually, I shall prevail and catch him, I have no doubt. Then we'll see him swinging from the nearest gibbet! So you need not be afraid of once more falling victim to the unconscionable rogue, Miss Collier, I do assure you."

"Since I am quite unlikely to be out and about in his lordship's carriage again any time soon, particularly at such a late hour, I have no fears on that score, sir."

Black Jack was not the only brigand to ride the hightoby in Cornwall, though. There were others, along with countless smugglers and even wreckers, as well.

During the reign of King Edward I, around 1300, Verity learned from the Colonel, a customs duty had been enacted, placing a fee upon the export of British wool, which was then in great demand throughout the Continent. It was not only the beginning of the first permanent customs system in Britain, but also of the clandestine industries of smuggling and wrecking—the luring of ships to wreck upon the rocks and reefs off the Cornish coast.

By 1671, when King Charles II established the Board of Customs, the illicit trade had grown to such an extent, Colonel Sherbourne elucidated, that the

Romney Marshes, in the county of Kent, had become the center of smuggling, with an estimated twenty thousand packs of wool being shipped across the English Channel to Calais, in France, yearly. During the 1700s, not only was wool being sent abroad, but tea, brandy, gin, rum and tobacco were also being unlawfully brought into Britain from the Continent, along with china, silks and cottons from the Orient. It was widely believed that until the end of the eighteenth century, approximately half a million gallons of brandy were being smuggled in through Cornwall alone annually.

Unfortunately, the Colonel explained to Verity, revenue officers often proved of little value in deterring smugglers, many of the former being all too willing, for a sufficient bribe, to turn a blind eye to all the latter's activities, or even to become actively involved themselves in bringing in the contraband. Nor were the revenue officers alone in their participation. Frequently, especially in Cornwall, entire communities—from the highest ranking members of society to the lowliest peasants—were in on the illegal schemes. Many poor farming, fishing and mining communities alike all supplemented their meager incomes with money garnered from smuggling. In fact, some families owed their riches and influence to a long history of piracy, smuggling and wrecking.

Much to Mrs. Wickersham's consternation, in addition to all these lawbreakers, it was believed that French spies were active in Britain, especially along the English Channel coastline. For although the Treaty of Amiens had been signed between Great

Britain and France earlier this year, it was not thought that the Corsican upstart Napoléon really intended to keep peacefully within his own borders. Instead, it was feared that war between the two countries might resume at any time.

It was equally difficult, Colonel Sherbourne explained, to apprehend any French spies that might be in the area, as there were so many immigrants who had fled from France to England to escape first the Reign of Terror and then the wars instigated by Napoléon that it was hard to know who was friend or foe. Further, the Colonel reported, it was not to be expected that the French upper classes, educated from youth in foreign languages, just as their English counterparts were, spoke English any less fluently than the English spoke French, which made detection of any French spies all the more onerous.

"And so, madam, as you can see, I have my hands full, trying to maintain law and order here in Cornwall," Colonel Sherbourne stated to Verity. "Not that I'm complaining, however. I know my duty, and I certainly intend to carry it out to the very best of my ability!"

The more she saw of him, the more Verity liked the Colonel. She thought him a handsome man, with a great deal of common sense, kindness and humor. So she looked forward to his visits and was always pleased to see him, to consult with him about the educational progress of Meliora and Bastian, who were his first cousins once removed, and, at his invitation, to walk with him through the gardens or park at St. Aubyn. Verity noticed that he was quite a favorite with Mrs. Wickersham and all the other servants, too, as well as with the twins, with whom he always spent some time, bringing them trifling little presents that, while inexpensive, were nevertheless sure to delight them.

Still, Verity must constantly remind herself, it would not do for her to become too much attached to or enamored of Colonel Sherbourne. He was the Earl's first cousin—and not for the likes of her. As the eldest son of a younger son, he must make his own way in the world. Thus, to please his family and to secure his own future, he was far more likely to choose as his wife a woman of fortune—not a plain, penniless governess who brought nothing but herself to a marriage, no matter how highly he might esteem her and enjoy her company.

Yet, against all her better judgment, Verity knew that if she were honest with herself, she must admit that some small part of her heart hoped otherwise. She had never before been in love. However, she feared she must be in grave danger of becoming so with the dashing Colonel, for she could not imagine why else she should always be so inordinately glad to see him.

She had hoped he would come to St. Aubyn manor today, for it was Saturday, when he could spend the most time with the twins. But after she had lingered around all morning and part of the afternoon, waiting for him, only to have her hopes dashed when he did not arrive, Verity abruptly realized how ridiculously she was behaving. Greatly annoyed with herself for acting like some lovesick schoolgirl instead of a sensible grown woman, she donned her spencer and a straw bonnet, and set out for St. Ives. Although she had no particular errands to run there, the long walk would do her good and help to take her mind off Colonel Sherbourne, she decided.

Instead of the bright, welcome summer sunshine they had experienced all week, the day had dawned with a pale, washed-out sun and a leaden sky that threatened rain, but which had yet to make its appearance. Still, the temperature had dropped several degrees from yesterday, so that Verity was glad of her light jacket.

She set a steady pace, not only to keep warm, but also so as not to tire herself. It was four miles to town, along a rough, narrow dirt track wending over hills and heaths, and it would take her more than an hour to get there. Overhead, as she walked, the sun continued its valiant struggle to penetrate the lowering clouds, staving off the promised rain for yet a little while longer, and beneath her feet, the ground was hard—and rich with the summer scents of blooming wildflowers, trailing broom and decaying manure left by the animals that grazed upon the commons. Along the earthen tops of the peculiar stone Cornish fences, the gorse grew thick, its evergreen tendrils spreading and clinging like leeches to the rocks.

In the distance, over the bays, seagulls flew and cawed, while others flocked along the shore, their cacophony piercing the summer air; and far below her, upon the turquoise waves, Cornish luggers and other small boats bobbed as they cast their hemp nets for fish and checked their baskets for crabs. Very faintly, Verity could hear the deep, tolling bell of the parish church strike the hour. Against her will, she wondered if, the drizzle having held off, Colonel Sherbourne had ridden over from Truro to St. Aubyn, after all. No, that would not do. She had promised herself not to think of him. Determinedly, she once more put him from her mind.

Presently, she reached St. Ives, where, having no special destination, she wandered along the narrow, twisting stone streets and alleys of the Downalong, and in and out of the various shops that lined them. Hungry and thirsty after her long hike, she bought some hot currant buns and a bottle of milk from a vendor, then carried her bounty away to the harbor wall, where she sat down in a vacant spot to enjoy her treat, tossing a bit of the bread to the occasional seagull that strutted at her feet, begging for a share.

Once she felt rested, Verity continued her excursion, spending some of her month's wages on a bolt of bombazine that had been dyed a soft dark brown and from which she intended to cut and sew a new gown for herself. That her sudden penchant for a new frock stemmed from the fact that she owned but two everyday dresses, both of them black and similar in style, and which were all that Colonel Sherbourne had ever seen her in, she impatiently thrust from her thoughts. Since coming to St. Aubyn, she had saved every penny she had earned, having no need to part with any of it. A new gown was required, if she were not to wear out her old ones before their time, she told herself firmly. To go with her new dress, Verity also bought a length of cream-colored muslin, from which to make a new tucker.

Then, as the hour had grown late and the pallid sun was beginning its slow descent into the ocean off Land's End to the west, she started the long walk home. By this time, the swollen grey clouds that had threatened rain all day had now fulfilled their promise, and drizzle had begun to fall, dampening the earth so that it was no longer hard beneath her feet, but increasingly miry. A clinging mist that tasted of brine upon her lips had blown in with the wind from the sea, too. She ought to have started back to St. Aubyn far earlier than she had, Verity realized, as she tramped along the uneven, narrow, serpentine path that snaked across the countryside. But nightfall came late to Cornwall during the summer, and would have done so today, had it not been for the overcast sky that had foreshadowed the rain that now spattered and sprinkled. Well, there was no help for it now. She must make her way home as best she could, hugging her parcels, wrapped in brown paper, close, to try to protect them as much as possible from the mizzle.

Eventually, as she strode across the rough terrain, the sun disappeared entirely; darkness fell swiftly; and the moon rose—a hazy silvery orb that was ringed and, now and then, occluded by wisps of drifting clouds. Unwittingly, Verity shivered when she spied it, for it reminded her of the moon that had shone in the dismal night sky when the Earl's carriage had been set upon by Black Jack Raven. Although she did not fear to be accosted by the infamous highwayman again, still, she knew there were other perils that came with darkness—smugglers and wreckers, for one.

On just such a night as this would they be out and about, the smugglers transferring their contraband from ships to secure places on land, and the wreckers beaming their false lights upon the shores, to lure unsuspecting vessels into smashing upon the deadly Cornish reefs, after which, the wreckers would wade into the tumultuous sea, clubbing to death all the survivors, then stealing their cargo. Verity did not want to inadvertently stumble upon any of this, for in the months that she had now lived in Cornwall, she had learned by heart—as everyone did—the old caveat, "Watch the wall, my darling," and she knew that those who were wise and wished to survive did exactly that, turning a blind eye and a deaf ear to the illegal activities of the smugglers and wreckers, who had been known to murder witnesses.

There were believed to be French spies in the area, also, who would be even more likely to deal her some mortal injury, should she chance upon them.

These terrifying thoughts now uppermost in her mind, Verity hurried onward, practically running across the uneven terrain, clutching her packages to her breast, breathing hard and fast, and cursing the drizzle and brume, the muck that sucked at her boots, and her own foolishness that had caused her to linger so long in St. Ives, in a deliberate attempt to deprive herself of Colonel Sherbourne's much yearned for company, in case he had happened to come to St. Aubyn today, after all.

At long last, much to her relief, she spied two bright flames flickering in the distance, and she knew it must be the great, twin brass lanterns mounted upon the tall, massive stone pillars that flanked the wrought-iron gates of St. Aubyn. She hastened toward them and, upon finally reaching them, paused there to catch her breath. Beyond lay the lodge, its curtains drawn tight, as usual, but still, soft lamplight spilled from the windows, and in the distance, at the end of the long, winding drive lined by the tall, twisted Cornish elms whose boughs contrived a leafy green canopy above, St. Aubyn waited.

From each huge old pillar on either side of the ornate gate, a stone wall curved down, then straightened out to form a fence marking the boundary. Upon the nearest one of these, Verity sat down for a moment to rest, laying her parcels to one side. Now that she was actually home, there was no longer any need to rush. She was safe on the grounds of St. Aubyn and could linger a while. The stone upon which she perched was chilly and damp from the mizzle, and her hands were cold, for she had worn no gloves. She blew on her numb fingers to warm them, then chafed her hands vigorously.

Below her, the hills and heaths all around tumbled down into dales and glens, with copses, fields and streams. Lights made blurry by the drizzle shone from the nearby villages, and smoke curled from their chimney tops to mingle with the moonlit mist. Except for the gentle pitter-patter of the rain, the quiet gurgle of the creeks in the valleys, and the rising and falling of the wind, all was hushed and still.

Tamsyn...Tamsyn...

The sudden soughing of the dead Lady St. Aubyn's Christian name sent an icy grue tingling up Verity's spine. Her heart abruptly thudding in her breast and her breath catching in her throat, she glanced around wildly, wondering whence the sound had emanated—for surely, she had not imagined it! But there was no one there that she could see and, as before, she finally decided it must be only the murmuring of the wind or the sea, coupled with her own wild fancies.

Tamsyn...Tamsyn...

The soft, eerie sighing of the exotic name echoed again, once more prickling her skin with gooseflesh, and now, for the first time, Verity thought to wonder if perhaps she were losing her mind. No, it was not so. Blessed with a vivid imagination, she might be, but...mad? No, she was as sane as anybody, and she would not accept that she was envisioning or hearing things that did not actually exist.

"Hello!" she abruptly called out sharply into the darkness. "Is—Is anyone there?"

There was no answer, but of a sudden, Verity felt hideously certain she was not alone, that she was being watched by someone—or some*thing*. Without warning, all of the strange, disturbing ghost tales related to her by the stranger at Jamaica Inn returned to haunt her. It was said, her interlocutor that night had told her, that Cornwall was the most haunted county in all of England, beset by giants and knackers, fairies and piskies, and spirits of all kinds, from forlorn specters to phantom coachmen.

Surreptitiously rising from the stone fence, Verity gathered up her two packages, still looking about her, but still spying nobody. Then, her heart pounding in her throat and her palms sweating, despite how she tried desperately to reassure herself, she started down the wending drive that led to St. Aubyn, her boots crunching—to her ears—loudly upon the crushed seashells in the silence.

At first, she forced herself to walk calmly in the middle of the drive, away from the towering, gnarled old trees, where there might be someone or some-*thing* lurking and from where she could be easily grabbed. But, then, all at once, several horrifying things happened.

She heard the name *Tamsyn* being softly cried again, and then again, the plaint growing ever more urgent on the moaning and rising wind, and from the corners of her eyes, she glimpsed something white and ethereal seeming to float and flutter like a wraith amid the dark, fiercely rustling Cornish elms along-side the road. Then, of a sudden, all the birds in the rookery took flight, cawing a raucous, vociferous ca-veat as they winged their way upward into the night sky, while, from behind her, there came a thunder-ous, ominous pounding, followed by an equally vi-olent and portentous scrabbling and scrunching upon the crushed seashells that paved the ribbon of drive, as though some ponderous, unknown, nameless and horrible *thing* had burst without warning from the darkness and mizzle, and were now chasing her.

Verity did not wait to hear any more.

She ran. She ran as though the devil himself pursued her.

All around her, the wailing wind shook the ancient, looming trees, and the whispering of the green wet leaves was like the rattle of dry old bones; the creaking of the overhanging branches was like the rasp of a huge coffin lid being closed on rusty hinges upon her, mottling the pale, shimmering silver moon that stretched long, dripping talons through the boughs. Decaying debris blown up by the gusts from the dank earth whorled around her, and the brume draped her in a diaphanous, chilling shroud.

As Verity raced on heedlessly, the ribands of her straw bonnet, bound in a loose knot under her chin, came untied, and the hat sailed from her head. The wind and rain ripped at her skirts and hair, tearing her hairpins free and loosening her chignon, so that the thick strands whipped about her face, blinding her. Pushing the wildly billowing tresses aside so that she could see, she lost hold of her parcels, and they tumbled to the ground. But she was far too terrified to stop to retrieve them, did not even consider or care about the expense, how much of her month's wages their precious contents had cost her.

For, whatever massive thing was behind her was now sweeping toward her at a furious pace, like some giant black bat on the wing, an enormous, amorphous shape she sensed at her back, gaining on her with every passing second that she fled. She would never outrun it, Verity thought, frantic with despair. She would never reach the manor—and help—in time. She had a painful stitch in her side, which was making it difficult for her to breathe, so that she gasped for air; and as though in some ghastly nightmare, her legs seemed to move slower and slower with every step she took, as leaden as though they were weighted down with heavy stones.

The drizzle stung her eyes and cheeks, mingling with her tears of fright, blurring her vision; and her skirts and the slick, broken seashells beneath her feet hampered her flight. Behind her, she heard whatever chased her snorting and snuffling forebodingly, then, hideously, felt its hot breath upon her nape. With heartbreaking desolation, Verity knew she could not escape from it.

So instead, at the last moment, she turned to confront the thing, and when she did, it shrilled long and loud, and rose up on its great, powerful haunches to tower over her menacingly. Huge, massively muscled, and as white as a phantom, the monstrous beast was—all rolling eyes, snapping teeth and flailing limbs, with a behemoth raven perched upon its back, colossal wings widespread and flapping vehemently in the shrieking wind. The bloodcurdling apparition meant to trample her under foot! As it lunged toward her, Verity screamed again, and then again, flinging her arms up piteously in a futile, last-ditch attempt to protect herself from the fateful, fearsome thing. Slipping and scrambling on the wet seashells, losing her footing, she stumbled backward, falling...falling....

Striking the ground so hard that her head swam sickeningly and the wind was knocked from her, she gazed up, dazed and petrified, at the demon creature looming over her, blotting out the inky night sky and the luminescent moon above, and poised to crush her savagely.

Then a merciful blackness swirled up to engulf her, and she knew nothing more.

Book Two

The Rising o' the Moon

I walk unseen
On the dry smooth-shaven green,
To behold the wandering moon,
Riding near her highest noon,
Like one that had been led astray
Through the heav'n's wide pathless way,
And oft, as if her head she bowed,
Stooping through a fleecy cloud.

L'Allegro
—John Milton

Six

The Homecoming

Turn up the lights—I don't want to go
home in the dark.

> *Last Words, June 5, 1910*
> —O. Henry (William Sydney Porter)

This be the verse you grave for me:
Here he lies where he longed to be;
Home is the sailor, home from sea,
And the hunter home from the hill.

> *Kidnapped (Requiem)*
> —Robert Louis Stevenson

Between the acting of a dreadful thing
And the first motion, all the interim is
Like a phantasma, or a hideous dream.

> *Julius Caesar*
> —William Shakespeare

St. Aubyn Manor
Cornwall, England, 1802

As Verity lay there, stunned and faint, upon the winding drive that led to St. Aubyn manor, with the rain spattering and sprinkling down upon her and the mist swirling around her, her dream, her nightmare—for, surely, that was what it was, she thought nebulously—continued unabated.

Mercifully, she was not trounced to death by the monstrous beast. Instead, miraculously, its deadly teeth and limbs missed doing any injury to her. But, then, to her everlasting horror, as the phantom creature stood snorting and snuffling above her, huffing its hot, cloudy breath upon her, the titanic raven clinging to its back suddenly swooped down to scoop her up from the ground, enfolding her with its massive wings and lifting her on to the great white specter.

"No...no, please," Verity entreated softly, her eyes closed and her head lolling as she began, however dizzily and weakly, to struggle against the huge bird of ill omen, ineffectively pummeling her fists against its broad chest.

"Devil take you, witch! Stop fighting me, or I'll beat your damned, otherworldly backside!" a low, authoritative voice abruptly growled ominously in her ear.

The next thing she knew, she was flying through the darkness, beneath the tortured Cornish elms whose branches devised a canopy over the drive to St. Aubyn. Her face was pressed close against the dire raven's breast, so that she could not see its face, and its wings battered about her wildly in the wind. Still, somehow, it held her fast, so that she could not escape, even had she attempted to do so. But she did not. Instead, mindful of its stern, frightening warning to her, Verity lay passively against it, her head aching, one ankle throbbing and her breath coming quickly and shallowly.

Dimly, she was aware of the strength of the enormous bird, and of the scent of it pervading her nostrils. It smelled strangely of tobacco and whiskey. And it had spoken to her. She was being kidnapped by a colossal raven that talked, she thought dully, in some shadowy corner of her mind, as she floated in and out of consciousness. No, surely, that was not possible, she then told herself. She must be imagining things. The blow to her head must have addled her wits. Yes, that was it. She was befuddled. It was the notorious highwayman Black Jack Raven who had snatched her up and who was now abducting her for some wicked purpose of his own!

But why was he riding a white horse instead of a

black one—and taking her to St. Aubyn? For, now, blearily, as she dared to peep from beneath her captor's cloak, Verity could see the manor looming ahead, its lamps shining softly in the drizzle and darkness. Much to her further surprise and bewilderment, the snowy steed galloped around the circle formed by the drive's terminus and came to a halt directly beneath the portico hazily lighted by the large brass lanterns hanging from the rafters and flickering on either side of the door.

Then, before Verity realized what was intended, she was swept down from the horse and up to the heavy oak portal, where the tall, dark, muscular man who held her captive in his strong arms pounded loudly with the brass, lion's-head knocker. After a moment, Mr. Lathrop flung wide the front door.

''My lord!'' he gasped out, as he spied Verity and her imprisoner on the porch.

Astonishing and perplexing her still more, instead of replying to this exclamation, the man who carried her as though she weighed no more than a feather swiftly and roughly shouldered his way past the openmouthed groom of the chambers and into the house, bearing her over the threshold and into the entrance hall.

''Miss Collier—I presume—has met with an unfortunate accident, Lathrop. Light the lamps and a fire in the library. At once!'' her captor demanded imperiously, as he strode inside, his black, many-caped greatcoat swirling like a cerecloth about him and Verity in the wind that whispered and keened past the open front door. "And see that Phantom is taken care of—not left to stand in the rain!"

"Y-y-yes, my lord. Right away, my lord, of course." Bowing and scraping obsequiously, the groom of the chambers scuttled away before them, calling loudly and sharply for assistance.

Within the time that it took Verity—belatedly and confusedly—to grasp the fact that her imprisoner was not the infamous highwayman Black Jack Raven, but, rather, her employer, Jago Ransleigh, Lord St. Aubyn, she was unceremoniously stripped of her spencer and installed upon a rich burgundy-leather chesterfield in the now brightly illuminated library, with a crystal snifter of sweet, mellow brandy pressed to her pale, tremulous lips and a fire blazing cheerfully in the grate to warm her.

"Drink, Miss Collier," the Earl commanded, his black eyes studying her ashen face intensely as he bent over her, glass in hand.

"No—No, please, I—I am unused to strong spirits, my lord," she protested feebly.

"Nevertheless, you are cold and wet through, and have experienced a bad shock, I fear. The brandy will restore you. Therefore, I am afraid I must insist."

Had she not realized it already from the servants' attitude as they hovered about, waiting for his orders to be relayed to them, Verity would have known, now, that the Earl was not one to brook resistance or disobedience. His manner alone toward her, although not intolerant, nevertheless made it plain that he was not accustomed to being defied. Without further ado, not wishing to anger him and painfully aware of the disruption she had already caused, she drank. The unfamiliar brandy tasted strange upon her tongue, although not unpleasantly so, and at Lord St. Aubyn's urging, she sipped slowly until, finally, the snifter was empty. By then, she felt wonderfully warm, and her headache and the pain in her ankle had diminished a little, so that she was able to make a proper physical evaluation—unclouded by terror— of her employer.

Like his cousin, Colonel Sherbourne, Jago Ransleigh was neither young nor old, but a man in his prime, tall, and dark like his twin children, with a disheveled mane of glossy black hair and a pair of penetrating, heavily lashed black eyes deep set beneath thick black brows that swooped like a raven's wings above them. His nose was aquiline, his mouth generous and carnal, and the thrust of his jaw arrogant and determined. His broad shoulders and chest tapered to a firm, flat belly, lean hips and long, muscular legs. An obviously expensive, well-tailored jacket of rich forest-green velvet fitted him like a second skin. Beneath it, he wore an elegant, striped silk waistcoat and a fine white cambric shirt with a forest-green neckerchief beautifully tied in a waterfall knot at the collar. Fawn-colored riding breeches hugged his corded thighs, and high black leather boots encased his legs. He was the epitome of a gentleman, although not a dandy, for his waistcoat bore only a single fob and seal, and aside from his gold pocket watch, his only other jewelry was a gold signet ring, which he wore on his left hand.

''Now that you are feeling somewhat better, let us

take stock of your injuries, madam. Do you hurt any-
where?'' the Earl inquired.

''My—My head. I struck it on the drive when I
fell. And my—my right ankle. I must have twisted
it somehow.''

Her head was examined by Lord St. Aubyn and
found to have a gash and a bump upon the back of
it. The cut, from the sharp edges of the crushed seashells of which the drive was fashioned, was duly
cleaned with an antiseptic. Then, despite her modest
demurring, the boot and stocking on her right foot
were ruthlessly, however impersonally, removed by
her employer.

''Now is not the time for missish airs, Miss Collier,'' he declared firmly, as he gently probed her
swollen and bruised ankle. ''Fortunately, you are
right, and it is only a bad sprain, rather than broken.''
He directed that a bucket of warm saltwater be
fetched and instructed her to soak her ankle in it.
''After that, some liniment and a bandage will suffice, I should think.''

''Yes, but these are all things I can take care of in
my bedroom, my lord, if only I may be allowed to
seek it,'' Verity pleaded, discomfitted and not wishing to be the cause of any more upset than she already had been.

''Presently, you shall be, madam, I do assure you,
so be at ease. However, although I confess I am
somewhat bemused as to why you were walking
down the drive after dark, the fact remains that I
nearly rode you down and am thus in no small part
to blame for what has befallen you. Therefore, you

will please permit me the salve to my conscience of ensuring that you have not suffered some permanent harm from the mishap.''

"No, my lord, I feel quite certain it is only a matter of a few bumps and bruises, from which I shall quickly recover. So I pray you, please do not trouble yourself any further on my behalf. It is really quite unnecessary, I assure you. As you observed, I ought not have been out on the drive after dark. But I had walked into St. Ives earlier to do some shopping and had got a rather late start home.... Oh, no! My—My parcels! I've—I've just now realized I must have dropped them on the drive when I—when I tried to flee from your horse. And my—my bonnet, as well.''

"Mrs. Wickersham—'' the Earl turned to the housekeeper, who stood to one side ''—please be good enough to send one of the footmen to search for Miss Collier's lost packages and hat.''

"Yes, of course, my lord.''

"I am curious, madam.'' Lord St. Aubyn redirected his attention to Verity. "Why *did* you run away from Phantom the way you did? Are you afraid of horses, perhaps? Was that the cause of your seeming panic? For, had you only stepped to the side of the drive, this entire unfortunate incident might have been avoided! As it was, I fear that your black gown and spencer proved a combination difficult to detect in the mist and relative darkness of the drive, beneath the elms. That is why I did not see you at first.''

"I understand that now, my lord, and I most sincerely apologize for having caused such a contretemps. But as I was walking along the drive, I—I heard a sound in the park, someone calling a—a name—or so it seemed to me at the time—and then I spied something...white and ghostlike, or so it appeared to me in the mizzle, floating through the woods. As you may guess, all this was...very unnerving to me, to say the least, so that when you and your horse burst so unexpectedly upon the scene, I'm afraid my imagination quite ran away with me. I mistakenly perceived your mount to be some monstrous beast bent on trampling me under foot and you yourself some giant raven perched upon its back, widespread wings flapping rampantly in the wind—the result of your caped greatcoat, I now recognize, my lord. Thus I fear that my only clear thought was to escape.''

''I see,'' her employer said gravely. ''But, surely, when I spoke to you, you must have realized I was a flesh-and-blood man—not some preternatural bird!''

''Yes, after a moment, I did. However, then, I believed you to be the notorious highwayman Black Jack Raven, intent on kidnapping me! Perhaps it was even the thought of him that caused me to so erroneously perceive you as a raven in the first place, my lord!''

''On her way from Jamaica Inn to St. Aubyn, Miss Collier was set upon in your carriage by the brigand, my lord,'' Mrs. Wickersham put in, to clarify the matter, in light of the Earl's apparent puzzlement.

''My coach...*my* coach was attacked and robbed?'' he asked, plainly surprised and outraged by the very idea.

"Yes, indeed it was, my lord," the housekeeper confirmed. "Fortunately, no one was hurt, and no money or other valuables were stolen. However, poor Miss Collier *was* subjected to the indignity of having the dastardly thief cut off a lock of her hair!"

"Well, then." The Earl spoke again soberly, after a long, contemplative moment. "No doubt that explains a great deal. Miss Collier—" he turned once more to Verity "—I fear you must have suffered a rather unpleasant and most distressing introduction to Cornwall…one from which you have not fully recovered. Thus, tonight, you wildly—although quite understandably—envisioned the rising wind to be someone crying a name, the drifting mist to be some apparition amid the trees, my horse to be some behemoth and myself to be both some gargantuan raven and the infamous highwayman who bears that name. No wonder your only thought was to flee!" Briefly, he paused, studying her reflective face. Then he continued. "You do not appear to be convinced, madam."

"Yes…no…I—I don't know." Verity sighed heavily. "It all sounds so very logical when you put it that way, my lord, that in truth, I realize it must be so. Yet I could swear that my eyes and ears did not so deceive me."

"Miss Collier—" Lord St. Aubyn now smiled wryly, with some amusement "—although named for the specter he resembles, Phantom is indeed a horse, I do assure you, and I myself am a man, not a raven—and unless you can think of some rational reason for why I should be running around the Cornish countryside, robbing even my own equipage—''

''Oh, no, my lord, of course not! I fear I must be more overwrought than I supposed.''

''Indeed,'' he responded dryly, although not unkindly. ''That being the case, let us complete the ministrations to your ankle, and then you shall be comfortably installed in your bedroom, and a supper tray brought to you—for I cannot think that under the circumstances, you would wish to join the others at table.''

''No, thank you, my lord, for your consideration.''

Despite her renewed protests, her employer insisted on rubbing the liniment on her injured ankle himself, then carefully wrapping a bandage firmly around it for support. After that, it was he who lifted her from the chesterfield to carry her upstairs to her bedroom, ignoring her continued demurring and asserting that she must not put any weight upon her ankle, lest it worsen the already bad sprain.

Verity was both mortified and terribly confused. She had never before in her life been subject to such attentions from a man, and she felt vaguely that there must be something improper about it all, despite the Earl's seemingly detached attitude toward her and Mrs. Wickersham's own continued presence as they ascended the staircase in the entrance hall, then made their way down the long passage to Verity's bedroom.

There, her chambermaid, Loveday, waited expectantly, having lit the lamps and the fire, and turned down the bed. Carefully, Lord St. Aubyn set Verity down upon this latter.

"In a few days, when you are feeling better, I shall look forward to meeting you more properly, Miss Collier," he remarked.

Then, after glancing around the bedroom and speaking to both the housekeeper and the chambermaid to assure himself that Verity's current needs would be satisfied, he nodded to her, then exited the chamber, followed by Mrs. Wickersham, who promised to send up her supper tray directly. After their departure, tsking and shaking her head over the mishap that had caused Verity to be injured, Loveday helped her undress and don her nightgown, then tucked her into bed.

"Surely, I would be better off at the table for supper." Verity indicated the small gateleg table between the two wing chairs at the far end of her bedroom.

"Nay, miss," the chambermaid asserted firmly. "That won't do a'tall. Thou heard his lordship, same as me, an' his instructions was most explicit. Thou art ta stay in bed till yer ankle can bear yer weight, an' thou art ta do nowt else in t' meantime, not e'en yer lessons with t' twins. His lordship said that whilst yer ankle is most like only sprained, it could have a slight crack in it. Do 'ee want it ta break, miss?"

"No, of course not, Loveday."

"Well, then, thou'd best do what his lordship told thee. 'Sides, miss, his lordship dunnat like ta be disobeyed. His word is law hereabout, an' there's few what would dare ta cross him!"

"Why? Is he a cruel master, then?" Verity queried, much startled. "But Mrs. Wickersham said he was a fair and honorable man!"

"Aye, miss, an' so he be, 'tis true. Still, that dunnat change t' fact that he's also got a wicked temper an' dunnat suffer fools gladly! So if'n I was thou, I'd not be wishin' ta make him angry at me, but would do whate'er he said, fer if'n thou dunnat an' make yer ankle worse, 'twill not go well fer 'ee, miss!"

Remembering now, of a sudden, how the Earl had ominously threatened to beat her when she had struggled against him upon his great white horse, Verity shivered.

"Yes, you're right, Loveday, of course. Very well, then."

Settling back among the pillows, Verity ceased her argument and attempts to rise. In truth, she still felt muzzy from pain and the brandy, so she was glad to lie there and rest, and to be waited on for a change. Presently, Bessie appeared with the supper tray, which she set on the bed, and upon ascertaining that there was nothing else that Verity wanted or needed, the two maids left her alone with her meal.

Once they had gone, she surveyed what she had been served. There was the ubiquitous hot pot of tea, a large, steaming bowl of hearty chicken soup, which smelled wonderful, a thick slice of fresh bread generously buttered and a small dish of strawberries topped with Cornwall's sweet, clotted cream. Verity ate slowly, not only to savor the tasty fare, but also because she was still a little shaken from her ordeal and did not want to be sick from the unaccustomed brandy. The tea and soup soon warmed her, however, and eventually helped to settle her slightly queasy stomach, too, so that, presently, she felt much better and was able to deliberate clearly on the evening's events.

Despite what she had told the Earl earlier, she was still not convinced that what she had heard and seen prior to his onslaught upon the scene had been only the wind or the sea and the mist. After all, Verity belatedly realized, she had heard the name *Tamsyn* being lamented before, when she had stood at the edge of the crumbling cliffs that overlooked the ocean at the rear of the manor, and elsewhere, in the gardens and the park. But, then, each of these times, she had spied no one about, although it had been broad daylight and not an early dusk beset by drizzle and brume. So perhaps the sound really *was* something peculiar to the restless Cornish wind or ocean, and the ghostly figure she had seen fluttering through the park had been nothing more than the drifting fog blown in from the sea, she finally decided, sighing. But still, despite her having reached this resolution, a niggling doubt continued to assail her, so that she even wondered if there were some mystery at St. Aubyn, of which she was unaware.

But, no, how could that be? Verity pondered. For everyone had been quite open with her, Mrs. Wickersham, upon being questioned, even relating the details of Lady St. Aubyn's untimely demise, although the memory was grievous to the entire household. Seemingly, there was nobody at the manor with anything to hide, so that, at last, Verity was compelled to conclude that those who were native to Cornwall knew much more than she about the peculiar effects produced by its wind, ocean and mist—and no doubt were not blessed with her fanciful imagination, either!

Verity was startled from her reverie by a quiet knock upon the bedroom door, then Loveday entered to take away the supper tray, and bearing a mahogany walking stick with an ornate brass handle carved into a horse head, and a leather-bound book.

"His lordship said thou art ta have t' use o' this, miss, in case thou need ta get up in t' night fer some reason." The chambermaid laid the cane upon the bed. "Also, he thought that since thou art unable ta come downstairs at t' moment, p'rhaps thou might enjoy passin' away the evenin' by readin' this novel." She set the book on one of the night tables.

"Oh, how very kind and thoughtful of his lordship! Please convey my thanks to him!"

"Aye, miss, that I will. Will thou be wantin' anything else?"

"Yes, Loveday, my hairbrush, please, so I can brush my hair before retiring, and a ribbon to tie up the braid, and then if you'll stoke the fire and blow out the all the lamps but those on the night tables for me, so I won't have to do that, I think I'll just be able to manage."

"Of course, miss."

Once the chambermaid had completed the requested tasks, then exited the bedroom, Verity took up the book that the Earl had sent upstairs for her.

She did not know what she had expected, but it was most certainly not the Gothic novel she discovered, written by Ann Radcliffe and entitled *The Mysteries of Udolpho*. As she leafed through it, Verity recognized that it was a work in four volumes, about a young woman who was imprisoned in a foreboding castle by her sinister guardian and who subsequently suffered one unnerving experience after another, all aided and abetted by her superstitious nature and wild imagination. Although she could not be certain, Verity somehow suspected that the Earl was privately amusing himself at her expense, that he had chosen the book solely because of the way in which her own unbridled fancy had run away with her earlier this evening on the manor's drive, causing her to envision supernatural beings that had not, in reality, existed.

Highly indignant, she almost tossed the novel aside. But the truth was that with her being stuck in her chamber as she currently was, there was precious little else to entertain her. She did not feel up to sketching or painting, nor to embroidering or any other fancy needlework, and there was no piano or other instrument in her bedroom. The book, then, would have to suffice. In fact, since it was quite long, she could probably make it last over the next few days, Verity reckoned, when she would have difficulty getting about, even with the aid of a walking stick.

She sighed heavily at the realization of this last, at the humiliating knowledge that she had only her own foolishness over Colonel Sherbourne—who had

not, it appeared, come to St. Aubyn today, after all—
and her own vivid imagination over the Earl to blame
for her present condition and confinement. Had she
not felt herself in such grave danger of falling in love
with the Colonel, she would not have gone to St. Ives
in the first place nor got such a late start home, and
had she not envisioned the Earl to be some behemoth
raven mounted upon some even larger, phantom
creature, she could, as he himself had earlier observed, have simply stepped to one side of the
manor's drive and thereby avoided the entire accident!

She wondered if the heroine of *The Mysteries of
Udolpho,* Emily St. Aubert, would prove to have
more in common with her than what she had already
grasped.

At that most provoking thought, but with a great
deal of curiosity and interest, nevertheless, Verity began to read: *On the pleasant banks of the Garonne,
in the province of Gascony, stood, in the year 1584,
the chateau of Monsieur St. Aubert...*

Utterly enthralled by Emily's adventures, Verity
read until the wee hours, when the candles had gut-
tered in their sockets and the fire had died to a bed
of glowing embers in the grate. She had not, as she
had planned, managed to save any of the novel for
later reading in the days to come, but, instead, consumed with desire to see what happened next, had
finished it to the very last, satisfying word. Now, as
one always does with a marvelous book that has
touched one deeply, she closed the cover slowly,
with the profoundest of reluctance, loath to admit

that she had, in fact, reached the end, that there were no more of Emily's and her dearly beloved Valancourt's adventures remaining to entertain her. Carefully, Verity placed the novel on one of the night tables beside the bed.

After that, still dwelling on the complex story, reliving it in her mind, she began to brush her long, soft dark-brown hair, bemoaning the loss of her hairpins, for although she had others, she had not so many that she could easily afford the loss of several. But there was no help for it now. Perhaps once her ankle no longer pained her, she could search along the drive, where she might be lucky enough to find at least one or two of the missing hairpins, she thought.

Laying aside her brush, she plaited her hair, braiding into it the long dark-red silk riband that Loveday had taken from a drawer of the dressing table and left beside the brush. Verity did not normally wear such finery, deeming it much too dear for every day and thus preferring her plain ribbons of black or grey. Indeed, she did not know what had ever possessed her to buy the crimson furbelow in the first place, except that the peddler who had persuaded her into making the purchase at the Belper market had been so very charming that in the end, she had not been able to resist. She did not know why Loveday had pulled it from the drawer. Still, Verity was not going to hobble across to the dressing table just to fetch another riband to tie off her hair.

Completing the bedtime routine and turning to blow out the lamps on the night tables, she caught a glimpse of herself in the gilt-framed oval mirror over the dressing table. For a long moment, she stared at herself in the looking glass, something she rarely ever did, vanity not being one of her vices and, even if it had been, honesty forcing her to deem herself far too plain and unremarkable to preen. So it was not her thick hair framing her heart-shaped face nor her wide, sootily lashed misty-grey eyes set beneath gently arched brown brows that captured and held her attention. Nor her finely chiseled, retroussé nose nor her sweetly vulnerable mouth nor her small, stubborn chin.

Rather, it was the fact that she had unwittingly plaited the dark-red riband threaded through her single long braid into a love knot.

One slender hand flew to the plait, to the intricate love knot that, in the diffuse half light, gleamed crimson against her dark-brown hair and pale-white nightgown, like a bright, lethal splash of blood staining her breast.

Why had she done such a strange thing? Verity did not know. She had not braided her hair in such a manner for years, had not until this very moment been aware that she even remembered how, for she had learned the way of it from some of the other girls at Trowbridge. It had been a silly enough ritual, performed at the stroke of midnight, around a single candle, in whose flame, it had been claimed, one would see a vision of one's true love after one had bound the love knot.

Now, as she stared into the mirror over the dressing table, Verity's gaze caught the flicker of her lamp beside her, and as she looked into the flame, unbidden in her mind rose the Earl's image bending over her, proffering her the snifter of brandy.

Drink, Miss Collier, she heard again his low, mellifluous voice command.

Was it only brandy he had offered her? she wondered now. Or something even stronger and more potent? A love potion—that she should have plaited the dark-red love knot into her braid, that his dark, handsome visage should have been conjured in the lamp's guttering flame?

Of a sudden, without thinking, Verity quickly bent over the crystal lamp and blew out its solitary candle, extinguishing its soft flame—and the Earl's image in her mind.

At long last, she slept—and dreamed highly disturbing dreams in which she was borne by a giant raven through the silvery, moon-raked night sky, and the rising, wild wind beneath the preternatural bird's great, soaring wings and the turbulent, foaming sea below moaned a strange, plaintive threnody of *Tamsyn, Tamsyn* in her ears, while she plaited a crimson love knot into her unbridled, unbound hair.

Seven

Along the Labyrinthine Drive

Misled by fancy's meteor ray,
By passion driven;
But yet the light that led astray
Was light from heaven.

The Vision
—Robert Burns

I fled Him, down the nights and down the days;
I fled him down the arches of the years;
I fled Him down the labyrinthine ways
Of my own mind; and in the mist of tears...

The Hound of Heaven
—Francis Thompson

The next few days passed quietly and uneventfully enough for Verity, although she knew from the reports carried to her ears by Loveday and Bessie that this was not true for the rest of the household. With the Earl's homecoming, it was as though the manor, previously slumberous, now stirred to wakefulness, as though it sensed, somehow, that its master was in residence.

He spent much time, Verity was informed, riding out with his steward, Mr. Drummond, over the extensive grounds of the estate, after which the two men were closeted in the Earl's study at length, going over the affairs of the manor and how best to deal with them. His business ventures were many, it appeared, encompassing everything from the raising of cattle, sheep and Cornish poultry—which provided beef, milk, mutton, wool, chicken and eggs, respectively—to china-clay mining and tin mining, from the former of which was derived kaolin, used in the manufacture of porcelain, and the latter of which product was employed in any number of industries. From generations of land ownership blessed with such enterprises was the Earl's fortune derived.

Now, too, came his tenants to the house, bringing both their news and their grievances to his attention, and other visitors arrived, too—local officials, dragoons and merchants, and even a fencing master, with whom the Earl practiced his swordsmanship. Every other hour, it seemed, there came the pounding of the brass lion's-head knocker upon the heavy oak front door or the clanging of the resonant brass bell that hung to one side in the portico. A steady stream of unfamiliar voices and footsteps echoed from the entrance hall, the small drawing room, the study and the library.

When not devoted to managing his business affairs, the Earl spent most of his time with his twin children, Meliora and Bastian, with whom he was very close. The three were most often to be found together in the library, whence had come *The Mysteries of Udolpho,* which book Verity, upon finishing, had duly returned to him via Loveday, charging the chambermaid to relate to him that despite how wildly improbable its convoluted plot had been found, how missishly given to swooning at the most inopportune moments its poor, beleaguered heroine had been judged, it had nevertheless been deemed quite an adventurous, mesmerizing novel, and had been much enjoyed and appreciated by its reader.

The result of the delivery of this sly piece of deliberate impertinence was that several more such books were immediately brought to Verity's bedroom for her perusal. From this, she knew for certain that the Earl had indeed been privately amusing himself at her expense when he had sent up *The Mys-*

teries of Udolpho to divert her, and that, now, apprized of the fact that she had not only got his joke, but also that she firmly disclaimed any resemblance whatsoever to *Udolpho's* Emily St. Aubert, his sense of humor was such that he wickedly offered her several more such heroines from which to choose.

Upon spying the stack of novels Loveday carried and upon ascertaining their contents, Verity could not help but laugh.

"Please inform his lordship that whilst I might once have been deceived by the twilight mizzle, I am not so insensible as to be so taken in again," she asserted ingeniously. "Please also say how grateful I am for his thoughtfulness and consideration, that it is clear to me that I shall not lack for entertainment during my brief confinement."

"Aye, miss."

In truth, Verity was vastly diverted, not only by the books, but also by the fact that several persons in the household took turns visiting her, including Mrs. Wickersham, the twins and Trueth, and Loveday and Bessie. As a result, Verity wanted for nothing and thus found little reason, aside from her daily ablutions, to rise from her bed, which would have placed a strain upon her injured ankle. Instead, she was able to rest, read, sketch and chat with her visitors—to the point that she felt almost guilty about so much attention being paid to her and for being as yet unable to resume her own duties.

But eventually, there did come the day when the swelling and bruising of her ankle finally subsided, and she was able comfortably to get up and about, hardly needing to rely at all on the cane the Earl had lent her. On that morning, Verity thought to be summoned into his presence, so she dressed quite carefully in one of her two black gowns and a clean white tucker. However, mildly to her surprise, no such demand to wait upon the Earl was brought to her, so that, instead, she was able to devote the entire morning to her lessons with the children in the schoolroom.

Afterward, she accompanied them downstairs to lunch, after which she had the remainder of the afternoon free. Upon learning from Mrs. Wickersham that the Earl had ridden out earlier with his cousin, Colonel Sherbourne, and that they had yet to return, Verity remembered her resolve to try to find some of her lost hairpins along the drive.

Donning her straw bonnet, which had been cleaned and returned to her, and her spencer, and with the Earl's walking stick in hand, she presently set off to this purpose.

It was a bright sunny afternoon, and after the days of her confinement, Verity was glad to be outside in the fresh, balmy summer air. She walked slowly along the drive, not only because she was uncertain as to just where she had lost her hairpins, but also because her ankle was still a trifle weak. However, she knew that now that the swelling and bruising had disappeared, it really needed exercise to strengthen it again. In a few more days, it would be as good as new.

Still, Verity realized it would be unwise to push

herself, so she took her time, pausing now and then to rest, and to savor the front gardens and park.

In the center of the drive's circle, the gargoyles of the great, central stone fountain gurgled, their waters streaming forth into the huge, fluted basin below, the ripples glinting diamond-like in the sunlight and the flowers planted all around blooming in a gay profusion of brilliant colors. The crushed seashells of the drive itself gleamed like pearls strewn across the lush green lawn.

Looking at them, Verity thought ruefully that her plan to try to recover her lost hairpins was probably a futile one. But as she had nothing else to do and the day was so very fine, she did not truly mind. While new ones would cost her, the sum was not so much that it represented any real hardship to her. Indeed, living at St. Aubyn, she had little enough to spend her wages on. So she strolled on, enjoying the scenery.

With the sun shining, it was now difficult for her to believe she had ever imagined that the mounting wind had sounded like the name *Tamsyn* being lamented in her ears, or that the swirling mist had appeared to her like some white specter floating and fluttering through the trees—much less that she had envisioned the Earl's powerful horse as some phantom creature bent on trampling her under foot and he himself as some unparalleled raven clinging to its back. Almost, now, she could laugh at the memory and her own foolishness. Today, even beneath the shadowy canopy fashioned by the gnarled, overhanging branches of the tall, twisted Cornish elms that

lined its verge, the drive looked perfectly ordinary—
not some dark, amorphous, frightening place of ban-
sheelike shrieking and of terrifying apparitions.

As she walked along, Verity diligently searched
for her lost hairpins. However, they were not to be
found, and at last, although she was doubtful about
the location, she decided that perhaps she had been
closer to the lodge when they had been torn from her
chignon by the wind during her flight from the Earl
and his huge white horse.

But now, for the first time that day, as she approached the lodge, Verity involuntarily shivered.
She did not know why. There was nothing in particular about the place to alarm her, especially in broad
daylight. Yet, even so, she felt strangely apprehensive. Despite the fact that, as usual, there was no one
in sight, and all the curtains were drawn tight at the
windows, she still had the uneasy feeling that someone was watching her—although why Lady Kenhebres or her servants, Mr. and Mrs. Ythnow, would
want to spy on her, she could not fathom.

Finally, remembering how her wild imagination
had so completely run away with her only some days
previous and what had proved the disastrous results
of that, Verity told herself severely that she was not
going to behave so ridiculously again. While she
might be young, inexperienced, romantic, fanciful,
and have, thus far, led a relatively sheltered existence
that had left her very unworldly and restlessly longing for some adventure and excitement, she was nevertheless neither a flighty nor an insensible woman.

Nor did she lack for courage. When the Earl's carriage had been held up by the notorious highwayman Black Jack Raven, she had not swooned, not even when he had so mortifyingly cut off the pilfered lock of her hair. And when she had realized she could not outrun the Earl's big horse, despite her thinking it was some monster and fearing to be trampled beneath its ponderous, flailing hooves, she had still turned to confront it.

Certainly, there was nothing for her to be afraid of now, Verity reminded herself sternly. The lodge was not abandoned and haunted, but, rather, inhabited, even if she had never seen its principal occupant. Nor was there even anything out of the ordinary about this last. Lady Kenhebres was elderly and an invalid, and while her servants, Mr. and Mrs. Ythnow, might not be very friendly, they were still flesh-and-blood people, not ghosts.

Thus resolved, Verity knelt upon the drive, using one hand to brace herself and running the other amid the crushed seashells to try to find her lost hairpins.

Tamsyn...Tamsyn...

As, without warning, the soft crying of the dead Lady St. Aubyn's name reached her ears, Verity felt an icy grue tingle up her spine, raising the fine hairs on her nape. Her heart leaped to her throat, pounding there horribly, and she froze where she was. This was not happening. This was not real, she tried desperately to tell herself. It was only the ceaseless Cornish wind rustling the leaves of the trees and rippling across the grass—nothing more.

Please God, nothing more.

Tamsyn...Tamsyn...your life is in grave danger. You must leave this place of death at once!

It was not the wind. Deep down inside, Verity knew that somehow, no matter how hard she attempted to reassure herself otherwise. But was it only her unbridled fancy? Or was she somehow going mad, she wondered, not for the first time, hearing voices where none existed? People did that, sometimes. She knew that. The famous French Maid of Orléans, Jeanne D'Arc, had claimed that various saints spoke to her.

But, no, Verity could not—*would* not—believe she was losing her mind. Covertly, from beneath the thick fringe of her sooty eyelashes, she glanced cautiously around the drive. But there was no one to be seen—only, after an instant, a vague, specterlike, gauzy fluttering of white amid the trees, and then, suddenly, much to her horror, a frantic growling and scrabbling in the undergrowth of the park, as though some wild animal would at any moment violently spring upon her from the thickets. This was followed by a thunderous, crunching sound, and as she looked up from where she knelt, petrified, she saw two horses galloping through the open wrought-iron gates of the manor, coming straight toward her.

Such relief overwhelmed Verity at this most welcome sight that she nearly sobbed aloud. Grabbing the Earl's cane, which lay on the ground beside her, she staggered to her feet, rattled but stepping mindfully, however awkwardly, to the side of the drive so that she would not be trampled under foot by the riders.

Spying her, the two men on horseback drew their mounts to a halt before her.

"Miss Collier," the Earl greeted her, as he reined in his prancing white stallion, Phantom. "Are you quite well? I saw you on the drive and feared that perhaps your injured ankle had given way, causing you to fall. You're looking very pale and shaken."

"Am I? I—I didn't realize, my lord—"

Hearing again the strange scuffling noise behind her in the park, Verity glanced fearfully over her shoulder. Then, as she tried furtively to move away from the edge of the trees and bushes, her walking stick unexpectedly slipped upon the crushed seashells of the drive, and she nearly lost her balance and fell.

"It is as I thought. You *are* unwell!" Lord St. Aubyn observed, swiftly getting down from his horse and hastening to her side to steady her. "Perhaps you ought not to have walked so far on your ankle and in this sun your first day out of bed. Hugh—" he spoke to Colonel Sherbourne, who had also dismounted "—fetch Miss Collier a glass of water from the lodge. Come, madam. Sit down over here."

Her employer led Verity to a bench outside on the front porch of the lodge, while the Colonel knocked peremptorily upon the door. After a long minute, it was answered by Mrs. Ythnow, who stared at them all impassively.

"Doryty," Colonel Sherbourne addressed the servant, the name quite startling Verity, "Miss Collier is ill and requires a glass of water. At once, if you please."

"No, really, I'm fine, Colonel, thank you," Verity

protested quietly, "although the water will be much appreciated, even so. I am perhaps a trifle thirsty from walking in the sun."

Wordlessly, Mrs. Ythnow vanished from the doorway.

"Are you certain you're all right, Miss Collier?" the Earl inquired. "Only a moment ago, you seemed to be afraid of something in the park, and you nearly fell again. Your face is still wan, and you appear as though you might faint. Has something alarmed you?"

"I hadn't fallen when first you saw me, my lord," she corrected him. "I had but knelt to see whether I could find any of my hairpins, which I lost here on the drive the night you returned home. However, it *is* true that whilst I searched for them, I—I saw something flash white among the trees and then heard what I believed to be some kind of wild animal in the brush, snarling and tussling about, and I feared it might attack me."

Anxious that Lord St. Aubyn not believe her to have permitted her vivid imagination to run away with her once more, Verity forbore to mention the eerie mewling of his dead wife's name that had come to her ears again or the strange, dire warning that had been issued to her. Before her employer could respond, however, Mrs. Ythnow returned to the front porch, carrying the requested glass of water. Silently, she handed it to Verity.

"Thank you," Verity said.

Her eyes oddly hard and watchful, the servant only

nodded mutely, then moved to go back inside the lodge.

"No, stay a moment, Doryty," the Earl commanded. "Miss Collier has reported that whilst she was in search of some hairpins she lost upon the drive earlier this week, she heard some wild creature growling and scrabbling in the park. Have you seen any such animal about?"

"Nay, m'lord," Mrs. Ythnow answered tersely. "Only yer great beast o' a dog, what tore down some clean laundry I had hung out back on t' line ta dry an' what, when I tried ta catch him, scampered off into t' woods, draggin' one o' t' bedsheets with him—t' nasty cur! I had quite a wrestle with him, I did, ta get me laundry back, so I'd appreciate it in t' future, m'lord, if'n thou would keep a better watch on him!"

"I'll do that." Lord St. Aubyn's tone and demeanor were such that, abruptly, Verity realized he was exceedingly angry. A muscle pulsed in his set jaw. Yet, much to her surprise, he did not reprimand the servant for her impertinent remarks. Instead, he stated coolly, "Thank you, Doryty. That will be all. You may go—and please, give my regards to Lady Kenhebres. She is well, I trust…?"

For an instant, Verity could have sworn that she glimpsed a flicker of fear in Mrs. Ythnow's cold dark eyes. But in the end, the servant only nodded again curtly.

"Aye, as well as she e'er is, m'lord."

Then, after dipping a curtsy to both her employer and Colonel Sherbourne, Mrs. Ythnow went back inside the lodge, her lips pressed together grimly as she shut the door loudly and firmly behind her.

"Well, really! What a very unpleasant sort of woman Doryty is!" the Colonel observed, once she had gone. "I honestly don't know why you keep her on, Jago—particularly when you know of her fondness for a pint of porter and after what happened because of it!"

"You mind your business your way, Hugh, and allow me to do the same," the Earl replied tersely. He paused for a moment, as though to check his emotions, then turned to Verity and, in a much lighter tone tinged with dry amusement, continued. "There, now, Miss Collier. You see? The whole incident is quite easily explained. So I trust you are not still imagining there are ghosts and hideous beasts prowling about the grounds of St. Aubyn."

"No, my lord. As I said, I merely thought the creature I had heard to be some kind of a wild animal."

"Good. Then, madam, if you are now feeling sufficiently recovered, I suggest you return to the manor. Hugh and I will accompany you."

"Thank you, but there's truly no need to put yourselves to such trouble, my lord. I can find my own way back."

"Yes, of course you can. However, we were ourselves on the way home when we chanced upon you."

"Indeed," Colonel Sherbourne put in, "and I, for one, would be quite delighted to continue there in such pleasant company as yours, Miss Collier—for in truth, Jago has not been at all at his best today. If

I didn't know better, I'd think he was dour Doryty's cousin and not my own!''

Lord St. Aubyn did not deign to reply to this. Instead, much to Verity's surprise, he abruptly whistled long and loud, and a few minutes later, a large, long-haired, wolfish black-and-tan dog burst without warning from the park on to the drive, to prowl about its master's boots. Her employer told Verity that its name was Styx and that she might safely pet it if she wished, which she did, scratching it behind the ears.

"You, then, are the culprit responsible for giving me such a fright and for making off with Doryty's clean laundry, too, are you?'' she queried to the dog, as she stroked its silky fur.

"Yes, I'm afraid so,'' the Earl confirmed.

Then, the two men leading their horses in order to walk beside Verity, and the dog following obediently at its master's heels, the party started down the drive toward the manor.

"I was sorry to learn of your indisposition, Miss Collier,'' Colonel Sherbourne commented, as they strolled along. "I trust your ankle is now much improved.''

"Yes, thank you, sir.''

"And how are my young cousins, Meliora and Bastian, getting on? As you probably know, it is some days now since I have seen them.''

"They are both quite well, sir, and their progress at their lessons improves daily. It is a real pleasure to teach two such youngsters, who are so well behaved and so eager to learn.''

"I'm very glad to hear it.''

Verity and the Colonel continued their polite colloquy in this vein, although Lord St. Aubyn contributed little to it, being content, it seemed, to inform Verity that he looked forward to meeting with her properly later that evening, at which time he hoped to see his children and also to hear more about what she was teaching them and what they had thus far learned.

The small party having then reached the manor, they parted company, going their separate ways.

Eight

Through a Glass, Darkly

When he be man, he takes a wife,
When he be beast, he takes her life.
Ladies, beware of him who be—
A silkie come from Sule Skerrie.

> *The Great Silkie (of Sule Skerrie)*
> —Traditional Orkney Islands Ballad

We know in part, and we prophesy in part.
But when that which is perfect is come,
then that which is in part shall be done away.
When I was a child, I spake as a child,
I understood as a child, I thought as a child:
But when I became a man, I put away childish
things.
For now we see through a glass, darkly;
but then face to face: now I know in part;
But then shall I know even as also I am known.

> *I Corinthians*
> —The Holy Bible

When Verity returned to her bedroom at St. Aubyn, she was of two minds. On the one hand, she was highly, however furtively, disquieted by the afternoon's events, for although the snarling and tussling she had heard in the park might indeed have been Mrs. Ythnow and the dog Styx wrestling over a bedsheet, that still did not explain the calling of Lady St. Aubyn's name nor the strange, disturbing warning that had been issued:

Tamsyn...Tamsyn...your life is in grave danger. You must leave this place of death at once!

What had it all meant? Verity wondered now, unwittingly shuddering. Was it possible that, attributing what had sounded like a lamented name to something other than the wind, she had grown frightened and simply misunderstood the words that had followed? That, in reality, what she had believed she had heard had actually been nothing more than Doryty threatening the disruptive dog for its misbehavior? Or was there, unbeknown to her, some dreadful mystery connected with Lady St. Aubyn's untimely death?

This last notion was truly chilling—however unlikely, she thought, in light of what Mrs. Wickersham had said about the matter. But still, while Verity could think of no earthly reason why the housekeeper would have lied to her, the fact that Doryty—the nurse who had drunk herself into a stupor at her post, thereby enabling the twins to creep outside on the tragic night that had brought about their mother's demise—should be caring for the invalid Lady Kenhebres at the lodge seemed exceedingly peculiar. Even Colonel Sherbourne had remarked on it.

But perhaps, despite what had happened on that night, Doryty had some kind of a claim on the Earl. However, if this were indeed the case, what could it be—and why, then, should she fear him, even while speaking so impertinently to him, as no servant ought to a master? None of it made any sense, Verity decided at last—although another idea now occurred to her.

Maybe it was Doryty who had cried out Lady St. Aubyn's name and issued the dire caveat. Doryty drank—that was certainly no secret at the manor— and perhaps when she did, she blamed herself for her mistress's death and, inebriated, confused and remorseful, forgetting that Lady St. Aubyn had lain in her grave now for the past two years, desperately sought to warn her of her impending doom.

Indeed, the more Verity dwelled upon this possibility, the more logical it seemed to her. Maybe the Earl even pitied Doryty and that was why he kept her on. It would, perhaps, not be out of character for him, Verity supposed, since he appeared to take a genuine interest in the welfare of all his staff. Witness his own kindness to and consideration for her, to the point of wishing to amuse her with the novels he had sent up to her during her confinement and that she had so enjoyed reading.

Verity was so comforted by this explanation that she was able to turn her mind fully to the other direction in which it pulled her, that of Colonel Sherbourne. How handsome he was—not in the dark, wild, brooding fashion of the Earl, but, rather, in an engagingly boyish and charming way that, coupled with his courtesy and congeniality, could not help but find favor and to please. She flattered herself that he had been sincerely glad to see her, although, still, she dared not hope that his amiable and interested manner toward her was indicative of anything more serious than that he found her pleasant company, as he had said.

Aware of how the Colonel was situated in life— that he was the eldest son of the Earl's mother's younger brother and therefore must earn his own livelihood in the world—Verity knew she would be very foolish indeed to fall in love with him, regardless of how her heart prompted her to do so. She possessed neither beauty nor fortune to tempt him, and, further, she was honest enough with herself to admit that had either of these alone been capable of attracting and fixing his interest upon her, she would have despised him for a lesser man than what she currently believed him, and she would not have daydreamed about him and fancied herself on the brink of losing her heart to him.

Having never been blessed—or cursed—with a romance, Verity had little experience of men. Still, she knew enough of her own character to feel certain she would not be happy in either love or marriage if she did not enjoy not only both the admiration and fidelity of her partner, but also his respect and a meeting of the minds with him. While she felt that all this she might indeed be able to achieve with Colonel Sherbourne, the fact remained that he was not likely to choose a plain, penniless governess as his wife.

That being the case, she would be well advised to put him from her thoughts, Verity told herself strictly, and not suffer herself to wear her heart upon her sleeve, thereby embarrassing both herself and him, and thus undoubtedly losing his good opinion and friendship, both of which, no matter what, she coveted for their own sakes. She had not so much the esteem of others and so many friends that she could afford to lose any.

A knock upon the bedroom door interrupted her musings.

"Yes, come in."

"Beggin' yer pardon, miss—" Loveday entered the chamber "—but Mrs. Wickersham has sent me ta tell thee that his lordship requests t' pleasure o' yer company an' that o' t' twins fer tea with him an' t' Colonel in t' small drawin' room at six o'clock this evenin'. Mrs. Wickersham further charged me ta say that thou should change thy frock, that 'tis customary ta dress fer t' evenin' when his lordship is in residence at t' manor, an' that t' twins should be at their best, also."

"Thank you, Loveday. Will you please go and inform Trueth to make the children ready accordingly, then return here to assist me in dressing?''

''Aye, miss.''

While the chambermaid was gone, Verity busied herself at her ablutions, then carefully took her pearl-grey silk gown from the wardrobe. Although she hated to wear it for any but the finest occasions, she had no other that would serve. Loveday, returning, helped her to dress, doing up the hooks and tying the long, trailing sash into a bow at her back. She hung her mother's prized gold locket around her neck, then sat down before the dressing table, so that Loveday, taking the hairpins from Verity's mass of dark-brown hair, could brush and sweep it up into a more formal coiffure than the plain, neat chignon she usually wore.

''Thou look very fine, miss!'' the chambermaid declared with satisfaction, stepping back, once she had finished, to admire her handiwork.

''In truth, I hardly recognize myself, Loveday. Until now, I had not thought it possible that I could be so much improved in appearance. You really are inordinately skilled at arranging hair and so forth, it would seem.''

''Aye, miss. I hope someday ta be a lady's maid if'n I can, so 'twere a real pleasure fer me ta help 'ee an' ta have someone else besides Bessie ta practice on fer a change. But, there, I'd best not keep 'ee, miss, fer 'tis nigh on six o'clock now, an' his lordship dunnat like ta be kept waitin'.''

''An impatient man, then, is he?''

''A stickler fer punctuality, I should have said,

miss, although 'tis true enough that he's not t' most patient master in t' world, either, fer as I've told 'ee afore, he dunnat suffer fools gladly, his lordship dunnat. But, then, again, I've seen 'im be as patient as Job when he was o' a mind ta be, with children an' animals, especially. Howe'er, I mustn't keep 'ee, miss, with me blather about his lordship, fer he surely would not approve o' thee being late because o' gossipin' with t' likes o' me!''

"No, I wouldn't think so. Very well, then. I'll go downstairs now. Thank you for helping me to dress, Loveday.''

"Any time, miss. As I said afore, I were glad ta do it.''

After collecting the twins from Trueth, Verity accompanied them downstairs to the entrance hall, where she was met by Mrs. Wickersham, who conducted them into the small drawing room. There, the Earl and Colonel Sherbourne waited expectantly, although not, Verity was gratified to discover, impatiently. For, just as she, the housekeeper and the youngsters entered the chamber, the tall, ornate mahogany grandfather clock that stood in the entrance hall struck six and, in its deep, resonant tone that echoed throughout the house, began to chime the hour. Verity was pleased to be right on time, so that Lord St. Aubyn would have no cause to be annoyed with her.

As they paused in the doorway, she surveyed her surroundings with interest, for the small drawing room was seldom used in her employer's absence and never in the evenings. But now, it was illuminated with candles burning in the crystal chandeliers and silver lamps, and with a fire blazing cheerily in the hearth, before which the dog, Styx, lay, chewing on an old ball.

All the walls of the chamber were tinted a pale, elegant French blue and accented with elaborate cornices, crown moldings, pillars and wainscoting painted a pure white and intricately carved with grapes, vines and flowers, which matched the ornate carvings on the white Parian mantel of the fireplace. The twin chandeliers dripped with crystal ropes and teardrop pendants, and were suspended from the centers of embellished, circular medallions in the ceilings. Rich, heavy dark-blue silk draperies that pooled upon the floor hung at the windows; beautifully colored tapestries and gold-framed mirrors, pictures and portraits bedecked the walls; and a thick Persian carpet in shades of blue, green, lavender and rose lay upon the dark oak floor, which contrasted strikingly with all the white trim. Fine wood furnishings of mahogany, rosewood and satinwood gleamed in the diffuse light, and sofas, chairs, benches and ottomans upholstered in chatoyant silks, satins, velvets and brocades filled the room. A pair of tall silver candlesticks and an ormolu clock sat upon the mantel, while Dresden figurines, snuff boxes and other bric-a-brac adorned the tables. A gorgeous Oriental screen with a lovely flower motif stood in one corner, and a variety of potted plants in Chinese porcelain containers were scattered about here and there.

A tea wagon laden with a silver tea service, china cups and saucers, silver spoons and an array of plates stacked high with small sandwiches, crumpets, biscuits, bonbons and other such scrumptious fare to tempt the palate completed the scene.

The Earl sat in a wing chair before the crepitant fire, Styx with the ball at his master's feet, while Colonel Sherbourne lounged on the couch.

Even upon observing them thus together, it was difficult to guess that the two men were cousins, for although much alike in height and build, they were otherwise as different as night and day. Lord St. Aubyn was as dark as a Gypsy, his sleek black hair longer and shaggier than his cousin's neat sandy-gold locks, and his mien arrogant, passionate and brooding, while the Colonel had a far more approachable, fairer, sunnier appearance.

Of the two men, she much preferred the latter, Verity thought, for despite her employer's kindness to her, she sensed that beneath his outwardly cool demeanor lurked a wild, savage edge that had given rise to the tales of his impatience and wicked temper—and she had not forgotten, besides, the sheer, brute strength it had taken to rein his great horse to a halt so that it had not trampled her under foot the night of his arrival, nor how he had swept her up from the drive as though she had weighed no more than a feather and threatened to beat her when she had struggled so pitifully against him.

He would not, she suspected, prove an easy man either to know or to love—although why this last should occur to her, she could not fathom, for surely, she was in no danger of losing her heart to her employer! Further, even if she had been, he, even less

than his cousin, could have no possible interest in
wedding a plain, penniless governess.

"Here are Miss Collier and the children, my
lord," Mrs. Wickersham announced, as the two men,
spying them, stood and, along with Bastian, bowed
politely, while, in response, Verity, the housekeeper,
and Meliora curtsied.

The amenities thus out of the way, the Earl bade
them all be seated—except that when Verity would
have chosen a corner chair somewhat away from the
rest and in the shadows, where she could remain in-
conspicuous, Lord St. Aubyn motioned her forward
instead, to the wing chair opposite his own before
the hearth. Reluctantly but obediently, she sat, bending to pet the dog, Styx, to cover her sudden confusion. She had thought that if her employer wished
to interview her, he would do so privately, but apparently, this was not to be the case.

Addressing herself to the tea wagon, the housekeeper did the honors, pouring the tea into the china
cups and filling the matching plates with the repast,
then handing them all around. While she did so, she
and Colonel Sherbourne entered into a polite but relatively trivial dialogue, occasionally directing a
query to the Earl or Verity, although the former's
attention was focused primarily on the youngsters.
For quite some time, he quizzed them on a number
of subjects and in a smattering of foreign languages—namely French, Italian, and German—to
test the progress they had made under Verity's aegis,
and he also instructed them to fetch their portfolios,

so that he could examine their drawings, and to play upon the piano that stood in one corner.

When he had finally finished with them, Lord St. Aubyn directed the twins to go and have their tea, after which, he told them, they could take Styx into the entrance hall if they wished and, there, play ball with him.

"I make you my compliments, Miss Collier," he then said to Verity. "You appear to have done very well with them in the short time you have been in my household and employ."

"Thank you, my lord. I am very glad that you think so."

"You came here in response to an advertisement I placed in, among other newspapers, the Derby *Mercury,* did you not?"

"Yes, my lord."

"I am curious, Miss Collier. Most young women would have little or no desire to come to an isolated manor in Cornwall, which caused me some difficulty in acquiring a governess, so that in the end, I was compelled to seek much farther afield to fill the position than I had originally thought would be necessary. What induced you to respond to my advertisement?"

"I—I wished to leave Trowbridge, my lord."

"Ah, yes. It is a semicharitable institution for girls, as I recall. You had no parents, then? You were an orphan?"

"Yes, my parents were killed in a shipwreck when I was young, and as my father's lands were entailed, his estate passed to a distant cousin whom I did not know and who, having no desire to be burdened with me, a mere child, installed me at Trowbridge and then promptly forgot I ever existed, I have no doubt, for I never heard so much as a single word from him afterward. Perhaps he considered that he had done his duty by me and that paying for me to be boarded at Trowbridge was, in effect, a kindness, since he need not have done so. I don't know. Certainly, neither at the time nor later did I ever perceive it to be so."

"I see. You were unhappy at Trowbridge, then, I gather?"

"I was indeed, my lord. It was a most miserable institution, run by a cadre of tightfisted administrators who grudged us so much as a candle stub and a few lumps of coal or peat on even the darkest and coldest of nights. We had little to eat—a bowl of thin gruel in the mornings, a slice of bread for lunch, and a bowl of broth in the evenings—so that we were invariably hungry, and we were kept at our lessons from dawn until dusk, after which, following our meager supper, we were compelled to listen to long readings by the director, Mr. Heap, from the Bible and other good works, and warned constantly that hellfire and brimstone awaited us if we did not moderate our behavior in all things, although Mr. Heap himself was so well fed that he was as plump as a partridge, drank to excess, was kept warm by a proper fire in all seasons and, among other unsavory vices, which I would not lower myself to mention, lined his own purse with the vast majority of the funds intended for our own upkeep, thereby cheating us all of what was rightfully ours.''

"Good God!'' Colonel Sherbourne expostulated, upon hearing all this. "The man ought to be dismissed and prosecuted!''

"So I have long believed, sir,'' Verity responded soberly, turning to him. "However, I have discovered that there is often very little recourse for the downtrodden against their oppressors in this world. We were, all of us, at Trowbridge both females and orphans, with no one who cared for us to look after our welfare and ensure our well-being. Is it any wonder, then, my lord—'' she redirected her attention to her employer "—that I should have yearned so very desperately to escape from Trowbridge, although I was no longer a pupil, but, rather, a teacher there? That I should have found even a desolate manor in the wilds of Cornwall far more preferable to a place I had long viewed as virtually a prison?''

"No, it is not.'' The Earl paused for a moment. Then he continued. "To the contrary, your answer explains even more than your desire to leave Trowbridge, for certainly, the treatment you have reported as suffering there easily accounts for your strange, fey nature and vivid imagination. No doubt, you escaped into your own mind and fantasies whenever you could.''

Verity blushed to hear herself so described.

"My lord, I suppose myself to be as down-to-earth as anyone else,'' she protested primly.

"Do you indeed, madam?'' Without warning, he laughed softly—a low, mocking sound that caused her cheeks to flame even more warmly. "Well, you suppose wrongly. Come, come, Miss Collier. This will not do. It will not do at all, I tell you. For I, more than anyone, know it to be untrue—and stand warned, I will always expect you to be scrupulously honest with me! Do you forget, now, that upon our very first meeting, you believed my stalwart horse, Phantom, to be some monstrous beast and myself a behemoth raven perched upon his back? No, I thought not! However, since it is scarcely chivalrous of me to take advantage, I shall play fair and confess that I myself perceived *you* to be some primeval silkie or kelpie stepped at the witching hour from the mists, the sea and the Otherworld into my own mortal one, with your dark, tangled hair streaming in the wind and your eyes the silver of the moon, and even when I lifted you from the ground, I was still not convinced otherwise—the result of my wild Celtic blood, I fear. For we are an unbridled, fanciful lot, we Celts, as you shall learn."

"My lord, I—I hardly know what to say," Verity stammered, much bemused.

"Then say nothing, Miss Collier," Colonel Sherbourne advised, with feigned gravity, for despite his seeming solemnity, a smile twitched about the corners of his mouth. "For you shall also learn that, like all Celts, poor Jago is moonstruck. It is best, when he is in such an odd mood, simply to ignore him and hope it passes quickly."

"Then so I shall, sir—for I now perceive his lordship to be making sport of me, as he did when, from the library here at St. Aubyn, he lent me *The Mys-*

teries of Udolpho and other such Gothic novels to
read for both my own edification and entertainment
during my brief confinement. I believe he wished me
to perceive some resemblance between poor Emily
St. Aubert and myself, although I saw none.''

"Did you not, Miss Collier?'' Lord St. Aubyn
queried, laughing softly again. "I wonder. Absolve
me at least of making a mock of you earlier tonight,
for no matter what you and Hugh may think to the
contrary, I assure you I was not. However, to the
latter charge, I will plead guilty if it suits you, for I
confess that under the circumstances, I could not resist the wicked impulse to tease you just a little. Still,
from all you have related to us tonight, it would appear that your own father, just like Emily St. Aubert's, was a man of property and some position, was
he not?''

"In truth, he was, my lord—a country squire in
the vicinity of Belper, which is a market town in
Derbyshire.''

"Yes, I am familiar with it. So…had he lived,
your situation would unquestionably have been
vastly different from what it became. You are, in
fact, a gentleman's daughter. I am not surprised to
hear it, as from the beginning of our acquaintance, I
have also thought there was a quiet air of gentility
about you, which was inbred rather than simply ac-
quired. And your mother?''

"She, too, was of a good family, my lord, but an
only child, and by the time of her death, my maternal
grandparents were already deceased, so that her in-
heritance, which would have been my own legacy

also and enabled me to live quite comfortably, had long been bestowed upon her. Unfortunately, however, I never received the bequest, as it was lost in some investments in which my poor father—who was ever too trusting for his own good, I fear—had been ill-advised.''

''Dear Miss Collier! You have had an exceedingly hard time of it, I'm very much afraid!'' Mrs. Wickersham exclaimed, glancing up from her embroidery, to which she invariably applied herself in the evenings. ''It is most fortuitous that you saw his lordship's advertisement and responded to it, for now, you are comfortable at St. Aubyn, I hope.''

''Indeed, I am, ma'am,'' Verity confirmed.

''I'm delighted to hear it,'' her employer remarked. ''Now, madam, I would be pleased if you would fetch your own portfolio for me, that I may see for myself what kind of hand it is that guides my children at their artwork. For whilst it is easy enough to determine that they can read, write, do arithmetic, and spout history, geography and a smattering of foreign languages, it is more difficult, without having inspected your own artwork, to judge whether their scribblings are merely the result of their as yet unskilled fingers or, rather, lack of talent in their instructor, which will require me to hire an art master. Well?'' He raised one black eyebrow inquisitively. ''Why do you hesitate, Miss Collier? Can it be that in this particular area, at least, you have misrepresented yourself, that you are, in fact, clumsy with both pencil and paintbrush?''

''No, my lord. I am competent enough with either,

as I informed you in my response to your advertisement. It is simply that I sketch and paint for myself alone and so would rather not display my artwork.''

"Nevertheless, I wish to see it and to make my own judgment as to its adroitness or lack thereof, so I will know whether an art master is needed here or not. I must therefore insist that you humor me.''

"Very well, my lord,'' Verity said at last.

Excusing herself, she went upstairs to her bedroom, where she retrieved her portfolio, then returned with it to the small drawing room. As the Earl opened the portfolio, the Colonel rose from the sofa to lean over his cousin's shoulder, and, too, Mrs. Wickersham laid aside her embroidery and drew her chair a little nearer to Lord St. Aubyn's own, so that she could also peruse the portfolio's contents, which were many, for Verity often sketched and painted at length to amuse herself.

Many of the pictures were of landscapes and seascapes, several done since she had come to St. Aubyn manor, and to none of these did she object showing. But the others were of fanciful and fantastic places and things that existed nowhere else but in her own thoughts. It was these that she had rather kept to herself, lest they be misunderstood and lend credence to her employer's belief that her imagination was not only vivid, but also worked overtime. However, much to Verity's dismay, it was precisely these sketches and paintings that the Earl lingered over, studying them with great interest.

"Your artwork is no less than I expected, madam,'' he observed finally, "for you do not lack either skill, creativity or imagination. Indeed, I see I was not far wrong, after all, in thinking you a silkie or kelpie from the Otherworld the night of my arrival home, for surely, that is what you have depicted herein.''

''If you say so, my lord, for I myself do not know this strange place of which you speak.''

''Oh, yes, you do—for right here before me is the proof of it, Miss Collier, which belies your words. The Greeks called it Elysium. We Celts know it as Avalon. But the name is irrelevant, for all are one and the same place—a paradise not of this world, but, rather, that belongs to the silkies, kelpies, fairies and other such creatures, and from which, should a mortal man happen to set foot upon it, he can never thereafter escape, for it is like a love knot, without beginning or end, binding him there forever....'' His voice trailed away, and abruptly, almost savagely, he closed the portfolio and laid it aside. ''I've seen enough...quite enough to satisfy me that you answered my advertisement truthfully—at least in this particular regard,'' he declared. ''Now, let us see if you play as well as you paint.'' He motioned toward the piano. ''I understand from Meliora that you are fond of Beethoven.''

''Yes, my lord.''

Obediently, Verity rose to take up a seat upon the bench before the piano, which was of the grand variety, rather than the cabinet style to be found in the schoolroom, and thus, as she ran her fingers experimentally over the keys, it produced a richer resonance that stirred and pleased her. As she had for

Meliora and Bastian, Verity played from memory the first movement of Beethoven's *Sonata quasi una Fantasia.*

When she had finished, Lord St. Aubyn commanded her to return to the wing chair before the fire.

"Is it only the first movement that you know by heart?" he queried.

"No, my lord. I know the second and third, as well."

"Then why did you not play them?"

"I—I do not know, my lord. There seemed no need, I suppose, the purpose of my performance being not to entertain, but, rather, merely to permit you to determine whether or not I am qualified to teach music to your children."

"Yes, you are quite right, and I do judge you to be a fit music instructor for them. You play beautifully and with rare emotion. I should very much like to hear you perform the entire sonata sometime— although not tonight, for the hour grows late, and it is high time the twins had their supper and then sought their beds. Good night, Miss Collier."

Thus, without fanfare, was she abruptly dismissed, and Mrs. Wickersham, too, it appeared, for upon hearing her employer's words, the housekeeper also stood, as did both men, and after the usual bows and curtsies had been dispensed with, the two women exited the chamber to see to the children.

When the youngsters had been fed and put to bed, and she had dined herself, Verity, carrying her portfolio, which she had taken away with her from the small drawing room, retired to her own bedroom for the night. Once there, however, she discovered herself to be strangely restless and excited, unable to sleep, despite the fact that her ankle had begun to throb dully again, the result of her having spent far too much time on it her first day from bed, no doubt.

She ought to get off it and try to sleep, Verity warned herself. But in truth, the idea of returning to the bed in which she had lain so unrelentingly the past few days held little appeal for her, and so instead, in the end, she set up her easel before the hearth and, opening her wooden paint box, started to work on a picture, in an attempt to occupy her mind and hands.

However, in reality, although she painted diligently, Verity scarcely paid any heed to the picture that gradually began to take shape upon the canvas, for this night, she worked in oils, with which she could take her time and to which she therefore need not devote her complete attention, as would have been required by watercolors, which dried so quickly that there was little opportunity to contemplate and linger over whatever one painted.

So, although her hands were busy, Verity found her thoughts drifting—returning time and again, not to Colonel Sherbourne, as she had expected, but to the Earl.

What a strange, dark, brooding, enigmatic, complex man he was! she mused. In just the short while since his arrival, she had already witnessed many intriguing aspects to his character, each more bemusing than the last, so that despite the time she had now spent with him, she felt she hardly knew him at all. Certainly, he had not his cousin's charming, easy manner, which never discomfitted her, as his own mercurial demeanor had tonight.

In all her life, Verity had never before heard herself likened to a silkie or kelpie, which, from the Earl's words, she had deduced must be some kind of a mermaid or other fanciful sea creature. Nor had she ever been told that her eyes were the silver of the moon. She did not know what to make of these compliments—if such they had indeed been. For, even now, despite his protests to the contrary, she could not help but think the Earl must have been making sport of her.

Yes, that must be the answer, she thought again, for his station in life was so far above her own that to believe he had any real interest in her, aside from how she taught his children, would be the height of vanity and arrogance on her own part.

Abruptly, Verity set aside her palette, placed the brush she had used into a small, open jar of turpentine, then closed the lid of her paint box and drew a clean cloth over the picture on which she had started work, but which, at the moment, seemed to her critical eye not to have any particular subject or design, but, rather, to consist mainly of random streaks and splashes of dark, amorphous color, as though she had had no clear idea whatsoever about what she had sought to bring to life on the canvas, but had painted aimlessly. Currently, her thoughts were too chaotic, it appeared, for her to concentrate properly on the picture.

Sighing heavily, feeling oddly despondent now that her earlier restlessness and excitement, having found no satisfactory outlet, had passed into frustration and suppression, she then completed her nightly ablutions and climbed into bed.

Still, it was a long time before Verity slept that night, and when she finally did, she tossed and turned fretfully, her slumber disturbed by strange, somehow troubling dreams seen as though through a glass, darkly—as shapeless and shadowy as the nebulous, embryonic picture that she had begun tonight, but that had yet to emerge into clarity and light.

Nine

At the Rhododendron Bower

The Soul unto itself
Is an imperial friend—
Or the most agonizing Spy—
An Enemy—could send—

No. 683
—Emily Dickinson

A thing of beauty is a joy forever.
Its loveliness increases; it will never
Pass into nothingness; but still will keep
A bower quiet for us, and a sleep
Full of sweet dreams, and health, and quiet
breathing.

Endymion
—John Keats

I sing of brooks, of blossoms, birds, and bowers:
Of April, May, of June, and July flowers.

I sing of Maypoles, Hock-carts, wassails, wakes,
Of bridegrooms, brides, and of their bridal cakes.

Hesperides
—Robert Herrick

The following afternoon, when her lessons with the twins had ended, Verity was summoned to the Earl's study. Upon her entrance, glancing up from where he sat at his ornate Louis XV desk, he bade her take a seat across from him, on one of the two bergère chairs beautifully upholstered in gold brocade, which were placed on the opposite side.

"Because of the injury to your ankle, I have not interrogated you previously, Miss Collier," he began, "about the assault of the highwayman Black Jack Raven upon my carriage the night of your arrival here at St. Aubyn manor. Whilst I understand that Hugh—that is, my cousin Colonel Sherbourne—has already interviewed you at length about the entire affair, I, too, would like to be apprized of any information you may have to impart in this regard. I confess I find the fact that Black Jack has grown so bold as to attack my own coach quite alarming. Who knows what such a scoundrel may do next? Thus it would seem best to take whatever precautions are necessary to protect both my staff and my vehicles."

"Indeed, yes, my lord."

So, once again, Verity related the tale of Black

Jack's accosting the Earl's coach, while he listened quietly, thoughtfully, occasionally interjecting a question or an observation. When she had finished her narrative, he thanked her, then turned his attention in another direction.

"Although, perhaps due to your recent confinement, you have yet to make any inquiries about your parcels lost the night of my own arrival home, Miss Collier," he said, "you have no doubt been wondering what became of them."

"No, my lord. When they were not returned to me, I simply assumed they could not be found, and I dismissed the matter from my mind," Verity explained.

"An understandable course of action. However, you are mistaken. Your packages *were* discovered. But unfortunately, unlike your straw bonnet, which was able to be salvaged and which I understand is now once more in your possession, the same cannot be said about the materials you had bought in St. Ives that afternoon. During the mishap, my horse trampled both parcels, utterly ruining the scrap of muslin and damaging the bombazine, too, beyond repair."

"I see. Thank you for informing me, my lord. Whilst I am, of course, most sorry to hear it, the truth of the matter is that since I had already resigned myself to the loss of the fabrics, along with my hairpins, my reconciliation is merely reinforced. Is there anything else, my lord?"

"Yes, madam, there is. You surely cannot think very highly of me if you believe that, having destroyed your purchases, however inadvertently, I would not make some restitution for it. I do apologize for not having done so before now, but as you know, since my homecoming, I have been much occupied with the business affairs of my estate.''

Turning in his chair, Lord St. Aubyn took a stack of packages wrapped in brown paper from inside the beautiful, burnished cabinet behind him and placed them on his desk.

''These are for you, Miss Collier. You will find that I have not only replaced all your lost articles, but also included a few others in recompense. Regardless of how it happened, the fact that I nearly rode you down and that you were injured in the process has grieved me sorely. So I beg you will accept these with no demurring.''

''I—I fear I am at a loss for words, my lord,'' Verity confessed, much surprised and greatly confused, for she felt it was most improper for her employer to be bestowing gifts upon her. Yet he had done so in such a fashion that she could hardly refuse without giving offense, which she suspected had been his intent. ''Since you put it that way, it would, naturally, be churlish of me to refuse your generosity. Thus, you leave me with little choice but to accept with pleasure and to thank you, my lord.''

At that, the Earl hooded his penetrating black eyes against her, so that she could not guess his thoughts, although a faint smile of satisfaction played about the corners of his mouth.

''Good. I am very glad to hear it. I shall look

forward to seeing to what use you put the parcels' contents. Good afternoon, Miss Collier.''

Dismissed, Verity exited the study, taking the packages away with her. She was inordinately curious to see what they contained. So she hurried upstairs to her bedroom, where she laid them on the bed to untie their strings and unwrap them one by one. In the first parcel, which was small, she discovered a packet of new hairpins to replace those she had lost, and in the second, which was only slightly bigger, a new length of cream-colored muslin. The third package, which was much larger in size, held a bolt of the same soft brown bombazine that she had bought at St. Ives.

So far, Verity thought, relieved, there was nothing inappropriate, but merely reparation on the Earl's part, as he had told her. But still, there remained three more parcels.

Picking up the first of these, she carefully untied and unwrapped it to reveal a bolt of dove-grey bombazine, from which she would be able to make yet a fourth everyday dress, and which she therefore very much appreciated.

The next package, however, caused Verity to cry out softly with pleasure, for it held a bolt of duskyrose silk so fine that she could scarcely believe it, for she had never before owned its like. Almost reverently, she stroked and caressed the material, already envisioning the kind of frock she could sew from it and determinedly thrusting to the back of her mind the stern, reproving strictures of the Trowbridge administrators, which rang in her ears.

No doubt, she should not accept such a present—
and a clearly expensive one at that!—from either a
man or her employer. But as she already had, the
damage was done, and to attempt now to return the
gift to the Earl would surely greatly displease and
offend him, she sensed.

When she opened the last parcel, Verity felt her
breath catch in her throat, for from the tangled string
and the brown paper spilled a bolt of chatoyant sea-
green silk so magnificent that it did not even seem
real, but appeared as though it must unquestionably
have come from the Otherworld of which the Earl
had spoken last night. The shimmering waves of the
fabric looked as though the ocean itself had rushed
inland to sweep over her bed, and from every angle,
they seemed to undulate like breakers.

It was too much, Verity remonstrated with herself.
She must return the material to the Earl at once! Yet
the notion of doing so and facing his censure caused
her to quail inwardly, particularly when she remembered the wicked temper Loveday had attributed to
him, and how, when he had swept her from the drive
the night of his arrival home, he had threatened to
beat her.

Verity was not a coward, but perhaps the Earl
would be so angry that he would not only turn her
off, but also do so without a reference—and then
what would become of her? She could not afford to
lose her position at St. Aubyn manor, for she knew,
given how her relative youth and inexperience had
been held against her previously, that if she were to
be fired and adamantly refused a testimonial from a

personage such as the Earl, no one else would hire her as a governess to their children. So in the end, after much wrestling with her conscience, she decided that the wisest course of action was to keep the fabric.

After all, she reasoned, it was a one-time present to compensate her for the injuries she had unwittingly suffered at the Earl's hands, and not as though he were going to be making a habit out of giving her such gifts.

Thus placating herself, Verity put the hairpins in a little silver-lidded crystal box upon the dressing table, then carefully rewrapped the muslin and all the bolts of cloth, placing them on the shelf in her wardrobe until such time as she would be able to devote herself to the cutting and sewing of the new gowns she planned to make from them. She would start with the dove-grey bombazine, she thought, for it was everyday dresses she most required, having a much rarer need of anything finer, unless the Earl should send for her again to take tea with him in the small drawing room.

It did occur to her that perhaps he would, that mayhap his entire purpose in giving her the bolts of material stemmed from the fact that he had guessed she possessed only the pearl-grey silk frock she had worn last evening, and he had wished to provide her with the means to fashion others suitable for such occasions, so that she would not be embarrassed by her lack.

But much to Verity's strange disappointment, in the coming days, the Earl did not send for her, or even for his children. In fact, she scarcely saw him, except in passing, when, if preoccupied by some business matter or another, he would merely nod to her silently and continue on his way, or if in a more expansive mood, he would smile in his own saturnine style and exchange a few pleasantries with her.

So she returned to the dull routine of her days, overseeing the twins at their lessons in the mornings, indulging in long walks and other pastimes in the afternoons, and cutting and sewing in the evenings, with the aid of Mrs. Wickersham and Loveday, who had offered to help her with the creation of her new gowns.

Meanwhile, all about Verity, life forged ahead.

News arrived at the manor via the Cornwall *Gazette,* which had begun publication last year, and from tenants and other visitors. Now and again, reports of another robbery by the highwayman Black Jack Raven—whom, unfortunately, Colonel Sherbourne still had yet to apprehend—reached the household, causing Verity to shudder and to shake her head sympathetically for those set upon by the brazen brigand, for she could not imagine that he treated all his victims as gallantly as he had her, even though he *had* mortified her by cutting off the lock of her hair.

Other accounts were even more unnerving, for despite the signing of the Treaty of Amiens by Great Britain and France earlier this year, relations between the two countries had not improved, and it seemed as though, sooner or later, they would go to war again. It was rumored even more strongly than before that there were French spies all over England, even in Cornwall, gathering information that would aid the French against the English. More than once, Mrs. Wickersham commented that she hoped there was no invasion and that all at the manor were not murdered in their beds by the French legions.

"Oh, surely, the French will not come here, ma'am," Verity tried to reassure her.

But the housekeeper was not so confident.

"I wish I could be as certain as you, my dear," she replied, sighing heavily. "But I don't trust the French. They've all gone stark, raving mad over there—chopping off the heads of their king and queen, and most all their lords and ladies, too. Why, it's exactly the same as though all of us here at the manor were to rise up against his lordship and cut off *his* head!" The elderly woman was indignant and horrified at the very idea.

"I suppose I hadn't ever thought about it that way before," Verity confessed. "But you're right, ma'am. Still, I believe it's highly unlikely the French will ever land upon England's shores, so you needn't worry."

"Well, I hope you are right, my dear. But even the notion that some of them are already here, spying on us, is most upsetting."

"Yes, it is indeed. However, Colonel Sherbourne and his dragoon guards in Truro—and, indeed, all over the country—are on the lookout for them and will protect us, ma'am. I feel sure we ourselves are quite safe here at St. Aubyn, besides which, I cannot think why the French would even come here to such a desolate and remote spot. What could they possibly hope to gain by it?''

''The same thing as the smugglers and wreckers, no doubt—a quiet, isolated place in which to carry on their nefarious activities, for who knows what they may be up to?''

With that observation, Verity was unable to argue. But still, although the thought of French spies in England was unpleasant, she remained doubtful of any real danger to the household at St. Aubyn, and so the idea did not trouble her the way it did Mrs. Wickersham. Why, if there were even one single French spy in Cornwall, Verity would be very much surprised, and even if there were, why on earth he would want to infiltrate or attack the manor, she couldn't imagine. Besides which, even if he did, what could a mere, lone man manage to accomplish against an entire household, which was composed in half by male servants?

Thus encouraged and assured, she pushed the entire notion from her mind and dwelled no more upon it.

It was some days after she, Mrs. Wickersham and Loveday had completed two of her new gowns that Verity chanced again to meet the Earl. It was a bright sunny afternoon, so she had taken the twins outside for a long walk in the gardens and park, so that Trueth might have some time to herself.

In the beginning, as she wandered along with the children, Verity took the opportunity to give them a botany lesson, pointing out and naming several of the flowers, plants and trees to be found on the grounds of the manor. Then she instructed the youngsters to gather specimens of those they found most pleasing, and to put them in the garden trug they had brought with them from the long conservatory at the rear of the manor.

"Once you have collected all your specimens, we will bring them inside to the schoolroom and press them between the pages of some of your schoolbooks," she explained to the twins. "Then, after the specimens have dried, we will place the best of them between two sheets of thin glass to preserve them. Would you like that?"

"Yes, Miss Collier," Meliora answered, and Bastian nodded.

He still did not speak as often as his sister, so that Verity had to spend much time coaxing him from the hard little shell he seemed to have constructed around himself for protection. But still, she did not mind. To her mind, he appeared, even so, to be less timid and withdrawn with her than when she had first come to the manor, so that she felt she was making good progress with him, however slowly.

After a time, when the children had chosen several flowers and leaves, and carefully laid them into the trug, Verity told the youngsters that they might play for a while, as long as they remained where she could see them. They especially liked a long grassy avenue lined with different varieties of great rhododendrons, all of which were now in full bloom, and so boasting a lovely profusion of blossoms that ranged in color from whites to pinks to lavenders. The twins enjoyed playing games here, where there was space for them, with sticks they picked up from the ground, to roll along old barrel hoops, a pastime that Verity had taught them one afternoon and thereafter encouraged, remembering Mrs. Wickersham's observation that they ought to behave more like children.

Now, their hoops in hand, Meliora and Bastian eagerly set off in search of appropriate sticks for their game, while Verity strolled sedately behind, carrying the trug and smiling gently to herself to see them acting more like youngsters their age should. On either side, the avenue had wooden benches nestled amid the rhododendrons, and when she reached one of these located midway on the wide grassy lane and thus providing an unobstructed view of it from end to end, she sat down to rest, placing the trug beside her. All around her on three sides, the rhododendrons formed a fragrant, flowery bower, and she inhaled the sweet scent deeply, reveling in it.

It was here that the Earl, out walking his wolfish dog, Styx, happened upon her, stepping from a small footpath opposite her into the avenue, then, upon noticing her, crossing the grassy lane to address her.

"Good day, Miss Collier," he greeted her, bowing, as she rose and curtsied. "Pray, be seated. It was not my intention to disrupt your reverie, nor you children at your games—" he turned to Meliora and Bastian, who, spying him, had come to stand before him, also making their obeisances. "Go back to your play. It is far too long since I have seen you both so animated and enjoying yourselves, and the sight greatly pleases me. Take Styx with you. Here is his ball. Throw it for him, Bastian, and he will fetch it for you.''

At once, the boy did as his father commanded, hurling the small ball as far as he could, and Styx, barking loudly, chased after it enthusiastically. Much to Verity's delight, Bastian's grave little face lit up unmistakably with pleasure, and after a moment, at Lord St. Aubyn's urging, he ran after the dog, Meliora following behind.

''You have worked very hard and managed wonders with my children since you came here, madam,'' her employer observed quietly to Verity, once the youngsters were away down the avenue. ''Your talents in this regard—and others—amaze and touch me. I am…most grateful and indebted to you.''

''It is no more than what you hired me to do, my lord.''

''Oh, but it is, Miss Collier. Therefore, I beg to disagree with you. For, as you yourself are aware from your own experience at Trowbridge, even the sternest of taskmasters can maintain discipline and also drum edification into the heads of their pupils— neither of which requires either the caring or the kindness that you have shown to the twins. You have a good heart—and seem to have a genuine liking and affection for them both.''

''Indeed I do, my lord. They are good children, well behaved, and eager both to learn and to please. What governess—what person, in fact—would not be proud of such charges entrusted to her care and would not also develop a real fondness for them?''

''There are those who would not,'' the Earl noted,

his tone suddenly—strangely—grim. ''No doubt, you were yourself a good child. However, that apparently did not endear you either to your distant cousin who inherited your father's entailed estate, thereby rendering you destitute, or to the administrators at Trowbridge. The world, you see, is so rarely as we might believe or would like it to be, madam. In light of your own past, you must know this to be so.''

''I...I suppose so,'' Verity replied slowly. ''However, the truth is that having led a relatively sheltered, however harsh, life at Trowbridge, I know so very little of the world, my lord, that I cannot think myself qualified to judge it. For all I am aware, both my distant cousin and the administrators at Trowbridge may have been anomalous in their natures. Certainly, I believed them to be so, for I felt most keenly that if I were no longer under their aegis, I would be much better off and, surely, could be no worse! Further, if anything, my experience here at St. Aubyn manor has only strengthened that belief. For I was warmly welcomed into your household and have been well and fairly treated here, from the lowliest of the scullery maids to your cousin, Colonel Sherbourne, to your own self, my lord. Indeed, I must thank you again for the bolts of cloth you gave me. They were really far too generous by way of recompense, but as you can see—'' Verity indicated the gown she currently wore, which she had fashioned from the dove-grey bombazine ''—I have put the material to good use.''

''Yes, so I noticed. It is a color that suits you, for it matches your eyes. I was right about them. They *are* the silver of the moon...the pale grey of the mist when it sweeps in from the sea to settle over the moors...quite an unusual and haunting hue. But I forget." Lord St. Aubyn smiled wryly, sardonically. "You are unused to compliments and will think I am making a mock of you, as you did before, when I likened you to a silkie or a kelpie."

"I am ignorant of what those are, my lord, although, from what you told me, I presumed them to be some kind of mythical sea creatures."

"In a manner of speaking. Silkies are seals, like those sometimes to be seen upon our Cornish beaches, and which are claimed to shed their skins and, taking human form, to dance beneath the moon. If, at such a time, it is said, you can find a silkie's discarded pelt and hide it, then the silkie will not be able to resume its seal shape, and it will belong to you forever, unable to return to the sea. A kelpie is a seahorse, to which similar tales are attached." Her employer paused for a moment. Then he continued. "Are you happy here at St. Aubyn, then, Miss Collier?"

"I...I fear your question took me by surprise, my lord, so that I hardly know how to answer," Verity admitted truthfully. "For, to be honest, I cannot say that I have given the question of my own happiness much thought. However, as I informed you earlier, I have no complaints to voice with regard to my treatment here at the manor. I am comfortable and content...so, yes, I suppose I am as happy as anyone in my position would be, although—" She broke off abruptly, biting her lower lip. Then she gave a little, self-deprecating laugh. "No, that won't do. It won't do at all!"

"What won't, madam?" the Earl inquired, his black eyes intense with curiosity.

"Nothing, my lord. It was wholly unimportant, I assure you."

"Come, come, Miss Collier!" he chided dryly. "It does not become you to be coy! You have piqued my interest, and now, I must have an answer."

"Oh, very well, then, if you insist, my lord. But you will only think me foolish and fanciful, which is precisely what I had hoped to avoid! It is just that, sometimes, I find that I feel...restless, somehow, as though there ought to be more to life than what I have thus far experienced. It seems, sometimes, as though my days run very much one into another, with very little for me to distinguish between them."

"Ah." Lord St. Aubyn laughed softly. "Now, I comprehend. You possess quite a lively, intelligent, curious mind, Miss Collier, and like any person gifted with such an intellect, you are bored by the routine of your days. You long for some adventure and excitement, some challenge to test your sharp wits against, some tantalizing dream to strive for! No, do not protest, for that is what, in essence, you have just now told me."

"Only to be made sport of for my pains, as I feared! It is easy enough for you to laugh, my lord, I suppose, for your own position in life is such that you may come and go just as you please, and as a result, no doubt, you have had many wonderful escapades and known much excitement. Mrs. Wickersham, in fact, has said that you have traveled widely, to the West Indies, the Continent and even to the Orient! What grand sights you must have seen! I should be glad, myself, to see such faraway, exotic places, although, in reality, I don't imagine that I shall ever do so, and thus must content myself with what I read about them in books—only, I am *not* content with that, even though I must be...if that makes any sense to you, my lord.''

"It does, and I was *not* laughing at you, however much you may believe to the contrary,'' her employer insisted. "I confess I am curious about you, madam. Your mind interests and intrigues me, for it is not at all common, not at all what one would expect to find in a governess—who are usually, I have discovered, rather dull, prim-and-proper sorts, with hardly a word to say to anybody beyond their pupils.''

"Perhaps you think so, my lord, only because you have never before troubled yourself to draw them out,'' Verity rejoined tartly, confused and discomfitted. "For, did you not choose to engage me in conversation, I daresay I wouldn't have hardly a word to say to you, either, beyond the customary courtesies. Nor am I a—a *specimen,* my lord, to be studied and examined for your own gratification and amusement! I am a human being, with desires and emotions, just as you yourself are—for in that we are no different, despite the chasm between our stations in life—and that I am not in a position to act upon those feelings that most bestir me is no fault of my own, besides, but, rather, due to the vagaries of fate that beset us all, whether we wish it or not.''

"*Touché,* Miss Collier...well spoken!'' the Earl declared, duly chastened. ''I perceive myself to have been put firmly in my place! However, on one point—and one point, only—I must beg to correct you. I do not in the slightest think of you as a *specimen,* to be studied and examined as one would an animal at a zoo or an object in a laboratory. That is not what provokes my interest and curiosity in you.''

"Is it not? Then you speak in riddles, my lord, and I do not understand you.''

"No, I don't suppose you do.''

Lord St. Aubyn fell silent and contemplative then, and Verity herself was equally so, too, mystified by what could have been his meaning.

What an odd, mercurial man he was! she thought. Not at all like his affable cousin. Still, she must admit that there was something about her employer that piqued her interest and curiosity, even so, as he had claimed she did his own, some indefinable emotion that drew her to him, like a moth to flame—and that left her feeling just as fragile and vulnerable. He disturbed her in a way that no one else before ever had, and that she could not explain, not even to her own satisfaction. It was as though, with all his mocking and probing, he tossed a pebble into the still, quiet pool of her being, causing ripples that disrupted the serenity and composure she always strove so hard to maintain.

Now, as the Earl stood over her, one booted foot planted on the wooden bench, his gaze fastened on his children, who played with Styx in the distance, Verity studied him surreptitiously from beneath her lashes. Undoubtedly, there were those who considered him handsome, she reflected, but she herself thought him too saturnine and swarthy to be deemed so. There was about him, for all his elegance and grace, a power and earthiness—and even a subtle menace—that troubled and agitated her. He was, she felt, as Loveday had told her, a man whom few would dare to cross and, so, not only accustomed to being obeyed, but also to getting what he wanted. Thus far, he had chosen to be kind to her, in however peculiar a fashion. But Verity sensed that, if necessary, he could also be cruel.

"What conclusions have you drawn, Miss Collier, from this tit for tat?" He abruptly jolted her from her reverie.

"I—I beg your pardon, my lord...?" she stammered, bemused.

"You have been studying and examining *me* now for quite some time—as though *I* were a specimen! No doubt, if you were able, you would tuck me into that trug, along with all the rest of the flowers and leaves you and the twins appear to have collected from the gardens and park, for some schoolroom purpose or another."

"A lesson in botany, my lord," she explained.

"A response that begs the earlier question. Do you believe me moonstruck, as my cousin, Hugh, told you?"

"I—I am not sure. Eccentric, perhaps. It is true

that you behave like no one I have ever before known.''

''Ah! I shall take that as a compliment, madam, whether it was meant as such or not—for in truth, I could not bear to think I were one of these unre-markable dandies or fops to be found in such droves in London and elsewhere, and that are currently all the crack. Such a thought would pain me greatly. I would far rather be my own man...unique.''

''Certainly, I did not intend to give offense, my lord.''

''No, I did not judge that you did. Therefore, none was taken. I am a man, you will discover, not given to placing blame, except where it is squarely due.''

''A wise policy, surely.''

''I have always believed so.'' Lord St. Aubyn paused for a moment, then abruptly changed the sub-ject. ''So, Miss Collier, you have a yearning to travel to the far-flung reaches of the earth, do you? What other aspirations do you hold? I wonder. Do you also long for a home, a husband and children of your own?''

''Do not all women, my lord?''

''No, they don't,'' he answered tersely, a suddenly serrated edge to his voice, and his dark visage once more shuttered against her, although a muscle throbbed in his set jaw, so that she was aware of some inner turmoil on his own part. But, then, after an instant, recovering his composure, he went on more lightly. ''That surprises you, I see.''

''Yes, it does...very much so.''

''That is because, as you yourself have observed,

having had such a circumscribed—however an austere—upbringing at Trowbridge, you know so very
little of the world. Yet, for all that, you hold decid-
edly firm opinions, particularly for one so young, do
you not? So, pray tell, what is yours of me?''

''My lord, that is scarcely a fair question,'' Verity
protested, in mild rebuke, ''nor one at all designed
to receive a scrupulously honest answer. You are my
employer. Therefore, you surely cannot expect me to
tell you other than that I hold you in the highest
esteem, even if I do not—and by that, I do not say
whether it is indeed so. Further, I cannot believe you
are so little admired by others that you needs must
court my own regard, which can be of no real importance to you, in any event.''

''So you would think me either vain or foolish or
both to seek your good opinion?''

''Since I do not yet know you well enough to
know what to think, I would merely wonder at your
motive.''

At that, much to Verity's surprise, her employer
suddenly threw back his head and laughed aloud—a
sound of pure amusement and delight.

''Devil take me, madam, but in truth, I am not at
all certain whether that is a genuinely honest answer—or simply a diplomatic one!'' he averred, his
dark eyes gleaming.

''Perhaps a little of both,'' she confessed, unable
to repress her own smile in response.

She had not heard him laugh before, and if she
were honest with herself, Verity must admit that she
found the sound pleasing, that their entire dialogue,

in fact, stirred her in some inexplicable fashion that enlivened and excited her—in a manner most unlike those conversations she so enjoyed with Colonel Sherbourne, which, while they warmed and comforted her, did not cause her pulse to race and herself to feel faint, as though she had run a very long way and could not now catch her breath.

"There. I have succeeded in coaxing a smile from you at last, Miss Collier," the Earl noted, with no small measure of triumph. "And a rare smile it is, too."

"What do you mean by that, my lord?" she inquired, her brow now knitted in a puzzled frown. "I am as much given to smiling as anyone, I hope."

"Are you? Perhaps so, although you strike me as a singularly strange, sober little creature, in your subdued frocks and with your outwardly calm demeanor. One could easily imagine you had been brought up in a convent, rather than a semicharitable institution for young girls. Had I not seen you looking so wild and fey the night of my arrival home, I should perhaps never have suspected what passion and tumult lie beneath your placid surface, madam. But that night, I saw that side of you, and as I told you once before, it was as though I had spied a silkie dancing beneath the moon…and now, I have seen your lovely siren's smile, also, which lights up and transforms your grave, heart-shaped countenance in quite a remarkable and fascinating fashion. It was that which caused me to comment upon its rarity—and not the fact that it is so seldom to be seen, although if that indeed is the case, then it must be considered all the more precious, and I am honored to have had it bestowed upon me."

"You flatter me—most outrageously, my lord!" Verity said, flushing hotly and nervously at hearing herself so enchantingly described. "As *I* have told *you* before, I am unused to such compliments as you pay me—if such they are, for I cannot help but suppose you are teasing me again."

"In that supposition, you are quite mistaken, Miss Collier, I do assure you." He paused for a moment. Then he continued abruptly. "But enough of this. The afternoon grows late, for the shadows lengthen. It will soon be time for tea."

As he had that day at the lodge, Lord St. Aubyn whistled long and loud, and in response, Styx came running and bounding to his master's heels, while Meliora and Bastian followed more slowly, their hoops and the dog's ball in hand. The youngsters' eyes were bright and their cheeks flushed from their unaccustomed exertions, and their small faces beamed with a rare pleasure and happiness that Verity was glad to see.

Picking up the trug, she rose from the bench that she had occupied at some length now, and, exchanging trivial chatter about nothing in particular, the small party walked back through the gardens to the manor together.

Upon reaching the house, Verity half expected her employer to invite her and his children to take tea again with him in the small drawing room. But he did not, and so she retired to her bedroom, feeling peculiarly deflated and disappointed of a sudden.

Ten

Footsteps in the Night

And all my days are trances,
And all my nightly dreams
Are where thy gray eye glances,
And where thy footstep gleams—
In what ethereal dances,
By what eternal streams.

To One in Paradise
—Edgar Allan Poe

Like dead, remembered footsteps on old floors.

The Pity of the Leaves
—Edwin Arlington Robinson

A dirge for the most lovely dead
That ever died so young!

Lenore
—Edgar Allan Poe

That night, Verity worked again on the oil painting she had begun some time ago now, but to which she had, since then, devoted only relatively little attention, having been more principally occupied with the cutting and sewing, from the bolts of material the Earl had given her, of her new gowns. However, the first two of these—the everyday frocks fashioned from the brown and the dove-grey bombazines—now being completed, she felt that she could take her time with the last two, for the remaining bolts of fabric were the beautiful dusky-rose and the chatoyant sea-green silks, and in all truth, she could not think when she would ever have occasion to wear anything so grand and lovely. As, despite all the compliments the Earl had paid her, he had not invited her to take tea with him in the small drawing room once more, it did not seem to her that she would ever again be required to dress for the evening.

Now, Verity carefully positioned her easel so that she could sit before the hearth, where a small fire burned, for even during Cornwall's summers, she had learned, nights were frequently chilly, particularly if the day had been damp with rain and mist.

Sitting down upon the bench at the foot of her bed, she then opened her wooden paint box and, after that, slowly turned back the cloth that covered the picture.

With a critical eye harsher than most would have proved, Verity studied the painting. Unlike the evening when she had first started work on it, it no longer appeared to her as a hodgepodge of random streaks and splashes of color, wholly anomalous and shadowy. Rather, now, in its lines, she could discern the beginnings of an otherworldly land and sea—not a paradise such as those the Earl had seen amid her sketches and watercolors the night when she had taken tea with him and Colonel Sherbourne in the small drawing room, but, instead, a strange, dark, atavistic place aeons old and possessing such a powerful force and magnetism that they were almost tangible, causing an icy grue to tingle without warning up her spine as she examined the picture.

As gooseflesh prickled her skin, unbidden in her ears rang the Earl's words to her of this afternoon in the rhododendron bower: *Had I not seen you looking so wild and fey the night of my own arrival home, I should perhaps never have suspected what passion and tumult lie beneath your placid surface, madam. But that night, I saw that side of you, and as I told you before, it was as though I had spied a silkie dancing beneath the moon....*

She had blushed, highly discomfitted, at hearing herself thus described by the Earl. But now, as she continued to gaze at the painting, Verity could no longer deny the truth of his observations. For, surely there *was* some such ilk somewhere deep inside her, for how else to explain what she saw within the painting?

It was as though the wild storm the night of her arrival here at the manor had wakened something within her that had until then lain slumbering inside her. Oh, perhaps, now and then over the years, she had suspected it was there, had even caught a glimpse or two of it. But always, before, she had determinedly closed her eyes against it, certain that if only she did not acknowledge its presence, it would disappear, never more to be seen. But now, somehow, her eyes had been opened wide to it, and there was no shutting them again.

It was this...this *thing* inside her, Verity thought now, that caused her to rebel against the seldom relenting tedium of her days and to long for some adventure and excitement, for something that was somehow more than what she had been allotted in life. It was as though ever since she had come to St. Aubyn, this thing, now wakened, had grown ever stronger, despite all her attempts to lull it once more into somnolence, so that it would no longer continue to agitate her, to make her dissatisfied with her lot.

But now, for the first time, Verity somehow knew that it would never sleep again, and that since it would not, she must find some constructive outlet for it, lest it otherwise drive her to despair and distraction, perhaps even to madness in the end. Mayhap it had even already started to do so, was this that had fueled her fiery imagination ever since her arrival at the manor and had caused her to hear the intermittent, eerie lament of *Tamsyn...Tamsyn...*in the rising of the wind and the murmur of the sea. She did not know.

The peculiar plaint was a curiosity that piqued her interest. But as she had, as yet, found no real explanation for it, even it did not represent the challenge that she craved.

Sighing heavily and taking her paintbrush from the small jar of turpentine in which she stored it to keep it clean and supple when she was not working, Verity started once more to daub colors from her palette onto the canvas. Growing increasingly absorbed as the picture began little by little to gain even further definition, she painted until nearly midnight, when, at last, she felt her eyelids drooping with tiredness.

Finished for the evening, she returned her brush to the turpentine and closed her wooden paint box. Then she once more perused the painting. Now, it consisted clearly of a night sky in which a storm seemed to be brewing, for a jagged trident of lightning split the firmament, and a full moon that was ringed and partially occluded by drifting, massing thunderclouds gleamed eerily. Beneath the tumultuous heavens, dark, looming cliffs hove up from the land, crumbling down onto a shingled beach, where white-foamed breakers of a roiling sea swept inland.

At this point, many people would have considered the picture complete. But instinctively, somehow, Verity knew it was not, that there was still a great deal more to be done with it before she herself would think of it as finished. What more it lacked, she did not at this moment know—only that she was still driven to work on it, as though her subconscious had some ultimate goal in mind that she was not currently cognizant of, but that would be revealed to her by and by.

Rising from the bench, she set about her nightly toilette, pouring water from the pitcher on the commode into its matching washbasin, so that she could have a sponge bath. Then she brushed her teeth and hair, plaiting the latter into its customary braid, tying it off with a simple grey riband. After that, Verity donned her nightgown, blew out all the lamps and climbed into bed, drawing the bed curtains around her for warmth.

For a while, she lay awake, going over again in her mind all that had passed that afternoon between her and the Earl in the rhododendron bower in the grassy avenue. How could she not doubt his interest in her? For although he had taken some pains to express it, she could not suppose he was in earnest, or even if he were, that his apparent fascination stemmed from anything other than some peculiar fancy on his part, which caused him to view her as some novelty, by which means he might divert himself. For despite his words to the contrary, what else could it be?

Had she possessed either beauty or title, fame or fortune, Verity might have believed the Earl to have become romantically enamored of her. But even as this thought crossed her mind, she dismissed it as being simply inconceivable. Plain and penniless, she could not imagine that there was anything whatsoever about her to awaken love or even lust for her in the Earl's heart. For nor did he appear to be a man given to dalliance with the household maids. No such rumors of that sort had reached her ears, and while Mrs. Wickersham would doubtless not have mentioned such to her, she felt certain Loveday would have.

Thus, greatly puzzled, Verity was at a complete loss as to how to account for the Earl's behavior toward her, other than to write herself off as providing some amusing, however transitory, entertainment for him.

Finally, she decided that there was nothing to be gained by teasing herself any further about the matter, and deliberately, however much with difficulty, she put it from her mind, closing her eyes and forcing herself to breathe deeply, in the hope that sleep would come and that the chaotic turmoil of her musings would then be settled, however temporarily.

She must at least have dozed, Verity thought afterward, for she did not remember being awake when the noise that disturbed her at last penetrated her consciousness. She heard it as though in a dream, off in the distance, and it was some time before it dawned on her that it was a real sound—the whisper of footsteps along the passage beyond her bedroom door.

Who on earth would be up and about at this late hour? Verity wondered, bewildered and sitting straight up in bed to listen. Then, after a moment, a wholly horrifying notion occurred to her, and hastily drawing aside the bed curtains, she fumbled in the semidarkness to light a candle, for her chamber was illuminated only by the silvery moonbeams streaming in through her windows. Rising from bed, she pulled on her wrapper, tying it about her slender waist, and hurried to her bedroom door. This, she never locked, for in all the time she had lived at St. Aubyn, she had never felt the need. Quietly, she opened it just a crack to peer out in the dark corridor beyond.

What she had truly feared to see was Meliora and Bastian creeping down the hall, intent on sneaking from the manor for some unknown purpose of their own. Instead, what Verity spied from the corners of her eyes was a tall figure clothed in a black French cocked hat, a black, many-caped greatcoat, and a pair of soft brown doeskin breeches and high black leather jackboots, clandestinely disappearing down the spiral staircase in the tower at the far end of the passage.

Some instinct warning her, she quickly shrank back into her chamber, closing the door furtively, her heart pounding and her palms sweating. She did not know who the man had been, but of one thing she was certain. Whatever he was about, he had not wished to be caught at it, for he had moved as silently as was possible and avoided using the grand, central staircase in the entrance hall, where he might have been observed by anyone in the household.

Who was it who had trodden so swiftly and softly down the east-tower steps? Although it was possible that one of the male servants had come downstairs from the second floor, Verity believed that was highly unlikely, since any of these could just as easily have gone straight down the tower stairs without ever venturing on to the first floor. That meant it

must have been one of the four men who had bedrooms on the first floor of the manor's east wing: the
steward, Mr. Drummond; the Earl's valet, Mr. Ashfield; the butler, Mr. Peacock; or the Earl himself.

Since the butler, Mr. Peacock, was short, rotund
and elderly, Verity dismissed him at once. His was
not the figure she had seen striding covertly down
the tower steps. That left the other three men. But
which of these it had been, she was unsure.

She lay back down in her bed, but did not blow
out her candle nor draw the bed curtains around her
again, for now, she was once more wide-awake.
There had been something disturbingly familiar
about the unidentified figure, she thought, which she
did not associate with any of the three men. But for
the life of her, Verity could not quite put her finger
on what it had been. Still, it niggled worrisomely at
the back of her mind, keeping her from drifting again
into slumber.

But eventually, all was once more still and hushed,
and as the too-fast beating of her heart gradually
slowed and her agitated nerves calmed, she felt her
eyelids begin to droop wearily again. Finally, she
slipped into a fitful, uneasy sleep, haunted by strange
and troubling dreams, so that she did not know when
she became aware once more of the light tread of
footsteps in the passage beyond her chamber.

At first, Verity thought she dreamed them. Then,
drowsily, she put them down to someone going into
one of the two shared baths before she remembered,
vaguely, that all the bedrooms were equipped with
commodes that held chamber pots, just like her own.

At last, however, after a long moment, it occurred to her that whoever had earlier crept down the tower stairs must now be returning.

In a dream, Verity saw herself again rise from her bed, pick up her candle and cross the floor to her bedroom door, which she surreptitiously opened a crack. Despite her caution, however, it creaked and groaned nerve-rackingly on its hinges as it swung wide, then once more closed. Then, almost soundlessly, footsteps advanced across the floor of her chamber, coming to a halt at the foot of her bed.

At that, of a sudden, Verity was again wide-awake, her heart thrumming hideously in her throat, her entire body bathed with sweat, gooseflesh prickling her skin, and she herself chilled to the bone as she abruptly realized that while she had actually only dreamed getting out of bed and opening her door, she had *not* imagined its scratching and moaning as it had slowly swung wide, then shut. Nor had she dreamed the footsteps entering her bedroom.

Someone—or some*thing*—was inside her chamber!

Desperately, she wanted to cry out for help. But for an interminable minute, she was utterly frozen with terror, not knowing who or what stood at the foot of her bed, watching her. Then, slowly, determinedly, she started to gather courage, and she thought it *must* be one of the three men whose own rooms were also on the first floor, although she knew, even so, that, if so, he could mean her no good— only a great deal of ill.

Covertly, she dared to risk a peep at her chamber.

But beside her, on the night table, her candle still burned, flickering and guttering in its socket, and blinded by its dying flame, she could make out but little, although what she did see petrified her even more.

Something gossamer and white seemed to float at the foot of her bed, no flesh-and-blood man at all, but an apparition!

Tamsyn…Tamsyn…your life is in grave danger. You must leave this place of death at once!

The soft, unnerving caveat caused Verity's heart to leap terrifyingly in her throat, as though she were being choked to death. Then, without warning, her guttering candle extinguished itself, and her bedroom was abruptly plunged into darkness.

She began to scream.

Eleven

Some Secrets Revealed

Three may keep a secret, if two of them are dead.

> *Poor Richard's Almanac (July)*
> —Benjamin Franklin

She is older than the rocks among which she sits; like the vampire, she has been dead many times, and learned the secrets of the grave; and has been a diver in deep seas, and keeps their fallen day about her....

> *The Renaissance, Leonardo da Vinci (Mona Lisa)*
> —Walter Pater

(1) Urge no healths; (2) profane no divine ordinances; (3) touch no state matters; (4) reveal no secrets; (5) pick no quarrels; (6) make no comparisons; (7) maintain no ill opinions; (8) keep no bad company; (9) encourage no vice;

(10) make no long meals; (11) repeat no grievances; (12) lay no wagers.

The Twelve Good Rules of the
Royal Game of Goose
—ascribed to King Charles I of England

Ominously, as the screams erupted from her throat, rending the night, footsteps seemed to rush at Verity from every direction, so that she did not know what was happening. The blood pounded in her ears, and it was an agonizing, seemingly unending instant before she realized someone was beating upon her chamber door. Then it was suddenly flung open wide, and light flooded her bedroom as the Earl and Mrs. Wickersham entered, candles in hand, while, in the passage beyond, Messrs Drummond, Ashfield and Peacock hovered, their own candles flickering brightly.

"Miss Collier! What is it? What's wrong? Are you injured or harmed in some way?" the Earl demanded anxiously, as he strode through her dressing room and into her chamber proper, his candle held high to light his path.

Abruptly conscious of the fact that she wore only her thin nightgown, Verity clutched the bedclothes to her breast to cover herself.

"No...no...I'm not hurt," she moaned. Then, between sobs of mingled fear and relief, she gasped out, "Oh, but, my—my lord! There was—there was someone…some*thing* in my bedroom! Standing there at the foot of my bed—watching me! It—It *spoke* to—to me! I thought at first that it must be a—a man. But it was a—a ghost!''

"Nonsense, madam! St. Aubyn manor is not haunted, I assure you! Ashfield, search Miss Collier's dressing room at once! Quickly, man!'' Lord St. Aubyn commanded curtly. "Peacock, fetch her a glass of brandy from the silver tray in my chamber! Drummond, rouse the lower staff, and check the remainder of the house! Find out whether or not there is an intruder upon the premises!''

As he rapped out these orders, Verity's employer moved rapidly through her bedroom, looking into every single nook and cranny, including the tower reading niche, and even under her bed, while Mrs. Wickersham, after lighting the lamps, came to sit beside her, assisting her into her wrapper and speaking to her softly and comfortingly.

"There's no one here,'' the Earl asserted grimly at last. "Ashfield, what have you found?''

"Nothing, my lord,'' the valet reported.

By now, Mr. Peacock had returned, bearing a snifter of brandy, which Lord St. Aubyn took and pressed upon Verity. But she still trembled so badly that she could hardly hold it, and in the end, Mrs. Wickersham had to help her, while her employer, satisfying himself that Verity had indeed suffered no harm and was in good hands, exited the chamber to interrogate the staff and oversee their search of the rest of the manor.

"Oh, you poor dear,'' the housekeeper crooned

soothingly, setting aside Verity's now empty glass
and solicitously chafing and patting her cold hands.
"What a dreadful fright you have suffered! You are
still shaking like a leaf!"

"It was—was just so—so terrible, ma'am! You
simply can't imagine...."

"I'm quite certain it was, my dear, for your
screams were so bloodcurdling that they chilled me
right through. Ah, Loveday! Thank goodness, you've
come! Stoke up Miss Collier's fire, and put some
more coal upon the grate. Her poor hands are like
ice, and despite the brandy, she cannot seem to stop
shivering. What is happening in the rest of the house?
Has any sign of a trespasser been found?"

"Nay, ma'am. But Ned is not in his bed, or so
Mr. Lathrop has told Mr. Drummond, an' his whereabouts have yet ta be determined."

"Why, where would a footman be at this late hour
but abed?" the elderly woman asked, obviously surprised by this piece of news.

"I dunnat know, ma'am," the chambermaid replied.

"Dear me! I truly hope nothing awful has befallen
him!" Mrs. Wickersham started now to wring her
own hands anxiously. "Have I not said time and
again that the French have all run mad across the
Channel, and that we shall all be fortunate not to be
murdered in our beds by their legions? Why, I shall
not be surprised to learn they have landed upon
Cornwall's shores this very night and invaded St.
Aubyn manor!"

"Surely not, ma'am," Loveday insisted stoutly,

being of a much more practical nature. With the small black shovel on the hearth, she ladled coal from the bucket onto the grate. "But if'n by some odd chance t' French *have* come here an' have t night done away with Ned—although why they should wish ta do such a thing, I'm sure I dunnat know—I, for one, should not shed any tears o'er it, fer he's as queer as a mad hatter, he is, always creepin' around, peepin' through keyholes an' listenin' at doors. He's a right nosy busybody an' gossip, is our Ned."

"For shame, Loveday! Why, the poor man might be lying in his grave, his throat cut by the French legions, even as we speak!"

"Fortunately, Mrs. Wickersham, St. Aubyn manor is not yet besieged by the French," the Earl assured her, as he returned in time to overhear the latter part of their conversation. "And the missing footman was found to be ill in the kitchen, where he had gone to get some mint leaves from which to make a tonic to settle his stomach."

"Then the house is secure, my lord?" Verity inquired, her voice tremulous. "It is as I told you, then. It was an apparition I saw at the foot of my bed!"

"Perhaps, Miss Collier, you but suffered a nightmare," he suggested gently, "and upon your awaking, your wild imagination ran away with you once more."

"No, my lord." She shook her head stubbornly, unwilling to be convinced of this again. "For, earlier, when I was definitely awake, I heard footsteps outside in the hall beyond my bedroom door, and, rising from my bed, I peeked out into the corridor to see a man—I know not who—garbed in a black French cocked hat and a black greatcoat, descending the spiral staircase in the tower at the far end of the passage.''

Lord St. Aubyn appeared much startled by this piece of information, and from hooded black eyes, so that Verity could not guess his thoughts, he suddenly glanced sharply, intently, at the Messrs Drummond, Ashfield and Peacock, all three of whom now stood just inside her chamber.

''That is quite easily explained, for it was I whom Miss Collier saw, my lord,'' Mr. Ashfield confessed, after a taut, speculative moment. ''I was preparing to polish your lordship's boots tonight when I abruptly realized I had absentmindedly left the blacking— which I had ridden into St. Ives earlier today to purchase—in my saddlebag. As it was so very late, rather than rouse any of the footmen and risk waking the entire household in the process, I decided simply to nip out myself to the stables to fetch it, my lord.''

''Thank you, Ashfield,'' Verity's employer said, then redirected his attention back to her. ''There, now, you see, madam? All is simply accounted for. Further, it would seem that at the time when you observed my valet, you yourself must not have considered him to be an intruder, lest, surely, you would have alerted the upper staff, at least, would you not?''

''Yes, indeed, I would have, my lord!''

''So you did not then judge that the manor had

been broken into or you yourself to be in any particular peril?''

"No...no, I didn't. It was only later, when the specter appeared in my bedroom, that I felt myself to be in dire jeopardy.''

"When you first saw this alleged phantom, had you fallen asleep by then, Miss Collier?''

"Well...yes, my lord," she reluctantly admitted.

"Ah. Let us hypothesize, then, shall we? Having slipped into slumber after spying my valet, you did then indeed embark upon a dream—no doubt even a nightmare, madam—and when, subconsciously, you discerned Ashfield's footsteps as he returned from the stables, you incorrectly believed someone had entered your chamber. You do not keep the door bolted?''

"No, my lord, I have never before felt the need.''

"Of course not. To continue, then, upon mistakenly thinking someone stood at the foot of your bed, you—dazed with sleep, petrified and doubtless hoping to go unnoticed—furtively opened your eyes just a little to peek about you, and as you did so, you observed the moonlight streaming in through your bedroom's north windows, casting an eerily shimmering silvery glow about the chamber, mayhap which was even intermittently obscured by drifting clouds, so that it appeared to you as though some pale, nebulous figure floated at the foot of your bed. Could that be possible, Miss Collier, do you imagine?''

"Anything is possible, my lord—except, you are forgetting that I distinctly heard the ghost speak!''

"Indeed? And what did it say to you?"

"That my life was in grave danger—and that I must leave St. Aubyn manor at once!"

"Miss Collier," the Earl rejoined gravely, his dark eyes once more shuttered and unreadable, and a muscle pulsing in his set jaw, "do you have any real and just cause to believe your life is threatened here, that anyone in this household wishes you either harm or gone from it?"

"No—No, my lord."

"Then do not you suppose that it was only the murmur of the wind or the sea that you heard, and that, in your great upset and understandable terror, you erroneously envisioned it as some phantom voice warning you of some menace to yourself?"

Abruptly, he strode to the north windows and flung one casement open wide, so that the cool night air swept into the chamber, causing Verity to shudder with cold, and from without, she could discern the soughing of the wind through the trees of the park and the inland rushing of the ocean, its billows breaking upon the rocks and shingled beach below the crumbling cliffs that hove up at the rear of the manor. Much to her surprise and discomfiture, all of this did indeed combine to sound as though some low, keening voice were moaning a piteous lament.

"Well, madam?"

Without warning, Verity buried her face in her hands, shaking her head confusedly.

"I don't know, my lord. I don't know," she whispered, her voice catching on a ragged note of dejection and bewilderment.

Firmly, he shut up the window.

"Pray, do not weep, Miss Collier," he now entreated kindly. "For it was not my intention to distress you still further, but, rather, merely to demonstrate what was not only possible, but also most likely to have occurred."

"I am—I am terribly sorry, my lord, for the contretemps I have caused," Verity apologized at last, mortified.

"Please, think nothing of it. You were alarmed by an unfortunate sequence of events that might have deceived anyone. Now, if you are feeling sufficiently recovered, I suggest that we all return to our beds. Loveday, perhaps you will be good enough to stay here with Miss Collier the remainder of the night?"

"Aye, m'lord. I shall be glad ta keep her company."

"Good."

At that, after bidding Verity good-night, the Earl exited her bedroom, followed by Messrs Drummond, Ashfield and Peacock, and Mrs. Wickersham.

Once Verity and Loveday were alone in the chamber, the latter, much to the former's surprise and everlasting gratitude, firmly bolted the door, then ensured that all the windows were locked up tight, as well.

"No point in takin' any chances, I always say," the chambermaid averred resolutely, blowing out all the lamps but one, then plumping up the pillows for Verity and climbing into bed beside her, settling the bedclothes snugly about them. "Mrs. Wickersham may go on all she likes about t' French legions, but

I meself know there's little danger o' our being invaded by *them,* fer they'd have ta cross t' Channel ta come here, would they not, miss? An' so we'd surely spy them long afore they stepped foot on our shores, an' we'd blast 'em clean out o' t' water with our canons! But no matter what his lordship claims ta t' contrary, there *are* such things as ghosts an' goblins. Why, e'en t' poor Lady St. Aubyn herself—God rest her soul—be a shade now, fer there's them what tells that she dunnat rest easy in her grave, an' will not till she's been avenged.... Not ta mention t' fact that there be just plain, queer doin's here at t' manor.''

"Why? Whatever do you mean, Loveday?'' Verity queried, much startled. ''What sort of queer doings?''

"Oh, like his lordship keepin' stout old Doryty on here, down at t' lodge, fer one thing, when everybody knows she does like her pint o' porter an' what 'appened ta her ladyship because o' it. An' odd comin's an' goin's at t' stables in t' wee hours...Ashfield creepin' out there in t' dead o' t' night—t' way he done tonight—or so he said! Who knows?'' the chambermaid speculated darkly. ''He's his lordship's man, isn't he? An' his lordship has been known ta keep peculiar hours, too, an' who can say fer what reason? An' then there's Ned, always skulkin' an' nosin' about like Mrs. Wickersham's sly, sneakin' cat, peerin' through keyholes and listenin' at doors—Ned, I mean, an' not t' puss. Why weren't he abed like t' rest o' us, where he ought ta have been, I ask 'ee? Fancy fetchin' a mint tonic fer his stomach, indeed! He were thievin' from his lordship's larder or wine cellar, more like, I'll wager—t' pilferin', pokin' an' pryin' noddy!''

"Loveday, you said there are those who claim Lady St. Aubyn doesn't rest easy in her grave and won't until she's been avenged. What did you mean by that?"

"Why...only that, miss. But, there, I've said more'n enough already. Thou mun be tired an' longin' fer sleep, an' here I be, keepin' thee awake with me blather. Thou mustn't pay any heed ta me. 'Tis all nowt save gossip, anyways, miss. I'm just wrought up, same as thee, no doubt.''

"Please, Loveday, tell me what you meant," Verity pleaded earnestly. "For reasons I don't wish to explain right now, it's very important to me to know. Truly, it is! Is there some mystery connected with Lady St. Aubyn's death? You need not think you are telling tales out of school, for Mrs. Wickersham has already spoken to me of what happened that tragic night...how the twins crept from their beds and sneaked from the manor, and how poor Lady St. Aubyn followed and, in her panic to find them, slipped and fell to her death from the cliffs. Is Doryty somehow even more to blame than I thought, drinking herself into a stupor and falling asleep at her post that night? Is it she on whom Lady St. Aubyn is believed to want to seek revenge?"

"Nay, miss," the chambermaid answered slowly. "But I dunnat know as I should say any more'n what I've already told thee, fer all I've heard be rumors only, an' p'rhaps nowt among us knows t' real truth o' t' matter nor shall e'er do. Still, if'n 'tis important ta thee ta know, I'd not like ta keep from thee what I've heard—fer I've noticed that his lordship seems ta take a particular interest in thee, miss, an', well, p'rhaps thou ought ta be warned...." Loveday's voice trailed away, and she was silent for a protracted minute, while Verity waited expectantly, almost breathlessly, for her to continue. Then, finally, glancing warily about the bedroom, as though to ensure they were not being spied upon and lowering her voice to an even softer pitch, the chambermaid went on. "'Tis about his lordship, miss, which is why I hesitate ta speak, fer I dunnat want ta lose me job. I need this position an' me wages—"

"Of course. I understand, but you can trust me, Loveday. I promise you that I shall not repeat what you tell me to another soul. Your secrets are safe with me."

"Aye...I do believe thou mean that, fer yer an honest sort, t' kind ta keep yer word, methinks. All right, then. 'Tis like this, thou see. There be those hereabout who whisper that poor Lady St. Aubyn's death weren't no accident at all, miss—that his lordship murdered her!"

Book Three

The Stroke of Midnight

Hence, loathèd Melancholy,
Of Cerberus and blackest Midnight born,
In Stygian cave forlorn,
'Mongst horrid shapes, and shrieks, and
sights unholy.

L'Allegro
—John Milton

Now, hast thou but one bare hour to live,
And then thou must be damned perpetually!
Stand still, you ever-moving spheres of Heaven,
That time may cease, and midnight never come.

The Tragic History of Doctor Faustus
—Christopher Marlowe

Twelve

The Fragrance of Memory

The jar will long keep the fragrance of
what it was once steeped in when new.

> *Epistles, I*
> —Horace

And a woman is only a woman, but a
good cigar is a smoke.

> *Departmental Ditties, The Betrothed*
> —Rudyard Kipling

Canst thou not minister to a mind diseased,
Pluck from the memory a rooted sorrow,
Raze out the written troubles of the brain,
And with some sweet oblivious antidote
Cleanse the stuffed bosom of that perilous stuff
Which weighs upon the heart?

> *Macbeth*
> —William Shakespeare

St. Aubyn Manor
Cornwall, England, 1802

The following day, after her lessons with the twins had ended, Verity determined that if she were to have any peace of mind whatsoever, then she must herself undertake an investigation into the matters that plagued her. For, after all that Loveday had revealed to her last night, she could no longer be certain there was not, in fact, some strange mystery surrounding Lady St. Aubyn's tragic, untimely death, perhaps even some terrible, deep dark secret that the Earl wished to keep concealed from her and everyone else at the manor, also—thus, whenever aught inexplicable and horrifying occurred, his continual attempts to convince her that she was simply imagining things.

But now, Verity felt sure that she was not. For her own sake, she must learn the truth one way or another, she thought grimly, however unnerving, hideous or grisly it might be. That the Earl had murdered his wife was a serious—although as yet unproven—charge. For some reason that she could not fathom, whenever she dwelled on it, she felt her heart tighten with an unbearable pain, as though some cruel fist were squeezing the very life from it. Deep down inside, Verity knew she did not want the horrible rumors about the Earl's having killed his wife to be true; she did not want to believe them.

What evidence, if any, was there to support such a dreadful accusation, in any event? That was what she must discover. Verity had decided to begin her search in her own bedroom, to try to figure out just what had happened last night, whether someone had really entered her chamber, or if, hearing the footsteps, she had only imagined or dreamed it. As the Earl himself had done the previous evening, she went through her bedroom from top to bottom, including the tower reading nook and the dressing room, where she opened the built-in coffers in the former and the wardrobes in the latter. She looked under the bed.

As far as Verity could judge, there was nowhere that anybody could have hidden to avoid detection during the Earl's own investigation. Nor could anyone have escaped through the windows, which had been closed and were on the first floor, besides, nor through the door, where Messrs Drummond, Ashfield and Peacock had stood. But, then, of course, she realized suddenly, they had not been there the whole time. Mr. Drummond had left to rouse the remainder of the household staff and to instigate a hunt for any intruder. Mr. Ashfield, after examining her dressing room, had entered her chamber to give his report to the Earl. And Mr. Peacock had gone to the Earl's own bedroom to fetch the snifter of brandy.

Now, contemplatively, Verity carefully inspected the door to her bedroom. It did not open fully, for the wardrobes in her dressing room lined the walls on either side of the portal, so that the door, when opened, struck the front edge of the wardrobe closest to it, creating between them a sheltered corner just large enough that someone could have hidden inside it, while the search was conducted, then slipped out when the steward, valet and butler no longer stood there, barring undetected egress. Probably, in all the uproar, Mr. Ashfield would not have thought to shut the portal and look behind it.

Yes, Verity reflected, it would have been a risky maneuver, but it would also have been possible, and she must presume that whoever had entered her bedroom had not lacked for either nerve or cunning.

Of the entire household's whereabouts last night, it appeared that only the footman Ned had initially been unaccounted for. However, according to Loveday, Ned was a busybody, gossip and petty pilferer of the Earl's larder and wine cellar—hardly the kind of person, it would seem, to be invading Verity's chamber in the wee hours and pretending to be a ghost. So, since he did not fit the bill, who did? She did not yet know. But she intended to find out.

Once leaving her bedroom, where had the trespasser gone? There were, of course, any number of rooms in the manor in which the interloper could have hidden, or, fearing discovery, he or she might have fled from the house entirely. Thus Verity's next objective was to search the manor as well as she could from top to bottom, bearing in mind that there were many chambers to which she could not legitimately gain access—all the bedrooms of the male servants, especially.

In the end, she found nothing, although since she had not really expected to, her hopes and intentions were not particularly dashed. Finished with the manor's interior, Verity then returned to her bedroom to don her straw bonnet and her spencer, after which she went outside to peruse the house's exterior. The intruder in her bedroom could have exited the manor through a window, she speculated.

"Do you mind if I inquire as to what you're doing, Miss Collier?"

"Oh! Good heavens! Colonel Sherbourne! What a start you gave me!" Verity laid one trembling hand upon her breast, where her heart now pounded far too hard and fast. "I did not know you were come to St. Aubyn today, sir."

"My deepest apologies, madam, for I had no intention of giving you a fright, I assure you. I've only just now arrived, and spying you poking and prodding about amongst the bushes, I thought that perhaps you had lost something and that I might be of assistance."

"No, I've lost nothing, thank you, sir. However, I would indeed be most grateful for your help, for no doubt, you know a great deal more about these matters than I do. I am looking for footprints or anything else out of the ordinary that might tell me whether or not anybody left the house last night via one of the windows."

"I see," the Colonel said slowly. "But...why? What has happened?"

A trifle breathlessly, Verity told him all that had occurred the previous evening—except that she did not reveal the rumors about his cousin, the Earl, which Loveday had imparted to her.

"So you see, sir, whilst it is undoubtedly likely that his lordship is correct, and it was all only my imagination or a dream...a nightmare, I should feel far easier in my own mind if I knew for certain one way or the other."

"Of course you would. So why don't we see what we can find, then, shall we?"

For perhaps twenty minutes or longer, they explored the grounds around the manor together, investigating shrubbery and flower beds until, at last, they were rewarded by the discovery of several footprints in the soft damp earth beneath the windows of the music room.

"Look! Someone *has* been here, sir!" Verity crowed triumphantly.

"Yes, however, do not get your hopes up just yet, Miss Collier, for there are a number of different sets of boots, all of which may belong to the gardeners."

"Oh. I—I confess I didn't think of that, but of course, you're quite right, sir. However, these footprints here...they are not boots, surely. In fact, they look like bare feet!"

"They are indeed—and what's more, they lead only away from the house, not into it, which means that whomever they belong to gained admittance to the manor by some other entrance, but then exited through the music room windows. And here, madam—'' bending forward, Colonel Sherbourne plucked a small piece of gauzy white fabric from where it was caught on the branch of a hawthorn bush ''—is another clue that perhaps your intruder was, in fact, real.'' He paused for a moment, contemplating the scrap of material thoughtfully. Then he continued. ''Tell you what, Miss Collier, why don't you allow me to delve into this matter a bit further for you? Perhaps it is nothing. But if it actually is something, then whilst it is in all likelihood no more than some kind of poor prank meant only to tease you, if by some chance it *is* something more serious than that, I should never forgive myself if I permitted you to expose yourself to some danger.''

''You are all kindness and consideration, sir. Thank you.''

''My pleasure. Shall we go inside now?''

Together, they went into the manor, entering by the front door.

''Well, Colonel,'' Verity said, as they stepped into the entrance hall, ''you will be wanting to see his lordship, I expect, and I've taken up quite enough of your time already. So…shall I attempt to discover his whereabouts for you, or will you announce yourself?''

''Why, we need neither of us do either, I see—for here is Jago now.''

At Colonel Sherbourne's words, Verity turned and saw the Earl approaching them from his study. Today, he was dressed in a black broadcloth jacket, a fine white cambric shirt with a jabot of lace at the throat and cuffs, a grey paisley silk waistcoat, and a pair of grey breeches and black boots. As always, he appeared to her the epitome of a lord and gentleman, rather than some common criminal, a murderer. Yet she knew that looks could be deceiving, although, even now, she found it difficult to credit the rumors Loveday had told her about him, that he had killed his wife. Surely, he had not! For she could not bear it if he had, Verity knew of a sudden, shaken and deeply confused by the realization.

"Good afternoon, Miss Collier," Lord St. Aubyn greeted her soberly, his black eyes flicking over her as though to satisfy himself that she had suffered no lasting ill effects from the previous evening. "I trust you are feeling better today."

"Yes, very much so. Thank you, my lord."

"Good. I am delighted to hear it. Hugh—" he turned his attention to his cousin "—I thought I heard your voice. Are you just now arrived?"

"Indeed, no. I have been here for half an hour or more, strolling in the gardens with Miss Collier, whom I chanced upon before coming inside. She has been telling me of last night's events. Such a stir! I hope things are more settled today."

"Yes, it would seem so. But, come. Do not let us stand about here in the entrance hall when we may be comfortable in the library. Pray, excuse us, Miss Collier."

"Of course, my lord."

Verity left the two men to make their way to the library, while she herself went along the west passage to the morning room, where she had earlier promised to join Mrs. Wickersham and Loveday—the house-keeper having insisted that they needed to begin cutting and sewing the gowns that Verity was to have from the dusky-rose and sea-green silks the Earl had given her. "For you do not know when they may be required, my dear," the elderly woman had declared to her, "and so it would be best to have them completed just as soon as we reasonably can."

Verity herself had not seen the need for any such urgency. However, believing that Mrs. Wickersham probably knew better than she did, she had willingly allowed herself to be guided by the housekeeper in the matter.

Upon entering the morning room, Verity found both the elderly woman and Loveday waiting for her.

"Ah, there you are, my dear," Mrs. Wickersham greeted her cheerfully. "I was beginning to wonder whether you had perhaps forgotten about our dress-making today."

"No, ma'am. I was but detained by a small, personal matter I needed to attend to, and then by Colonel Sherbourne, who arrived a little while ago and, chancing to spy me outside in the gardens, took a short turn around them with me. I beg your pardon if I am late."

"No, do not fret yourself—for we had set no specific time this afternoon," the housekeeper reassured her. "It is only that I feel we should get started on your two finer gowns just as quickly as we can, the sooner to finish them both. For, as it is now midsummer and the Season in London has ended, it may be that his lordship will choose to entertain guests here at the manor presently. Whilst it is true that he has not done so since her ladyship's untimely death, she has been gone two years now, so the official period of mourning has long passed, and for all that he loved her deeply, his lordship does not, I do not believe, contemplate never resuming a normal life.''

"Did his lordship and her ladyship entertain often, then, before she died?" Verity inquired.

"Oh, yes!" the elderly woman confirmed, her face lighting up with pleasure at the memory. "Why, hardly a day at all went by in the summer when we did not have some party or fête or ball when her ladyship was alive, for she was much esteemed by everyone wherever she went, and all the young ladies and gentlemen flocked to her side. She never lacked for cicisbei—although his lordship did not much care for them, I don't believe, for he is possessed of a jealous nature and did not like to share her. But, there, young ladies must have their admirers, or so her ladyship always insisted, and declared there was no harm in it, that it was most unfashionable to be escorted about by one's husband wherever one went.''

"Indeed?" From where she bent over the bolt of dusky-rose silk spread upon the table they were employing to trace the pattern and cut it, Verity glanced up reprovingly. "Well, whilst I do not profess to know what is customary these days, ma'am, for my own part, had I a husband, I should be both proud and glad to be seen on his arm wherever I went, and not needing a court of dandies and fops about to constantly flatter and amuse me!''

"Well spoken, Miss Collier!" From where he stood in the doorway with his cousin, Colonel Sherbourne, the Earl eyed her with a great deal of approval, his dark eyes gleaming as they raked her with interest and speculation.

"My—My lord, I did not know you were there," she said, flushing and biting her lower lip anxiously. "I was not presuming to criticize—"

"I know you were not, so pray, do not apologize—but *do* forgive our intrusion, for, I assure you there was no help for it! Hugh would have it that I am very dull company today, I fear, and thus incessantly urged that we join you and Mrs. Wickersham, from whom, I have no doubt, he hopes he may wrangle an early tea."

"Jago has the right of it, indeed!" The Colonel laughed gaily, unabashed, as he advanced into the morning room. "My dear Mrs. Wickersham, I beg you have pity on me! Due to my onerous duties in the dragoon guards, I've had no luncheon today, and although I thought to partake of it with Jago, I got an inordinately late start from Truro, so missed out here, as well. As a result, I am utterly famished. If Cook could only be prevailed upon to lay out an early tea, along with some Cornish pasties, you and he both would have my undying gratitude!"

The housekeeper smiled, beaming with pleasure at the Colonel's teasing antics, for she had known him since he was a child, and he was a great favorite with her. Laying aside her scissors and sewing box, she stood.

"I will see what I can manage, sir," she told him.

"But in recompense, I charge you and his lordship both to give some direction to Miss Collier about her gowns—for despite the quality and elegance of the silks, she will insist on having everything simple and austere, when I am persuaded that a bit of ribbon or lace would make all the difference and would not need to be in the least fussy, besides."

"Have no fear on that score, then, ma'am," Lord St. Aubyn replied, a faint smile of his own playing about the corners of his sensual mouth. "For, as you know, Hugh and I both have not some inconsiderable notion of what is *au courant,* and we will certainly endeavor to set Miss Collier straight."

At that, Verity looked up again, much alarmed, her cheeks once more staining with color and her heart beating far too quickly and shallowly in her breast. For, despite the fact that the Earl's tone had been light and even mocking, it had also been implacable, and with a sinking feeling, she realized he did not now intend—and perhaps had never intended—that she fashion anything the least bit plain and unadorned from the bolts of silk.

"My lord, surely, it is for me to judge what is or is not suitable for me and my station." She spoke quietly but firmly.

"I beg to disagree, madam," her employer rejoined, his mellifluous voice low and pleasant, but holding an even greater note of adamance, nevertheless. "For, as you yourself have noted, your sheltered upbringing at Trowbridge has left you relatively ignorant of the world, so that you can have little notion at all of how to get on in it." Quite easily but authoritatively did he thus dismiss her own preferences. "Are you done tracing and cutting the pattern, Loveday? Good. Then pin it upon the dressmaker's mannequin, and Hugh and I shall instruct you from there."

Mrs. Wickersham returned, with the footman Ned trailing in her wake, bearing the requested early tea and Cornish pasties, which repast Ned laid out upon a sideboard, seeming to dawdle so long at the task that, finally, the Earl reprimanded him coolly.

"Have you quite finished up there, Ned? Yes, thank you, that will do. Be about your other duties, then. Mrs. Wickersham shall do the honors."

"Aye, m'lord." The footman bowed low, then moved to close the doors to the morning room at his departure.

"No, leave them open," Lord St. Aubyn commanded tersely. "For it may be that Hugh and I will desire to indulge in a cigar, and it will not do for the smoke to fill up the room, offending the sensibilities of Mrs. Wickersham and Miss Collier."

"Very well. As thou wish, m'lord." Bowing again, Ned prepared to take his leave of them, only to be halted again briefly by his employer.

"And send up to the nursery for the twins," the Earl directed, "for Hugh and I would be pleased to see them."

"Aye, m'lord."

Shortly thereafter, the children appeared, with the dog, Styx, following at their heels, and quite a merry little party ensued, thanks in large part to Colonel Sherbourne, whose joviality would not be suppressed. He kept them all laughing with his tales and jests, so that even Meliora and Bastian caught his mood and were moved to glee as they played happily with the dog and with Mrs. Wickersham's cat, Calico, which bestirred itself to chase after a ball of yarn for them.

All the while, Lord St. Aubyn and the Colonel gave instructions and suggestions for the making of Verity's two silk gowns, which, much to her dismay, grew increasingly modish and fine, although she was highly relieved to see that, even so, both her employer and his cousin possessed unimpeachably impeccable good taste, and that, thankfully, their idea of what was fashionable and elegant did not extend to frills and furbelows.

"You are in very good spirits today, sir," the housekeeper observed of Colonel Sherbourne. "May one inquire as to the reason?"

"Indeed, you may, ma'am," he answered, smiling. "Still, it is for Jago to share the felicitous news, I think, if he will."

"My cousin refers to the fact that I have at long last decided to reopen St. Aubyn manor to guests, Mrs. Wickersham," the Earl explained, with an understatedness calculated to de-emphasize this piece of information, as though it were of no importance. "I am even now forming a small party that is to be made up of several of my and Hugh's acquaintances, including his both lovely and lively fiancée, Miss Nightingale."

"Oh! I knew it would be so!" the elderly woman exclaimed, with obvious delight, clapping her hands

together like a child and sighing deeply with pleasure. "For I was telling Miss Collier only this afternoon what grand entertainment we used to have here
at St. Aubyn manor, and how I hoped and believed
that perhaps now that the Season in London had
ended, your lordship would finally wish to have parties and fêtes and balls here again! Was it not so, my
dear?" she asked of Verity.

"Yes, it was, ma'am." Verity obligingly confirmed, feeling, however, abruptly and painfully deflated, unable to share in the other's happiness. Still,
somehow, she managed with composure to say to the
Colonel, "I did not know you were affianced, sir."

"Yes, for nearly a year now, after which Miss
Nightingale's parents have consented that we may be
married. I am quite sure you shall like her, Miss Collier, for I'm certain there was never a more agreeable
or merrier soul than my Kate!"

"I shall very much look forward to meeting her,
then," Verity forced herself to reply with warmth,
determinedly putting from her mind all her secret
hopes and aspirations where Colonel Sherbourne was
concerned, glad and grateful, now, that she had
wisely kept her own counsel and not permitted herself to wear her heart upon her sleeve. For, clearly,
in light of his declaration, any feelings Colonel Sherbourne might cherish toward her own self were but
those of a friend who enjoyed her acquaintance and
company. "For, already, I feel sure she is everything
you claim."

"Who else shall compose the party, my lord?"
Mrs. Wickersham queried.

"Oh, I am not yet certain of all the rest." He waved one hand carelessly, as though this, too, were as unimportant as his news. "But the Marchmonts and Avondales, undoubtedly, and also Lord Lindley, Messrs Tucker and Grainge and Captain Pettigrew. Naturally, we shall make up a list and devise some simple entertainment for the days when our guests will be here at St. Aubyn...pheasant hunting, fishing and billiards for the gentlemen will do nicely, and perhaps walking, reading and sketching for the ladies during the daytime, and, as expected, cards, charades and some music and dancing for all in the evenings. Nothing elaborate, ma'am, so I pray you, please do not put yourself into a dither—although, of course, all the spare bedrooms must be readied in preparation."

"And when shall those invited to St. Aubyn manor come, and how long shall they stay?" Plainly, the housekeeper was already brimming with plans and excitement.

"Within the fortnight, and not above three or four days, I should think."

Reaching into the inner pocket of his jacket, Lord St. Aubyn drew forth a fine, engraved gold case, from which he casually extracted a slender cheroot. This—their early tea now having been consumed— he lit and began to smoke, his indolent, graceful action abruptly causing Verity to start a little in her chair, the foreignly exotic fragrance evoking a sudden memory as it wafted to her nostrils.

"Is something the matter, Miss Collier?" Her employer lifted one eyebrow inquiringly. "Do you find the smoke of my cigar distasteful? Would you prefer it if I took myself back to the library to indulge?''

"No, my lord—for it would surely be presumptuous of me, would it not, to place my own preferences above yours, in your own home?"

"Yes, it would." As he spoke these words, a sardonic smile curved his mouth, and then he laughed softly, insolently, as though he were well aware of their arrogance and how that would pique her. "However, if despite the open doors, you truly cannot abide the smoke—"

"No, it is not that, my lord. It is only that, just now, I was suddenly and strongly reminded of the time I spent at Jamaica Inn, whilst I waited for Howel to collect me on my way here to St. Aubyn manor. As Colonel Sherbourne is aware, at the inn, I chanced to share the parlor with a stranger—a well-spoken, well-educated man who proved an excellent raconteur and with whom I eventually exchanged some light, intriguing and entertaining discourse whilst I applied myself to my supper. He smoked a cheroot whilst we talked, and the aroma of your own made me recall the incident, that is all."

"I see." The Earl's dark visage was now suitably impassive.

But for whatever strange, unfathomable reason, Verity abruptly had the most distinct, perturbing impression that he was still laughing at her.

Thirteen

An Ostentation of Peacocks

Remember that the most beautiful things in the
world are the most useless; peacocks and lilies
for instance.

> *The Stones of Venice*
> —John Ruskin

I heard them cry—the peacocks.
Was it a cry against the twilight
Or against the leaves themselves
Turning in the wind,
Turning as the flames
Turned in the fire,
Turning as the tails of the peacocks
Turned in the loud fire,
Loud as the hemlocks
Full of the cry of the peacocks?
Or was it a cry against the hemlocks?

> *Domination of Black*
> —Wallace Stevens

With the Earl's return to St. Aubyn, Verity had thought the slumberous old manor had stirred to wakefulness. But that was nothing compared to the hustle and bustle with which the house was now beset in preparation for the forthcoming activities and the welcomed, expected guests so soon to arrive to partake of them.

Was there ever such a great stir? she wondered, astounded. If so, she had certainly never before beheld its like. For, despite the fact that the manor was always kept clean and tidy, it was now scoured and shined from top to bottom, as though it had never previously seen a scrub brush or a polishing cloth.

In every single chamber, from the servants' quarters on the second floor to the reception rooms on the ground floor, draperies, bed curtains and carpets were beaten to relieve them of dust; windows and walls were washed; and floors were swept. Furniture was rubbed with beeswax and buffed until it gleamed, and mirrors and silver were polished until they shone. Every chimney, mantel and hearth was cleaned, and coal buckets were filled.

On the ground floor, the grand pianos and the harp

in the drawing and music rooms were tuned; new decks of cards were placed in the card room; and the smoking room was supplied with cigars of every sort.

In the bedrooms upstairs, featherbeds and pillows were fluffed and aired; linens were laundered; and writing desks were outfitted with ink, quills and paper. Cots for abigails and valets to sleep on were erected in dressing rooms; the cedarwood lining of wardrobes was lightly sanded to renew its pungent fragrance; and sweet lavender sachets were placed on the shelves. Every commode and bathroom was scrubbed and stocked with pristine towels and scented soaps.

Everywhere, doors and windows were flung open wide to let in light and fresh air, and cut flowers were brought in from the conservatory and gardens to be placed in vases and bowls.

Everyone tread softly in the kitchen, where Cook, easily excitable and enraged under even the best of circumstances, was now in a veritable uproar, plucking chickens, hanging hams and trussing game, chopping vegetables and preparing soups, salads, sauces and gravies, and baking custards, cakes and confections, puddings, pies and pastries, and breads and buns of all kinds. In the larder, provisions were replenished and more stores added, and in the basement's wine cellar, the butler, Mr. Peacock, carefully selected and dusted off bottles of claret, hock, port, sherry and champagne, as well as bottles of brandy, cordial and ratafia, for serving with suppers and after dinner.

All in all, there was such a hubbub that Verity had

a difficult time keeping the twins focused on their morning lessons, for even they two had been affected, agitated and animated by this lately unprecedented change in the household.

"Shall we see for ourselves all the fine ladies and gentlemen who are coming here, madam?" Meliora asked, her eyes sparkling with anticipation at the thought.

"Yes, I should imagine you will at some point," Verity confirmed. "Perhaps during the day or the early evening."

"Oh, not during the day, madam, please," Bastian entreated quietly. "For I do not wish to go hunting with the gentlemen and to kill the birds for sport!" he abruptly cried, distressed and on the verge of tears at the very idea.

It was the longest speech he had ever made to her, and in that instant, Verity dared to draw him upon her lap, to cuddle him close, and to tousle his hair gently.

"I promise you will not have to go hunting, Bastian, nor kill the birds—although perhaps you might go fishing with your cousin, Colonel Sherbourne, if you like. However, you must remember that men do not hunt just for sport, but also to put food upon the table. There is no waste here at St. Aubyn manor, for your father does not hold with killing animals just for the sake of it."

"I'm glad!" Bastian declared, his lower lip still trembling. "For I quite like the deer and the rabbits and the birds—although perhaps not the boars, for they are mean and ugly!"

"Indeed they are!" Verity agreed, laughing at the notion, and, to her delight, earning smiles from both children as a result.

Meliora, in fact, had crept nearer to snuggle b neath Verity's arm, as well, evidently wishing for her own share of hugs and affection. Never before had Verity felt as close to the youngsters as she did in that moment, and she sensed that at long last, the final barriers the twins had erected for protection about themselves had fallen, that she had succeeded in winning not only their trust and liking, but also their hearts. At that emotional thought, she felt her own heart well inside her, and she realized then that she had come to love and care for them as deeply as they did her.

The three of them passed the remainder of the morning more happily together than they ever had before, with a new, however unvoiced, understanding of their relationship that profoundly pleased and contented them all.

The fortnight before the invited guests were to arrive at St. Aubyn manor passed swiftly in the great flurry of activity, and before Verity knew it, on the Wednesday afternoon that followed, there sounded the unmistakable clatter and crunch of carriage wheels coming up the long, winding drive that terminated in its circle at the front of the house.

From the minstrel gallery on the first floor, through the lozenged lead-glass panes of the narrow Gothic windows on either side of the circular stained-glass window set in the center of the exterior wall, she and the twins watched the arrival of the guests as the vehicles conveying them to the manor drew one after another to a halt beneath the portico, after which it was impossible to see them anymore. Until then, however, glimpses could be caught of the elegantly bonneted and attired ladies seated at the windows of the closed coaches or upon the benches of the open carriages, parasols in hand to shade them from the sun that shone brightly and warmly that day, and of the equally fashionable gentlemen who rode alongside on horseback.

The groom of the chambers, Mr. Lathrop, stood in the entrance hall to receive the guests, along with Mrs. Wickersham, several of the footmen and maids, and the Earl himself. When those who had been invited to the manor had arrived and been greeted by its lord and master, Mr. Lathrop and Mrs. Wickersham then conducted the gentlemen and ladies, respectively, upstairs to their bedrooms, while the footmen and maids followed behind, carrying baggage and bandboxes.

At this point, however, Verity insisted upon removing her young charges from the minstrel gallery, thinking it was not meet that they should be discovered spying upon and ogling the guests. Returning the twins to the nursery, she then waited for the house to quiet again, so that she was certain all the ladies and gentlemen had retired to their bedrooms to rest and to change for the evening tea, before seeking her own chamber via the east-tower stairs, by which means she hoped to avoid running into any of the guests who might still be wandering about.

There were, Verity knew, no spare bedrooms remaining at the manor. Even the empty one next to
her own, which, had the Earl still possessed a living
wife, would have belonged to the Countess's abigail,
had been given over to Colonel Sherbourne for the
duration. The Colonel's fiancée's parents, Mr. and
Mrs. Nightingale, had been installed in the large
apartment next to the Earl's own, while all the rest
of the guests were lodged in the west wing, along
with their own valets and abigails. In the west wing's
two large apartments were Sir Charles and Lady
Marchmont and Mr. and Mrs. Avondale. The first set
of the six smaller bedrooms housed the Marchmonts'
two daughters, Gwendolyn and Juliet; the Nightin-
gales' only daughter, Katherine, who was Colonel
Sherbourne's fiancée; and the Avondales' three
daughters, Blanche, Elizabeth and Sophia; while in
the second set were Lord Peregrine Lindley; Katherine's brother, Harry, and Captain Fitzpatrick Pettigrew; and Messrs Robert Tucker and William
Grainge.

As at most such occasions in the country, the party
was an eclectic mixture of personages drawn ᵢrom
neighboring estates and elsewhere, so as to make a
lively, entertaining group. However, that first night,
Verity did not meet any of them, for, much to her
confusion and disappointment, she was not summoned downstairs, as she had half expected to be—
for why else had Mrs. Wickersham insisted on the
two new silk gowns being finished? Instead, although
Verity waited for a good long while in her bedroom,
unsure whether or not to dress for the evening, no

invitation to join the guests was brought upstairs to her—although a supper tray was, from whose appearance, bewildered and crushed, she correctly deduced that her presence at the party was neither expected nor desired.

You silly, stupid girl! Verity chided herself most bitterly and violently. *How could you even imagine that you would be one of those privileged to be present at his lordship's party? You, a mere, plain, penniless governess, go into society as though you were the equal of everyone else and had every right to be among them? Why, what a notion! What foolishness! What utter nonsense! What sheer vanity and arrogance on your own part!*

Still, although, logically, Verity knew all this to be true, she had dared to hope—for, besides her two new silk dresses, had there not also been the expectation raised by Colonel Sherbourne of her meeting his fiancée, Katherine? And was it not true, too, that she, Verity, was as well born as the vast majority of those at the party and that had it not been for the caprices of fate, she would have been found among their ranks?

But somehow, the knowledge of this last only worsened her feelings of hurt and dejection, and although she valiantly fought the tears that threatened to spill over, in the end, Verity succumbed to them and was unable even to try to choke down any of her supper, which she left untouched on the tray, despite the fact that with it, irascible Cook had clearly attempted to please. After that, her eyes red and swollen from her crying and her head pounding with a sickening migraine, Verity lay down, still fully clothed, upon her bed, trying hard not to listen to the—to her—painful sounds of bright gaiety and amusement that drifted upstairs to her ears from the chambers below.

Turning her face into her pillow to muffle her sobs, she wept again, silently cursing both the Earl and Colonel Sherbourne, whom, for their many kindnesses toward her, how they had jested and teased her when directing the styling of her two new silk frocks, she had dared to believe her friends. In reality, she was nothing to either of them, Verity thought now—too distraught even to wonder why, strangely enough, the loss of the Earl's liking and approval should matter far worse to her than Colonel Sherbourne's.

At last, worn out by her grief and throbbing headache, she slept—not even bothering, for the very first time in her entire life, to undress.

For the first time since arriving at St. Aubyn manor, when Verity awakened in the morning, she did not at first know where she was, but imagined herself still at Trowbridge instead, so that when she gazed around her bedroom, she was initially bemused by how it had been transformed overnight. Then, finally, she remembered that she had left Trowbridge behind forever, and that she had been governess to the Earl of St. Aubyn's twin children, in Cornwall, for many long weeks now. After that, the events of yesterday afternoon and last night came flooding back to her, and she discovered that she had slept in her clothes.

Thank heavens, Verity thought, that it was still early enough that Loveday had not yet come to make up the chamber! Or perhaps, more likely, she was busy in the guest bedrooms.

Rising from her bed, Verity hurried to divest herself of the garments she had slept in, sponge bathing at the washbasin on the commode and cleaning her teeth. Then she dressed herself carefully in her new brown bombazine gown and cream-colored muslin tucker, after which she brushed her hair, coiling it into its customary chignon at her nape.

Spying her supper tray, whose contents she had not touched, and fearing to hurt and anger Cook otherwise, she flung wide her rear window and emptied the plates and bowls into the shrubbery below, so that he would not know she had not eaten what he had so temptingly prepared for her the previous evening, as though to lessen the blow to her sensibilities that she had not been invited to be one of the Earl's party.

Then, cracking open her chamber door, Verity peeked out into the long passage beyond. Observing no one about, she gathered up her supper tray and slipped out into the corridor to the east-tower stairs, which she descended to the ground floor below. Hastening along the main hall, she was abruptly halted by the sound of the Earl's voice calling out to her from the billiard room.

"Yes, my lord?"

She stepped inside the chamber to find him leaning

nonchalantly against the green-baize billiard table, one of the slim brown cheroots he favored in hand. He was dressed in a fine white cambric shirt with a burgundy silk cravat tied in the mailcoach style, a burgundy-and-tan kerseymere waistcoat, and a pair of soft buckskin breeches and black leather Hessian boots. A burgundy jacket, also of kerseymere, lay to one side on the billiard table.

"Miss Collier, I have just now witnessed one of the strangest sights I have ever before seen in my entire life, and I was hoping you could perhaps explain it to me."

"Indeed, my lord?"

"Yes, I was sitting in the smoking room, enjoying a cigar, when all of a sudden, a great mess of food rained from the sky, past the windows, and into the shrubbery."

As she heard these words, Verity was not only rendered speechless, but also a deep crimson flush stained her cheeks, and she was painfully aware of the now-barren supper tray she carried, providing obvious evidence of her crime.

"My—My apologies, my lord," she stammered, at last. "But I suffered an unaccustomed migraine last evening, and discovered that I was not hungry as a result. Since I didn't want to offend Cook—"

"Pray, do not fret yourself, madam. Your secret is safe with me, I assure you, for I quite understand and am very sorry to learn you've been unwell." Lord St. Aubyn's dark eyes searched her face intently. "You do look pale and unrested. I hope you feel better presently, for there is to be dancing tonight and the next two nights after that, also, and you will be needed to make up a full complement, so that none of the gentlemen will lack for a partner.'' He extinguished his cheroot in a nearby ashtray and shrugged on his jacket. Then, coming forward, he deliberately took the supper tray from her hands. ''You have three fine gowns appropriate for the occasion, do you not, Miss Collier?'' he inquired, with a curious gentleness.

At that, all of a sudden, Verity realized why she had not been included last night. The guests were to stay until Sunday afternoon, and she had but three suitable frocks for evenings, not four. By not requesting that she join the party last night, her employer had kindly spared her from the embarrassment and humiliation of appearing in the same dress twice.

''Yes, my lord, I do,'' she answered gratefully, her eyes speaking volumes as she and her employer walked slowly down the passage toward the kitchen together. ''And I am honored and delighted to be invited to join your guests.''

''Good. I'm very glad to hear it. Then, shortly before dinner ends tonight, please bring Meliora and Bastian down to the small drawing room and, there, await us.'' Pausing at the kitchen door, he handed her back the supper tray. ''I shall look forward to this evening.''

''As shall I,'' Verity said quietly, blushing again beneath the Earl's scrutiny and faint smile of satisfaction, her eyes now modestly downcast and her heart beating strangely quick and light in her breast of a sudden.

"Good morning, Miss Collier." He gave her a slight bow.

"Good morning, my lord." She curtsied.

Then he disappeared down the corridor, in the direction of the offices of the upper staff. Utterly bewildered by her own abruptly chaotic, tumultuous emotions in that instant, Verity stood and watched silently until he was out of sight.

That evening, Loveday once more came to Verity's bedroom to help her dress and to arrange her hair, which was braided and threaded with a pale grey riband, then swept up and secured atop her head. Since it was the first night—but not the last— that she was to attend the party, Verity donned her pearl-grey silk frock, deeming it the least fine of her three evening gowns and wishing to save the best, the chatoyant sea-green silk, for the final night. She had no other jewelry but her mother's gold locket, which she hung around her neck, but as it was pretty enough and a cherished heirloom, she wanted no other.

After that, collecting Meliora and Bastian, who were also garbed in their finest, Verity took them downstairs via the east-tower steps, from which she and the twins could enter the small drawing room without passing through the entrance hall, where they might have been spied by those assembled in the dining room for dinner. For, now that the moment of her debut, such as it was, into society had arrived, Verity was suddenly stricken with self-doubt and trepidation. Well born, she might be, but a governess she was. Perhaps she would be snubbed by the grand company who would shortly ingress the small drawing room.

She bit her lower lip with anxiety at the thought, feeling abruptly sick to her stomach. Earlier, she had been far too nervous and excited to consume anything on the tray that had been sent upstairs to her chamber, and now, she was glad of it, for she felt certain that if she had eaten, she might well now be ill as a result of it. She sat down in a chair in a corner, where she thought that perhaps she might go unnoticed, and instructed Meliora and Bastian to sit quietly, as well, so that they would not crease their clothes.

"You shall not be long here, you understand?" Verity told the children. "Not above an hour or so, I should think, after which Trueth will come downstairs to fetch you up to bed."

They nodded gravely, but there was no time to speak further reassurances to them, for just then, the small-drawing-room doors from the entrance hall were flung open wide by two of the footmen, and talking and laughing gaily, the ladies of the party made their way into the chamber.

How beautiful they all were, Verity thought as she spied them, like an ostentation of strutting peacocks or a field of swaying lilies in their colorful finery as they invaded the small drawing room. The older females—Lady Marchmont and the Mmes Avondale and Nightingale—wore gowns of deeper hues, elaborate fringed shawls, and turbans with plumes, while the younger women were all dressed in white or pastels with lace and ribbons.

As the ladies glanced around the chamber and noticed her and the youngsters, Verity rose and curtsied, as did Meliora, while Bastian bowed. A few of the younger females nodded to them in response, but the rest only stared, then resumed their colloquies, gathering in groups upon the sofas and chairs, and around the fireplace. Only one—a cheerful redhead with bright green eyes and a smattering of freckles across her retroussé nose, and dressed in an ice-green gown—came forward, smiling merrily and with her hands warmly outstretched.

"You must be Miss Collier. I'm Katherine Nightingale, Colonel Sherbourne's fiancée—and these must be Meliora and Bastian. My goodness, how the two of you have grown since last I saw you! I'll wager you don't remember me, however, for we met only once and not for any duration. It is a pleasure to see you again, and also to meet you at last, Miss Collier—for the Colonel has told me so much about you!"

"I cannot imagine that there was very much to tell, Miss Nightingale, surely." Verity smiled, liking Colonel Sherbourne's fiancée at once.

"Only that you are quite good and kind, and have worked wonders with the twins, and here at the manor elsewhere, as well, and indeed, I can already see for myself that all this is so."

Settling herself comfortably on a chair beside Verity, Miss Nightingale thereafter engaged to draw both her and the children out, chatting amiably to them all, so that they were soon put at their ease. Just shortly, they were joined by Mrs. Wickersham, also. Thus, what might have proved a rather uncomfortable, lonely interval for Verity was instead passed in pleasant dialogue, and somehow, she knew she had not only the Colonel, but also the Earl to thank for Miss Nightingale's attention, at least.

Presently, the footmen arrived with coffee, and the gentlemen were called from the dining room, where they lingered over port and cigars. With the exception of Colonel Sherbourne and Captain Pettigrew, who were in their uniforms of the dragoon guards, the males of the party, which now included the steward, Mr. Drummond, were all similarly attired in black jackets, fine white cambric shirts with white neckerchiefs, and white breeches and black pumps—to these last of which some, like the foppish Lord Lindley, had added buckles or other ornaments.

Spying Verity from across the chamber, the Earl approached and made her known to the rest of his guests. Much to her surprise, instead of presenting her as the governess, he introduced her as "Miss Verity Collier, daughter of the late Squire Collier, of Belper, in Derbyshire." He said nothing more—as though nothing more, in fact, need be said, so that there were those who must have wondered about her exact position in his household. Yet, despite the fact that the guests would certainly be apprized of her status by their own servants, Verity was still deeply touched and gladdened by Lord St. Aubyn's introduction, his determination to make it known to his guests that she was of good family and background—

although why this should have mattered to him was a mystery to her.

Still, it made the party aware that, as Messrs Avondale and Nightingale were, her own father had been landed gentry, a country squire; and since Lord St. Aubyn was not only the guests' host, but also the highest ranking gentleman in the room, followed by Lord Lindley, a viscount, and Sir Charles Marchmont, baronet, his example was sure to prevail.

"Miss Collier was unable to join us last night, I'm afraid, due to being indisposed with a migraine," her employer further elucidated. He turned to Verity. "However, I trust you are now much improved, madam?"

"Yes, my lord, thank you."

Because the party was not at all large, it was confined to the small drawing room, where the furniture had been moved to clear a space in the center for the dancing that was to be the primary thrust of the entertainment, although decks of cards had been set out on tables for those guests who did not care to participate, and Mrs. Wickersham had retired to a corner with her embroidery.

After the coffee had been served all around and the twins much made over and then sent off to bed, the musicians engaged for the evening began to play, and partners were chosen for the first dance. For this, Verity promptly found her hand claimed by Harry Nightingale, and for this courtesy, too, she thought she must thank not only the Earl and Colonel Sherbourne, but also Miss Nightingale.

Mr. Nightingale was a pleasant, charming young

man, and so Verity was happy to stand up with him, while the Colonel led out Miss Nightingale herself, and Lord St. Aubyn partnered Miss Gwendolyn Marchmont. Yet, strangely enough, Verity found that while the sight of the former did not discompose her as she had expected, that of the latter did. In Verity's opinion, Miss Marchmont, although the most beautiful of all the young ladies in the chamber, was also the haughtiest. There was in her manner a distinct air of superiority and even of malice toward the others of her own sex, and she could not be satisfied if she were not the center of attention. No doubt, she felt this last was no less than her due, since she was the eldest daughter of a baronet and thus the highest ranking of all the young ladies present. But for her own part, Verity could not like her.

However, as Miss Marchmont was tall, slender, blond and blue eyed, as Lady St. Aubyn had been, Verity supposed that her employer must prefer such looks, and however much she was loath to admit it, she must acknowledge that the Earl and Miss Marchmont made a very striking couple as they executed the intricate steps of the dance. Still, for some inexplicable reason, it pained Verity to see them together, and in an attempt to stifle her feelings of conflict and confusion, she forced herself to concentrate on the dance, so that she did not misstep or clumsily tread on her partner's toes.

After she had danced with Mr. Nightingale, Verity then found herself paired with Captain Pettigrew, and then with each of the other young gentlemen in turn, until the last dance—the Sir Roger de Coverley—for which Lord St. Aubyn finally stood up with her.

This was quite a lively dance that often traditionally served as an evening's finale, so Verity felt honored that her employer had chosen to dance it with her. He bowed; she curtsied. Then they began to move in time to the music, and she found that, oddly enough, it was not only her feet that seemed so light and soaring that they hardly touched the ground, but also her heart that felt as though it had wings. The Earl's hand held hers firmly when they touched, as they so seldom ever had before, and his dark, gleaming eyes and roguish smile signaled his earnest approval of and liking for her, causing her to blush and her heart to beat more quickly and shallowly than even the dance steps could account for as he led her down the line. Verity felt most unlike herself, giddy and gay, as though she could have danced with him forever.

But eventually, much to her disappointment, the last notes of the spirited music died away, and although it was now but one o'clock in the morning, the evening was at an end, for this was not a party where late hours were to be kept, so that supper must be served before dawn. As did the rest of the party, Verity retired from the small drawing room, to the grand staircase in the entrance hall, thence to seek her own chamber.

However, once safely ensconced in her bedroom, she discovered that she was still much too restless and excited to sleep, and after undressing and then donning her nightgown and wrapper, she sat down on the bench before the burning hearth in her chamber and directed her attention to the picture on her easel. Her head in such a whirl, her thoughts in such a turmoil, that she was scarcely even aware of the movements of her paintbrush upon the canvas, Verity painted until the wee hours of the morning.

Then, at last, exhausted, she climbed into bed, where she slept so deeply that if she dreamed at all, she did not remember it afterward.

Fourteen

Of Storms and Sonatas

When storm-clouds brood on the towering heights
Of the hills of the Chankly Bore.

The Dong with the Luminous Nose
—Edward Lear

So what is the incomprehensible secret force driving me towards you? Why do I constantly hear the echo of your mournful song as it is carried from sea to sea through your entire expanse?

Dead Souls
—Nikolai Gogol

Believe me, if all those endearing young charms
Which I gaze on so fondly today,
Were to change by tomorrow and fleet in my
   arms,
Like fairy gifts fading away,
Thou would'st still be adored as this moment
   thou art,

Let thy loveliness fade as it will,
And around the dear ruin each wish of my heart
Would entwine itself verdantly still.

Irish Melodies: Believe Me, If All Those
Endearing Young Charms
—Thomas Moore

Friday night at St. Aubyn manor passed much as Thursday night had done, except that Verity donned her new dusky-rose silk frock instead of her old pearl-grey silk gown that she had worn the previous evening. As before, Loveday came to her bedroom to assist her in dressing and arranging her hair, braiding it and, this time, threading it with a pale rose riband before once more sweeping it up and securing it atop her head.

Then, again, Verity collected the twins and accompanied them to the small drawing room just before dinner ended.

She was much less nervous than she had been the night before, even though she felt sure all the guests must now be aware that despite her breeding and background, she was nothing more than a mere governess at the manor. Still, with the exception of the Misses Marchmont, who had had very little to do with her previously, in any event, no one treated her any differently. So she was able to be at her ease and to enjoy herself even more than she had on Thursday—although she must own that she was surprised by the amount of flirtation and gossip that the young ladies, especially, indulged in, their dialogue covering everything from cicisbei and the latest fashions to the highwayman Black Jack Raven and the possibility of French spies being in England.

"I would not say it is only a possibility, Miss Marchmont," Colonel Sherbourne observed in regard to this last, to the elder of the two sisters. "I believe there can be no doubt whatsoever that French spies are among us here in England. It is only a matter, rather, of determining where."

"Indeed? Well, then, perhaps this brigand Black Jack Raven, whom we have heard so much about lately as terrorizing Cornwall, robbing coaches, is one of them!" she suggested. "If so, that is all the more reason, Colonel, one would suppose, why he ought to be caught and hanged!"

"I think it most unlikely that any French spy is going about the countryside posing as a common thief, madam." Colonel Sherbourne smiled with some amusement. "Black Jack's interest lies in obtaining money and valuables—not information and secret documents."

"Well, I, for one, do not at all like to imagine that there are actually French spies here in England—much less Cornwall," Mrs. Wickersham chimed in, obviously upset by the turn the conversation had now taken. "I've said it before, and I'll say it again. We are all apt to be murdered in our beds by the French legions!"

Although all the young ladies shrieked with fright and dismay at that, the gentleman only laughed before issuing stout reassurances to the contrary, thereby mollifying the housekeeper, who had got rather indignant at perceiving herself the butt of their merriment. Not wishing to see her further discomposed, the Earl abruptly but smoothly changed the subject, signaling to the musicians to strike up the first song of the evening, and the dancing that was the main thrust of the entertainment commenced with a gaiety that dispelled any other thoughts.

As before, Verity danced with all the young gentlemen in turn, once more closing the evening as the Earl's chosen partner, to the strains for the Sir Roger de Coverley.

On Saturday, the weather, which had heretofore continued bright and sunny, turned dark and cloudy again, with a pale-grey mist blowing in from the sea and the lowering sky promising rain. Although by late morning it had begun to drizzle, this still did not deter the gentlemen from their hunting party. However, it put a significant crimp into the plans of all the ladies, who had intended to enjoy an alfresco luncheon in one of the gazebos in the gardens. Instead, the females were confined to the house, unable even to take their embroidery hoops, books or sketch pads and paint boxes outdoors.

Lady Marchmont and Mmes Avondale and Nightingale prevailed upon Mrs. Wickersham to make up a fourth at cards, but the younger ladies were disinclined to play, and eventually, grown bored with sitting around the small drawing room, chatting, sewing, reading or playing upon the piano, Miss Gwendolyn Marchmont at last suggested that they take one of the carriages into St. Ives, where they might at least walk about and do some shopping.

This scheme at once met with approval from her sister, Miss Juliet Marchmont, and from the three Misses Avondale. Miss Nightingale, however, observing that Verity was not invited, was reluctant to go until, to spare Miss Nightingale any further discomfort, Verity excused herself, falsely claiming that she had some letters to write, and retired upstairs to her bedroom. A short while later, she heard the young ladies, having changed into their walking dresses, leave the house.

In truth, although she had no one to whom she could have penned a note, Verity *was* tired from the late hours she had kept the past few nights, and so she decided to lie down for a nap until just before tea time. Fully dressed, she lay down upon her bed. Presently, she dozed.

When she awakened, it was nearly tea time, and the day had grown dark with an early dusk and rain that now pitter-pattered against the windows. But that was not what had roused her. Rather, she had heard something...a low moan—or perhaps the rising wind outside or the turbulent sea breaking upon the rocks along the shore, Verity thought, shivering at the idea and freezing of a sudden where she lay in her bed as she waited breathlessly, expectantly and fearfully to hear *Tamsyn...Tamsyn...* softly lamented. Instead, much to her surprise, the groaning sound came again.

Someone was in pain!

Reaching out, Verity fumbled to light a candle. Then, leaping from her bed, candlestick in hand, she hurried across her chamber to crack open the door, where she stood, listening intently. Yes, she was right. There *was* someone in pain—perhaps ill or even injured—in the east tower! Holding the candle high to light her path, she hastened out into the passage beyond and then into the tower itself.

"My lord! Oh, my lord! What is it? What—What is wrong?" Verity paused on the landing, thinking, mortified, as she spied him staggering up the steps, that perhaps the Earl might be drunk. "Are you— Are you ill? Oh, no! You're hurt!" she cried, stricken, as she suddenly saw that where his right hand was pressed to his left shoulder, blood was slowly seeping. "Stay where you are, my lord, and I'll go summon help immediately!"

"No! No, Verity, for God's sake, don't call anyone!" Lord St. Aubyn ordered harshly, his breath coming in hard, labored rasps. "Come here! Come here right now, and let me lean upon you so I can get to my bedroom!"

Biting her lower lip hard, confused as to why he did not want her to seek assistance and thinking that perhaps he was feverish and delirious as a result, she hesitated momentarily, torn by indecision.

"Verity...Verity, please, I've no time to explain, but you must trust me, and do as I command you. My very life is in your hands at this instant, I promise you!"

At that, still carrying the candle, she hastened to her employer's side, not at all understanding his last, cryptic words, but nevertheless persuaded by the urgency in his voice. When she reached him, he directed her to stand to the right of him, after which he wrapped his good, right arm around her shoulders.

"You must bear my weight as best you can, I'm afraid," he told her.

"I will, but, oh, my lord, how came you to be injured? Was it a hunting accident?"

"That doesn't matter right now. Just help me to my chamber before anyone spies us!"

With difficulty, they started up the stairs together, halting upon the landing, where the Earl bade Verity leave him to determine whether or not the corridor beyond was empty. Upon learning that it was, he then had her assist him down the hall to his bedroom.

"Now, do you go across the passage, and fetch Ashfield for me. Permit no one to see you. Once you have sent him to me, go to your own chamber, and wash the blood from your gown. Do it yourself—don't leave it to the laundry. If anybody asks about it, say that you accidentally spilled paint upon it and did not wish it to stain. That's another frock I owe you, by the way. After that, you must clean up any traces of blood in the east tower. It is vitally important you speak to no one—I repeat, *no one!*—about what has happened, for I wish nobody in the household to learn of it, save for my valet. Do you understand me, Verity?"

"Yes, my lord." She nodded, deeply puzzled but still willing to obey.

"One more thing—no matter what you might hear later, you must trust me, and remember that things are not always what they may at first appear. Can you do that for me? Promise me that you will do that for me! Swear it!''

''Yes...yes, of course, my lord, I promise...I swear it!''

''Good...good. I knew I could count on you! I've known from the start that you are a good, loyal lass—not like to desert me at the first sign of trouble. Go now, then. Check the corridor first, to be certain there is nobody in it.''

Verity did as requested. Upon observing that the hall was still vacant, she hurried across it to Mr. Ashfield's bedroom and rapped softly upon the door.

''Miss Collier?'' The valet opened the portal, clearly surprised by her presence.

''Shhh.'' Verity held one finger to her lips. ''His lordship has been wounded somehow. He's bleeding and in a bad way. You must come quickly!''

Mr. Ashfield needed no further urging. Swearing under his breath, he hastened across the passage to Lord St. Aubyn's bedroom, knocking gently before swiftly stepping inside. Verity longed to accompany the valet, to discover whether or not her employer was all right. But, mindful of his words to her, she instead retired to her own chamber, there to fetch what she needed to clean the east-tower staircase, as directed, not knowing how long she had before the young ladies returned to the manor and everyone retired upstairs to change for dinner.

Her thoughts churning, her pulse racing and her hands shaking, Verity worked feverishly but competently, scrubbing the stone steps from top to bottom, until she was certain no trace of blood remained on them. Then, returning to her bedroom, she flung open the rear window and poured the bloody water in the washbasin out, hoping none of the gentlemen in the house had adjourned to either the billiard room or the smoking room directly below, or that if they had, they would mistake the sudden gush of water for downpour from one of the gutter spouts. In one of the two shared bathrooms in the first floor's east wing, she then rinsed out the washbasin and carried it back to her bedroom, along with a pitcher of fresh water.

Once back in her chamber, Verity hurriedly moved her easel near to the fireplace and placed her paint box on the cushioned bench at the foot of her bed, to lend credence to the false tale of her having accidentally splattered the dress with her paints and having wished to remove the splotches as soon as possible. Then she stripped off her soiled gown and, with hands that still trembled, began to wash the traces of blood from it, which had been made by the Earl's right hand when he had leaned on her for support, and also from her cleaning of the east-tower stairs.

As she stood at her commode, scrubbing her frock in the washbasin, Verity heard a sudden commotion downstairs, a gaggle of female voices raised shrilly in some obvious distress. Her heart constricted painfully in her breast, for she feared that something further had befallen the Earl, that perhaps his injury had proved mortal, and for some unknown reason, that thought was like a wooden stake being driven into her very soul. The blood roaring in her ears, she hastily finished with her dress, then hung it on the hearth to dry.

After that, cursing her fingers that fumbled with unaccustomed nervousness and clumsiness at the fastenings, Verity frantically donned a fresh gown and descended to the entrance hall below, where, in the small drawing room, she discovered several of the manor's guests assembled, and Miss Gwendolyn Marchmont lying prostrate on one of the sofas, a vial of smelling salts being wafted beneath her nose by Miss Nightingale.

"Oooh, it was horrible…just horrible, I tell you!" Miss Marchmont moaned, as she reclined among the pillows upon the couch, her left arm now flung dramatically across her forehead. "Was ever there a more fearsome sight? *I* surely never saw one! That hideous black mask! Those terrible dark burning eyes! That supercilious mouth! Those lethal pistols— pointed straight at me! Oh, my delicate sensibilities! I thought I would expire right there on the spot!"

"My poor, dear child." Her ample breast swollen with unconcealed outrage and shock, Lady Marchmont held and patted her elder daughter's right hand solicitously. "Oh, but this is all simply monstrous…infamous! It is not to be borne! It *must* not be! Colonel Sherbourne—" she turned to that gentleman, who stood nearby "—what is to be done? Surely, this notorious highwayman Black Jack Raven must be tracked down, captured and hanged immediately! Don't you agree, Sir Charles?"

"Yes, quite, madam," her husband stoutly replied.

By these statements, Verity correctly deduced that

the carriage the young ladies had earlier traveled to town in had, upon its return home from St. Ives, been set upon and robbed by the very same brigand who had held up the Earl's coach on the night that she herself had been en route from Jamaica Inn to St. Aubyn manor. Now, as she thought of the Earl himself and of the wound he had so recently suffered, a dreadful, terrifying suspicion crept unbidden of a sudden into Verity's mind. She would have dismissed it at once, however, as being ludicrous in the extreme, except for Miss Marchmont's next words.

"Oh, yes, the thief *must* be caught and hanged, sir! For not only did he steal my beautiful pearl necklace and brooch, but, also, I have no doubt whatsoever that we should all have been murdered afterward, had it not been for the gallant bravery and quick thinking of one of the footmen who accompanied us into town," Miss Marchmont, now sniffling tearfully but prettily into her lacy handkerchief, declared to the Colonel. "For, upon being commanded by the rogue to drive on, this footman—Ned, by name, I am informed—had the sharp presence of mind to take up one of the coachmen's pistols, which had earlier, upon orders of the scoundrel, been cast down upon the ground, and as we drove off, the footman turned from his perch at the rear of the carriage and fired upon the blackguard, wounding him, I think!"

"No, you don't say!" Colonel Sherbourne expostulated, plainly startled by this piece of information.

"Yes, indeed, sir, I'm quite sure it must be so," Miss Blanche Avondale chimed in. "For when I heard the report of the pistol, I glanced out the coach window and saw the highwayman falter a little in his saddle, as though he had been struck, before he set his spurs to the sides of his black stallion and decamped with all our money and valuables!''

"Have no fear, ladies." The Earl spoke smoothly and coolly from where he now stood in the doorway between the entrance hall and the small drawing room. "My apologies for not having sought to comfort and reassure you earlier. However, after returning from hunting this afternoon and learning what had befallen you, I deemed it both prudent and expedient to send for both the coachmen and footmen who accompanied the carriage, so that we might receive a full report of the matter, and also to dispatch a rider to Truro immediately, Hugh, to inform the dragoon guards, so Lieutenant Butterworth may, weather permitting, institute a search for the assailant at once."

"Oh, that was very quick-witted and well done of you indeed, my lord!" Miss Marchmont exclaimed, abruptly recovering her composure. Rising from the sofa, she hurried to his side, laying one hand upon his left arm. "How glad I am that you are come! For, as you may imagine, I have been *most* distressed by this entire ghastly business! But now that you are here, I shan't be afraid any longer, for I know that *you* may be counted upon, not only to protect us, but also to ensure that this notorious highwayman is put an end to!"

"I shall, of course, endeavor to do whatever I can toward achieving those lofty, noble goals, madam,''

Lord St. Aubyn answered, leading Miss Marchmont back to the couch. "But you are still most pale, and I fear you are not yet fully recovered. Pray, be seated again. Perhaps a small sherry or cordial to revive you? Mrs. Wickersham—" he addressed the housekeeper, who hovered to one side, anxiously wringing her hands over this sad turn of events "—please be good enough to arrange for some sherry and cordial to be brought for the young ladies, and also some refreshment for the rest of our most welcome guests. In fact, as it is nearly tea time now, there can surely be no objection under the circumstances to its being served a trifle early. We can dress for dinner afterward."

As, from the corner in which she sat, unnoticed, Verity watched her employer carefully, she could scarcely believe that only a short time before, he had been in such a bad state as to require her assistance up the east-tower steps. Had she not aided him and seen for herself the blood seeping from his injured shoulder, she would certainly not now have guessed him to be wounded. He had apparently been cleaned up, patched up and dressed by Mr. Ashfield with an amazing speed that was a testament not only to the valet's skills, but also to the Earl's own strength and sheer force of will and determination.

Not by so much as a flicker of an eyelid had he flinched when Miss Marchmont had laid her hand upon his left arm. But still, Verity knew that the action had pained him, that he could not, in fact, bear Miss Marchmont hanging upon him, and that it was for this reason that he had therefore escorted her back to the settee and bade her be once more seated. Verity marveled at his calmness and coolness, even as she was aghast and stricken by the stunning notion that Lord St. Aubyn and Black Jack Raven must be one and the same man!

For, how else to so satisfactorily account for so many different things that now fell so neatly into place in her mind? The stranger at Jamaica Inn and the cheroots he had smoked—the very same as those of her employer, she would now be willing to wager. All the Earl's arrangements for her at the inn, and her interlocutor's convenient appearance before her in the parlor, as though he had been purposefully waiting there for her, she decided now, upon further reflection in this new and terrible light. The many questions he had asked of her over supper, so seemingly innocuous at the time, but, in reality, cleverly designed to draw her out and illicit any useful information from her. The highwayman's having reminded her somehow of the mysterious stranger himself, and the thief's so gallantly relieving her of naught save a lock of her hair.

How very peculiar it would have seemed, Verity realized now, if every single carriage of any import in the Cornish countryside were to be robbed save for Lord St. Aubyn's own. Yet, if he were, as she now suspected and believed, the infamous brigand himself, then there was no way he could have both set upon his own coach and been inside it himself at the same time. Thus, he had required some other victim to be in his own vehicle when he had performed the dastardly deed—and how well she had served that purpose!

Oh, these were all highly dire and disquieting thoughts! She should not be having such about her employer, Verity chided herself sternly. For, surely, she must be mistaken in her suspicions and beliefs! But still, they continued to flood into her mind—and would not be banished.

One more thing—no matter what you might hear later, you must trust me, and remember that things are not always what they may at first appear. Can you do that for me? Promise me that you will do that for me! Swear it! the Earl's voice rang again in her ears.

"Well, 'pon my word, this is all devilishly unpleasant business!" Lord Lindley observed, before she could ruminate further upon this memory. "Sink me, if I don't feel as though I could do with something a bit stronger than tea myself, St. Aubyn! A brandy, at the very least!"

Mr. Peacock was promptly dispatched to the wine cellar to choose some more potent libations for the gentlemen, while Lord St. Aubyn motioned forward the two coachmen and two footmen who had been waiting quietly but expectantly in the background and who had attended his carriage into St. Ives. Verity did not stay to hear the interrogation of these, but instead slipped from the small drawing room to return to her own chamber, her head in such an agitated whirl that she paced the floor restlessly as she tried desperately to restore order to her chaotic thoughts.

Why had she not denounced the Earl as Black Jack

Raven immediately? she asked herself, stunned and distressed. Why had she instead kept quiet and helped to cover up his crimes? This was unpardonable, surely. Miss Gwendolyn Marchmont's pilfered pearl necklace and brooch were undoubtedly quite valuable, Verity supposed, and the stolen jewelry of Miss Juliet Marchmont and the Misses Avondale and Nightingale was probably equally as precious. Perhaps, when the entire affair was finally exposed, as Verity felt certain it must be in the end, she would be charged as an accomplice for her part in it—and perhaps even put into prison! she thought, distraught and frightened by the notion. She was neither a judge nor a magistrate, so she did not know the law and how it would treat her in such a situation.

What on earth should she do? she wondered. What action should she take? She considered applying to Colonel Sherbourne, laying the whole before him, and seeking his advice. But the fact that he was the Earl's cousin and therefore might not even believe her gave her pause, and in addition, she did not wish to place the Colonel, who had been kind and a friend to her, in a difficult position. Besides, what proof did she have of anything? Verity asked herself. While she could claim the Earl was wounded, he might sneer at the very idea, accuse her of lying and simply refuse to have his person examined. Then she would merely be made to look ridiculous, a complete fool, and nothing would be gained by her deed, except, unquestionably, her prompt and uncompromising dismissal from her post as governess here at the manor.

The thought of that alone wrenched painfully at Verity's heart, for even could she have borne to lose so highly valued and well-paid a position in such a pleasant household, she could not help but wonder what would become of poor little Meliora and Bastian, who had come to love and care for her as deeply as she did them.

One more thing—no matter what you might hear later, you must trust me, and remember that things are not always what they may at first appear. Can you do that for me? Promise me that you will do that for me! Swear it! the Earl had demanded of her.

And so she had promised and sworn. How could she now renege on her solemn vow—and without even speaking first to the Earl? Would it not be far better to wait and talk to him about the matter, to hear what explanation, if any, he might have to offer for his strange and reprehensible, criminal conduct? Yes, surely, that was the wisest course of action, Verity decided at last.

She had no time for further contemplation, which would, perhaps, have changed her mind, for just then, her reverie was interrupted by Loveday knocking gently upon the door, then entering her bedroom to assist her with her toilette. As they chatted about the afternoon's events and Verity made mention of the paint she had spilled upon her everyday frock, the chambermaid helped her to dress in the shimmering sea-green silk gown she had saved for tonight, knowing it to be the finest of all three such dresses she now possessed. Once she was arrayed in its long, lustrous folds, her hair was braided and threaded with a matching silk riband by Loveday, then artfully swept up and fastened securely into place with hairpins. As she had on the previous two nights, Verity then hung her mother's gold locket around her neck.

"Oh, miss, thou look t' finest I have e'er seen thee look!" Loveday exclaimed, well pleased with her handiwork.

"Thank you, Loveday. I am very glad to hear it, for I fear that all the upset this day has quite set my nerves on edge. No doubt, I shall dance most clumsily as a result, and tread on my partner's toes!"

"Nay, thou'll do no such thing, miss—fer, given all t' excitement caused by t' carriage being held up today by that 'orrible highwayman Black Jack Raven, an' fearin' 'twere going ta blow up such a storm as now howls outside, besides, his lordship sent a rider earlier ta tell t' musicians not ta come ta t' manor tonight, that all t' young ladies was so torn up an' wearied by t' day's events that they didn't feel up ta dancin' this evenin', anyways."

For a moment, Verity sat poised at her dressing table, abruptly filled with confusion.

"But, then, surely, I am not needed downstairs tonight to make up a complement," she said, at last, disappointment sweeping over her.

"But thou art, miss, fer his lordship charged me most particularly ta say that thou art ta come down an' join t' party, just as thou have these last two nights, an' that he looked forward ta hearin' thee play upon t' piano, if thou will. So I gathered that music an' cards an' such art ta be t' thrust o' t' evenin', fer all t' young ladies shall surely do nowt but chatter away endlessly about t' robbery—fer they've talked o' nothing else e'er since it happened, so that if'n thou ask me, miss, now that 'tis o'er an' they art safe an' unharmed, they art most happy ta dwell on it, an' ta fawn upon t' gentlemen fer protection an' comfort, an' ta bemoan t' loss o' their valuables, no doubt with t' aim o' receivin' more ta replace them what was stolen by t' dastardly thief! Why, only imagine that pokin' an' pryin' busybody noddy Ned havin' had t' gumption ta shoot him, miss—an' 'tis thought he actually hit t' rascal, too, no less!''

"Yes, so I've heard. I've no doubt at all that you're quite right about everything, Loveday," Verity responded, for with her words, the chambermaid had painted a most vivid and seemingly accurate picture. "Am I to bring the children with me, also, then?"

"Nay, his lordship said 'twere not necessary fer t' twins ta come down, that talk about t' coach havin' been held up would only upset them an' might e'en give them nightmares."

"In truth, I should not be at all surprised if that were to prove the case. Very well, then. Thank you, Loveday. That will be all."

The chatoyant sea-green silk rustling gently around her as she moved, Verity descended to the entrance hall to take her accustomed seat in a corner of the small drawing room. As she did so, she observed that the chambermaid was correct, that there was indeed to be no dancing tonight, for the furniture was placed as usual, rather than cleared from the center of the room, and more decks of cards than were normally placed about were in evidence on the tables. A fire blazed brightly in the Parian hearth, to mitigate the chill that had crept inside the manor as a result of the storm that raged outside, the wind keening like a banshee and the rain pelting against the lozenged lead-glass panes of the windows. Candles burned all around.

Verity had been not long seated when the ladies emerged from the dining room, looking, as always to her eye, like an ostentation of peacocks in the pure whites, soft pastels and brilliant colors of their gowns. Their conversation and laughter filled the air as they swept into the small drawing room, casting themselves down upon sofas, chairs and ottomans as though the short walk across the entrance hall had exhausted them all this evening. As was customary, Verity stood and curtsied, receiving a like obeisance in response from Miss Nightingale and a few desultory nods from one or two of the others. Miss Gwendolyn Marchmont, however, eyed her with displeasure.

"I fail to understand what need we have of the governess tonight, Mama," she commented to Lady Marchmont, as though Verity were not present, "for as there is to be no dancing on account of our shattered nerves and fatigue, what purpose can her being here possibly serve?"

"I believe his lordship said she plays the piano," Lady Marchmont replied.

"Oh, what governess doesn't—a little? For they

all play a little, do they not, so they may teach their pupils? But one can hardly think she is a master. Why, no doubt, any one of us is more accomplished and may play for his lordship's divertissement, if he so desires. I play exceptionally well myself, you know.''

Under normal circumstances, Verity would have been deeply hurt by these observations. As it was, since there was no apparent reason, aside from sheer jealousy, for Miss Marchmont's peevish remarks, Verity instead was beset by not only amusement, but also puzzlement. For, surely, Miss Marchmont had no need to envy her simply because the Earl had twice danced with her and, tonight, had requested that she entertain his party by playing the piano. That she, a mere plain, penniless governess, could be thought to have engaged the Earl's interest, perhaps even his affection, seemed to Verity such an impossibility that she could scarcely credit it, and she simply could not believe that anyone else would, either.

Evidently, however, Miss Marchmont was so out of sorts from her ordeal this afternoon that she perceived Verity as a threat and a rival for the Earl's attentions.

''Perhaps his lordship thought to spare you tonight, Gwen,'' Miss Juliet Marchmont stated, ''for the shock to all our sensibilities has much affected us. Miss Collier, however, as I understand it, was not so deeply distressed when his lordship's own carriage was robbed whilst she was in it, so that one may presume this afternoon's events to have had no affect upon her whatsoever.''

''Which only goes to prove a sad want of delicacy and feeling!'' Miss Gwendolyn Marchmont cried. ''For had I not been in the coach myself today, I should not myself feel any less affected by the suffering of those who were!''

Much to Verity's relief, no more was spoken in this regard, for just then, coffee was served by the footmen, under the aegis of the butler, Mr. Peacock, and the gentlemen were summoned from the dining room, where they had lingered at length over their port and cigars—doubtless to escape from the endless chatter about the robbery. If they had indeed wearied of this particular subject and now considered it tiresome, however, nothing of this showed upon their faces as they crossed the entrance hall to enter the small drawing room and join the ladies.

Instead, when the topic was brought up yet again, the gentlemen each took pains to reassure the ladies that everything that could be done to recover their stolen valuables and catch the highwayman was, in fact, being done—although, now, realistically, little hope was held out for success, due to the storm's interference, which would clearly make any tracking of the brigand impossible. Both Colonel Sherbourne and Captain Pettigrew were compelled to endure extensive interrogation as to why the dragoon guards had thus far failed to apprehend the rogue, but under the circumstances, their replies that he was a clever, cunning scoundrel, employing myriad means to elude them, could not be deemed satisfactory.

"Do you not agree that such excuses simply cannot answer, my lord?" Miss Marchmont inquired archly of the Earl.

"No, I don't," he rejoined bluntly. "Do you forget, madam, that Hugh is both my cousin and a colonel? I find naught about which to fault him in this matter, nor Captain Pettigrew nor the dragoon guards, either. As Hugh and the Captain both noted, Black Jack Raven is not a fool, but, rather, a highly dangerous man possessed of both intelligence and daring. He wears a mask and a domino always, so that nobody has ever seen his face, and since he has never killed anyone, only robbed his victims—and only the rich ones, at that—the common people have little incentive to betray him. Further, to the great credit of the dragoon guards, in so far as I am aware, every single coin and valuable ever stolen by the thief has eventually been recovered by them and returned to its rightful owner. Therefore, none of you ladies needs must continue to fret about your lost money and jewelry, for I've no doubt at all that they, too, shall be found and reclaimed."

"But...how is that possible, my lord?" Miss Marchmont queried, plainly puzzled by this assertion.

"That, I cannot tell you, madam, for to do so would be to betray the very methods and means by which the dragoon guards intend to capture the wicked culprit who plagues us all. So I fear you must content yourself with the idea that your pearl necklace and brooch will soon be once more in your possession, and be satisfied. Now, I pray you, let us not permit this subject to continue to cast a pall upon our party, but, rather, let us have some music, at least, to entertain us.''

''I should be more than happy to oblige, my lord.''

So saying, Miss Marchmont quickly rose and stepped over to the grand piano, where she seated herself on the bench and began to run her fingers deftly over the black-and-white keys. Then, after choosing some music from the many sheets arrayed upon the piano, she commenced the piece. As she had boasted earlier, Miss Marchmont did, in truth, play well, although not, as she had declared, exceptionally. Instead, her execution, while technically proficient, without a single flaw—she neither slurred her way through any of the more difficult passages, nor skipped them entirely—lacked any hint of passion or other emotion. In short, Miss Marchmont did not actually play; she *performed*—and she did so with every intention of impressing her listeners with her expertise, rather than with any great depth of feeling or proper interpretation of the music. It was, Verity thought, like watching an automaton.

After Miss Marchmont had performed for a while, courtesy and propriety dictated that she allow the other young ladies present a turn to demonstrate their own particular skill if they wished, and so, as though

determined to prevent Verity from playing, she summoned her sister, Juliet, to the bench, and then the
three Misses Avondale, each of whom appeared increasingly less adept upon the keys than the last. Finally, Miss Marchmont entreated Miss Nightingale
to perform.

"No, I'm afraid I must beg to be excused," Miss
Nightingale demurred, shaking her head and with a
rueful smile upon her face, "for it would be the
height of cruelty to inflict my own small talent—
which, I assure you, is very small indeed!—upon
everyone else present. Therefore, I must relinquish
my own place to Miss Collier, whom I have been
told plays beautifully and so whom I have been most
anxious to hear."

As these words had been carefully chosen and
voiced in such a manner that Miss Marchmont could
not look other than rude and hateful if she spoke
against them, she was forced to swallow with seemingly good grace any protests she might otherwise
have made and, however inwardly she might seethe,
to summon Verity to the piano bench.

"What music will you have, Miss Collier? I will
turn the pages for you as I have for all the rest,"
Miss Marchmont offered, with such feigned sweet-
ness that Verity correctly suspected that the lady's
idea of turning the pages for her would be to do so
in such a way as to cause her to stumble through any
piece she might select, thereby showing her at a disadvantage, embarrassing and humiliating her, as in-

deed perhaps Miss Marchmont had slyly done to all the others. Verity would not have put it past her.

"Thank you, ma'am, you are most kind. However, I do not require any music, for I shall perform a piece I have committed to memory."

At that, Miss Marchmont had no choice but to take a chair, which did not sit well with her, as her statuesque form had been shown to great advantage in the lamplight while she had been either seated or standing at the piano. Thus she had been certain of having all eyes—including those of the Earl—on her there. Now, she must sit down and thereby lose the focus of all attention. Still, not one to give up easily, she assumed a chair by the Earl's side, leaning over to speak with him, in an attempt to distract him from Verity's performance, only to be politely censured by Miss Nightingale, who declared that she wished to hear the music.

After that, Verity struck the opening notes of Beethoven's *Sonata quasi una Fantasia,* so softly that everyone in the room had to grow quiet to hear them. Outside, peculiarly enough, came a lull in the storm, too, which lasted through the first movement, played *adagio sostenuto*—a strange, lovely melody that, as Verity performed it, seemed as haunting as mist drifting across the moors. Then, as the rain began once more to pitter-patter almost teasingly against the windows, so, too, did the keys of the piano move beneath her deft fingers as she slid effortlessly, lightly, into the second movement, played *allegretto* and which was lively, saucy and coquettish, like the wind that danced upon the hills and heaths. Finally, just as the storm released its full fury again, so did Verity unleash all the potency and passion of the third movement, played *presto agitato* and into which she poured every last ounce of wild, pent-up emotion inside her, so that the music was as powerful as the roiling sea rushing inland onto the shingled beaches. And all the while, the storm outside raged in the night, and even the candles of the small drawing room flickered in their lamps as though beset by some draft that had swept into the manor.

There was not a single sound in the chamber besides the strains that issued forth from the piano within and from the storm without. Decks of cards lay unshuffled upon the tables; drinks sat untouched on their trays; snuffboxes remained closed; and cigars smoldered in ashtrays, unsmoked. All was hushed and still as Verity's nimble fingers traveled furiously up and down the keys, until, at last, she struck the final chords as forcefully as she had the opening notes gently, and the sonata was finished.

"Brava! Bravissima!" she heard the Earl shout, and then the small drawing room erupted into thunderous applause such as she had never before received in her life.

Blushing deeply with pleasure and triumph, Verity stood and curtsied low before the party. When she rose and glanced up, she saw that they were all on their feet, still clapping appreciatively. But there was only one whose face she sought in the chamber. Her eyes met the Earl's own, and such was the expression on his dark, saturnine visage then that her heart swelled and turned over tumultuously in her breast, and Verity knew suddenly and with certainty that when she had lost herself in the music, she had done so because she had played for him—and him alone.

In that moment as highly charged and shattering as the night sky and lightning beyond the windows, she realized that somehow—she knew not how—she had fallen deeply and irrevocably in love with him, with all her heart.

Fifteen

Portrait in Passion

Every man's work, whether it be literature or
music or pictures or architecture or anything
else, is always a portrait of himself.

> *The Way of All Flesh*
> —Samuel Butler

Know then thyself, presume not God to scan;
The proper study of mankind is man.
Placed on this isthmus of a middle state,
A being darkly wise and rudely great:
With too much knowledge for the skeptic side,
With too much weakness for the stoic's pride,
He hangs between; in doubt to act or rest;
In doubt to deem himself a god, or beast;
In doubt his mind or body to prefer;
Born but to die, and reas'ning but to err;
Alike in ignorance, his reason such,
Whether he thinks too little or too much;
Chaos of thought and passion, all confused;
Still by himself abused, or disabused;

Created half to rise, and half to fall;
Great lord of all things, yet a prey to all;
Sole judge of truth, in endless error hurled;
The glory, jest, and riddle of the world!

An Essay on Man
—Alexander Pope

No, it simply could not be true that she was in love with the Earl! Verity thought, stricken, as, after the party had ended, she hurried upstairs to her bedroom, wanting to escape from the small drawing room as quickly as possible, lest he should guess the fateful secret she now harbored deep in her heart.

But how could she be so very certain of this new and wholly unbidden emotion herself? she wondered, she, who had so little experience of men. Previously, she had imagined herself on the verge of falling in love with Colonel Sherbourne, had she not? Perhaps this, too, was but a passing fancy, born of the Earl's kindness and amity, and which would presently dissipate as easily as her feelings toward the Colonel had done. But no, that was not true, Verity realized slowly, for if she were honest with herself, she must admit that her emotions toward the Colonel were the same as they had always been. It was just that she had not hitherto recognized that they were composed of the warmth and affection that she would feel for anyone whose friendship she valued highly, and that, indeed, she felt for Mrs. Wickersham, and that, these past few days, she had come to feel also for Miss Nightingale.

However, try as she might, Verity could not equate these same emotions with those she now felt toward the Earl. Her feelings for him *were* different, somehow. For when she had learned that the Colonel was affianced, her pain and disappointment, in truth, had been due more to the bursting of the bubble of her innermost hopes and dreams than from any real loss of the man himself, whom she had never believed would ever belong to her, in any event. Rather, she had envisioned a suit of shining armor in her mind and placed Colonel Sherbourne into it, whether it had fit him or not. But that was not the fairy-tale guise in which she viewed the Earl, and the idea of him perhaps marrying Miss Gwendolyn Marchmont, who had undoubtedly set her cap for him, was like a sharp blade being stabbed deep into Verity's heart.

So, Miss Collier, you have a yearning to travel to the far-flung reaches of the earth, do you? What other aspirations do you hold? I wonder. Do you also long for a home, a husband and children of your own? the Earl's words to her that day in the rhododendron bower now echoed once more in her ears.

Do not all women, my lord?

No, they don't.

Was it of Miss Marchmont that he had spoken that day? Verity wondered curiously now. Did he perhaps erroneously believe that any addresses he paid her might ultimately prove in vain, or did he recognize, as Verity did, and despair at the thought, that Miss Marchmont yearned not for a home, but a mansion;

not for a husband, but a provider; and not for children, but for baubles?

Verity did not know. She knew only that she loved him, that it was this that had kept her tongue still when she might have cried out the true identity of the infamous highwayman Black Jack Raven, thereby exposing the Earl and his crimes.

The thought of these last gave her pause, but then she remembered that he must have some good cause for the deeds, however unknown to her at this moment, and that he had claimed that all the stolen money and valuables were always returned. As the Colonel had not denied this, it must be true. What, then, could be the Earl's motive? Of this, too, was Verity in ignorance. It did not matter, she thought. She would surely learn the answer when she confronted him and requested an explanation. Until then, she could not, would not, believe ill of him, who had somehow grown so very dear to her heart.

Thus reassuring herself, Verity undressed and pulled on her nightgown and wrapper. Then she sat down upon the cushioned bench at the foot of her bed, before the easel upon which stood the picture that had been slowly progressing over the passing weeks.

Lifting the cloth that covered it, she contemplated the painting silently. Then, after a time, taking her brush from the small jar of turpentine and opening her paint box to remove her palette, she set to work again, painting until the wee hours of the morning, as the storm continued unabated outside. She worked on the picture just as she had played the sonata, as though possessed by some strange force stronger than her own self, pouring forth all her wild, passionate emotions, the secrets of her heart.

At long last, she paused. Did she require any further proof of her own feelings, it was to be found here, Verity realized. For now, she observed that to the painting's shingled beach swept by the breakers, she had at some point—she did not remember when—added a female silkie dancing with wild abandon beneath the moon, her seal's pelt tossed to one side upon the rocks. The silkie was naked, wrapped only in the strands of her long dark-brown hair the color of her soft sealskin, one thick tress of which was braided and threaded with a crimson rib- and tied in a love knot. Above, on the crumbling cliffs, a tall dark man spied upon the silkie, poised to creep down to the shore to steal away her seal's pelt and hide it forever so that she could never again return to the sea, but must stay with him always.

Somehow, Verity knew the picture was finished now—and that it was the best work she had ever before done. In all her life, she perhaps would never again paint anything so powerful and beautiful as this haunting, otherworldly picture. Dipping the end of her brush into black paint, she carefully signed her name in the lower, right-hand corner.

In some dim corner of her mind, she recognized that her love for the Earl was as futile as would prove the silkie's quest to return to the sea once her seal- skin had been stolen and concealed. For what was she, Verity, to him?

Naught—nor would she ever be.

* * *

The following afternoon, after attending church, then returning to the manor for a late breakfast, the guests departed, and the household quieted as it had not done since their arrival. But despite the pall that now seemed to hang over the manor, Verity was not sorry to see them go. Only the loss of Colonel Sherbourne and Miss Nightingale did she regret, and these two, she hoped to see again, although she did not yet know when that might happen.

The Earl himself, she did not chance to meet for several long days afterward, nor was she summoned into his presence. Instead, he remained closeted in his study or library, and when she thought about it, Verity supposed he must be resting, rather than working, for she felt certain it had cost him an almost superhuman effort to appear before his guests as though nothing were wrong, when, in fact, he had been painfully wounded and weakened by loss of blood. But as he often worked at length in either his study or his library, the Earl's long hours there were not remarked upon by any in the household, and so she presumed that he and Mr. Ashfield, the valet, had succeeded in covering up his injury from all save herself.

Life went on as before, and Verity was as content—or discontent—as she had ever been, happy to be at the manor and thus near to him who owned it, but yearning restlessly, as always, for something more than what was her own lot in life.

When her afternoons were free, she walked in the gardens and park, upon the hills and the heaths, and to St. Ives, where she wandered along the narrow, twisting cobblestone streets of the Downalong and sat upon the harbor wall with the old men who smoked their pipes, watching the fishing boats and the dolphins in the bays, the seagulls that flew overhead and strutted upon the shore, and the sailors and miners who came and went at the Sloop, where they imbibed a pint or two of ale. But never again did Verity linger so late that she must walk back to St. Aubyn manor in the dark or pass by the lodge after nightfall. In that regard, she had learned her lesson. Even in the daylight, she generally tried to avoid the place and its odd, taciturn servants, Mr. and Mrs. Ythnow, who looked after the Earl's invalid mother-in-law, Lady Kenhebres.

Whenever she spied the lodge in the distance or was compelled to pass by it on her way to and from St. Ives, Verity wondered what kind of a life the poor, elderly lady must live there inside its four walls, with all the curtains always drawn tight and such a peculiar couple to wait upon her. Perhaps there were some things worse, Verity reflected, than being a plain, penniless governess with only a few talents to recommend her.

Of the guests who had spent four days at the manor, she heard little. Nor, much to Mrs. Wickersham's disappointment, were any more invited. "For I did so hope there would be others," the housekeeper said, sighing, "and that Miss Marchmont, at least, would return, for his lordship seemed much taken with her, I believed. Physically, she is much

like the poor Lady Tamsyn was—God rest her soul—
and perhaps in other ways, as well.''

But for herself, Verity could only be glad that Miss
Marchmont had not come back to the manor, and she
thought Mrs. Wickersham very much mistaken in lik-
ening that haughty, spiteful lady to the deceased
Lady St. Aubyn, whom the Earl had so dearly loved
and lost to such a terribly tragic, untimely death.

One day, once more dwelling upon this last, Verity
found her way again to the cemetery on the grounds
of the manor, to Lady St. Aubyn's great stone sep-
ulcher. There, pushing open the ornate wrought-iron
gate, which was not locked, she carefully descended
the treacherous, mossy, crumbling steps into the dank
cold vault and, once her eyes had adjusted to the
relative darkness within—for the mausoleum was illuminated only by the sunlight that filtered inside
from the gate—approached the solitary crypt that
was Lady St. Aubyn's own.

No granite effigy was carved upon this. Instead,
the heavy slab that sealed the stone coffin was
smooth, chiseled only with Lady St. Aubyn's name
and the dates of her birth and premature death, followed by the words *Rest in peace,* nothing more.
Dust layered the tomb; cobwebs draped its ceiling
and corners; and it smelled of moisture, mold and
decay. Save for Verity's own, no footsteps had trodden herein for quite some time. She found that
strange, and despite how much she longed not to believe it, she could not now help but remember the
rumor Loveday had imparted to her, that the Earl had

killed his wife. Verity shuddered at the notion. Surely, it was not true!

Yet she could not forget the fact that he and Black Jack Raven must be one and the same man. So, of what other crimes he might indeed be guilty, she cringed to think.

Earlier, she had cut a bouquet of flowers from the gardens, and this, she now laid upon the top of the crypt's stone slab. Then she ascended once more into the pale sunlight of the summer that stretched even now toward autumn and, in doing so, brought days that were often damp and chilly. Shivering in the wind and drawing the pelisse she wore more closely about her, Verity walked on through the gardens that sloped down to the dark, jagged cliffs that climbed above the ocean's edge, until, at last, she stood upon these, looking down at the rocks and shingled beach below, to where Lady St. Aubyn had, two years ago, fallen to her death.

It was here that the Earl had found her—and where he found Verity, too. Above the sounds of the wind and the sea, she did not hear his approach or his calling of her name, so that when she turned and spied him walking toward her, carrying a parcel wrapped in brown paper, she was startled. Unbidden into her mind came again Loveday's assertion that there were those who speculated that the Earl had murdered his wife, and of a sudden, it occurred to Verity that if he were indeed the notorious highwayman Black Jack Raven, as she suspected and believed, he might have good cause to kill her, too.

At that idea, she unwittingly flinched and shrank

away, and as she did so, her line of vision shifted so that, without warning, she became disoriented. Her head swam dizzily with vertigo, and then she staggered and fell. As she pitched forward, she caught a glimpse of the Earl's utterly stricken countenance as now, hoarsely shouting her name and dropping the package he held, he desperately raced toward her.

"Verity! Oh, my God, Verity! I thought—I thought—"

"Shhh. Hush, my lord, please. You must not carry on this way. I know what you thought, so there is no need to explain. However, as you can see, I am perfectly all right—just a little shaken, that's all. I'm absolutely terrified of heights, so I was never close enough to the cliffs' edge to topple over, and I wouldn't even have stumbled and fallen down if I hadn't been so surprised to see you that I momentarily lost my bearings, for I did not hear you approach."

"No, you were gone far away from me—into the Otherworld, whence you come, I fancy, for there was upon your face and in your misty eyes that strange, fey expression I sometimes see when, in your mind and imagination, you have slipped the bounds of this earthly world and ventured into that other."

"It is as Colonel Sherbourne once told me—you are moonstruck, my lord."

Gradually, Verity became aware of how Lord St. Aubyn held her in his strong embrace where they knelt upon the damp ground, and although she was loath to move from the circle of his arms, she knew she must, that she could not answer for the consequences otherwise. For there was upon his own dark visage such an expression of intensity and passion when he gazed at her that it both frightened and excited her beyond all measure. Her heart beat too swiftly and erratically in her breast, and her breath came quickly and shallowly, as though she had run a long way.

Confused and agitated, her eyes suddenly downcast and a tide of crimson sweeping across her cheeks, she attempted to rise, but for an interminable moment as fraught with portent as the air before a storm, her employer tightened his grip upon her, holding her still where she was. For one wild, utterly thrilling instant, Verity thought that he meant to kiss her. But finally, instead, he assisted her to her feet, then reluctantly released her. Retrieving his parcel and laying it on a rock at his feet, he stood beside her, staring down at the shingled beach just as she herself had only minutes before.

"I trust you suffered no lasting injury, my lord, and are now mended." Verity spoke at last, hesitant to disrupt his contemplation, but wanting to broach one of the subjects uppermost in her mind, even so.

"Yes, thank you, madam. The wound has healed and no longer troubles me, and I am indebted to you for your assistance on the east-tower stairs and afterward, and for your silence, too." The Earl paused for a moment, as though collecting and ordering his thoughts. Then he continued. "No doubt, you have been wondering how I received my injury, and because you are by no means a fool, you will most likely have examined in a new light things that perhaps have puzzled you in the past, and also things to which, for your own sake, Miss Collier, I most earnestly wish you were not privy.''

"Is it—Is it as I suspect and believe, then, my lord? Are you—Are you and Black Jack Raven one and the same man?''

"How to answer that question? Am I a highwayman, a robber, a thief, who preys upon unsuspecting vehicles to relieve their occupants of their money and their valuables? No, that is not I, madam. Rather, it is but a dangerous, daring role I have for some time now assumed and played to the very best of my ability, like an actor upon a stage.''

"But...why?'' Verity's brow was knitted in a puzzled frown.

"To tell you that, Miss Collier, would perhaps imperil your life, as well as my own, and that, I would never willingly choose to do. However, it may be that without a clear knowledge and understanding of what I do and its critical importance to England, you will either inadvertently or deliberately betray me in some manner, and that, also, is a risk I cannot afford to take. Thus am I torn in two directions and know not what course of action to follow. Which is the lesser of the two evils? I ask myself. To speak or to remain silent? In my mind, which, as you have doubtless observed, is cool, detached and logical, I am quite certain of the answer. But in my heart, which is as yet unknown to you, I feel desperately that I must choose the other option.''

"You speak in riddles, my lord, and so I do not comprehend you. But in any case, to follow the dictates of one's own mind and conscience must always be thought the wisest path,'' Verity advised, ''for the heart is foolish and capable of deceiving us and leading us astray.''

''Yes, that is true—although I know my own heart to be free of any imprudence or guile. Now, madam, suppose you were offered such a devilish choice as I am faced with, where you could save the lives of many who were wholly unknown to you or the life of a single one who had grown as vital and necessary to you as the very air you breathed. What would you do?''

''I...well, I should try to save them all, my lord. But if I could not, then, of course, I would choose to save as many as I could, however dear the cost to me.''

''Ah, Verity, Verity—whose name means Truth! With its keen blade do you pierce my very heart and soul! Would that I could save but that essential one! That I could cast off all my duties and obligations, and tell the rest of the world to go to the devil and be damned! But you would not respect me if I did, I fear. So, very well, then. Let it be thus. I will speak—and be honest in the telling—and then, upon these small shoulders of yours—'' firmly but tenderly, he laid his hands upon them ''—you must bear a portion of the weight that I myself have carried these past months, and carry still. But in truth, I know you are strong enough for the task, for have I not twice now witnessed your bravery, when you refused to part with your locket to Black Jack Raven, and when you turned to confront me and my horse upon the manor's drive, believing us some ghastly apparition?

"This, then, is my tale. Hugh and Mrs. Wicker-sham have got the right of it—there *are* French spies here in England, and one of the cleverest and most cunning of these calls Cornwall his base of operations. In the hope of catching him, the War Office in London, to which, as you will no doubt remember, I am attached, devised a plan whereby I would pose as the highwayman Black Jack Raven, in which infamous guise I could safely mingle and pass amongst thieves, smugglers, wreckers and others of such ilk, and thereby attempt to ferret out the spy here in Cornwall—one Fouquet, by name, although, naturally, he does not go by it here, but has assumed an alias. Since my cousin, Hugh, as you know, is colonel of the dragoon guards stationed at Truro and a part of the scheme, that is the reason why Black Jack has never been captured and hanged.

"Recently, I have got quite close to discovering the identity that Fouquet is employing here in Cornwall, although I've yet to nail it down in total. But of course, the nearer I come to learning what false role he plays here, the nearer he undoubtedly comes, as well, to learning my own true one. That is why I could not afford to allow anyone in the household save you to find out I had been wounded at the same time as my own carriage had been robbed and my footman Ned had fired upon Black Jack Raven, hitting him. Whilst I might easily have accounted for the coincidence to my guests by claiming a hunting accident or by some other such story, it is possible that Fouquet would have heard of the incident and guessed the real truth of the matter. That, I could not afford, for my entire purpose in setting once more upon my own coach, with all the young ladies who were my houseguests in it, was to divert suspicion from myself, thus making Fouquet doubt any ideas he might possess that I and Black Jack Raven are identical.

"I could have shot Ned, thereby disabling him— for I am an expert marksman and can drill the pip out of a playing card at fifty paces. But as, naturally, I had no desire to shoot my own footman, and it seemed most unlikely to me that he, a mere footman, would actually be able to wound me, I resisted the uncharitable impulse—only to get a bullet in my shoulder for my pains! Quite a lucky shot, it was, that Ned fired!" Once more Lord St. Aubyn paused, gathering breath and his thoughts. Then he went on.

"Now, Verity, you know what is in my mind— but not yet what is in my heart." Slowly reaching into the pocket of his waistcoat, her employer drew forth his gold pocket watch and, pressing its clasp, sprang open the cover. "When I informed Miss Marchmont and the other young ladies that all the money and valuables pilfered by Black Jack Raven had always been located, reclaimed and returned to their rightful owners by Hugh and the dragoon guards, I lied. There is one treasure that I kept for myself." He showed her his open pocket watch, where, inside the gold cover, the lock he had stolen from her thick dark-brown hair nestled, bound with a short, slender crimson silk riband tied into a love knot. "This, I could not bring myself to part with.

"I was fascinated by you that night at Jamaica Inn—by your quaint, charming manner, by your obviously intelligent interest in all the wild tales that I spun for you then, and, most of all, by your strange, fey countenance with your eyes the silver of the moon, the color of the mist blown inland from the sea. But it was in that moment when I held up the carriage and when, despite having my pistol aimed straight at your heart, you dared to defy me and refuse me your mother's locket that I first began to love you, I think. And then, that night when I nearly rode you down upon the drive and, afterward, lifted you in my arms, and you lay with your long, soft dark-brown hair wrapped around you like a silkie's pelt, I knew that you belonged to me and no other— for I had stolen your sealskin, you see, and hidden it away in my pocket watch forever."

With a sharp little click, the Earl suddenly snapped shut the gold cover, returning the pocket watch with its secreted lock of hair to the pocket of his waistcoat. Then he bent and picked up the package he had earlier laid upon the rock at his feet.

"That afternoon you helped me up the east-tower stairs to my bedroom, I told you that I owed you another frock. This is the material I bought for it."

Breaking the strings that bound the parcel, then unwrapping the brown paper, he showed Verity the bolt of cloth he had purchased for her. Involuntarily, her breath caught in her throat, for the fabric was even finer than the sea-green silk—a shimmering satin the soft, lustrous white shade of mother-of-pearl.

"Marry me, Verity," he said.

Sixteen

The Interloper

Ominia tempus revelat (Time reveals all.).

> *Apologeticus*
> —Tertullian

Terror in the house does roar,
But Pity stands before the door.

> *Poems from Blake's Notebook:*
> *Terror in the House*
> —William Blake

Go! you may call it madness, folly;
You shall not chase my gloom away!
There's such a charm in melancholy
I would not if I could be gay.

> *To—*
> —Samuel Rogers

Verity was stunned and rendered speechless by the Earl's demand. At first, she thought she must not have heard him aright, that some trick of the wind or the sea or both had distorted and obscured his true words. Finding her tongue at last, she asked him to repeat them, and when he did, she was immediately silenced once more. For in that moment, she was filled both with unbearable joy and an equally unbearable agony. She hardly dared to breathe, to hope that he was serious. She thought that if she dared to draw breath, she would surely shatter some dream so beautiful as to be wholly unimaginable, and she would be abruptly cast into rude, pitiless awakening. She thought that if she dared to hope, he would surely laugh at her, telling her that it was but a jest, and that she ought not to have aspirations above her station.

"Verity, I am in torment! What is your answer?"

At that, tears brimmed suddenly in her eyes, and although she tried to hold them back, they spilled over to trickle slowly down her soft pale cheeks.

"My—My lord, I do most earnestly entreat you... I sincerely and ardently pray you...please do not tease—tease me in this fashion, for if you are not—not serious, I do not think I can endure it! But still, I know that, somehow, I—I must, for in truth, you cannot mean other than to—to make a mock of me!''

''The devil, you say! I mean nothing of the sort!'' Lord St. Aubyn growled, looking so very dark and fierce in that instant that he frightened her. ''Do you intend to stand there and tell me no, madam, that you will not marry me, that you have no love for me, that you feel nothing in your heart for me beyond what a governess should feel for her employer? Deuce take it! I shan't believe it if you do, Verity, I promise you! I shall have an honest answer, by God, and hear what I know to be the truth—that you feel as I do and long for this marriage just as fervently as I do— or else I shan't be responsible for my actions!''

So saying, he tossed the opened package he held back down upon the rock at his feet, then, without warning, seized her and pulled her to him roughly, despite how she struggled against him, like some small, trapped wild bird beating its wings desperately and helplessly against a glass, not understanding why it could not fly onward.

''Verity...Verity,'' he muttered against her hair, his voice harsh with emotion, as he clasped her to him, compelling her arms to her sides and kissing her face and mouth in a way that left her even more breathless. ''Be still...be still, for I do not mean to hurt you. Nor to make sport of you, I swear it!''

''How can I believe you?'' she cried, sobbing violently against his broad, comforting chest. ''For none knows better than I the difference in our stations, the fact that I am poor and plain, with naught but a few hard-won talents to recommend me! What am I, compared to someone like Miss Marchmont?''

''A rose as to a thorn. That is your answer. I have no need of fortune, and beauty in things exists in the mind which contemplates them. You are as beautiful as the moon over the moors to me, and that is all that is important. As for your talents, I cannot myself count them as but few, for in my own mind, they are so many as to be countless. What are you, compared to Miss Marchmont and others of her ilk? A rare diamond among a handful of paste jewels, that is what. I warn you, I *shall* have you. Do you forget? I hold your sealskin, my dearest silkie, and because of that, you can never more slip away into the mists and sea of the Otherworld and be lost to me forever. I shall bind you to me and tie the silken skeins into a love knot, without beginning or end. Marry me, Verity! Marry me!''

In the face of all this and his urgent demand, Verity could no longer go on blindly doubting hiᶜ sincerity, and she ceased trying to fight against him and, sighing deeply, laid her head upon his shoulder.

''Yes…yes,'' she answered ardently, in response to his proposal. Then, ''Can this indeed be true?'' she asked, bemused. ''That you really want me for your wife? For it seems like but a dream to me, my lord, from which I keep thinking I shall at any instant awaken, finding you and everything about us evanesced like brume beneath the sun—or vanished into

the mists themselves, like the Otherworld of which
you speak.''

''It *is* true, I assure you. I am no vision from your
dreams, but a flesh-and-blood man, as real as you.
Do you not feel my heart beating against your
own...our two hearts beating as one?'' Clasping her
hand, he pressed it against his chest, over his own
heart, to demonstrate the truth of his words. ''Come.
Walk with me—for this is a place that haunts me
still, although it shall have a happier memory now,
as well, and glad I am of it.''

The reference to his first wife cast a shadow over
what was otherwise the happiest day of Verity's entire life. The knowledge that the Earl had loved
someone else prior to her was a terrible pang in her
heart. Despite what he had told her, how could she
possibly ever hope to measure up to one such as
Lady St. Aubyn must have been? Verity had seen the
portrait of her dead rival, hanging in that lady's old
bedroom, and she thought she could not hold a candle to that incomparable beauty fashioned in the tall
blond mold of Miss Marchmont, but with such gra-
ciousness and goodness that, even now, Lord St. Aubyn did not want to be reminded of her and how and
where she had died.

At the realization, Verity began once more to be
beset by uncertainty. But somehow, her employer
sensed this and reassured her so fervently and kindly
yet again as they strolled through the gardens toward
the manor that she felt ashamed of herself and earnestly resolved to doubt him no more. They did not
linger longer, however, for the chill and dampness of

the wind that swept in from the ocean was such that the Earl did not wish Verity to be exposed to it, and he escorted her into the house, declaring that she must change for the evening, anyway, as he wanted her and the children to dine with him tonight.

"We will be a real family," he said, his black eyes gleaming with both love and desire as they surveyed her.

Once inside the manor, he called for the entire staff to be assembled in the entrance hall, where he announced that Verity had done him the honor of consenting to be his bride. Clearly, the servants were very startled by the news, but they duly offered their congratulations and best wishes for their lord and lady's happiness, and in the end, the awkward moment passed off as well as could be expected under the circumstances. After that, Verity retired to her bedroom to prepare for dinner, and just shortly, Loveday arrived to assist her, plainly all agog at the notion that Verity was to be the Earl's wife.

"What are they all saying downstairs, Loveday?" Verity inquired anxiously. "Do they think his lordship has taken complete leave of all his senses? That I have forgotten my place and become an upstart like the little Corsican dictator across the Channel in France?"

"Well, there be no denyin' that they was mostly all taken by complete surprise, miss," the chambermaid reported, as she fastened up Verity's sea-green silk gown. "But ta tell 'ee t' truth, I dunnat believe they know what ta think! Thou art respected an' well liked in t' household, o' course, fer thou've nivver given yerself airs nor treated anyone differently from another, not from t' lowliest scullery maid ta Mr. Drummond himself. So that makes it more difficult fer them ta criticize his lordship's choice—not that anybody would, naturally, except behind closed doors, where his lordship would not be bound ta hear. Howe'er, all things considered, everyone knows that thou was gently born an' bred, an' that 'twas due ta yer father's estate havin' been entailed when thou was a child that thou was left destitute an' turned out by yer distant cousin. So there can be no objections on that score, an' as fer anything else, why, I'll wager his lordship is rich enough ta do as he pleases an' not ta have ta worry about what anybody else might think o' him, including his servants. Fer meself, I wish thee well, miss, an' if'n 'twill not be thought too bold o' me, may I say that when thou chooses yer lady's maid, I hope thou will remember me.''

"Oh, Loveday! Of course I will! For how could I possibly forget all you've done for me ever since I' came here to St. Aubyn manor? I promise you that if I have any say at all in the matter, the position will be yours just as soon as such things are decided, for I cannot think of anyone else more deserving of the post, nor who would suit me so well nor serve me so loyally.''

"Thank 'ee, miss. I appreciate that more'n I can say. An' in that event, will thou—will thou teach me ta speak proper, miss, like yerself? Fer I'd not e'er want ta be thought not fit ta be yer abigail nor ta

embarrass thee amongst all t' other fine ladies an'
their maids.''

"Yes, Loveday, it would be my pleasure to teach
you—and even to instruct you in French, so that you
may also drop the occasional French phrase now and
then, the way Mr. Ashfield does, and thus be thought
all the crack!''

Governess and chambermaid both laughed at that,
as though they were but engaging in idle chitchat and
impossible daydreams, not poised on the threshold of
something real and momentous, which would change
their lives forever.

Her toilette completed, Verity collected the twins
from Trueth.

"Is it true, madam, that you're to marry Papa?''
Meliora queried, as they went downstairs to the small
drawing room.

"Yes, it is.''

"And then will you be our mama?'' Bastian
asked.

"Yes, she will,'' the Earl, overhearing the question as he entered the chamber, replied firmly, "and
somehow, I think you shall both like that very much,
won't you?''

"Oh, yes, Papa!'' they cried, much to Verity's
delight and suddenly tearful emotion, for she was
deeply touched by the youngsters' attachment to her.

Approaching her, Lord St. Aubyn lifted her hand
to his lips, kissing it, before drawing her into his
arms and kissing her again lightly on the mouth.

"I thought we would dine in here, in the small
drawing room,'' he explained, "where we can be

cozy, for the four of us would be lost in the dining room.''

"I agree. I have, in fact, been quaking in my slippers at the very thought of eating in there,'' Verity confessed, "for I'm afraid all this is still quite new and rather unreal to me, so that I should feel like an interloper in the dining room.''

"There is no rush. You will grow accustomed to everything in time, and when you are more comfortable, we will entertain guests here at the manor together, as well...not many at first, until you are certain of yourself, but some I think you will enjoy— Hugh and Miss Nightingale, for a start.''

"Indeed, I would be so pleased to see them both again.''

"And so you shall. But tonight, it will just be the four of us—a family.''

"That is very important to you, my lord, is it not?''

"Yes...there has been no real family here at St. Aubyn for...quite some time now. I want a wife. I want a mother for my children. We—I and the twins—have mourned far longer than we ought. But now, it is time to start anew, for all of us to build a future together as one and to seize the love and happiness that we deserve. This, we shall do, Verity, I promise you—for I will let nothing and no one stand in our way. Ah, dinner is served. Come. Let us eat, and then, afterward, we shall have some music to entertain us.''

The Earl was determined to brook no delay in the wedding. It was to take place the week after the banns had been read. So preparations for it began at once, with a whirl of activity commencing that did not cease for a month. As it had been before the party, the manor was thoroughly cleaned from top to bottom, and Cook was kept busy in the kitchen, cooking and baking an endless assortment of foods, while the butler, Mr. Peacock, once more descended to the basement's wine cellar to choose appropriate libations.

Previously, Verity had assisted with all the work undertaken in the household. Now, as its soon-to-be mistress, it was her responsibility instead to oversee its every aspect, consulting with both Mrs. Wickersham and Mr. Peacock as to what was required, while the Earl spent equally long hours with Mr. Drummond, the steward, riding out over the estate and attending to matters concerning its various enterprises and tenants. Verity's regular morning lessons with the twins were discontinued, although she always made time to read to them and play the piano with them in the evenings, and an advertisement was drafted for insertion into London's *The Times* and *The Gazette,* and county newspapers far and wide, in search of a new governess to replace her in the schoolroom.

Verity often thought about this last, wondering if in some small market town like Belper, in Derbyshire, in some semicharitable institution for girls, like Trowbridge, another young woman huddled in her cheerless cubicle, examining the local newspaper for just such a listing as she herself had searched for.

How frequently she wished she could whisper in that young woman's ear and tell her how happy she would be at St. Aubyn!

For Verity *was* happy—ecstatically so. She was young and in love, and not a day went by, now, that she was not made aware of the fact that she was equally beloved by the object of her affection and adoration. Long-unworn jewels that were Ransleigh heirlooms were bestowed upon her, and bouquets, sweetmeats, love notes and other trifles were regularly left upon the pillows of her bed. A steady stream of merchants and mantua makers came to the manor, from which she selected materials and designs for the gowns, undergarments and other essentials that would comprise her trousseau; and from the bolt of mother-of-pearl satin the Earl had given her, her wedding dress was fashioned, to be adorned with lace and hundreds of seed pearls. No expense was spared.

Yet, sometimes, despite everything—or perhaps because of it—Verity felt overwhelmed, as though she were unequal to the role she sought to play, the tasks she undertook. At such times, she would think that, surely, all was but a dream and that if only she pinched herself hard enough, she would awaken in her bed at Trowbridge to discover that she had lain ill, feverish and delirious for months now, and that no such place as St. Aubyn manor even existed in reality.

"It is not the Otherworld I have come from," Verity told the Earl one night, as they sat before the granite fireplace in the library, "but that I have some-

how crossed over into, as your Celtic ancestors traveled in their swan boats through the mists to that
paradise, never to be seen again. I wonder if I have
simply vanished from the real world, and I think that
even if I have, I shall not be missed there. No one
shall search for me or ponder what has become of
me. How sad it makes me to know that!''

''Then do not dwell upon it, my love, for it is not
true, in any event,'' Lord St. Aubyn declared, glancing up from the chessboard between them, where he
was teaching her how to play the game. ''For if,
somehow, you were indeed to slip from this world
into the Otherworld, you should be missed by everyone here at the manor—most particularly by the children, and by me most deeply of all. And I should
search ceaselessly unto the very ends of the earth for
you and ponder endlessly what had become of you.
Now, do you take heed, my darling, for you do not
concentrate upon our game, and as a result, your
queen is in jeopardy.''

''Oh!'' Hastily, Verity picked up her endangered
queen and moved it to a safer square upon the chessboard, shivering of a sudden, as though a goose had
just walked over her grave.

''What is it? What's wrong?''

''Nothing...just a chill from a draft, I suppose.
The weather worsens. Summer is gone, and autumn
is upon us, I fear.''

From where it lay upon the burgundy-leather chesterfield, the Earl solicitously picked up one of Verity's new fringed cashmere shawls and draped it
around her closely so that she would be warm. Then

he stoked up the fire himself and placed more coal upon it, so that it burned brightly again. "For it will not suit me at all for you to catch cold and fall ill right before our wedding day, my sweet," he told her.

At this, with all its attendant implications, Verity blushed deeply and cast her eyes down modestly, her heart thudding hard and fast in her breast. Having no mother's hand to guide her and having had so little experience of men, she was woefully ignorant of much, save for the things she had heard at Trowbridge, from the gossip of the other girls. While she understood that her marriage must be consummated, Verity was not fully certain about what all that entailed, and deep down inside, she was a little frightened by her own nescience and worried that perhaps she would not please her husband.

Her husband! How strange—and yet how very exciting—those two words seemed to her! In just a few short days, she would be Lord St. Aubyn's wife! Even now, that fact did not seem quite real to her. When the evening had ended, she retired to her bedroom, still feeling as though she must be dreaming it all.

Outside, beyond her windows, the constant Cornish wind rose and fell as it swept and keened across the moors and marshes, snaked its way around distant tors and the nearby hills, and whispered to the soughing ocean whose white-foamed waves swelled, heaving and dipping before they surged inland to dash against the black rocks and to rush over the shingled beaches. Drizzle tapped like ghostly fingers against the lozenged lead-glass panes of the windows, and mist wafted amid the gardens. From the rookery in the park came the cawing and croaking of the night birds crowded for warmth and protection amid the gnarled old trees, and over all, the hazy, ringed moon kept silvery, silent watch.

As she climbed into bed, Verity hoped a storm were not blowing up again, for the Earl had informed her that those of autumn and winter were far worse than what she had already experienced thus far in Cornwall, and one day, in St. Ives, he had pointed out to her how the houses that had been built too near to the shore along the Downalong had had to have all their lower windows tightly and stoutly boarded shut, to prevent the maddened, roiling sea from crashing through and pouring inside when the fierce, thunderous tides of winter rolled in. Now, remembering, she shuddered and huddled more deeply beneath the bedclothes, as though they would somehow defend her from the inhospitable elements and anything else that might threaten in the darkness.

After a long while, Verity slept. But it was a fretful, uneasy slumber, for dreams came to her once more that night...strange, disturbing dreams that eventually metamorphosed into nightmares, in which she was chased by monstrous beasts and phantasmic creatures along endlessly twisting dirt roads and narrow, labyrinthine cobblestone streets until she came to a long, serpentine seashell drive, at whose circular terminus loomed a great, grim, forbidding manor constructed of solid grey slate and surrounded by a terrible, thick, tangled brier amid which blowsy dusky-rose blossoms billowed, shedding and scattering their silken petals upon the brown-grassed lawn, and huge thorns as hard as horn burgeoned, as though to pierce the lowering pewter sky....

Behind her, the gruesome, otherworldly beasts and creatures came on, snorting and snuffling, their breath blowing ominously in her ears and hot against her nape as she ran on desperately toward the portentous, dark-stoned house in the distance. Overhead, the knotted, tortuous branches of the towering, distorted trees standing like dour, giant, misshapen sentinels along the verge fashioned a shadowy woven canopy through which the moonbeams dripped like silvery blood as she raced beneath, her legs growing more leaden with every step she took. The soft-glowing candlelight spilling from the lozenged lead-glass windows of the manor to filter diffusely through the dreadful, choking bramble made this last appear as though it were ablaze, engulfing the house with wildly flickering tongues of flame.

Still, somehow, Verity knew that she must reach it or die, for the hideous, ever increasing pack of beasts and creatures behind her drew ever nearer, harrying her heels, sharp teeth and claws tearing at her hair and plucking menacingly at her cloak. Gasping for breath, a painful stitch in her side, she slogged on, the crushed seashells like marshland beneath her feet now, muckily sucking them under. Ahead, a gargantuan stone fountain rose before the house, fiendishly grinning gargoyles spewing venom from their gaping mouths into the enormous, overflowing basin below, so that Verity thought she would be swept away by

*the vehement, vitriolic outpouring. But still, she
strove ever onward, swimming through the churning
gush of seething poison—although she knew not how
to swim—and then hacking and scrabbling her way
through the treacherous, trailing brier until, at last,
she achieved the manor.*

*Frantically, she pounded hard upon the heavy oak
door. But without warning, its brass, lion's head
knocker came alive beneath her hand, swelling and
expanding to a hundred times its normal size. Snarling and roaring, it lunged toward her, its ferocious,
yawning maw swallowing her whole. When she
emerged from the horrible blackness within, she
stood inside the house. But an eerie pall lay about
it, as though it had slept for a thousand years. Gossamer cobwebs hung from the chandeliers and in the
corners; layers of pale-grey dust enshrouded the
grand staircase and floors; and white sheets swathed
all the furnishings. There was no one home—nor had
there been for aeons. No footsteps trod within, save
for Verity's own as she hurried upstairs to her bedroom, got into bed, and, like a frightened child,
pulled the covers up over her head.*

*For an eternity, it seemed, she lay breathless in
the darkness, suffocating beneath the bedclothes,
waiting with agonizing expectancy...her palms
sweating profusely, her heart thudding horribly in
her breast, her nerves stretched taut and silently
screaming for release, and her ears straining to hear
above the pounding and roaring of her blood. Then,
of a sudden, she heard it! Footsteps sighing and
slithering their way along the passage beyond, until,*

finally, they came to a halt just outside her door. Gooseflesh prickled Verity's skin, and her heart leaped to her throat as the knob rattled, then slowly turned, and then, creaking and groaning on its hinges, the portal swung open wide, then once more closed.

Stealthily, the footsteps advanced across the floor. Someone—or something—was inside her chamber!

In some dark, obscure corner of her mind, she realized she had dreamed this nightmare before, and, desperately, she tried to wake herself up, in the end, by sheer strength of will forcing her eyes open. To her horror, by the shimmering silver moonlight that streamed in through the windows, she observed something diaphanous and white, and that seemed to float at the foot of her bed—an apparition!—one arm outstretched, hand ending in a long, thin, gnarled, bony finger that pointed straight at her.

"Tamsyn...Tamsyn...your life is in grave danger. You must leave this place of death at once!"

As she had once before, Verity began to scream, and to her vast relief, moments later, both the Earl and Mrs. Wickersham, candlesticks in hand, entered her bedroom, while Messrs Drummond, Ashfield and Peacock hovered in the doorway, their own candlesticks held high to illuminate the chamber.

"My love...my love, it's all right. It's all right," Lord St. Aubyn murmured comfortingly, as he gathered her into his strong embrace. "It was only another bad nightmare, that's all."

"No...no, it wasn't!" Verity insisted stubbornly, shrugging on her wrapper and struggling to rise from bed. "Light the lamps! I want my room searched! Please, my lord. There *was* someone here, I just know it!"

"Very well, then. It will do no harm to look, I suppose, and if it will set your mind at ease, my darling—"

"It will."

All the lamps were lit, and a methodical search that left no closet, cabinet or coffer unopened was diligently undertaken of Verity's entire bedroom, including the tower reading nook and her dressing room. In the end, however, much to her despair and disbelief, no one was discovered lurking in her chamber. But then, suddenly, she remembered her bedroom door and how it butted up against the corner of one of the wardrobes when open, creating a hidden niche.

"Wait!" she cried, scrambling from bed and running frantically toward the dressing room. "Wait!"

Grabbing hold of the portal, Verity abruptly slammed it shut, gasping aloud in shock as her action revealed an unknown woman standing concealed and trembling violently behind the door. The stranger was tall, thin and elderly, with long, wispy grey hair that straggled wildly from her head and with pale-blue eyes that glittered like ice as they stared confusedly at everyone now crowded incredulously and accusingly about her. She wore a long, gauzy white nightgown that was torn at the hem, which floated and fluttered when she moved, and her feet were bare.

"Good God!" the Earl expostulated, as he spied her. "Lady Kenhebres!"

Seventeen

The Earl's Tale

The splendor falls on castle walls
And snowy summits old in story:
The long light shakes across the lakes,
And the wild cataract leaps in glory.
Blow, bugle, blow, set the wild echoes flying,
Blow, bugle; answer, echoes, dying, dying, dying.

> *The Princess: The Splendor Falls*
> —Alfred, Lord Tennyson

Ask me no more: thy fate and mine are sealed:
I strove against the stream and all in vain:
Let the great river take me to the main:
No more, dear love, for at a touch I yield;
Ask me no more.

> *The Princess: Ask Me No More*
> —Alfred, Lord Tennyson

Now lies the Earth all Danaë to the stars,
And all thy heart lies open unto me.

The Princess: Now Sleeps the Crimson Petal
—Alfred, Lord Tennyson

"Tamsyn...Tamsyn...your life is in grave danger. You must leave this place of death at once!" Lady Kenhebres, the Earl's mother-in-law, chanted again her strange lament, in her eerie, melancholy voice. Then, suddenly, seeming to recover her wits, she pointed straight at Verity and said, "You cannot marry him—for he will murder you, just as he did my daughter!"

Gasps all around greeted this announcement, and when Verity glanced up at Lord St. Aubyn, who stood at her side, she observed that his dark, saturnine visage was filled with fury, and that a muscle pulsed alarmingly in his set jaw. Still, when he at last spoke, it was kindly enough.

"Lady Kenhebres, you are ill and should not be out of your bed, especially in your nightgown and with your feet bare, and in such inclement weather, besides. Mrs. Wickersham shall take you into her chamber, where you may warm yourself by the fire, and then I will have the carriage drive you back to the lodge." Turning, he addressed the housekeeper. "Mrs. Wickersham, please be good enough to conduct Lady Kenhebres to your bedroom, and there, see to her comfort. Do not permit her to leave your chamber, for, as you know, she has long been unwell and may do some injury to herself or perhaps even others in her current state. I will station Mr. Ashfield to guard your door, in case you should have need of assistance.''

''Yes, my lord. Thank you, my lord. I appreciate that, although, in truth, I doubt that poor Lady Kenhebres will cause any more trouble tonight. She is usually docile enough if one deals with her gently. Come, my lady,'' the housekeeper urged the elderly woman quietly. ''It is I—Agatha Wickersham—you remember me, don't you? Come, and let me take you into my room, where you can sit before the fire and have a cup of tea.''

Mutely, Lady Kenhebres finally allowed herself to be led away.

''Go with them, Ashfield,'' the Earl directed. ''Drummond, be good enough to nip upstairs and instruct Lathrop to have the lamps and a fire lit in the library, and Cook to prepare a light repast...some tea and soup or sandwiches, whatever may be on hand and quickly and easily made ready. Peacock, send one of the footmen down to the lodge to wake Ythnow and his wife, and to inform them about what's happened. Have a second footman go out to the stables to tell Howel that he's to take the coach down to the lodge to fetch the Ythnows, then come back here to collect Lady Kenhebres.''

''Yes, my lord. At once, my lord.'' Bowing, the butler departed to carry out his orders. But only moments later, he returned, the Ythnows hard on his heels. "It would seem, my lord, that Ythnow and his wife discovered Lady Kenhebres's absence from the lodge and immediately instituted a search for her," Mr. Peacock announced. "Spying all the lamps being lit throughout the manor, they surmised that perhaps she had come here."

"Aye, we was worried about her." Eval Ythnow shuffled his feet nervously and licked his lips. "There be strange comings an' goings an' doings here at t' manor, m'lord. I've seen 'em fer meself! An' we didn't want owt ta happen ta poor Lady Kenhebres."

"Yes, well, I fear it is Lady Kenhebres herself who has proved responsible for any peculiar goings-on here at St. Aubyn, Ythnow," the Earl declared firmly. "She is in Mrs. Wickersham's chamber now, so you and Doryty may see to her there. Ned—" he directed his attention to the footman, who had appeared on the scene "—do you have something to report?"

"Aye, m'lord. Cook says ta inform thee that t' refreshment thou requested is nearly ready, an' does thou want it served in t' library or elsewhere?"

"The library." The Earl turned once more to Verity.

"Verity, my sweet, get dressed, and then join me downstairs in the library, please—for I've no doubt whatsoever that you are consumed by curiosity and perhaps not a little fear at this moment, and I will not have you lie here in increasing anxiety until dawn, wondering if what Lady Kenhebres told you is true and I murdered my first wife."

''Thank you, my lord. Give me but a few minutes, and then I shall be there directly.''

After he had left her, Verity clothed herself more rapidly than she had before done in her life, riddled—as the Earl had suspected—with doubts, suspicions and fright, and silently cursing her trembling hands, which fumbled helplessly at the fastenings of her dove-grey gown. It was the first one she had happened to take from her wardrobe. She felt as though she were still in the throes of some nightmare, and she wondered, horribly, if the only reason the Earl had asked her to marry him was, in fact, to ensure her silence about his masquerading as Black Jack Raven, until he could get rid of her permanently at some later date, without rousing any suspicions.

At last, Verity managed to finish dressing, but in the interests of time and her nerves, she did not even try to brush out her hair and pin it up in the neat chignon in which she usually wore it. Instead, she left it in the braid into which she customarily plaited it at night, before bed. Then, taking a deep breath in a futile attempt to calm herself, she descended the grand staircase to the entrance hall, whence she made her way to the library.

There, the Earl awaited her, garbed soberly in black and grey, and holding a snifter of brandy in one hand. A lock of his black hair fell carelessly across his forehead, shadowing his face racked with emotion, and he looked more drawn and wearier than she had ever seen him, more so even than when, wounded and bleeding, he had struggled to climb the steps in the east tower. At the sight of him, Verity felt her heart lurch and turn over in her breast.

"My lord—" she advanced into the room, closing its doors behind her "—I came only to tell you that your fears, while understandable, are ungrounded. I do not believe what Lady Kenhebres told me. I know you did not kill your first wife—that you loved her deeply."

At that, Lord St. Aubyn swore softly, shaking his head slowly in despair and disbelief before running one hand wildly through his shaggy black hair.

"Loved her? *Loved* her?" Much to Verity's utter confusion and distress, he laughed tersely, mirthlessly, at her well-intentioned words. "I *loathed* her!" he abruptly ground out. "Utterly and vehemently!"

Then, downing in one long swallow what remained of his brandy, he violently dashed the empty glass upon the granite fireplace, where it shattered into a million pieces. The expression on his dark visage in that moment was that of some demon, some burning-eyed fiend! Horrified, Verity gasped, her hands flying to her open mouth, as though to prevent the sound from escaping, so as not to draw any attention to herself. Wide-eyed with sudden apprehension, remembering how, on the night of his arrival at the manor, he had threatened to beat her, as well as all of Loveday's warnings about his black temper, Verity took a step back from him, and then another.

Observing this, the Earl suddenly buried his face in one hand, sighing heavily. When he once more glanced at her, his face looked a good deal less satanic but no less anguished.

"Sit down," he commanded, and then again when she hesitated, "sit down, Verity. I'm not going to hurt you, I swear it!"

Thus reassured, she finally did as he instructed, gingerly taking a seat upon the burgundy-leather chesterfield. Her fringed cashmere shawl, which he had wrapped around her so tenderly only a short while earlier that evening still lay there, and, tears starting in her eyes at the sight of it and at the memory it evoked, Verity gently gathered it up and pulled it close about her. A timid knock upon the door interrupted her reverie, and at Lord St. Aubyn's "Come," Mr. Peacock and the footman Ned entered the chamber, bearing tea and the light repast that had been ordered, all of which they set down upon a round table that stood between two wing chairs.

Spying the splintered glass scattered all over the hearth, Ned inquired, "Shall I clean that up, m'lord?"

"No, the housemaids can do it later. Leave us, and see that we are not disturbed hereafter," Lord St. Aubyn directed curtly. Once the two servants had gone, he poured a cup of tea and filled a plate for Verity, then handed them to her. Then, seeing that she was comfortably situated, he said, "I must apologize, madam, for my earlier outburst. However, I believe that once I have related my sad story, you will understand. So...let me tell you now the real truth about my marriage to Tamsyn Kenhebres and what happened that night she died." The Earl paused, now pouring himself a cup of tea, also, as he collected his thoughts. Then, slowly sitting down in one of the wing chairs, he continued.

"I met Tamsyn several years ago, in London. Her parents, Earl and Countess Kenhebres, had brought her to town for the Season. At the start, I was much taken with her, and despite the fact that she had numerous admirers, it was I whom she finally accepted and wed.

"I like to think we were happy together for at least a little while, but the truth is that we really never were, and after the twins were born, during the second year of our marriage, things went steadily downhill. For beneath her beautiful facade, Tamsyn was everything I would have despised if only before marrying her, I had grasped her true nature—which she had most carefully and artfully concealed from me, however. Vain, selfish, disloyal, unfaithful...suffice it to say that my list of grievances against her is quite a long one.

"Worst of all, however, was the fact that she was a most exceedingly unnatural mother, who never wanted any children—despite that she knew full well before we wed that I required and hoped for an heir. She actively disliked the twins from the very moment of their conception, I do believe, and although I hoped this was merely the result of her confinement and would pass after their birth, that was, tragically, not to prove the case, as you shall hear.

"Instead, the older the youngsters grew, the more Tamsyn loathed them, for in her weak, spiteful brain, she saw them as a reminder that she, too, inevitably aged and would not be young and beautiful forever, and unfortunately, that was everything to her. She had never cultivated either her mind or that black marble stone she called a heart, so what talents and accomplishments she could indeed boast of were along lines similar to those of Miss Marchmont. Like all young ladies, Tamsyn sketched and painted, but there was no animation to her pictures. She played the piano, but without emotion.

"Her principal goal in life had been to catch a rich husband by whatever means she could, even if it meant duping him in the process, and thereafter to indulge herself however she pleased, acquiring a plethora of servants, gowns, jewels and all the other fancy trappings that such women feel are vital and necessary to their importance and well-being.

"With the exception of her perverted attitude toward the twins—which, whilst inexcusable and highly disturbing to me, I could nevertheless control and counteract by simply ensuring that she never had any contact with them—I could have borne most of Tamsyn's excesses with impassivity, if not gladness, for, as you yourself know, Verity, I am not poor, and I would have taken unrelenting steps to curb her before being brought even close to ruin, besides. Had she truly loved me, I would have grudged her nothing. Even as it was, I did my duty by her. For as I saw it—however bitterly, by then—I had made my bed, regardless of how stupidly, and now, I must lie in it.

"What I could not swallow, however—as could no man with any pride in himself, his rank, and his

achievements—were Tamsyn's countless infideli-
ties.'' Here, the Earl paused to sip from his teacup
and also to light a cheroot, which he drew on deeply
before he went on. ''By this time, I was increasingly
away from home a great deal...attached to the War
Office in London and burying myself in my work in
order to escape from the sorry marriage I had made.
And for a while, fearing the consequences to herself
otherwise, Tamsyn was clever and cunning enough
to ensure that no rumors of her misbehavior reached
my ears.

''Things came to a head, however, when I finally
learned the truth. I was in London at the time, whilst
she was here at St. Aubyn manor. In my own carriage—the very same one that bore you here—I left
the city immediately, traveling swiftly, halting only
to change horses along the way, and I eventually arrived here late in the evening a day or two afterward.
I had deliberately not notified anyone beforehand of
my coming, so Tamsyn had no warning of it. Upon
being informed that, ill with a migraine, she had already retired upstairs to her bedroom, I instantly went
up, resolved on confronting her, regardless.

''What I discovered was her *flagrante delicto* with
her current lover. Upon spying me, he speedily
yanked on his breeches, grabbed up the rest of his
clothes and decamped through her window, irrespec-
tive of its height from the ground below and hanging
on to the ivy to break his fall. I paid him no heed,
for whilst I sincerely hoped he had broken his neck,
I knew that if he hadn't, I could deal with him later—

and would have, except that to avoid dueling with me, he fled to the Continent the very next day.

"As you may imagine, an extremely unpleasant row ensued between Tamsyn and me, at the end of which I informed her in no uncertain terms that I intended to divorce her, and that I expected her to make whatever arrangements she needed to be gone from the house by the time I awakened in the morning. I then went downstairs to my study, where I sat fuming, smoking and drinking at length."

Once more, Lord St. Aubyn paused to wet his throat with another long swallow of tea and to light a second cheroot.

"What happened after that is so unimaginably evil that I can hardly bear to speak of it! Realizing she had pushed me too far, that I would not be swayed from my purpose, Tamsyn decided to get cruelly even with me before leaving the house. As I mentioned earlier, her mind was not strong, and I truly believe she must actually have been insane by then. Aware that Doryty, who, as you know, was the twins' nurse at the time, drank and habitually had a pint of porter around ten o'clock at night, Tamsyn intercepted the kitchenmaid bringing the tray upstairs, taking it to deliver herself instead. Before doing so, however, she poured a measure of laudanum into the jar, in order to drug poor, unsuspecting Doryty—who, unfortunately, has been compelled to bear the brunt of the blame for that night ever since.

"Once Tamsyn was certain Doryty would not rouse, she crept upstairs and removed Meliora and Bastian from their beds, coaxing them into their clothes and into remaining silent by telling them that she was taking them to see the fairies dancing on the lawn beneath the moon, and that they must be very quiet, so as not to frighten them away. She then took the twins downstairs, opening the front door to deceive me and the servants into thinking she had gone out that way, whilst she herself went out through the conservatory and into the gardens at the rear of the manor. From there, she hurried the children on toward the cliffs at the edge of the sea.''

"Oh, no..." Verity murmured, stricken. "Oh, no..."

"Yes," the Earl continued grimly, inexorably, as though she had not spoken. "She had always hated them, and she fully intended to murder them both, to revenge herself on me. Fortunately, from the windows of my study, I had observed the three of them in the gardens and, knowing in a way that utterly chilled me to the bone that Tamsyn meant to hurt or even to kill my children, I had run out after them all. Eventually, of course, she saw me coming, and although she rushed on headlong toward the cliffs, she could not carry both the twins, and now, doubtless sensing that something was wrong, neither of them would easily walk along at her side anymore, so that in the end, she was forced to abandon poor little Meliora. Bastian was my heir, you see—as though I could have endured the grievous loss of my daughter any less, even so!

"Tamsyn scooped up my son and bore him away to fling him over the cliffs. However, by that time— thank God!—I had reached her side, and a terrible struggle for control of him ensued. At the last moment, I succeed in snatching him from her grasp, but as she fought to retain her hold on him, she lost her balance, stumbled and fell over the cliffs herself on to the rocks below."

For an interminable minute, Lord St. Aubyn fell silent, lost in his painful memories, and Verity, too, was quiet and still, shocked and horrified by all she had been told. Then, finally, he resumed his tragic tale.

"I've always thought quickly on my feet—which is one of the reasons I'm attached to the War Office—and that night was no exception. I wanted no scandal, and there was always the chance that the real story would not be believed. I had, after all, been furious with Tamsyn and threatened to divorce her, and it was possible that the servants knew of the lover in her bedroom and also that they had overheard the row. So I hid the children in the gardens, charging them most strictly to remain there until they were discovered, and coaching them both as to what they must say when they were found by the servants.

"Afterward, I closed up Tamsyn's chamber, moved myself into the east wing, and installed Lady Kenhebres—by then a widow and who lived with us at the time—in the lodge. For upon the death of her only child, she had suffered a mental decline and begun accusing me of murdering her daughter. As Doryty—who has always been stout and has a hard head for liquor, and who is thus never done in by a mere pint of porter—guessed that she had been drugged and suspected something of the real truth of what had occurred that night, I set her and her husband, Eval Ythnow, to watch over Lady Kenhebres, who, unfortunately, however, is as clever and cunning in her own way as Tamsyn was, and so who sometimes manages to escape from them, and whom, I'm very sorry to report, is obviously the person who has been haunting you ever since you arrived here at the manor. I imagine it's quite clear to you, now, why I felt it necessary to deceive you into thinking her voice you heard now and again issuing her mad warning was nothing more than the wind or the sea.

"Now, Verity, there is an end to my sorry tale. You know the whole of it—and perhaps you can understand now why the twins were as you found them when you came here, and, too, why Miss Marchmont could never hold any attraction for me, why it is you, and only you, whom I love and hope to marry, if you will still have me...."

"Oh, my lord..." Rising, ashamed, now, that she had ever doubted him, had ever—even for one single moment—thought him capable of having murdered his wife, she went and knelt at his feet, pressing his hand to her soft pale cheek, which was wet with the tears she had shed for him and for Meliora and Bastian, as well. "My lord...my dearest Jago...yes, I will still have you—more than ever now. How could you ever doubt it? Do you not yet know how much I love you and the children? You and they are all my heart and happiness."

What they said then was only for lovers to know, but they talked until the pale-grey dawn broke on the eastern horizon, and afterward, there were no shadows between them.

They were married in a quiet celebration two days later in the St. Aubyn family chapel, with Color Sherbourne and Miss Nightingale as their witnesses; and when, on their wedding night, with sweet, tender fierceness, Jago drew Verity into his arms and lovingly taught her the full measure of her womanhood, her heart and soul were replete.

Eighteen

The Hanged Man

Marriage and hanging go by destiny;
matches are made in heaven.

> *Anatomy of Melancholy*
> —Robert Burton

Humanity with all its fears,
With all the hopes of future years,
Is hanging breathless on thy fate!

> *Evangeline*
> —Henry Wadsworth Longfellow

Death...on his pale horse.

> *Paradise Lost*
> —John Milton

Because of the uncertain situation on the Continent, which the Earl feared might erupt again into war at any moment, leaving them stranded there, he took Verity away instead to Brighton for their honeymoon. Located on the Sussex coast, the town had long been a popular seaside resort, frequented by the Prince of Wales and many others of the *haut ton.* There, for a fortnight, Lord St. Aubyn rented a luxurious suite at the Castle Inn, where he and Verity embarked upon a social whirl guaranteed to delight her.

The Assembly rooms were presided over by a master of ceremonies, Captain Wade, and balls were held every Wednesday and Friday at both the Castle Inn and its rival hotel, the Old Ship. Other entertainment included the Prince of Wales's Pavilion, the theater on New Road, the racecourse, which hosted the race for the Brighton Cup, and, for gentlemen, the White Hart, which boasted a cockpit for cockfights. The two lending libraries, Donaldson's and Fisher's, offered a wide selection of newspapers and books. At precisely nine o'clock every day, it was fashionable to stroll along the Steyne, which had originally been a marshland, but which at some point had been drained and, with the addition of wide avenues, gardens and a huge central fountain, turned into a stylish promenade.

While the Earl had seen it all before, he found renewed pleasure in sharing it with his bride and introducing her into society. Verity enjoyed every single minute of it, but still, when their time at Brighton had ended, she was not sorry to return home to St. Aubyn manor, and to Meliora and Bastian, whom she had missed—although Loveday, who had not only been promoted to the position of her abigail, but was also now learning to speak properly, would have been glad to stay another fortnight at least. "For I learned ever so much from the other ladies' maids about all the latest styles and what else is currently fashionable, m'lady! For instance, did you know that 'tis all the crack now to decorate one's chambers in a Chinese mode?"

Shaking her head, Verity was forced to turn away to repress a smile. It was clear to her that, having attained the post of her abigail, Loveday was determined not only to fulfill her responsibilities with distinction, ensuring that her lady was never to be seen at a disadvantage, but also to advise on household matters pertaining to decorating. Verity had no doubt that were Loveday to be given full rein, the whole of St. Aubyn manor would soon look like an Oriental pagoda.

"So I understand," Verity responded at last to her abigail's question. "Still, however tempted, we must not give way at every single turn to what is considered *au courant,* Loveday—for only think if we were to redecorate the entire house in the Chinese manner, only to discover at the end of our labors that it had grown passé virtually overnight?''

"Why, I hadn't thought of that, m'lady. Perhaps only touches here and there, then, in case styles should change...?''

To this, Verity could agree, although she pointed out that because of how widely Lord St. Aubyn had traveled over the years, the manor already contained a tastefully eclectic mixture of furnishings in modes from all over the world. However, there was one room that she did decide to redecorate in its entirety. This was the former Lady St. Aubyn's old apartment in the west wing.

Previously, the Earl had kept it intact to remind himself of how beauty could deceive the eye of its beholder and conceal a treacherous heart. But since this was now no longer a consideration, Verity wished to rid the house of all traces of her hateful predecessor. This scheme, with Lord St. Aubyn's consent and blessing, she undertook to carry out immediately upon her return home from Brighton, disposing of all the apartment's furnishings, save for the former Lady St. Aubyn's portrait, which she had placed in one of the storerooms on the second floor of the manor, in the event that, someday, Meliora or Bastian might desire to remind themselves of what their mother had looked like.

Of her own parents, Verity had no portrait, not even a miniature, and she had always regretted this, for she had been so young when they had died that, sometimes, she could hardly recall their faces. She did not want Meliora and Bastian ever to feel this same lack.

Thus did Verity begin her new life at the manor, where, as the days passed and autumn drifted toward winter, she was now happy in every respect, save one. This last was that the Earl continued his shadowy second life as the notorious highwayman Black Jack Raven. It was a bone of contention between them, with Verity worrying that the Earl might be killed, and he himself insisting that he could not, in all good conscience, forgo his obligations to the War Office and his attempts to ferret out the French spy he felt sure was using Cornwall as a base of operations.

In the end, Verity was compelled to give way before the Earl's quiet but earnest explanations and reassurances, recognizing that regardless of her own anxieties on his behalf, she could not demand that he behave in any disloyal or cowardly fashion by resigning his post. His sense of honor, duty, loyalty and bravery were too high, and his work was too important, for that. But still, she fretted for his safety, and she was only slightly mollified and comforted by his promise to take care.

Now, as she sat at the desk before the windows of her new, large apartment next to the Earl's own in the east wing of the manor, Verity sighed, laying down the quill pen with which she had been composing a letter. Gazing out through the lozenged lead-glass panes at the front lawn and the park and rookery beyond, she thought that life would be perfect if only her husband could capture the French spy! Then the Earl could stop masquerading as Black Jack Raven, and he would no longer be in danger. Ah, well. At least she had the solace of knowing he was growing increasingly closer to unmasking the wicked culprit, and one of the reasons she loved the Earl, Verity must admit, was because of his deep sense of commitment to what was right. She could not ask him to compromise that, no matter how much she might worry about him.

Once more picking up her pen, she finished the letter she was writing to Miss Faith Ivers, a sensible young woman of good breeding, character and education, who was presently residing in Cottam, Nottinghamshire. Miss Ivers was to be the new governess to Meliora and Bastian, and Verity was in the process of outlining all the travel arrangements she had made for the young woman's journey to Cornwall and St. Aubyn manor.

After dusting the completed letter lightly with sand to dry the ink, Verity slowly folded it up and sealed it. The Earl, being a member of Parliament's House of Lords, would frank it for her later, so that she would not need a stamp. Smiling gently to herself, she wondered if Miss Ivers possessed an adventurous spirit and a longing for some escapade and excitement.

A soft knock at the door interrupted Verity's reverie, and at her low-voiced "Come in," Loveday entered the chamber.

"Begging your pardon, m'lady, but there's a bit of a dustup in the kitchen, I'm afraid, as the menu you approved this morning for dinner this evening has gone sadly awry, for somehow—'tis not known how—Mrs. Wickersham's cat, Calico, has managed to eat the fish, and Cook is in such an uproar over it that he's threatening to take a meat cleaver to the poor creature! Naturally, as a result, Mrs. Wickersham has gone all to pieces. I thought you'd want to know.''

''Yes...oh, dear,'' Verity said, rising from her chair before the desk. ''Yes, I suppose I had better go down at once.''

Cook had such an excitable, volatile personality that everyone walked on eggshells around him under even the best of circumstances, and although Verity was no exception, still, she knew it was now her duty as the lady of the manor to confront him and prevent him from possibly making mincemeat out of Mrs. Wickersham's beloved cat, Calico. So, with Loveday trailing along in her wake, Verity descended the grand central staircase in the entrance hall to make her way down the west corridor to the kitchen.

There, she discovered Cook, meat cleaver in hand, chasing Calico around the chopping block and under the table, while Mrs. Wickersham stood by helplessly, pleading with Cook to spare her cat and wringing her hands with anguish.

''Cook...*Cook!*'' Verity spoke sharply, causing the big man to draw up short and, spying her, to pour forth a vitriolic account of all his sufferings in the kitchen, which culminated in the fact that Calico had made off with his lordship's dinner for the very last time. ''Yes, perhaps, but I assure you that I cannot and will not stand idly by and permit you to do away with Mrs. Wickersham's poor cat, Cook,'' she insisted bravely, eyeing him, and the meat cleaver he brandished, askance.

"But, m'lady, what's ta be served fer dinner now, I ask 'ee, now that t' miserable beast has made off with t' fish? If'n it won't cease its evil ways an' quit snatchin' food from t' choppin' block an' t' table when no one is lookin', then it ought ta be got rid o', I tell 'ee!''

"I'm certain Mrs. Wickersham will keep a better watch on it from now on, Cook,'' Verity replied firmly. "And one of the footmen can go to St. Ives for more fish, or else you can substitute some other dish for dinner. But Calico is not to be harmed. I'm quite certain his lordship would be most angry if he learned you had taken a meat cleaver to Mrs. Wickersham's cat.''

At last, nodding in agreement, although, still, he grumbled under his breath darkly, Cook returned to his pots and pans, banging them about with a great deal of violence and relish, while the housekeeper tearfully scooped up the errant Calico, declaring that she did not know how she could ever repay Verity for saving the creature.

"I don't believe Cook would really have hurt your cat, Mrs. Wickersham,'' Verity told her comfortingly. "I think he only wanted to scare you, so you would keep Calico out of the kitchen henceforth. It *was* very naughty of her to have stolen the fish for dinner, you know.''

"That's true—I can't deny it, my dear. Oh, I just

don't know what gets into her sometimes! She's usually so well behaved.''

''Yes, well, do try to keep her out of trouble if you can, ma'am, and see that she is fed tidbits and treats more often. Perhaps that will cure her of her penchant for his lordship's dinner!''

''A most excellent suggestion, my dear. I shall indeed give it a try.'' Still expressing her gratitude, in between scolding the mischievous cat, the elderly woman carried Calico away to the morning room, where they settled themselves comfortably before the fire in the hearth.

Shaking her head over the contretemps and once more smiling to herself, Verity returned to the entrance hall, telling Loveday that she was going for a walk. After that, donning her new sealskin pelisse, matching bonnet and woolen gloves, and gathering up her new sealskin muff, as well, to keep her hands warm, she let herself out the front door, into the late wintry afternoon air.

Since marrying the Earl, Verity had made it a habit to call now and then on Lady Kenhebres at the lodge, to see how the poor old Countess was getting along and to attempt to reassure her that the Earl had not murdered her daughter, that the former Lady St. Aubyn's death had been a tragic accident, nothing more—although Verity never revealed to her what had really happened that dreadful night nor the dead Lady St. Aubyn's true nature. She did not know whether her visits to the lodge did any good or not, but as she thought Lady Kenhebres always seemed relieved to see her alive and well, she continued to drop in on her.

Cornwall in winter was a dismal, desolate place, and today was no exception. Without its summer flowers and greenery to brighten and soften it, the manor looked even more forbidding, as did the park, where the deciduous trees had shed their leaves to reveal their gnarled old branches. The naked boughs presented stark, eerie silhouettes against the backdrop of the leaden sky and the swirling brume, as though all the trees had been long dead. Only the stands of evergreen yews here and there retained their soft, short needles, giving much needed color to the sodden brown lawn and park.

At the center of the circle formed by the long, winding drive's terminus, streams continued to pour forth from the gargoyles of the great stone fountain into its large, fluted basin below, for the weather had not yet turned cold enough to freeze the water, although Verity's breath was cloudy, and a thin layer of hoarfrost limned the trees and ground, adding to the surreal quality of the scene.

Somewhere in the distance, she could hear the Earl's dog, Styx, howling—a strange, plaintive lament that for some unknown reason made her shiver suddenly, as though a goose had just walked over her grave. The sound seemed to be coming from the general direction of the lodge, and she strolled more briskly that way, wondering if aught were amiss.

More than once as she tramped through the trees, along the narrow, muddy, serpentine paths that wound through the park, Verity thought uneasily that she was being watched, and it occurred to her that perhaps Lady Kenhebres had managed to sneak away from the lodge again. If she had, then perhaps something untoward had befallen her! That notion now uppermost in her mind, alarming her, Verity hurried on, abruptly crying out, startled, when, at her approach, the birds in the rookery suddenly shrieked and took flight, the fluttering of hundreds of wings sounding like the beat of ominous drums, echoing weirdly, almost frighteningly, through the stillness of the woods and the drifting mist that played will-o'-the-wisp among the barren trees and clung thickly to the hollows of the land.

In a raucous black cloud, the birds rose up, winging their way skyward, blotting out the pale, sickly sun that strove valiantly to pierce the dark gloominess of the firmament and the park, but that fought an ever losing battle with the lowering pewter thunderheads that intermittently spat drizzle and with the stands of trees that seemed to huddle together even more closely in the chilly air, as though to derive what warmth they could from one another.

Only the thick, spreading yews stood bright and defiant against winter and its inhospitable elements, their boughs soft and soughing gently when Verity brushed against them as she pushed her way deeper into the park, toward the direction from which Styx's mournful baying continued to emanate. Perhaps the dog had only cornered some small creature, such as a fox or badger, she now thought, trying to reassure herself. But still, the inexplicable sense of dread that had first touched her with icy fingers at the sound grew increasingly stronger the nearer she drew to the place where Styx was.

Then, at last, Verity broke through the yews to a small glade where a tall, knotted, dead old Cornish elm towered, and without warning, her fear metamorphosed into a frozen fist that grabbed her cruelly and began to squeeze. Unwittingly, she started to scream, the tortured wails issuing from her throat mingling with the howls of the dog who sat there, staring up at the horrible, misshapen object that hung by a stout rope from one naked, gnarled branch of the elm, slowly turning and twisting in the wind.

It was Eval Ythnow—and he had, it seemed, been dead for quite some time.

Nineteen

Treacherous Traitor

Life is short, the art long, opportunity fleeting,
experience treacherous, judgement difficult.

Aphorisms
—Hippocrates

I wish to leave the world
By its natural door;
In my tomb of green leaves
They are to carry me to die.
Do not put me in the dark,
To die like a traitor;...

A Morir (To Die)
—José Martí

Nine coaches waiting—hurry—hurry—hurry—
Ay, to the devil....

The Revenger's Tragedy
—Cyril Tourneur

St. Aubyn Manor
Cornwall, England, 1802

As long as she lived, Verity would never forget the ghastly sight of Eval Ythnow's hanged body swaying in the wind, or the awful baying of the Earl's dog, Styx, at the corpse, as though to sound a warning and alert the manor of what had happened. At first, not understanding what had occurred, Verity had thought Eval had killed himself, although she had not known why.

It was only later, long after the Earl had arrived on the scene, accompanied by his cousin, Colonel Sherbourne, who had ridden over from Truro that day, and they had cut Eval's body down and sent Verity back to the house, that she had learned that the dead man had been tortured and murdered. That was why Eval's corpse had appeared so misshapen. He had been brutally beaten and hacked with his own ax, which had left him cut, bloody, bruised and swollen, before, unconscious, he had been strung up from the heavy rope tossed over the branch of the Cornish elm. Apparently, he had been in the park, chopping and gathering wood for the lodge, when he had been set upon by some unknown assailant, for some equally unknown—but clearly sinister—purpose.

However, now, several weeks later, nothing more than that had been discovered, despite a full investigation undertaken by both the Earl and the Colonel. As a result, the normally happy household was subdued, and the frightened servants crept about, whispering among themselves and starting violently at any unexpected noise—and avoiding the kitchen at every opportunity, obviously suspecting that the easily excitable, volatile Cook might have had something to do with poor Eval's demise.

"I wouldn't put it past, Cook," Loveday said quietly to Verity, on one occasion. "He's a big, strong man, and the way he beats those pots and pans of his around so violently and brandishes that meat cleaver of his like an ax when he's in one of his towering rages is enough to make a body think he isn't all there...that he's gone clean out of his head, that's what! Why...wasn't he going to make mincemeat out of poor Mrs. Wickersham's cat that time before you stopped him? And how do we know it was Eval's own ax what was used on him—and not Cook's meat cleaver?" the abigail suggested darkly.

"Eval's ax was covered with hair and blood," Verity replied, unnerved. "Loveday, I simply cannot and will not believe Cook murdered Eval. For one thing, what reason would he have for doing such a terrible thing?"

"He might have got in an argument with Eval.

You know how Cook gets riled up about the least little thing. Maybe Eval filched some apples for some pies or tarts Cook was fixing to bake or something. It wouldn't have been the first time Eval had dropped by and taken something from the kitchen or the larder, which Doryty needed for Lady Kenhebres but had forgotten to buy at the market in St. Ives—being too busy imbibing a pint of port at the Sloop!''

"Oh, Loveday, you mustn't say such things," Verity insisted firmly. "Really, you mustn't. And you mustn't be so hard on poor Doryty, either. She's had a bad time of it, first for her part in that tragic night when the Earl's first wife died, and then, afterward, looking after poor, mad Lady Kenhebres all this time, and now losing her husband, Eval, under such dreadful circumstances. It's no wonder Doryty drinks now and then. Besides which, Lady Kenhebres is welcome to anything we might have in our kitchen or larder, and Cook knows that. So I just can't believe he would have murdered Eval over a handful of apples or something! Cook's high-strung, yes, but I truly believe that, in reality, he's all bluster...that he wouldn't actually hurt anyone."

"If you say so, m'lady." Plainly, Loveday remained skeptical.

In light of such rumors, Verity was glad and grateful that at least the new governess, Miss Ivers, who had at last arrived at St. Aubyn manor and now been in residence for the past fortnight, had proved as sensible as she had appeared in her response to the advertisement placed by the Earl in the country's various newspapers. Otherwise, the young woman would surely have upped and left the moment she had set foot in the house, learned what had so recently occurred on its grounds and been made privy to the servants' gossip about Cook.

But try as she might, even Verity herself was not immune from the fearful pall that seemed to hang over the manor, as though it had fallen under the spell of some evil sorcerer, as, upon her first coming to the house, she had half fancied, and now, more than ever, she longed fervently for the Earl to give up his secret role as the highwayman Black Jack Raven.

"For how do you know Eval's horrible murder is not, in some fashion, connected with your masquerade as Black Jack?" she asked her husband, one evening in the library, again expressing to him her concern that he would perhaps be wounded once more or even killed by some unsuspecting coachman or footman—or ruthlessly murdered by the treacherous French spy, Fouquet, whom he sought to ferret out in Cornwall. "How do you know this insidious Frenchman whom you are after has not uncovered Black Jack's own true identity already—or that, at the very least suspecting you, he did not torture and kill poor Eval in an attempt to gain information about your comings and goings, and anything else that might be of use to a spy? Eval was our lodgekeeper, was he not? Who else to know better than he, then, whether and when you ride out at night."

"Sometimes, my love, I fear you are far too intelligent for your own good." Smiling ruefully, the Earl sighed heavily. "I had hoped to keep the knowl-

edge from you, to spare you from any further alarm
and upset on my own behalf, especially. But now, I
see there is no help for it, and I must tell you the
truth. You have, I'm afraid, hit the nail on the head,
my darling. For I *do* believe Eval was killed exactly
how and why you have just said—which is all the
more reason why I cannot, *will* not, resign my post
with the War Office and cease playing the part of
Black Jack Raven!'' the Earl stated decisively. ''I
cannot, as Lord St. Aubyn, expect to mingle with
thieves, smugglers, wreckers and the like, and to ac-
quire any knowledge whatsoever of any import about
Fouquet. Only as a highwayman do I stand any
chance at all of learning the identity Fouquet has
assumed here in Cornwall. However, you need not
fret yourself over my safety, my sweet, for as I have
informed you before, I feel certain I am very near
now to completing my task of unmasking and cap-
turing the interloper—clever, cunning, dangerous and
unscrupulous though he may be.''

''Yes, but you've also said this Fouquet must be
equally close to uncovering your own true identity,
Jago—indeed, he may know it already!—and who is
to say whether, upon learning it, he may not make
some attempt to assassinate you as cruelly as he murdered poor Eval, before you can expose him and have
him arrested?''

''Please be good enough to give me some credit,
my love.'' The Earl smiled at her wryly, however
fondly. ''I did myself think of the deadly possibility
you have just now voiced to me, and, possessing my
own share of intelligence and guile, to guard against

it, I arranged with Hugh to pose as Black Jack Raven whilst we ourselves were known to be away in Brighton on our honeymoon. It is my earnest hope that this will have thrown Fouquet off the scent entirely, or, at the very least, have momentarily bewildered him, compelling him seriously to rethink any ideas he may have harbored that I and Black Jack Raven are one and the same man. My only regret is that, in all probability, it was this very confusion on Fouquet's part that led to his brutal attack upon Eval.''

"Even so, Jago—" Verity bit her lower lip anxiously "—I cannot like this scheme, and I don't understand how you can be so very sure that you are so near to learning this Fouquet's alias here in Cornwall. For, surely, if he is as clever and cunning as you say, he has more than one!''

"Yes, indeed, he does,'' Lord St. Aubyn confirmed, setting aside the teacup from which he had been drinking and rising from the wing chair he had occupied before the hearth, beginning to pace the floor. "However, regardless, there are still a number of clues I have come across, which have eventually enabled me to deduce certain aspects about the various roles Fouquet has chosen to play here. For instance, he keeps rather odd hours for a smuggler. In my guise as Black Jack Raven, in St. Ives, at the Sloop and other such establishments, where I go to peddle my alleged booty—in reality, baubles I myself have purchased quite legitimately—I have learned of a supposed smuggler who is known simply as the Jester. What interested me about this man was his alleged name, for in French, as, being fluent in that language yourself, my darling, you are unquestionably aware, the word *jester* is *fou*—which also means *mad*—whilst *quet* is a common suffix.

"Now, when one undertakes to assume a role such I myself have played as Black Jack Raven, it is always wise to choose an alias that one will remember to associate with oneself and thus will respond to naturally. So, since my given name is Jago, which is Cornish for Jacob or James, I decided to use the diminutive Jack. The Raven surname also derives from my own true one, Ransleigh, which means 'from the raven meadow,' whilst the Black part of my alias I adopted to add a certain flavor to my character and selected because that is the color of my horse Mephisto, whom I ride on those occasions when I am posing as a highwayman."

"I see," Verity announced, utterly fascinated, despite her anxieties on his behalf. "So you thought that perhaps this Fouquet had contrived something similar!"

"Yes, indeed, I did. Now, to continue, upon further investigation, I discovered that the so-called Jester comes and goes at the Sloop and elsewhere usually only on certain days, at certain hours. Once I was finally able, after a long period of time, to establish a pattern to these movements, it naturally occurred to me that, probably, it indicated that he was otherwise employed at some perfectly valid post that required him to maintain a relatively regular schedule. Although, as you know, my love, there is nothing particularly unusual about this, since a great many persons of even the highest order involve themselves in smuggling here in Cornwall, I *was* led to wonder what sort of regular position the Jester might hold. What kind of legitimate work might he actually do?

"Both discreet observation and casual inquiries informed me that he was no manual laborer, for however much he may wish to do so, a man cannot reasonably alter the nature of his hands, and on the one or two occasions when I was fortunate enough to spy the Jester without his gloves, I saw that his own hands were well kept. Further, for obvious reasons, as I disguised my own self when in St. Ives and elsewhere, he himself always wore a wig, a black patch over his left eye, and other such accoutrements designed to camouflage his real appearance, but of which, even given his alleged smuggling activities, he actually had no need, for even persons well-known to be smugglers here in Cornwall are scarcely ever arrested. So his physical artifice was another point that attracted my attention to him, making me believe he perhaps had other—sinister—grounds for wishing to conceal his true self."

"Indeed!" Verity exclaimed, suitably impressed by the Earl's perspicacity.

"There were, of course, countless possibilities with regard to the Jester's seemingly authentic employment. So, eventually, I realized I must approach the matter from its opposite end...meaning that with regard to Fouquet himself, I was able to rule out any number of these possibilities on the basis that they would have either have left his nights, at least, generally free, enabling him to venture abroad as he pleased—which meant he and the Jester were probably not one and the same man—or else would have required specialized knowledge. It was highly unlikely that, in addition to a smuggler, Fouquet was also posing as a solicitor, for instance, as one could not assume him to be adequately enough skilled in English law to pass himself off in such a manner. I chose to be a highwayman because I could not expect as a smuggler to conceal my own real identity for any great length of time, since I am well acquainted with far too many people here in Cornwall who are engaged in that illicit activity, and also because I am a crack shot and swordsman—talents well suited to a life on the hightoby.

"Finally, just recently, in fact, from information obtained by the War Office via its own spies in France, I learned Fouquet to be a gentleman and thus well acquainted with a gentleman's household and how it is run. For this reason, I then deduced that perhaps he might have sought work as a servant in such an establishment. Were that indeed to be the case, and were Jester and Fouquet identical, as I had come to suspect and believe, Fouquet's employment as a servant would then satisfactorily account for his peculiar comings and goings as the Jester, for he would not be able to venture abroad at will, but only on his days and nights off, or else—at some considerable risk to himself of termination without a reference at best, and of complete discovery of his true occupation at worst—by slipping from the house or his room when he was required to be on duty or else abed with the rest of the servants."

Pausing in his explanation, the Earl withdrew his gold cigar case from his jacket, casually extracted a cheroot and lit it, his head bent intently to the flame as he inhaled deeply. Then, after blowing a cloud of smoke into the air, he continued.

"Now, my darling, upon further consideration, it seemed to me that there were but a few such gentlemen's establishments here in Cornwall where Fouquet might have applied for a post—and only one wherein he might also truly have legitimately hoped to attain valuable information about England's covert activities with regard to France. Because of my attachment to the War Office, that household was none other than my own!"

"No...oh, no, Jago!" Verity cried, stricken. "Surely, that cannot be! Good heavens! Why, poor Mrs. Wickersham would be utterly horrified and no doubt faint dead away on the very spot if she even for one minute thought—much less learned for certain—that we had a French spy in our very midst! Oh, I just can't imagine who it might be. All our servants are good and loyal. No...no, it simply cannot be true, Jago!"

"I assure you it is, my sweet," Lord St. Aubyn rejoined grimly, abruptly flinging his cigar into the hearth and snatching up a piece from the chessboard that sat upon a nearby table. "For in French, as you know, the word *fou,* besides meaning 'jester,' also refers to a bishop in a chess game—and this particular match, I swear, is now drawing to an end!" So saying, he violently threw down the bishop he had moments before plucked from the chessboard and waved about furiously. Then, deliberately, he trod upon the piece as he strode rapidly to the library doors, which he ripped open wide to reveal the footman Ned, still bent over in the entrance hall, where he had unquestionably had his ear pressed to the portals' keyhole only moments before. "Checkmate, Ned Bishop!" the Earl snarled, with triumph. "Or should I say...Edouard Fouquet?"

For an eternity, it seemed to Verity, the footman she had believed to be only the "pilferin', pokin' an' pryin' noddy" that Loveday had called him stood there, stunned and speechless with surprise. Then, at last, he must have realized the game was, in truth, at an end, as Lord St. Aubyn had declared, for without warning, his eyes narrowed, glittering like shards in the lamplight, and he smiled superciliously as he bowed low, with exaggerated courtesy to the Earl.

"Mai, oui, Monsieur le Comte, je m'appelle Edouard Fouquet," the footman confirmed. "But, yes, my lord Earl, I am called Edouard Fouquet— and proud I am of it! *Vive la France!"* he shouted, before he turned and ran.

Lord St. Aubyn dashed after him, with Verity following hard on their heels, and as she reached the entrance hall, she observed, to her horror, that both men were now armed with rapiers hastily jerked down from where they had previously hung crossed on the wall above one of the four fireplaces in the entrance hall.

Briefly, mockingly, the two combatants saluted

each other. Then they began the lethal ritual of feinting, lunging and thrusting, and of parrying and riposting, the blades flashing so quickly and wickedly that Verity could hardly keep up, could not believe this was happening. She thought it must be a dream—a nightmare!—and she prayed desperately to awaken, safe in the Earl's arms and bed. But no such comfort commenced. Instead, the deadly duel continued mercilessly, weapons scraping steel upon steel, foible upon foible, forte upon forte, as each man struggled grimly to best his opponent.

However, it appeared that neither would prevail, for both men were evenly matched in height, weight and skill, well trained by their respective fencing masters and at fencing schools such as Angelo's Haymarket Room in London and the Académie d'Arms de Paris. As she watched, riveted to the ominous, unfolding scene, Verity felt her heart leap to her throat, for more than once in Brighton's Assembly rooms, she had heard it remarked that the French excelled at swordplay and, more often than not, defeated their English rivals in duels.

Numbly, in some dim corner of her mind, she thought she should go and fetch help, but when she finally did galvanize herself toward this end, Lord St. Aubyn, divining her intent, growled at her to stay close behind him, lest she be taken hostage and used against him. Because the two men battled so savagely back and forth across the breadth of the entrance hall and up and down half its length, with Fouquet cleverly keeping the Earl pinned down behind the grand staircase, she could not seem to find any opening through which she might pass safely. Nor, in light of Lord St. Aubyn's caveat to her, did she deem it wise to try to run back into the library, whence she might reach the main east passage, at least, for fear that Fouquet, discerning her aim, would chase after her and capture her before she could ascend the steps in the east tower.

Verity did call for assistance until she was nearly hoarse from it, but the manor was large, and all the servants were either in the kitchen and servants' hall, preparing dinner and clattering pots and pans, and crockery and silver, as a result, or else upstairs getting dressed for the evening. So no one heard her cries for help, much less responded to them.

Now, Fouquet attempted to thrust through the Earl's guard, but, much to Verity's relief, with no success. Lord St. Aubyn swiftly countered, the muscles in his arms and back rippling, his corded legs quick to shift his weight against his foe. And so the mortal battle raged on, rapiers feinting in high carte and thrusting in low tierce, blades clashing and scratching, then once more parting, only to come together in feint and thrust, parry and riposte yet again.

Had Verity not hideously grasped the fact that the Earl's very life was at stake, she would have greatly admired the superior skill of two such outstanding swordsmen. As it was, she could only be terrified by the macabre, mesmerizing duel. But even the fear she now felt was not equal to that which abruptly seized her with an unbearably cruel fist when, in some obscure part of her consciousness, her ears distinguished the happy chatter and gay laughter of the new governess, Miss Ivers, and her two young charges as they descended the grand staircase for dinner.

After that, everything happened so very fast that Verity could hardly take it all in. As Miss Ivers heard her new mistress's hoarse, agitated shouts of warning, she ran down the steps to see what was amiss, Meliora and Bastian following rapidly behind. As they reached the foot of the stairs, Fouquet, having observed the three coming down and having maneuvered himself in that direction, suddenly flung away his weapon, sending it bouncing and crashing across the floor into one wall, and, from beneath the jacket of his livery, drew forth an evilly gleaming dagger. Then, roughly shoving the tearfully confused Miss Ivers aside, he grabbed up Bastian, who was now screaming shrilly, sticking the short blade to the little boy's throat.

"Step back, St. Aubyn!" the French spy spat. "Step back, or you'll soon need another heir!"

By this time, other servants, at last hearing all the commotion, had come running. But it was too late. Nobody—not even the bold Earl himself—dared to move in the face of the dire threat to Bastian's young life.

"You—" Fouquet motioned to Cook, who had arrived from the kitchen, excitedly bearing his meat cleaver in one hand "—put that down, and open the front door!"

"What means this? What art thou doing?" Cook growled, nervously dancing from one foot to the other. "Have thou gone off yer head, Ned?"

"His name isn't Ned," Lord St. Aubyn stated quietly. "It's Edouard Fouquet, and he's a French spy. It was he who tortured and murdered poor Eval Ythnow, to try to gain information about my comings and goings here at the Manor. He's utterly ruthless. So do what he says, Cook. Put down that cleaver, and open the front door."

Upon hearing all this, Mrs. Wickersham, who stood poised halfway down the grand staircase, promptly swooned and was saved from falling down the steps only by Mr. Drummond's having the presence of mind to catch her. Obediently tossing his cleaver to the floor, Cook flung wide the heavy oak portal, and Fouquet backed slowly toward it, his knife still at Bastian's throat. Then, upon attaining the doorway, the French spy abruptly raced out into the mizzle and darkness, carrying the little boy away with him. Seeing this, the Earl turned without warning and, much startling everyone present, ran into the library. Not understanding his action, knowing only—horribly—that Bastian's young life was in danger, Verity determinedly gathered up her skirts and chased out into the night, after Fouquet.

Once she got outside, she observed by the light of the moon that shone hazily in the dark firmament that the French spy was swiftly and furtively making his way not toward the stables, as she had fully expected, but, rather, around to the rear of the manor. Bastian now made no sound, being borne like a sack of potatoes under Fouquet's strong left arm, and Verity did not know if the child was alive or dead, although

she believed—she *must* believe!—the former, for
otherwise, surely, the French spy would have discarded the body. Perhaps Bastian had fainted, she
desperately reassured herself. In any event, he had
doubtless been warned by Fouquet to cease screaming and struggling, lest he have his throat cut immediately.

As she plunged on through the mist and drizzle,
Verity felt her heart turn over with agony in her
breast, for she could only imagine the little boy's
terror, how, if he were conscious, he must be reliving
that terrible night when his unnatural mother had carried him away into the night, just as the French spy
now did. Worse, dashing through the gardens at the
back of the house, Verity saw, to her horror, that
Fouquet, too, now rushed headlong toward the cliffs,
and in some dark portion of her brain, she surmised
that he must have a boat hidden somewhere on the
beach below, in the event that he needed to make
just such a quick escape as this and flee across the
Channel to his homeland. He must not reach his concealed vessel! she thought. He might take Bastian
with him and, when the child was no longer of any
more use to him, throw him overboard to drown.

This ghastly idea driving her forward like a vicious, pitiless whip, Verity ran on, gasping for breath
and with a painful stitch in her side. In her terrified
mind rang a line from Tourneur's *The Revenger's
Tragedy,* tauntingly repeating itself over and over, a
fearsome refrain: *Nine coaches waiting—hurry—
hurry—hurry— Ay, to the devil....*

Now, Fouquet had gained the great, jagged cliffs

that hove up like dark, crouching behemoths at the edge of the mortal black rocks, the roughly shingled beach and the frothing, restless sea far below. Finding a steep, narrow, treacherous slick footpath amid the shadowy, crumbling cliffs, he started down to the shore. Shortly thereafter, Verity herself stood upon the cliffs, staring down at the French spy as he slowly descended, unwilling to relinquish his hold on Bastian and not wanting to slip and fall to his death, either. Her head swam dizzily with vertigo as she gazed over the edge of what seemed to her an endless abyss, and she staggered upon the wet grass, strove frantically to retrieve her lost balance. But in the end, her weak, shaking knees gave way beneath her, and she sank down upon them, closing her eyes to try to stop the earth's sickening spinning.

From somewhere behind her, she could hear Meliora's high, thin screams piercing the night air. But Bastian remained frighteningly silent. Breathing hard, Verity forced herself to rise again, glancing back over her shoulder, hoping desperately that help was at hand. Cook, wildly brandishing his meat cleaver, maddened with rage at the discovery of a traitor in their midst and Bastian's abduction, was running toward her frantically, followed by others of the servants. But they would perhaps not arrive in time to save the little boy, and the Earl was as yet nowhere in sight.

She alone might prove Bastian's salvation.

At that terrifying but nevertheless galvanizing realization, her heart in her throat, her body trembling uncontrollably, Verity deliberately forced her footsteps along the same inauspicious trail that Fouquet followed.

In the end, such was her terror of heights that she clambered and clawed her way down the precipitous, slender, hazardous moist track, finally losing her grip on the rocks to which she tried so desperately to cling, and falling, sliding along the damp earth until she smashed into the French spy some short yards below, causing his dagger to fly from his hand and sail down to the beach to clatter upon the rough shingle.

"Imbecile!" he hissed, incensed. "Do you want to kill us all?"

"Give me Bastian!" Verity cried, struggling to her feet and grabbing hold of the little boy. "Give him to me, you monster! You don't need him anymore, and if you give him to me, you can make good your escape! You've hidden a boat down there, somewhere, haven't you?"

"Oui...but the child is my assurance that the Earl does not follow me—for I heard him that night in the library, when he told you the tale of his mad first wife. He will not wish to risk the life of his son and heir. So, now, let go of the boy, you stupid witch! For *you,* I don't need!"

With that menacing announcement, Fouquet started shoving her violently, trying to push her off the perilous, precipitous slope of the cliff. But as she struggled frantically with the French spy, Verity clung like a leech to Bastian—and then, suddenly, an explosion reverberated in the night, and to her everlasting horror, seconds later a bloody black hole burst open in Fouquet's forehead. He stared at her—wide-eyed and openmouthed with shock and incredulity—before he inexorably toppled backward, falling from the cliffs to the malignant rocks far below.

Her arms locked around the unconscious child she had torn from the French spy's slackened grasp, Verity pitched forward on the footpath, pressing Bastian to the damp earth so that he would be safe beneath her, one hand stretching out then to grab hold of a stony outcrop just above to prevent them both, too, from tumbling to their deaths.

"Verity! Oh, my God, Verity!" Lord St. Aubyn shouted from the top of the cliffs, where he had watched her desperate fight for her and his son's life, and from where, having retrieved one of his dueling pistols from the library, he had fired the fatal shot that had given them both a chance to survive. Beside the Earl stood little Meliora, for although her small, beautiful face was pale with fear and wet with tears that glistened in the moonlight, she had dared to run after her father, to try to save her brother. "Verity...Verity, are you and Bastian all right? Oh, thank God! Don't try to move, my dearest love! Stay where you are! Drummond and I are coming down!"

Epilogue

The Love Knot

All Kings, and all their favorites,
All glory of honors, beauties, wits,
The sun itself, which makes times, as they pass,
Is elder by a year, now, than it was
When thou and I first one another saw:
All other things, to their destruction draw,
Only our love hath no decay;
This, no tomorrow hath, nor yesterday,
Running, it never runs from us away,
But truly keeps his first, last, everlasting day.

The Anniversary
—John Donne

The Silkie's Spell

O hark, o hear! How thin and clear,
And thinner, clearer, farther going!
O sweet and far from cliff and scar
The horns of Elfland faintly blowing.

The Princess
—Alfred, Lord Tennyson

One day I wrote her name upon the strand,
But came the waves and washed it away:
Again I wrote it with a second hand,
But came the time, and made my pains his prey.
Vain man, said she, that dost in vain assay,
A mortal thing so to immortalize,
For I myself shall like to this decay,
And eke my name be wiped out likewise.
Not so, quoth I, let baser things devise
To die in dust, but you shall live by fame:
My verse your virtues rare shall eternize,
And in the heavens write your glorious name,

Where when as death shall all the world subdue,
Our love shall live, and later life renew.

Amoretti
—Edmund Spenser

St. Aubyn Manor
Cornwall, England, 1808

Sometimes, on a wintry eve, when the wind was high and blew like a torrent among the rustling trees of the park, and the moon was hazily ringed and tossed among ghostily drifting clouds; when the ocean along the treacherous rocky coast maddened and roiled, and swept, white-foamed, over the deceptive reefs and shingled beaches, the grey rain came hard, and the gossamer mist cloaked the hills, the moors and the marshlands of Cornwall, Verity would remember that perilous night when she had braved her own terror to descend the crumbling black cliffs at the edge of the sea and, there, fought so desperately for both Bastian's life and her own.

At such times, she would, of a sudden, shiver violently, and the Earl would know she recalled that terrible night, and he would hold her very tenderly and close in his strong embrace until, at long last, the memory passed and her trembling subsided. But nor did he himself forget—how he had shot Fouquet to save Verity's life and that of Bastian, and then had borne her up the steep, slippery slope of the cliffs, in the wake of Mr. Drummond, who had carried the unconscious child.

Both Lord St. Aubyn and Verity were deeply grateful that of that dire night's events, Bastian recollected nothing after the French spy had taken him from the manor, and that Meliora had arrived at the cliffs after Fouquet had fallen to the fateful black rocks below. As yet, neither Jowanet nor Kittow, the now five-year-old daughter and four-year-old son whom Verity had borne to the Earl since their marriage, knew anything at all about that night, although someday, when they were older, Verity would tell them—just as she would tell Meliora and Bastian where their dead mother's portrait was tucked away in one of the storerooms on the second floor of the manor, in case they should ever wish to see it, although she did not believe they would.

Now, as she stood in the doorway of the library, surveying her family, Verity sighed quietly, and tears of deepest joy brimmed in her eyes. Above the granite hearth hung her own painting—of the silkie who danced on the moonlit beach and the man who watched from the cliffs above, poised to creep down and steal her sealskin, so that he could bind her to him forever, preventing her from slipping away back into the mist and sea whence she had come. Verity had given the picture to Lord St. Aubyn as a wedding present, and he had had it mounted in a gold frame and hung it where he might see it always.

Beneath the painting sat the Earl himself, surrounded by their four children in a circle, and as she gazed at them, her heart welling over in her breast, Verity thought how like a love knot they were, all their lives interwoven into a whole without beginning or end—generations stretching back through the ages and ahead into the future—as God, in His infinite wisdom and grace, had intended families to be, bound together by blood and by marriage, and, most of all, by love.

One hand crept to her breast, where, hanging from its delicate gold chain around her neck, her mother's filigree gold locket lay. Once, a long time ago, it had been empty inside, without even a miniature portrait of her parents to comfort her. Now, however, it held something equally precious to Verity, although even Lord St. Aubyn did not know what, or how she had stolen it from him...how she had so carefully and lovingly cut it from his head, and bound it with a short, slender crimson silk riband tied into a love knot, one night while he had slumbered deeply—and dreamed himself a silkie lord of the Otherworld, enchanted by a mortal maid with long dark-brown hair that tangled in the wind and eyes the silver of the moon, the color of the mist upon the moors.